CRITICAL PRAISE FOR THE WRITING OF TERRY C. JOHNSTON

"RICH AND FASCINATING . . . There is a genuine flavor of the period and of the men who made it what it was."
—*Washington Post Book World*

"COMPELLING . . . memorable characters, a great deal of history and lore about the Indians and pioneers of the period, and a deep insight into human nature." —*Booklist*

"MASTERFUL!"
—John M. Carroll,
historian and renowned expert
on the American Indian wars

"A winner!" —*The Buckskin Report*

"EXCELLENT . . . very forceful and moving." —Turner Kirkland, *Dixie Gun Works*

"The battles are described, and detailed, in an excellent manner." —*The Heliograph*

"AN UNFORGETTABLE ADVENTURE!"
—*Rocky Mountain News*

THE PLAINSMEN SERIES BY TERRY C. JOHNSTON

SHADOW RIDERS

THE SOUTHERN PLAINS UPRISING, 1873

TERRY C. JOHNSTON

St. Martin's Paperbacks

SHADOW RIDERS

ISBN: 0-312-92597-2

Printed in the United States of America

St. Martin's Paperbacks edition/December 1991

10 9 8

for
Audie,
because you helped me
feel again and showed
me just how much a miracle
loving someone can be

My people have never first drawn a bow or fired a gun against the whites. There has been trouble on the line between us, and my young men have danced the war dance . . . Two years ago I came upon this road, following the buffalo, that my wives and children might have their cheeks plump and their bodies warm. But the soldiers fired on us, and since that time there has been a noise like that of a thunderstorm . . . The blue-dressed soldiers . . . killed my braves . . . They made sorrow come in our camps, and we went out like buffalo bulls when their cows are attacked. When we found them we killed them, and their scalps hang in our lodges. The Comanches are not weak and blind, like the pups of a dog when seven sleeps old. They are strong and farsighted, like grown horses. We took their road and we went on it. The white women cried and our women laughed.

—Ten Bears
Yamparika Comanche

I have heard that you intend to settle us on a reservation near the mountains. I don't want to settle. I love to roam over the prairies. There I feel free and happy, but when we settle down we grow pale and die . . . A long time ago this land belonged to our fathers; but when I go up to the river, I see camps of soldiers on its banks. These soldiers cut down my timber; they kill my buffalo; and when I see that, my heart feels like bursting; I feel sorry . . . Has the white man become a child that he should recklessly kill and not eat?

—Satanta
Kiowa chief

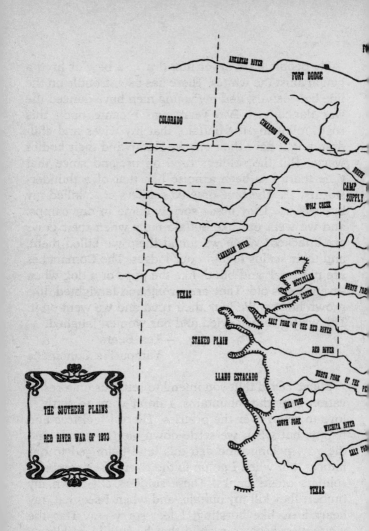

Map drawn by author, compiled from contemporary sources. Graphics completed by Sandra West-Prowell.

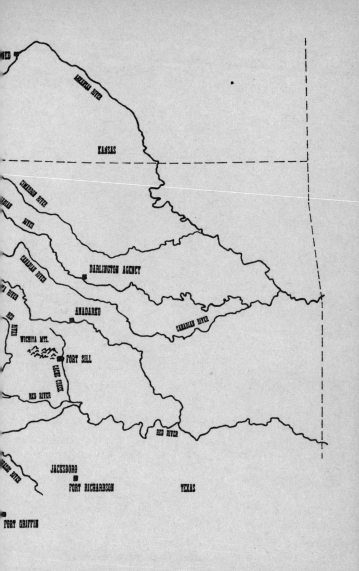

Author's Foreword

A warfare in which the soldier of the United States had no hope of honors if victorious, no hope of mercy if he fell; slow death by hideous torture if taken alive; sheer abuse from press and pulpit, if, as was inevitable, Indian squaw or child was killed. A warfare that called us through the cliffs and canyons of the southwest, the lava beds and labyrinths of Modoc land, the windswept plains of Texas, the rigors of Montana winters, the blistering heat of midsummer suns, fighting oftentimes against a foe for whom we felt naught by sympathy, yet knew that the response could be but deathless hate . . . A more thankless task, a more perilous service, a more exacting test of leadership, morale, and discipline no army . . . has ever been called upon to undertake than that which for eighty years was the lot of the little fighting force of regulars who cleared the

way across the continent for the emigrant
and settler.

So penned Lieutenant Robert G. Carter, serving in
Colonel Ranald S. Mackenzie's Fourth Cavalry stationed on the frontier of west Texas. A most dramatic
statement I wanted to use in beginning this foreword.
Carter served the Army of the West with honor for
much of the entire era of the Indian Wars.

As much as this time was one of supreme drama
and romance—we must not forget that we are talking
about real heroes, both red and white. Not the cellu-
loid heroes Hollywood would have us believe peopled
the West. Instead, I'm speaking of the faceless men
and women who became heroic solely because they
were called upon by circumstances to forge this nation's destiny across the trackless frontier . . . or
they were called upon to resist that westward migration of a foreign and incomprehensible race.

Both races played lead roles in the most astound-
ing drama played on any world stage at any time in
our collective history—the American West.

Indeed, the American frontier West was an experience both of extremes and of complexities. Not an
easy story to tell simply, but one I hope will be worth
your experience in reading—this whole-cloth tapes-
try of a dramatic and most romantic time. And perhaps nowhere else in the West did two of the greatest
symbols of the American frontier confront one another but there on the southern plains, beginning in
the early 1870s. Contrary to what most people believe, it would not be farther north in the land of Red
Cloud and Sitting Bull and Man Afraid that we find
this dramatic, last-ditch effort. Nowhere else but in
that region of the southern prairie did those two

great enemies stare one another in the eye so fatefully: the free-roaming Kiowa-Comanche and the buffalo hunter.

Besides the singular icon represented by the frontier horse soldier, these are the two most potent symbols of the West in our collective imaginations: the naked warrior on his small, quick pony . . . and the hardy men who ventured onto the central and southern plains to begin the final chapter for the nomadic warrior tribes by hunting the buffalo for only the hides (and perhaps a few tongues).

Ironic too that in the mind of the Indian the buffalo hunter came to symbolize everything he could hate in the white race.

As this story will soon unfold, you will meet Billy Dixon, hide hunter. Nothing less than a real hero in my eyes, head and shoulders above so many—although most of the time, young Billy just happened to be in the wrong place at the wrong time. Through Dixon's role in this story, I will begin to tell of the buffalo hunters' era on the southern plains, a story that will continue right in the next book, *Dying Thunder*, Volume 7 of the Plainsmen Series. Billy Dixon will be back with Seamus Donegan at the Battle of Adobe Walls, where twenty-nine white buffalo hunters held off untold numbers of Comanche and Kiowa and Cheyenne for five days. But first you'll read the background to the entire conflict, allowing me to set the stage for this novel, *Shadow Riders*.

These hide-men were not that different from the "long-hunter" who haunted the Appalachian and canebrake country two centuries ago to hunt for game and new homes for their family. Nor were they that different from the Rocky Mountain fur trapper who came in search of beaver. Each of them, like the last to come—the buffalo hunter—were of a kind: a fiercely independent breed. A spearhead of the nation's destiny.

The only matter of any consequence that differed the hide hunter from those who had gone before him was that men like Billy Dixon were hunting buffalo, an animal irretrievably associated with the frontier, with the Myth of the West, and with the rise and fall of fortunes for the nomadic red man of the West. In killing off the buffalo to advance their own personal gain in addition to the larger fortunes of eastern entrepreneurs, the buffalo hunter unwittingly accomplished much more than his fair share to bring about the settlement of the plains.

This novel starts off at the beginning of that era of this ofttimes mythical creature—the buffalo hunter—who descended upon this fringe of the western frontier like the locusts of ancient Egypt descended upon the Pharaoh. From 1871 through the winter of 1873, the period encompassed by what you will be reading shortly, these hide-men killed those great, nearly blind, massive-headed beasts in such astonishing numbers that one fact is likely to be incomprehensible for you to understand: that a relatively small group of white men armed with extremely accurate and powerful weapons began killing buffalo at the rate of what works out to be some two hundred per hour, spread out over a twenty-four-hour period per day, until, by the spring of 1874 (when the next novel in this series will take up this dramatic story), there were complete sections of the central and southern plains where a man could no longer find any of the beasts which had once blanketed the prairie from Canada to northern Sonora.

Dying Thunder, that next installment in this ongoing series that I envision encompassing some twenty-two novels, will tell the story of not only the waning days of the buffalo hunter on the central and southern plains, but the last days of the great horse-mounted cultures who once upon a time built their entire culture around the nomadic journeys of the buffalo—using the animals for food, shelter, weapons, tools, and not the least as an object of worship.

When the buffalo were taken away from these horsemen, there was little culture left for the Indian to hold on to. The buffalo hunter—not the frontier army—ultimately drove the last of the southern tribes, those once-great warrior cultures, into the reservations to feed their families.

In the end, as I have said before, both sides in this conflict underestimated the resolve of the other. The buffalo hunter cleared the plains for the settler who came in his wake. And the Indian understood neither of them—he was baffled by just how great a value the white man placed on the material ownership of the land. Yet, as I have mentioned before, the white man in turn failed to comprehend to what extremes the Indian would go to maintain the universal freedom of the land.

And in this case, we're talking about two tribes who had been driven and harried and pushed to their limit for at least two centuries before the era of the great buffalo wars. Here was the place. And both the Kiowa and the Kwahadi Comanche understood this to be their clarion call to a final, desperate last stand —to defend at all costs their dying way of life.

This, even though by the time the buffalo hunters were done slashing their way through the great herds, both the Kiowa and the Kwahadi were no more than mere shadows of their previous greatness: hence our title, *Shadow Riders*.

Perhaps I should remind those who have been diligent in reading the previous five volumes in the

Plainsmen Series, along with informing those readers for the first time joining up with Seamus Donegan in what will be his twenty-four-year odyssey across the length and breadth of the American West, that above all, this is the story of a time and characters largely forgotten what with the pace of our supremely comfortable, relatively untroubled lives. I do so hope I have been able to convey with my story what must have been the very real pathos, the genuine human drama and conflict and passions of men colliding at destiny's siren call.

But I do want the newcomer to this iron-assed trail ride Seamus Donegan takes us on to know of my keen desire to go beyond the mere *retelling* of history. As a historical novelist, it is up to me to add something that history and historians alone cannot convey to the reader: that imminently warm, throbbing pulse that not only makes the reader a spectator to the drama, but for once and all time allows the reader to truly *relive* a moment in history.

The fevered romance of that quarter century is what I believe I have recaptured for you here in the Plainsmen Series—a fever that made the Indian Wars a time unequaled in the annals of man, when a vast frontier was wrenched from its inhabitants, in a struggle as rich in drama and pathos as any the world has known.

There is no richer story than to peer like voyeurs into the lives of people under the stress of life and death. Wondering, as only a reader in the safety of your easy chair can, if you would have measured up.

Important too is that the reader realize he's *reliving* the story of real people. In the cast of characters that accompanies the front material for this novel, a few of the names appear with an asterisk. They, and only they, are fictional characters, brought in by me for the use of a subplot that flows along elbow to elbow and stirrup to stirrup with the main storyline—the buffalo war of the great southern plains. Remember that all the rest were real, breathing human beings— on this stage at the time of this story. It is really the actual, documented events of their lives that form the backbone of this story. Not the dalliance of this historical novelist.

Into the midst of this tragic drama of the *Shadow Riders*, I once more send my fictional character, Seamus Donegan, late of the Union Army of the Shenandoah, cavalry sergeant turned soldier-of-fortune. (At this point the reader should be reminded that Seamus—Gaelic for James—is pronounced *Shamus* . . . just as you would pronounce Sean as *Shawn*.) Over the twenty-two volumes that will encompass this era of the Indian Wars, you will follow Seamus Donegan as he marches through some of history's bloodiest hours. Not always doing the right thing, but trying nonetheless. As those of you who have read the first five volumes in the series know already, Donegan was no "plaster saint," nor was he a "larger-than-life" dime-novel icon that Hollywood seems so dead set on portraying for us in our western themes.

History has plenty of heroes—every one of them dead. Seamus Donegan represents the rest of us. Ordinary in every way, except that at some point we are each called upon by circumstances to do something extra-ordinary . . . what most might call heroic.

Over the past year and a half since the publication of Volume 1, *Sioux Dawn*, I have been deeply gratified at the rousing success of this singular character, who, by the way, ended up being far different than I had first envisioned him. Seamus is, above all, his own man—and won't even let this author tell him what to do. Let me heartfully thank those of you who I've met at book signings from Canada to Texas, from California to the Atlantic Coast states, and from the Great Lakes down to the Gulf Coast—thank you for your fond acceptance of Seamus as not only a character you've come to identify with . . . but a man so many of you have come to regard as real and as a friend.

I find that reaffirming—because Seamus Donegan is very much a friend of mine.

We've all spent enough time in the saddle together, around winter campfires and hunkered down in little patches of what shade the great plains had to offer us, haven't we?

So what you will follow here in the *Shadow Riders* is, after all, a compelling story of something inevitable. Something of destiny's impelling course sweeping us up in its headlong rush into the future. But that has always been the story of man at war—of culture against culture, race against race. And remember this: that in this story, we stand but three short years from celebrating our nation's centennial, a time of scientific marvels, the beginning of our great Industrial Revolution.

Think of that: our Grand Republic speeding ever onward toward her Centennial birthday!

While out west, the unsung, lonely soldiers of the army of the frontier were called upon to wage a costly, inefficient, and thankless war against a stone-age people. A stone-age people who time and again confused, outmaneuvered, and downright defeated the cream of our military machine.

This time rather than going into detail on the books I drew upon for the factual history, the background, the color of that era, I'll just be content to list those titles I recommend, should you wish to learn more of the conquering of the southern plains.

The Conquest of the Southwest by Cyrus T. Brady

Conquest of the Southern Plains by Charles J. Brill

Fighting Indian Warriors—True Tales of the Wild Frontiers by E. A. Brininstool

Bury My Heart at Wounded Knee by Dee Brown

Crimson Desert—Indian Wars of the American Southwest by Odie B. Faulk

Soldiers West—Biographies from the Military Frontier edited by Paul Andrew Hutton

Carbine and Lance: the Story of Old Fort Sill by Colonel Wilbur S. Nye

Death Song—The Last of the Indian Wars by John Edward Weems

The Indian Wars of the West by Paul I. Wellman (currently reprinted in two volumes: *Death on the Prairie* and *Death in the Desert*)

Satanta—The Great Chief of the Kiowas and His People by Clarence Wharton

Even more so, the twelve volumes I returned to again and again in the late hours of each night when this story would not be denied, those same books I returned to again and again early each morning when I had no trouble getting up before dawn to write once more, ready to ride again that day with Seamus Donegan or the Tenth Negro Cavalry or Ranald Slidell Mackenzie's Fourth Cavalry—those twelve volumes I treasured most during the writing of this story:

The Life and Adventures of a Quaker Among the Indians by Thomas C. Battey

On the Border with Mackenzie—Or Winning West Texas from the Comanches by Robert G. Carter

The Buffalo War—the History of the Red River Indian Uprising of 1874 by James L. Haley

The Comanches—Lords of the South Plains by Ernest Wallace and E. Adamson Hoebel

The Buffalo Soldiers—A Narrative of The Negro Cavalry in the West by William H. Leckie

The Military Conquest of the Southern Plains by William H. Leckie

Five Years a Cavalryman by H. H. McConnell

The Kiowas by Mildred P. Mayhall

Plains Indian Raiders—the Final Phases of Warfare from the Arkansas to the Red River by Wilbur Sturtevant Nye

The Buffalo Hunters—the Story of the Hide Men by Mari Sandoz

Quanah, Eagle of the Comanches by Zoe A. Tilghman

Ranald S. Mackenzie on the Texas Frontier by Ernest Wallace

And if you have time to read but one book on this period beside Mari Sandoz's monumental work, to get a sentimental look at the hide-men and their era, you must read:

Life of "Billy" Dixon—Plainsman, Scout and Pioneer by Olive K. Dixon

With these sources at my fingertips, what remained was for the novelist in me to again do my best to flesh out the story with muscle and sinew, giving these faceless ghosts from our past voice once more. And distinctive voices is what I tried to give each of them, voices that would ring in your mind's ear long after you have finished the last page of *Shadow Riders*, voices that will express better than I ever could the mood and flavor of both that time and that place.

If I make you feel the bone-numbing cold so much

that you know you'll never be warm again . . . then you will begin to understand what it must have meant to a plainsman, despairing of ever again warming his frozen fingers over a fire. If I can make you feel the sheer panic and gut-wrenching fear it must have been to find yourself in the path of a raging prairie fire hurtling itself across the plains with a mindless destructive abandon . . . then you might begin to understand just how frightened these frontier-hardened men could become of something they could not understand, much less control.

For many of us, at those crucial turning points in our lives, fear is our most intimate companion. An enemy who will either break us . . . or a friend who will see that we survive, in the end a little stronger the next time we watch the sun rising pink and orange across the endless plains.

So go ahead as you turn the pages . . . sniff the air—you'll likely smell the stinging, pungent fragrance of gunpowder so hot it burns going down. Or you might smell the earthy perfume of a buffalo chip fire—if you've been savvy enough to lay in some against the coming blizzard. Those buffalo chips just might be the only thing between you and becoming a pile of bones come next spring when the wolves find what's left of your carcass at the first thaw. When your hands are cold enough, when your tongue is too numb to talk—you'll likely not care what it is that keeps you warm, and thank the great herds of buffalo that passed this way.

If one thing is constant and to be counted on out here in this country, it's that the wind will blow. The wind is like a constant companion, always at your ear, so constant you don't listen to it anymore. But that wind becomes a terror when it drives before it a frightening prairie fire . . . or with fury swirls the arctic winds into a plains blizzard.

So, you best saddle up, my friend. Seamus is waiting to ride out and there's no time to waste. You'll be knee to knee as he gallops for his life before that prairie fire and rides face-on into the jaws of the winter blizzard. If you look over at him now, you'll see how the wind and the sun, the wind and the cold, the wind and the caking dust mark a man living out his days on the plains. Tossing his long, curly hair, filling his nostrils with the wildness of this land.

And just like there's more than enough land to go around, there's enough wildness here as well.

Saddle up . . . we're riding to Texas.

—Terry C. Johnston
The Staked Plain
Panhandle of Texas
June 20, 1991

Characters

Seamus Donegan

Civilians

Thomas Brazeale
Nathan S. Long
Henry Warren
Sharp/Abner Grover
Lawrie Tatum—agent to
  the Kiowa-Comanche
  (resigned: 3/73)
S. W. T. Lanham—District
  Attorney, Jacksboro,
  Texas
Judge Soward
James Haworth—suc-
  ceeded Tatum as agent
  to the Kiowa-Comanche
John D. Miles—agent to
  the Southern Cheyenne

Billy Dixon
Mike McCabe
*Rebecca (Pike) Grover—
  Sharp Grover's wife
*Samantha Pike—Rebecca
  Grover's sister
Governor Edmund J. Davis
  —Governor of Texas
E. P. Smith—U.S. Indian
  Commissioner
Enoch Hoag—Superinten-
  dent of Central Superin-
  tendency, U.S. Indian
  Bureau
*Simon Pierce
*William Graves

Army

General William Tecumseh
  Sherman
Colonel Ranald S. Macken-
  zie—Fourth Cavalry
Colonel Benjamin H.
  Grierson—Tenth U.S.
  Negro Cavalry (Compa-
  nies: B, D, E, L, M)
Captain Louis H. Carpen-
  ter—H Company, Tenth
  Cavalry

Lieutenant L. H. Orleman
  —H Company, Tenth
  Cavalry
Lieutenant R. H. Pratt—D
  Company, Tenth Cavalry
Lieutenant Robert G.
  Carter—Fourth Cavalry
Lieutenant Peter M.
  Boehm—Fourth Cavalry
Captain E. M. Heyl—
  Fourth Cavalry

Lieutenant Colonel John W. Davidson—Tenth U.S. Negro Cavalry
*Lieutenant Ben Marston—commanding first Stillwell escort
Sergeant Reuben Waller—Company H, Tenth U.S. Negro Cavalry
*Lieutenant Harry Stanton—commanding second Stillwell escort
General Philip H. Sheridan

Scouts and Interpreters

Horace Jones—Grierson's interpreter at Fort Sill
Philip McCusker—interpreter at Medicine Lodge Treaty ceremonies
Jack Stillwell

Kiowa Indians

Satanta/White Bear
Kicking Bird (chief)
Satank (chief)
Big Tree (chief)
Mamanti
Lone Wolf
Yellow Chief
Eagle Heart (chief)
Big Bow (chief)
Red Otter
White Horse—well-known horse thief
Tau-ankia—son of Lone Wolf
Gui-tain—nephew of Lone Wolf

Kwahadi Comanche Indians

Quanah Parker
Wanderer/Peta Nocona

Comanche Indians

Cheevers—chief
Black Horse

Prologue

Moon of Plums Ripening
1866

"We have seen the wagons, White Bear!"

The stocky, muscular Kiowa chief watched that young, grinning rider bring his snorting pony to a halt before him. On all sides milled anxious warriors, warmed by the sun of this late summer day.

"The others you left behind will not be seen by the white men with those wagons?" asked the chief.

The young messenger shook his head, smiling in the brilliant, late-morning light. "It is a long snake of wagons . . . crawling slow as a sand tortoise. The white men will not know we are even in the country, White Bear—until we are on top of them!"

At that, the rest of the ten-times-ten hooted, shaking their bows, a few old muzzle-loaders held aloft in the hot August air among the warriors waiting down in the cottonwood and alder of the Llano River.

"They will stop soon, perhaps at the river crossing not far from here," White Bear told the warriors he hushed with a single wave of his hand. "The white man always stops to eat."

"We will strike them before their mouths are empty —and give them a bellyful of death!" shouted Big

Tree, a young, proven warrior who had become one of White Bear's trusted lieutenants.

The chief turned once more to the young scout who had galloped in with the good news. "Take us to the others now. So that we may see for ourselves this long snake of wagons you have found for us."

"Our ride will not be long, White Bear," the young one replied, pointing overhead. "From where the sun now hangs, it will not yet be at mid-sky when we reach the river crossing where the white men wait."

Without another word, the Kiowa war-chief turned and by stabbing the hot, still air with his long medicine lance ordered the hundred to follow. No squeak of leather saddles. No noisy strike of iron horseshoe on pebble. No rattle of bit-chains. Instead, these were proven warriors raised from birth in the hunt and chase of buffalo and enemy alike, at this moment nestled bareback atop war ponies, a single rawhide or buffalo-hair halter lashed securely to the animal's lower jaw. Silently they moved out: a fighting force on the move across the heart of the southern plains.

It was home to White Bear, better known to the hated white man by his Kiowa name—*Satanta*.

Born on the fringes of northern Mexico in the early winter of the year those white men designated as 1807, Satanta was the son of a Kiowa warrior and a Mexican woman. As a young child she had been captured on a raid made deep into the Saltillo country of Mexico in the late 1700s. Like so many others, she was raised as a Kiowa so that their wombs eventually bore the seed for many warriors.

She bore one son—White Bear.

It was his eyes that would see the greatest of days for the Kiowa people. Generations before, the Kiowa had been the first to see the white men marching north out of the hot lands far to the south, dressed in their heavy, sun-gleaming clothing, riding their tall elk-dogs.

And the Kiowa would be one of the last to give up to the white man. More pale-skinned enemies would fall to Kiowa bullets and arrows, lances and clubs, than to any other tribe on the southern plains.

Yet little did White Bear know as he rode down to the Llano Crossing this day, that his eyes would see the sunset of that greatness.

Long, long before any man's memory, the ancient Kiowa had lived in a land of cold, never-ending winters near the headwaters of the Missouri River, between the Flathead to the west and the Crow to the east. On the north roamed the far-ranging, war-loving Blackfoot confederation. It was in that country, during an autumn antelope hunt, that two rival Kiowa chiefs argued over possession of a young doe, her sides still warm as she lay among the sage. Arrows from both bows bristled from her side. Both chiefs claimed the doe, along with the prized udder, filled with the warm, rich milk considered a delicacy among their people.

Instead of bloodshed, the chiefs and their followers went their separate ways. One band wandered northwest, never to be heard from again. The other migrated south and east some, toward the headwaters of the Yellowstone River, eventually moving on to live in the shadow of the Black Hills, where they traded in peace with the Crow—until the white man far to the east began pushing the Dakota Sioux onto the northern plains, four generations before Satanta's mother was captured in Mexico.

A small tribe compared to the mighty Lakota bands, the Kiowa were once more pushed out of the way, this time farther south. Into the land of the Apache and the fierce, war-hungry Comanche. For many summers the Kiowa battled the Comanche, until both tribes made what was at first an uneasy truce, then eventually forged a strong and lasting alliance that would see them into these final days of their greatness as warrior societies on the southern plains.

From the Comanche the Kiowa first acquired Mexican mules. It wasn't long before the Kiowa became eager customers for Mexican prisoners—children and women only. A child might be worth at least ten dollars in blankets and beads, vermillion and tobacco . . . while a Mexican woman would be worth much, much more in trade goods. As was their custom, the Kiowa tattooed many of those captured Mexican women. Because of that disfiguring ornamentation and their new families created among a primitive people—few of these women chose to return to Mexico if rescue presented the opportunity.

"They are on their way to the new fort the soldiers are building," Satanta told the warriors—speaking of Fort Concho, being built here in the tough reconstruction months following the end of the Civil War.

He had reined them up some distance from the Llano Crossing, then sent two scouts ahead to find out what the wagon men were doing. "The white man used to fight among himself. Now they come to settle and raise their spotted cattle on our hunting land. We must show them this land will never be theirs—the price we will demand in blood for this ground must be too high for the white man to pay!"

Just prior to the early 1820s, the Kiowa saw their first Americans, traveling in long mule trains back and forth along the Santa Fe Trail, crossing the Cimarron and the Arkansas. A decade later the tribes of the southern plains were told some white traders had built a mud fort far up on the Arkansas, in sight of the tall, blue mountains. But few Kiowa and Comanche journeyed that far to trade: it would mean riding into Arapaho and Cheyenne country.

For many of those early years, the Kiowa and Comanche preferred instead to raid into Mexico.

Then in 1834, the "Summer of the Girl Returning" in Kiowa winter counts, the tribe was first visited by the Americans' warriors. General Henry Leavenworth led a sizable force of Mounted Dragoons to the southwest, land of the Kiowa and buffalo. Even more telling, Leavenworth had brought his riflemen to accompany the return of a Kiowa child to her people, a girl who had years before been captured by the Osages. The old chief, Dohauson, was much impressed with the effort taken by the white man and his warrior society to return this one small child to her people. The Kiowa pledged their undying friendship to the Great Father far to the east where the sun was born each day.

A decade later, in 1844, a white man came among them, sent by "Hook Nose Man" Bent, the trader in the mud house far up on the Arkansas. This old man who now built the log and mud trading house a few miles above the old Adobe Walls, west of Indian Territory, was named "Wrinkled Neck" by the Kiowa. Here the tribe traded for looking glasses and brass tacks, powder and lead for their old muzzle-loaders, iron barrel hoops for their arrow points. Still, Bent's trader lacked one thing most desired by the Kiowas: Mexican captives.

For nearly twenty years Wrinkled Neck's trading house flourished, until cholera spread its deadly scourge across the southern plains in the winter of 1861–62. The disease that no man feared in the morning while taking his breakfast, yet left that same man dead by supper, had been carried north by the Kiowa gone south to raid into Mexico. On their win-

ter count robes the tribe called this time of despair,
dying and stinking bodies in the camps . . . the
"Spotted Winter." Cholera finally died out, but not
until it had killed nearly a fourth of the tribe and
scattered the rest to the four winds in fear and super-
stition.

It was a time too that the white man had made his
presence known in Colorado Territory, coming for
the tiny yellow rocks. So many white men marched
greedily west that the buffalo were being pushed farther east along the Arkansas.

Satanta recalled the following winter, when the
warrior bands were camped on upper Walnut Creek,
which flows into the Arkansas at the great bend the
river makes in Kansas Territory. The snow came so
early that season, drifted so deep and stayed so long,
that the Kiowa remembered the year as the "Winter
When Horses Ate Ashes."

As soon as the white man stopped fighting himself
far to the east, the many tribes on the plains were
instructed that they would now be compelled to make
peace with the Great Father in Washington City.
Soldiers were coming to enforce that peace.

By this time there were few Indians who had not
learned of the massacre of Black Kettle's Southern
Cheyenne on the Little Dried River—what the white
man called Sand Creek.

Yet in the autumn of 1865 five warrior bands
warily met with white peace-talkers at the mouth of
the Little Arkansas. Only Kicking Bird, a courageous
chief who throughout his life counseled for peace, favored holding talks with the Great Father's representatives. Lone Wolf and Satanta sneered at any
suggestion that the Kiowa must fear the white man
and his soldiers.

At that council Satanta told the white man, "There

are three chiefs in the land of the Kiowa: the Spanish Chief, the White Chief, and now me. The Spanish Chief and me are men. We do bad toward each other, sometimes steal horses and take scalps from men, but we do not get mad and act the fool. The White Chief is a child and gets mad quick when my young men, to keep their women and children from starving, take from a white man something so simple as a cup of sugar or coffee or flour. The White Chief is angry and threatens to send his soldiers. He is a coward. Tell your White Chief what I have said."

That's why now, in Satanta's fifty-ninth summer, he was leading this raid on the white man's wagon train. This was, after all, what his people had done for as long as any man now alive could remember. To make war—as a man.

"White Bear—the wagons have stopped!"

"How far?"

The young scout pointed downstream. "My pony is hardly winded from the ride."

"It is time I had a look myself."

Minutes later Satanta inched on his belly to the crest of a hill and peered over. Below him stretched the timbered valley of the Llano, like a cool, beckoning ribbon here at midday in the late summer's heat come to roast the southern plains. The tall grass in the meadows, waving as far as the eye could see, had already been touched by the scorching heat come to stay this late in the season. He saw, smiled, then turned and retreated down the gentle slope to his expectant warriors.

"The white man is eating his noon meal," Satanta explained. "The animals are no longer tied to the wagons and are inside the ring made for their safety."

"Those wagons will not be enough to save them this day!" shouted Big Tree eagerly.

"Now is the time to finish making your medicine and painting your ponies. Very soon we must ride through that gap in the hills and come up behind the white men," he said, gesturing toward the saddle in the low hills.

It was through that gap that Satanta led the hundred, for the most part concealed behind the skimpy timber offered along the river's course. By the time he stopped the warriors and called his two hot-blooded lieutenants to his side, the moment of attack had arrived.

"They have seen us, my brothers," Satanta explained, his eyes not straying from the ring of wagons where the white men had suddenly exploded into action upon spotting the Kiowa, yelling, darting about, frantic like a prairie dog town under siege.

"It does not matter," said Yellow Chief with a smile.

"You are eager, aren't you?"

"I smell blood on the wind, White Bear," the young warrior answered.

"It is good. You will take half the warriors. Big Tree will lead the rest today."

Big Tree nudged his pony closer, an eager darkness crossing his face. "You are not leading the attack?"

Satanta shook his head. "I have lived many winters and taken many scalps. I will direct the attack from here." Reaching behind his shoulder, the Kiowa chief pulled up a shiny bugle he slung over the shoulder on a rawhide loop. "Each time I blow, I want the attack cut off and you both to ride to me. Is this understood?"

They nodded.

"It is good. Go now—see what the white men have for us in their wagons!"

With a whoop, both young war leaders leapt away, quickly dividing the hundred warriors. Big Tree sent a wild cry aloft as he led his band to sweep around the left side of the wagon circle. Yellow Chief led his warriors to the right.

All the white men had abandoned their tiny meal-time fires and now lay on their bellies in the shade beneath their wagons, their long guns ready.

For those first minutes, Satanta watched the young warriors hurl themselves down on the wagons, circling the white men, whirling past one another in two blurred rings of noise and terror as they pushed their ponies to great speed in that arc of spraying sand and brilliant summer sunshine. Closer and closer to the wagons they rode with each circuit, firing their arrows from short, Osage-orange bows, then quickly dropping to the off-side so that the white man had no more target than a heel hooked over a pony's backbone or a brown hand tangled in the pony's mane.

For a long time the white man did not fire, seemingly content to watch the brown-skinned riders and their lunging, sweating ponies, content to listen to the arrows hiss overhead and clatter into the branches of the trees where they had circled up for the noon meal. More arrows tore through wagon canvas. Iron-tipped wasps stung the mules kept at the center of the ring, making the animals noisy in their braying, thrashing, crazy dance of confusion and fear while the white man waited safely beneath his wagons.

Satanta put the bugle to his lips and blew three loud notes.

It was enough of a call on that dry, hot wind to bring about a pause in the raucous attack. Yellow

Chief, then Big Tree, clattered to a halt at the chief's side.

"Arrgghh!" cried Yellow Chief in frustration. "They will not shoot at us, White Bear!"

"The white man will not fire unless he is afraid," Satanta explained. "You haven't made him afraid yet. When I was a young man, I rode right into the jaws of my enemy's might. I stared at his arrow point, the sharp end of his lance, the gaping mouth of my enemy's rifle. If you want your young warriors to respect you—show them your courage . . . now. Only then will we be able to end this racing in circles and get down to lifting the white man's scalps!"

"Aiyeee!" shouted Big Tree as he reined away in a tight circle.

"We will not fail you!" roared Yellow Chief as he hammered heels into his pony's ribs.

Big Tree had the lead now, his warriors following him in ever nearer to the wagons. No longer content to shoot from a safe distance, the young Kiowas raced closer and closer to the white men on their bellies in the shadows. Then Yellow Chief saw that he must do even better as he thundered in with his half-a-hundred. He would ride into the jaws of those guns and make the white man's bowels run cold with fear.

"Close enough that you see the fear in their eyes, Yellow Chief," said Satanta softly as he witnessed the wild, noisy race.

Then suddenly the ring of wagons erupted with explosions. The white men were shooting their guns at last.

He nodded. "It is good! Now you ride close enough to make the white man's heart turn to water."

Thirty guns roared, booming low there beside the Llano in that circle beneath the trees where the gray-white gun smoke clung just above the dirty canvas of the wagons. While some of the white men frantically reloaded their rifles, others continued to aim and shoot their pistols at the charging horsemen.

In a spray of sand and grit and tufts of summer grass, a warrior spilled from his pony. Tumbling through the dried, yellow stalks—his shoulder and chest already slicked with crimson.

Then another pony faltered, stumbled and spilled its rider. That animal . . . and another . . . then a third never rose from the grassy sand. In agony the riders crawled on their bellies away from the stinging smoke and spitting fire of the white man's guns.

Satanta could hear Yellow Chief exhorting his warriors now, goading them into wilder bravery. The attack was taking longer than he had expected—and still the white man remained safe inside his ring of wagons. Satanta had not seen one of the enemy fall, dead or wounded. He blew his bugle once more.

When the two war leaders halted before him, Satanta said, "We must get inside that ring of wagons. The white man is like a field mouse burrowed under the shadows. The only way is the way of the badger— go in and get him out!"

With resolve, the two looked at one another. Then without a word, they reined away to their warriors.

Now the end would come, Satanta felt certain. All they needed to do was ride close enough, shoot many arrows then leap among the wagons. It would be over soon enough—this smashing the war clubs into the faces and driving the tomahawks into the backs of the heads until no white man remained alive.

It must be done fast, as he had learned many, many winters before. A long battle only meant many Kiowa dead and wounded. In his youth Satanta had learned the fight must be quick and furious to be a victory.

The white man's rifles erupted with a deafening roar once again.

As he watched, Satanta saw Yellow Chief sweep in from behind the ring, daring closer than any of the rest, his small rawhide shield held up to cover him as he waved the stone-headed club at the end of his arm.

Then the warrior was spinning backward off the pony. And the animal was rearing back as well, flinging its rider into the grassy sand like a child's doll. The pony landed atop Yellow Chief's legs.

Satanta's lungs did not breathe, watching the young war chief's hands claw desperately at the crusty earth, raking at the grass, trying to yank himself free as frothy blood gurgled from his lips.

His insides are torn!

As Satanta yanked the bugle to his lips, he saw Yellow Chief stop moving, his two hands slowly opening, freeing the unyielding earth and grass beneath him.

Before the Kiowa chief's bugle call was finished, two more warriors had spilled from their ponies. As that pair of horsemen crawled away from the deadly wagon ring, their ponies thrashed and kicked in death throes . . . then lay still, raising only their heads as they cried out in a pitiful, humanlike scream of torment.

When the two young ones believed they were safe enough, both clambered to their feet and dashed toward the trees.

Bullets found them both in a renewed frenzy of firing from the wagons.

Satanta felt each body go down in a bloody splatter, as if it were his own.

"Big Tree!" he shouted. "The toll is too great."

"You are calling off the attack?"

He nodded. "We will find some other white men, another wagon train to attack. We leave now, but not

until you have first sent your men to get those who
have fallen!"

Big Tree looked over his shoulder at the open
ground sloping down to the Llano Crossing where
the white men huddled in the midday shadows with
their big, long guns. "We can get four. Yet . . . Yellow Chief—he is too close to the wagons."

Satanta tore his eyes from the white men and the
greasy white smoke that hung in a hot, bitter-smell-
ing cloud over the wagon ring. Now he glared at the
young war chief.

"I am an old man. I have fought many battles in my
many summers of raiding. Yet you are sitting here,
telling me none of these young men will ride in to
rescue the body of Yellow Chief?"

Big Tree wiped his lips. "He is . . . surely he is
dead, White Bear."

"Here!" Satanta snapped, pulling the rawhide loop
from his shoulder, removing the bugle and flinging it
at Big Tree. "I will show you the true courage of a
Kiowa warrior! Watch—all of you! And behold your
chief!"

With a cool, arrogant courage, Satanta slowly led
his prancing war pony within rifle range of the thirty
white men, then suddenly hammered his heels into
the animal's ribs and in a burst of furious speed tore
straight for the body of Yellow Chief. As he neared
the fallen pony, Satanta gripped the reins in one
hand, his heel locked on the pony's hip, inch by inch
leaning to the side, his fingers raking the brittle,
bloodstained grass.

For some reason, the white men did not fire their
weapons at that lone horseman. Perhaps they were
awed with his courage, presenting his full, brown
body to their long guns. Then only one man fired, and
that shot went wild. In the next instant he was over

the bloodied body, reining his heaving pony to a stuttering halt.

Satanta grasped on the warrior's arm with the strength of two men and with a mighty shout pulled the broken, crimson-smeared body from beneath the dead pony. As the white men began urging one another to shoot, the Kiowa chief slung Yellow Chief across the back of his pony, gave the wagon ring a sneer and a profane wave of his arm, then reined for the timber at a lope, presenting his wide, brown back to his enemy.

"We go now, warriors!" Satanta said as he let two others take the body of Yellow Chief from him. Clearly, most of the hundred still burned with battle fever.

"Do not worry, my brothers," the Kiowa chief told them as they abandoned the white man's wagons and the Llano Crossing. "Someone . . . and soon . . . will pay in blood for the life of Yellow Chief!"

Chapter 1

Moon of Ducks Coming Back
1871

Satank gazed into the sky overhead, so incredibly blue now that the spring storm had passed and the thunderstorms had rolled on to the east where the civilized Indians lived on their reservations, pretending to be white men.

The ducks were coming back. They and the geese filled the sky these lengthening days, flying north in great, dark vees against the pale, azure blue of the sky reflected in the small ponds and puddles of water left after each passing spring thunderstorm.

The old man liked this time of the year best. It made him feel like a randy young colt again.

Bald Head, the white Indian agent over at Fort Sill, called this time April.

Satank liked his way better. It was this time of the year he remembered the tingle of juices flowing in his veins and the strength of mating surge through his loins. Ah, the ways of a young man!

And for the first time in his life, Satank actually grew jealous of his own grown son, married now, with two sons of his own.

Among his people, the Kiowa, Satank's name meant "Sitting Bear."

And sitting was something he most enjoyed these days. He drank deep of the clean air left behind in the storm's wake as the dark clouds cleared off and rumbled eastward. It was near here that he had been born nearly seventy winters before. This was the land they had fought the Comanche for, the land they held along with the Comanche across many summers of hunting buffalo. And riding side by side, the two tribes had struggled against the hated white Tehannas.

Even the merest thought of the white man spoiled Satank's mood. That thought come here now to cloud up the sky of his mind and moods like the dark thunderclap clouds so full of noise and wind and fury.

The Mexicans far to the south and west had rarely ventured this far into Comanche and Kiowa land. And if they had, it was only to trade along the well-established routes carved out long winters beyond remembering across the high Staked Plain. Yes, the Mexicans came to trade in cattle and horses stolen from the white man. And there were occasionally the Comancheros who dared ride into the land of the Comanche and the Kiowa to trade as well—to trade in human captives.

A life his grandsons would not have for their own, this chasing after the buffalo for all the Kiowa needed to survive in this great land where they had come from the far north. Yet it was here, among the Republican and Arkansas herds of the shaggy, black beasts, that the Kiowas and Comanches did not yet realize they were playing out the final acts of a great tragedy like no other in the history of the world.

The first act in that long played-out drama had seen the coming of the strange, pale men out of the south armed with powerful weapons, some marching on foot, others riding atop the big elk-dogs. It was the

coming of the horse that ushered in the second act of
the tragedy. For now the Kiowa and others had their
first guns. More important—now at last they rode as
true kings of all they cast their eyes upon.

It was the horse that evolved the Kiowa into a truly
nomadic people, free and wild—yet a people in every
way totally dependent upon the buffalo season after
season after season, dependent for food, and shelter
and clothing, and for the very purpose to their lives.
The Kiowa was as irretrievably bound to the buffalo
as much as any prisoner was shackled by irons to his
cell. No matter that for Satank's people the cell had
no roof save that of endless powder blue overhead,
no walls save that of the far horizons at the curve of
the earth in all four directions.

They were locked in this prison, unaware that the
death of the buffalo would soon spell the death of
their culture. Yet, for the last five winters, Satank's
spirit helper had been telling the old man to listen
fervently to the wind. But the old man had laughed at
that—simply because the wind always blew out here
on the plains!

Still . . . when he did listen, Satank heard the
faintest whisperings of the spirits long gone the way
of breath-smoke, telling him the final days had come
and were now upon his people. With the going of the
buffalo, they told him, so would go the Kiowa. The
bones of his people left to bleach in the sun on the
high prairie like the carcasses left to rot by the few
white hunters who were bravely daring to cross the
Arkansas into the last sacred hunting ground guaranteed the Kiowa and Comanche by the treaty-talkers.

Long, long ago, nothing had been so complicated
as this. He was a young warrior then, like his son
now. Satank had taken his first wife and they had
been joined by two small children come to bless their

lodge. Days filled with nothing more worrisome than
raiding and hunting the buffalo with his bow. Each
summer, he purged himself at the sun dance the medicine men held along one creek or another in this
vast, rolling grass kingdom ruled by the brown-
skinned sovereigns of the southern plains. It had
been so good . . . but only for half his life, Satank
remembered.

Even when his enemy was as bloodthirsty as was
the old Kiowa chief, it was good, simply because a
warrior clearly understood his enemy—the Mexican.

The dark-skinned men marching out of the south
and west of the great Staked Plain would often talk
soft and sweet while stroking their dark beards or
smoothing their dark mustaches when they coveted
something dear to the Kiowa. Satank himself had immediately liked the long, scraggly mustaches of the
Mexicans—so grew one himself—an oddity among a
warrior society that normally plucked every single facial hair, including eyebrows. He wore his mustache
as proudly as any symbol of manhood.

While the Mexicans often talked sweet when they
wanted something, on the next occasion of meeting
with the Kiowa, the Mexican could be as brutal as
any warrior: butchering the Indian men, women and
children without qualm or remorse. What bothered
most Kiowa about the Mexicans was that the dark-
skins would lure the Indians into their villages and
settlements with promises of barter and trade-goods,
and once the gates were shut, those Mexicans would
slaughter the ignorant bands as retribution for past
raids upon herds of cattle and horses or for carrying
off a few women and children to become new members of the tribes.

The Kiowa learned quickly to hate the Mexican,
and hate him with everything he had. But unlike the

white American who had for so long had little to do in this great kingdom of grass and hills, the Kiowa did understand the Mexican. They were alike in many ways.

Then the white man began to arrive in such numbers, no longer just content to push down from the land of the Lakota and Osage and Pawnee, crossing the Arkansas, the Cimarron and the Canadian on his way only to trade with the Mexicans in Santa Fe. Now the white man came out of the east, his walking soldiers in blue uniforms and his rolling wagon guns rumbling along behind, marching to fight the Mexicans, to take land away from them.

Just like the white man had later begun taking this grand, grass kingdom of rolling hills from the Comanche and the Kiowa who had ruled it from atop their fleet ponies.

In those years following the white man's war with Mexico, the number of Tehannas multiplied like puffballs on the prairie after a spring thunderstorm. Not that they were there to kill the buffalo, no—instead these built their lodges beside the creeks and scratched at the earth and raised their animals and kept to themselves while the Kiowa most loved to be in the company of one another. This was something hard for Satank to comprehend—that the Tehannas would want to set themselves off from others of their own kind.

Twenty winters after the white man's war on the Mexicans, in the summer after Yellow Chief was killed, word came to the Kiowa that the treaty-talkers wanted again to speak to the warrior bands. Two years before, they had met with the white man and received his presents and signed his talking paper at the mouth of the Little Arkansas. Now again, there was to be more talk far to the north, on Medicine Lodge Creek.

That was four winters ago by Satank's count— when the bands gathered for the great peace council not far from Fort Larned in the white man's Kansas Territory. Many miles to the south on the Cimarron River, and refusing to yet come in to talk, were camped the might of the Southern Cheyenne, more than 250 lodges in all. Skeptical, they waited far from the reach of the white man's soldiers should this treaty-talk prove to be a ruse and a trap.

On the other hand, Black Kettle's twenty-five lodges of Southern Cheyenne marched right to the banks of Medicine Lodge Creek itself to camp. Below them stood more than a hundred lodges of Comanches. And downstream from them were raised the camp circles of some 150 lodges of Kiowa, along with eighty-five lodges of Kiowa-Apache—warrior bands under Satank, Satanta, Big Tree, Big Bow, Lone Wolf and Kicking Bird. Camped closest to Fort Larned were some 170 lodges of Southern Arapaho.

All told, an impressive gathering of more than eight hundred lodges, each camp in a joyful mood, for the hunting had been good in recent days. What was more, word had it the soldiers at the nearby post had just received shipments of the goods soon to be brought out to the great encampment in wagons: coffee, sugar, flour and dried fruits; in addition to blankets and bolts of colorful cloth, there were to be surplus uniforms from the white man's recent war among himself, uniforms the War Department had in the last few months turned over to the Interior Department. And on its way as well was a sizable herd of the white man's cattle to feed the gathering bands.

When the white commissioners arrived at the scene on the fifteenth of October, they and their military escort of the Seventh Cavalry camped across the creek on the north side of the Medicine Lodge. Row upon neat row of soldier tents were erected across the grassy prairie for time beyond memory dotted with dried buffalo chips. Nearby stood a long train of the freight wagons bulging with the very presents for those who would sign the talking paper with the Great Father back east. Closest to the creek were the tents erected for the commissioners themselves.

In that flat meadow between their tents and the stream bank, the great council got its informal sessions under way on the seventeenth of October. Two days later the visiting chiefs began making their formal speeches.

Behind the commissioners seated at their table hung a large canopy beneath which the many stenographers sat over their paper and pens, recording the proceedings word for word. There too gathered the many newsmen here to record for their curious readers back east this momentous gathering with the warrior bands of the Great Plains.

On each subsequent morning the council assembled, the Cheyenne and Arapaho chiefs seated themselves on the right hand of the white men, or on the west. To the left sat Satank along with the other Kiowa and Comanche leaders. In a sweeping crescent behind these chiefs sat the old men, councilors and leaders among their people. Behind them, beside the stream itself, the young warriors strutted in all their martial glory—feathers and bells, paint and totems, in no way shy in showing off their weapons.

That first day Senator John B. Henderson had proposed to the assembled chiefs that the Cheyenne and Arapaho bands be moved south to the Arkansas River while the Kiowas could settle on land farther south along the Red River for their permanent reservation.

As soon as the head men would agree to this proposal and formally touch the pen, Henderson told them, the army would distribute the promised goods. Woman's Heart and Kicking Bird were the first of the Kiowa to step to the tables and again make peace with the white man as they had so often done in the past.

Satank and the rest of the chiefs did not.

When it came time for the old chief to speak, he told the white commissioners, "The white man grows jealous of his red brother. The white man once came to trade. Now he comes as a soldier. He once put his trust in our friendship and wanted no shield but our fidelity. But now he builds forts and plants big guns on their walls. He once gave us arms and bade us hunt the game. We loved him then for his confidence. He now covers his face with the cloud of jealousy and anger and tells us to be gone, as an offended master speaks to his dog!"

Then came a few of the Comanche, followed by the Arapaho, and finally—after many days of debate—the Cheyenne agreed to the white man's terms.

Their job done, the commissioners informed the chiefs they were ordering the distribution of the promised presents. High-walled army freight wagons groaned into the meadow, emptying their contents into three huge piles: on the west, a pile for the Apache and Arapaho; in the center, a pile for the great Cheyenne of the central plains. And, on the east, a pile for the Kiowa and Comanche of the southern plains.

There was so much there and the celebrating so great—Satank remembered now how the warrior societies were ordered forward to see that a fair distribution was made among the people. One by one the women were handed a kettle and an axe, blankets and the white man's clothing, coffee and sugar and flour and much more.

Sitting Bear recalled that day—remembering it as the first time he had ever thought that the white man just might number like the stars in the sky. What sadness it had caused him too—while there was such celebration in the camps.

No man, no woman nor child, was able to ride from that meadow back to their villages. Every pony and pack animal the Kiowa put to use hauling their new riches, stacked high and cumbersome and wobbly on animal backs or swaybacked on groaning travois. No woman muttered complaints of having too much.

With the days growing shorter and the nights colder, Satank had watched as the other bands wandered off onto the mapless prairie, slowly marching into the four winds. Along the bank of Medicine Lodge Creek that last morning before the Kiowa themselves marched away, the old warrior had found the stream slicked with a thin, fragile layer of ice scum. Winter was due on the high plains. Winter would not be denied.

Satank felt it in his heart again, even now, that coldness of winter as he stroked his scraggly mustache.

It hurt too, remembering that happy time for his people before they were ordered onto their reservation, recalling how the great cloud of dust rose into the clear, autumn-cold sky above the rear marchers of Arapaho and Southern Cheyenne and Comanche, each taking a different trail to find their own winter camps.

He gazed now at this small campsite, remembering that great, empty campsite along the Medicine Lodge four winters gone, strung as the campsites were up

and down the banks of the little stream, the tall grass
trampled and pocked with hundreds of lodge circles
and blackened by hundreds of fire pits, pony drop-
pings and bones and the remains of willow bowers
used by the young warriors too old to live any longer
with their families but too young yet to have a wife
and lodge and children too.

His eyes stung him for a moment as Satank swallowed down the pain of loss, remembering the old
days—knowing his grandchildren would never know
such joy as he had known in days gone, and never to
hold again in his hands. A pain like a deep wound
within him refusing to heal, seeping a poison with
such a stench that it made his nose wrinkle.

Little more than a year after Medicine Lodge, the
Yellow Hair Custer had marched into Indian Territory and massacred Black Kettle's sleeping village
camped but a few miles down the Washita from the
Kiowa. Then a moon later the Yellow Hair had
marched once more, this time after the Kiowa themselves. Custer and Soldier-Chief Sheridan had caught
Satanta and Lone Wolf on Rainy Mountain Creek and
held the pair hostage until the rest of the bands came
in. Although the chiefs were prepared to die and had
told their people to flee to the faraway Staked Plain,
Big Tree and Satank and Woman's Heart decided to
do as the soldiers demanded. In desperation, the Kiowa were made to promise they would stay on their
reservation in the shadows of the newly constructed
Fort Sill.

Yet it made his heart swell to think back that the
next spring the young men were riding off again, to
raid into the land of the Tehanna for cattle and
horses, even riding north to steal mules from the
soldiers at Camp Supply.

From time to time a visitor came from the Cheyenne or the Arapaho, telling of the slaughter of the buffalo north of the Arkansas River. The visitors spoke of how the air stunk with the rotting meat left behind for the fattened buzzards and the four-leggeds who lived on stinking carrion. The white hunters took only the hides, perhaps a few tongues, and left the rest to rot and bleach and foul the clean prairie air.

"It does not matter," Satank had assured them, as only an old warrior could. "The treaty-talkers told us —this is our land down here. These are our buffalo and we can hunt them as long as there are buffalo. The white man will never cross south of the Arkansas to kill the buffalo—for our children's children will have the rich, juicy meat for their bellies many winters yet to come."

"What becomes of us if the white man kills all the buffalo north of the Arkansas and he wants our buffalo?" asked young Mamanti, a brave war-chief preparing to lead a party of 150 warriors south into Tehas, where they would raid farms and settlements and perhaps a wagon train or two.

Satank laughed easily, showing some of the gaps in his teeth. What teeth he had nowdays were sore, and he remembered how he used to chew on buffalo hump-meat barely seared over a flame.

"Do not worry, Mamanti," he said, reassuring the war-chief. "The treaty-talkers promised us the soldiers would keep the white man north of the river. You would be foolish to think that the white hide hunters would ever dare cross south of the Arkansas."

Chapter 2

May 18, 1871

"$\mathcal{W}$e don't start making better time, we won't see Salt Creek tonight," said the young teamster to the older man on the bench beside him.

Thomas Brazeale had been working for civilian Henry Warren for two years now, back and forth, up and down this road, in and out of the Indian Territories, on contract to haul supplies for the forts of west Texas: Richardson, Griffin and Concho.

The old man wiped a sweaty hand along the butt of his Spencer repeating rifle and flung a long brown curd toward the tail of the leeside mule. He connected, center.

"Don't know what you're fretting about, son. It don't matter much to me where I sleep tonight. One piece of ground just like the next."

They had just entered the Salt Creek prairie, and weren't making the kind of time they should be on this part of the haul. At least Thomas knew that. "I figure we got ten more miles till we reach Salt Creek. It's the next water we'll see."

"And if we don't, Warren's see'd to it we've got water in them barrels lashed to every wagon. Now shut-up and drive, boy—what you paid to do," the old man snapped.

Brazeale didn't like this old rifleman assigned to his lead wagon for this trip west from the rail depot at Weatherford, Texas, burdened under a load of corn for the army. Ten wagons, forty mules, and a dozen employees. And Thomas had to ride with this old, snarling bastard through luck of the draw—just because Brazeale always drove lead wagon. Knowing, as he did, the road, and landmarks, and places to noon and where to water the stock, along with where the good grass could be found come time to make camp for the night.

Two days back they had been late leaving Fort Richardson farther down on the Brazos River. And that had made Warren late ever since. Now they were a good twenty miles west of Richardson, Brazeale spotting some horsemen far ahead, across the grassy plain.

"Riders."

"I see 'em, boy. You just tend to your driving."

The horsemen turned out to be the advance of a military escort for no less than William Tecumseh Sherman himself. The general stopped for but a few minutes to shake hands all around with the teamsters, veterans of the Confederate Army to a man, thanking each one of them for the job he was doing, declaring that his escort was lagging behind him a few minutes on this leg of his journey to Fort Richardson.

"All's well down at Griffin," Sherman reported, turning his back on the old rifleman who refused to budge from the wagon seat. "Believe me, I know about long and delicate supply lines . . . what with that goddamned Georgia campaign. Bloody plain you men are the backbone to keeping this frontier open. My congratulations to you."

Sherman saluted the civilians, then remounted and promptly rode off with his dozen soldiers, having caught up, continuing east.

Thomas Brazeale climbed back aboard the high-walled freighter, glanced over his shoulder, eased off the brake and slapped leather against mule hide. The wagons rumbled into motion once more.

"Why didn't you get down to shake hands with the general?" Thomas asked the old rifleman.

He spit more brown juice into the spring wind. "Son of a bitch can die with a bullet between his goddamned eyes, for all I care."

"That was General—by God—Sherman!"

"And during the goddamned war I done my best to make things hard on that poke-stealing bastard," he snarled.

"Didn't know you was so hard again' the Union."

The old man stared at Brazeale, incredulous. "I'm from Texas, boy. There ain't no doubt of that, is there?"

"No, sir."

"So there damned well better be no doubt where my heart laid when it come to that goddamned war."

"Sounds like the war ain't over for you."

The old man finally glanced over and caught the grin on Brazeale's face, then smiled with one of his own. "Shit—if I was still of a mind to fight the war . . . there'd be one less Yankee general right now . . . and one more dead body to lay a'bleaching in the middle of this Jacksboro road!"

Thomas had to laugh at the old man, the way he said it, and the way he stroked the butt of that scuffed and worn but well-oiled Spencer repeater. Seven shots, and seven good Injuns, the old man had said days ago when they first loaded up at the rail siding in Weatherford, on the other side of the Brazos River, last stop on the line coming west from Dallas.

"All seven red niggers got a real good chance of spending eternity in Hell, I got anything to say about it!" the old Texan had spouted.

He was a sour one, Thomas thought, most of the time—but he could smile if he had to. And the old man would do to ride with all the way to Fort Griffin and back.

"You think General Sherman got more soldiers riding his rear guard?" Brazeale asked less than an hour later as the wagons lumbered closer and closer toward the Salt Creek Crossing.

He had to nudge an elbow into the old man's side to roust him from his sleep.

"What's that?"

"Look yonder," Thomas said, pointing. "You figure that's some of Sherman's rear guard?"

The old man didn't reply at first, merely squinting and peering through the shimmering afternoon sunlight, studying the road far ahead.

"First off, son—there's too damned many of the sonsabitches to be soldiers."

Brazeale swallowed hard. "Not . . . not soldiers?"

The old man was rising from the bench seat, turning to signal back to the other nine wagons and teamsters. "Find us a good, open spot to corral these wagons up, son. And you best make it fast. We don't have time to be lollygagging."

Brazeale felt his heart rise in his throat as he read the look of something strange, foreign, in the old man's eyes. Then he glanced on down the road at that dust cloud and the wavy horsemen beneath the sun and shadow and haze of the Jacksboro-Belknap

Road. Not that he hadn't seen Indians before, even Kiowa. Shit, he worked for Henry Warren of Weatherford—and if that didn't mean hauling supplies north to the Nations where the government had the Indians on reservations, why . . . but this group of horsemen was something else. More warriors coming on at that easy pace, just coming and coming on— more than young Thomas Brazeale had ever seen.

And these didn't look like no reservation bucks neither.

There was no time lost in rumbling those ten wagons into a crude circle, wagonmaster Nathan S. Long yelling orders and nobody really listening as they all scrambled to unhitch the mules from the trees, confining the forty-one animals inside the circle while the teamsters pulled rifles and ammunition from beneath the seats and made themselves small under the wagons just as a bugle blast split the air and more than a hundred Kiowas gave a war whoop, pounding heels into their war ponies.

In the shadows of that wagonbed, Thomas felt he was choking on his own belly-bile. Cursing himself, he knew it was better than wetting himself.

Those painted, screaming warriors were not content to merely circle the wagons this time out. Instead, they rushed headlong at the dozen white men as if they intended to overrun the ring of wagons in one swift and bloody charge.

Just like a nighthawk, Thomas thought as the screeching brown horde thundered in. Like a nighthawk sweeping down on a moth or wren or tiny sparrow.

As those dozen teamsters opened fire into the brown mass of that first wave, Nathan Long and four others were either killed or wounded.

Thomas watched the screeching, red wave pass,

the sting of burnt black powder making his eyes water, pungent on his tongue. Behind him some of the teamsters were yelling again, nonsense. Then someone was pulling on Thomas's leg. He jerked around to find one of the older men motioning him out of the wagon shadows.

"Let's get!"

"Where?"

"We're going to the trees, by God!"

Brazeale glanced over the scene. Five men down: two staring at the sky, motionless. Another two facedown in the grass and dust, barely breathing. The old rifleman was the fifth, sitting slumped against a wagon wheel, his legs akimbo, his head slung low between his shoulders. On his chest glistened a bright red rosette. As Brazeale crouched beside him and pulled the old man's head back, the wrinkled eyelids fluttered.

"I'm done, boy. Just don't let them bastards get me alive. You . . . you gotta kill me 'fore you go."

"C'mon, Thomas!" rose the shout from others.

He gazed back at the old man.

"Gimme my gun, boy—you don't got the stomach to kill me yourself, much as I'd beg you."

Brazeale found it in the nearby grass, slapped it in the old Texan's hand. For the first time those wrinkled eyes softened.

"I don't want you to watch—now get and save your hide!"

Brazeale was pulled onto his feet by two others anxious to escape. He found himself running, eyes stinging as he glanced one last time at the old man, watching the Texan jam the muzzle of his rifle under his chin, stretching down for the trigger guard. He squeezed off the tears and turned around as the three of them vaulted over the wagon tongue.

The rifle exploded like spring thunder behind him. Brazeale did not look back.

One teamster spilled a few yards ahead of him, whimpering in pain from the first arrow that fluttered between his shoulder blades.

They would never make the trees ahead.

He leaped over the wounded man, squirming still, his hands red as he struggled to grasp the arrows bristling high in his back. Crying out, like the gutted pigs back home—crimson streaming down his wrists.

When Thomas reached the trees, he was gasping, sliding in among the late shadows with the rest. How many he did not know at that moment. Only that there were five back there at the wagon ring where the warriors closed in now. And two out there in the dry grass, having tried to make it to this stand of trees. His mind scratched at the calculations the way he would scratch at the damned chiggers troubling his sweating body this time of the year. That made five of them left out of the twelve . . .

The guns opened up in a sporadic rattle of fire within the ring, warriors screaming in victory, ponies whinnying. The mules braying as the first fell.

The red bastards were shooting the mules.

Then Thomas saw one of the two bodies moving out on the Salt Plain, there in the tall grass. Slowly crawling, crawling toward the trees.

A blast from a bugle drew Brazeale's attention from the wounded teamster in the grass. By lord, he prayed—it might be soldiers!

But as the huge, stocky, bare-chested Indian rode into sight and reined up, Thomas saw the bugle hung from the war-chief's neck. Whoever he was, he was shouting orders, stopping the slaughter of the noisy, scree-hawing mules.

Overhead the storm clouds had rolled in so quickly

that Thomas had not even noticed. Black, roiling, fluffy and full of terror. The kind of clouds a twister would drop out of—

His attention was brutally yanked back to the grassy plain where three warriors had discovered the wounded teamster among the tall grass. With a shriek from the white man, the three dragged their captive back toward the wagons, shouting joy at finding one of their enemy alive.

Thomas swallowed hard, choking on the sour ball in his throat. He understood enough to know why the warriors were celebrating now. It wasn't for the wagons and their booty. It wasn't for stealing the mules. No . . . instead, they had them a white man now. Alive.

Young Brazeale squeezed his stinging eyes shut and turned around to find the other four teamsters gone. He could not hear them answer when he whispered for them. Thomas could not see them anywhere in the shadowy timber nearby. Gone.

But that's where he wanted to be.

Long gone from this bloody meadow . . .

"Looked like Spencers, sir," gulped the young Texan.

General William Tecumseh Sherman fumed to his core as he tore his eyes from the young teamster's face.

Just minutes ago the civilian had stumbled into Fort Richardson on foot, grimy and soaked to the hide with the driving rain, his eyes wide with fear, wide with what he had witnessed. Telling any and all listeners about the raid on Henry Warren's wagon train some twenty miles back on the Jacksboro-Belknap Road.

Shadows lengthened in the room with that first fuzzy texture come to early evening here on the

southern plains, the air stirring enough to cool things
quickly what with the passing of the noisy, crashing,
prairie thunderstorm. Sherman had to admit, he
liked the weather farther north. Farther still than St.
Louis, where he had moved his command headquarters after he found his craw filled with that strutting
peacock of a Secretary of War Belknap and the rest
of those starched collars who sucked up to one another like a bunch of gelded, bawling calves.

"How many, son?"

The teamster shook his head, swiping his rain-
dampened hair from his eyes as the post surgeon
gruffly attended to bandaging the gash the youngster
had along his side. "Don't know, General. A lot."

"Colonel Mackenzie," Sherman said grittily,
turning to the commander of the Fourth Cavalry
headquartered here at Richardson, "those red sonsabitches got those Spencers up on the reservation—or
Bill Sherman doesn't have balls. By Jupiter, we've
got to cut off this trade in weapons and powder—but
first, we've got to get you following these murderers."

"Yes, sir," answered the tall, handsome, mus-
tachioed Mackenzie. "From what the civilian here
tells us, there were between a hundred and a hundred fifty warriors. I've already sent my adjutant to
have four companies stand ready to horse, General."

"Good. Pack thirty days rations," growled Sherman, stuffing the damp stub of his cigar back in his
yellowed teeth. He gazed at the young teamster a moment, then his eyes found Mackenzie staring at him.
"You know, Colonel—I passed that train with my escort minutes before they were jumped."

Mackenzie nodded. "It must surely have a sobering
effect on you, General. To think that those raiders
could be carrying your scalp on their belts now."

Sherman snorted, running a hand over his thin-

ning hair, half-bald already, what there was turning
to gray bristles on top. "Shit, Mackenzie. I thought
these Kiowa and Comanche down here were warriors. This scalp of mine isn't fit for a real fighting
Injun's lodgepole!"

"We don't find a trail to follow, you want us to stay
out for the thirty days, General?"

"I want you to do your goddamndest to find the red
bastards! If you can do it, and strike them hard inside
those thirty days—then do it. Cut those warriors off at
the knees!"

"I'll send word back when I've found them."

"Where will you head from here, Colonel?"

Mackenzie did not hesitate. "There's only one direction that bunch will go, I'm afraid. They'll ride
north."

Sherman fumed, his ruddy cheeks puffing. "Back
to the God-blamed reservation?"

"Yes, General. Back to Fort Sill."

Chapter 3

May 27, 1871

"*T*his New York paper claims I should be President, Mr. Tatum," announced the graying General Sherman as he laid the *Herald* on the civilian's small desk in the middle of his cramped office.

Lawrie Tatum, agent for the Kiowa-Comanche reservation located just outside Fort Sill, nodded. He was Society of Friends—a Quaker. "Yes, General. If the Almighty has that in His plans—you will be President of the United States."

The civilian watched the easygoing Sherman wrinkle his eyes at that and step over toward the window, gazing out on the wide, tree-ringed meadow. Agency storehouses stood in a short row to his right, a small chapel to the left of this tiny clapboard office house built for the government's agent.

"Grant may like you Quakers," Sherman said with his back to Tatum, "but—for the record—I don't."

"It's plain to see, General."

"These bands don't respond to anything but force. And when they don't respond to that, then they must be eliminated."

Tatum coughed nervously, swallowing down his temper. He could feel his ire rising, and reminded

himself to stay calm. This was one of the most powerful men in Washington City, well known for his
strong, unvarnished views on dealing with the western tribes.

"Then we know where we both stand, General."

Sherman turned. "Yes we do."

"You don't like the President's policy of dealing
even-handedly with the tribes, do you, General?"

"Haven't I made that abundantly clear?"

Tatum nodded. "You have. But I don't think you've
given Grant's and Secretary Delano's policy time to
work."

Sherman snorted, yanking the cigar from his teeth
and patting his pockets for a sulfur match. Disgust-
edly, he waved an arm out the window. "You tell me
. . . just try to tell me, Mr. Tatum, that you have control of your goddamned wards."

"I . . . I can't—"

"Damned right, you can't!" Sherman shouted.
"Both the Kiowa and Comanche are free to jump this
reservation whenever it pleases them to. I heard reports from at least a hundred civilians down in Texas
regarding depredations committed by your wards on
this peace-loving reservation."

"Do those people have proof it was—"

"To hell with proof, Mr. Tatum!" Sherman
snapped. "Mackenzie rode in here yesterday morning
with enough proof for me—for any right-minded
man, by God. That teamster roasted alive over a fire
. . . every one of the bodies unspeakably butchered.
Good God, man! You heard the colonel's report same
time I did. And you still don't think it was your Kiowas?"

Tatum felt like a cornered rabbit. How he had
prayed to make this a model of reservation life since
the day he had arrived here from the east, 1 July

1869, relieving General William B. Hazen from what had been a temporary civilian post. In a flurry of activity and stoic Christian resolve, Lawrie Tatum had immediately let contracts to have several stone buildings erected for the agency, before hurrying east to Chicago where he purchased a steam engine, a shingling machine and other materials to construct a sawmill, along with huge millstones for grinding corn. With the power of his love and his faith in God alone, Tatum believed he could bring his wards away from the blanket and to a pastoral, farming life.

Whereas Hazen was a military man who had run his Indian affairs from his headquarters at Fort Sill, Lawrie had located his agency buildings on high ground overlooking Cache Creek. It was there he built the first schoolhouse for teachers Joseph and Lizzie Butler, after completing living quarters for agency employees. From the ground up, Lawrie Tatum had built a small community he prayed would forever remain rooted in love between red men and white.

There was no fear in the man. Some might look at Lawrie Tatum and say it was because he was Quaker. But those who really knew him realized the agent was a courageous soul in his own right. Time and again in his two years here, the Kiowa and Comanche chiefs and warriors had tried bullying and bluster, if not outright intimidation. None of it worked. Tatum, the man the Indians nicknamed "Bald Head," would not be bullied. Instead, they had grudgingly come to respect him in their own way, knowing Bald Head did not lie, and never skirted around the truth.

He was exactly the sort of man the Society of Friends had cast their nets for when the newly inaugurated President Ulysses S. Grant accepted the

Quakers' peace plan. Grant had begun by appointing as Commissioner of Indian Affairs a full-blooded Indian, Brevet Brigadier General Ely S. Parker, an attorney who had served on Grant's own staff during the Civil War. Parker's board of commissioners was established to advise Secretary of Interior Columbus Delano on appointment of agents for the western tribes. From their own headquarters at Lawrence, Kansas, the Society of Friends operated under the watchful eyes of Enoch Hoag, who firmly believed, like Tatum, that the red man would respond to love and respect if treated with sympathy and dignity.

Over time, Tatum believed, his Kiowa and Comanche wards would come to the light of God's path, living by Christian virtue. It was a policy and a belief that often put the Quakers at direct odds with Grant's War Department and the no-nonsense commander of the army itself: General William Tecumseh Sherman.

"Mr. Tatum?"

Turning, the agent found one of his civilian employees at the open doorway, pulling his hat respectfully from his head.

"Yes, Ross?"

"The chiefs are here, Mr. Tatum."

"Chiefs?" Sherman asked, his interest suddenly pricked as he strode from the window.

Tatum nodded. "It's time to hand out the annuities, General."

Sherman sputtered. "Annuities? To these murderers?"

How Tatum wanted to tell the unpolished general what he thought of his bluster and his tobacco-reeking mouth and the way the general openly drank his whiskey—like the rest of those soldiers he had met in the past two years he had spent out here.

"Surely you understand the women and children must live on something—"

"By damned, you're right, Tatum! They've got to have something to live on while their men are off raiding and stealing, killing and raping and kidnapping."

Tatum suddenly leaned forward on both arms, elbows locked as he rocked forward across the small, wobbly desk. "Listen, General—if I believed as you did, no one would be trying to do what's right out here."

"Tell me, Mr. Tatum—what's right?" Sherman scoffed.

"Your government's clearly failed in its job, General. As many soldiers as you want to send out here—you still can't get the job done. Now shut up and let me talk!" he growled sternly when Sherman opened his mouth. "I didn't come here to make my fortune, like most agents could do before the President turned over control to the Quakers. Corruption, bribery—it's all plainly here for the man who wants to make a quick fortune, General. But if I did not believe that virtue is its own reward, I would not be here trying to help these Indians, trying to work with your soldiers."

"Then help me round up the troublemakers—"

"I'm not finished, General. Just look around you. Look at these luxurious accommodations I live in. You think I'm here, like the others, to divert money from this agency into my own pockets?"

"I haven't accused you of—"

"By rights you'd better not! A man out here will never eat high on the hog, General." He turned to his employee. "Mr. Ross, be sure everything is prepared in the warehouses for the distribution. Set up the tables, then return here for the rolls."

Ross had disappeared before Sherman strode purposefully to the desk, his eyes narrowing beneath the bristling eyebrows. "You're still going to issue the goods to these people?"

"That's my job, General. Our government wants these people to live on these reservations, far from the buffalo they want and need to hunt for their subsistence, to turn themselves into farmers. I must do my part in seeing that I smooth the road to a farming life for them—"

"They don't stay on the reservations, can't you see?" Sherman asked, sweeping his hat from Tatum's desk. He appeared to pause for an answer, and when one was not forthcoming, the general strode to the open doorway. "I'll be at the post. Colonel Grierson's office—should you decide you have need of more frank talk, Mr. Tatum."

"You're not staying to witness the issuance, General?"

A dark look crossed the soldier's face. "The only thing I want to give these Kiowa is an empty bowl and a hanging rope."

What made Lawrie Tatum shudder as he watched Sherman stomp away to rejoin his escort and ride off to the fort was that the agent was afraid he understood. While he and the Indian Bureau might feed and clothe these Kiowa and Comanche, Lawrie Tatum and the rest were nonetheless powerless to make their wards behave.

He stood at the window, watching the white employees, good Friends all, shuffle supplies and tables into place. Stacks of blankets, piles of sugar and coffee, canvas britches and cotton shirts, bolts of cloth and fifty-weight of flour. In the agency corral stood some skinny cattle that would soon be nothing more than bone and gristle as the hungry Kiowa butchered their allotment.

The women and old ones and children were the first to appear from the trees this morning. It was some time before the warriors stepped from the leafy shadows. The chiefs came only when all were settled on the ground before the tables.

"Mr. Jones," Tatum called out as he stepped onto the porch. Colonel Grierson's Kiowa interpreter, Horace Jones, came over. "Tell Satanta and his head men I want an audience with them in my office. Right away."

Jones gestured vainly at the distribution tables. "Now?"

"Now."

Tatum retreated into the shady, spring coolness of his tiny office and shuffled papers on his desk, his back to the door of purpose until he heard Horace Jones's boots on the floor behind him, a gentle cough announcing their arrival. Then he slowly turned.

"Satanta!" he said enthusiastically, trying to hide his anxiety at the prospect of having this Kiowa chief lie to his face. "It is good to see you!"

Tatum stepped to the stocky chief and shook hands. Down the line he went, shaking with Big Tree, Lone Wolf, Eagle Heart, Big Bow, Woman's Heart and Satank, the oldest of them all, who sported a scraggly mustache while every other Kiowa plucked facial hair, even eyebrows. He thought it such a savage custom.

"Please, sit," he told them.

When Jones made the translation, the chiefs spread blankets and settled to the agent's floor.

"I do not want to smoke with you this morning," Tatum started abruptly. "And what I have to say will not take long—but it is of great importance . . . to us both." He drew himself up and sighed. This was already proving extremely hard on him.

"The soldiers have told me of a wagon train that was raided a few days ago. Down in Texas. Seven white men were killed—horribly tortured and mutilated." He waited for the interpreter to catch up as he watched the Kiowas' eyes for any betrayal.

"I know you were off the reservation, Satanta. Perhaps the rest of your chiefs as well. The soldiers have asked me if you have been gone from this place—and I cannot lie to them. Tell me, from your own lips so that my heart will be at rest. Tell me you did not have anything to do with this raid on the white man's wagons."

An immediate rustle of shock went through the chiefs, and suddenly Satanta arose before any of the rest could speak.

"My heart is strong," said the Kiowa leader. "So I too do not lie. I will not lie to you, Bald Head." He tapped his broad chest. "I led that raid. Again and again I ask for weapons and powder and lead—but you do not give it to us. We ask for other things that are promised to us by the white treaty-talkers. But the white man keeps his hands closed to the Kiowa. You keep your ears closed to our pleas."

"You do not need the guns if you will only grow crops and raise the cattle."

Satanta sneered. "We do not want your skinny spotted buffalo! We will hunt buffalo the way we always have. But now the white man is laying the tracks for another smoking horse to cross our buffalo land to the south. We will stop these men who lay the iron tracks. I—White Bear of the Kiowas—I took these other chiefs," and he swept a thick, muscular arm toward the open door, "and those young warriors out there . . . I took them all to Texas to show them how to fight the white man!"

Tatum felt his heart seize in his chest. "You led the raid on the wagon train?"

"I did. And I watched my young warriors count many coup."

"The rest—these went with you?"

Satanta appeared to strut standing there before the agent, proud to anoint himself the leader of the whole thing. "Yes. They went with me: Satank, Big Bow, Fast Bear and Big Tree. We killed seven of theirs," as he held up the fingers. "But they killed three of our warriors and wounded two more. We call it even now."

Then Satanta walked over to Tatum and clamped a dark hand on the agent's shoulder. "But do not worry, Bald Head—we will not be raiding around here this summer. We will only raid into Texas. To stop the white man and his smoking horse."

Tatum, unable to speak, glanced over the other chiefs seated on the floor.

"Do not look at them, Bald Head," Satanta said with a menacing growl. "They did not lead the raid. I did. They came to learn from me how to fight the white man and his many-shoot guns. If any other man claims he led that raid—he is a liar!"

From the looks on the faces of the rest, Tatum could see that Satanta must be telling the truth. None of them would dare claim leadership of the raid on the Warren wagon train—none but Satanta himself. Yet the agent realized the rest were every bit as guilty of bloody crimes.

"I . . . I believe you, Satanta," Tatum muttered, his eyes going to Horace Jones. "Tell the chiefs they are free to go now. It's time for them to receive their annuities with the rest of their people."

When the interpreter had translated, Satanta returned to Tatum's side. "Bald Head does not want to know anything more about my raid on the wagon train?"

"No." Tatum blanched, shaking his head as he turned away to his small desk. He could not look at the chiefs any longer without betraying what revulsion he felt inside for them and their heinous crimes. Most of all, the agent was fearful that the pit of him contained more than revulsion—afraid that he might actually hate these chiefs for what they had done.

And hate was a luxury a Quaker could not afford.

Without turning around as the Kiowas rose from their blankets and shuffled out the door, Tatum said, "Horace, when the chiefs are settled outside, come back. I have something you'll need to take to the post for me."

When Jones stepped back into the agency office, Tatum was seething with anger—an emotion so foreign to him that it scared the man down to the soles of his feet as he penned the final words of his note to the commander of nearby Fort Sill.

> Col. Grierson
> Post Comd.
>   Satanta, in the presence of Satank, Eagle Heart, Big Tree and Woman's Heart, in a defiant manner, has informed me that he led a party of about 100 Indians into Texas, and killed 7 men and captured a train of mules. He further states that the chiefs Satank, Eagle Heart, Big Tree, and Big Bow were associated with him in the raid. Please arrest all of them.
>
> Lawrie Tatum
Ind. Agent.

Chapter 4

May 27, 1871

*W*illiam Tecumseh Sherman had to admit this was turning out to be a damned lucky week for him.

First off, he and his escort had themselves narrowly missed getting chewed up and possibly losing their scalps down on the Jacksboro-Belknap Road where the Kiowa had hit Henry Warren's wagon train. And now the butchers who had murdered the wagonmaster and his six teamsters had openly admitted to their crimes before that Quaker Lawrie Tatum just moments ago.

Sherman handed the agent's note back to Colonel Benjamin H. Grierson, commander of the Tenth U. S. Negro Cavalry, Fort Sill, I.T. Indian Territory.

"By Jupiter, Colonel—your brunettes will have this play," Sherman said.

"I'm hopeful this can be done with as little bloodshed as possible, General."

Sherman would have grown exasperated had he not been so excited. "You call the plan, Colonel. Whatever you want. I don't care how you have your brunettes play it out. Only one thing I want to see happen: capture those guilty for the butchery!"

Grierson nodded. He turned to Inspector General

Randolph B. Marcy, who was accompanying Sherman on the general's inspection tour of southwestern posts. "I think you'll both be proud of the Tenth Cavalry when this day is done."

Sherman huffed, "Proud or not, Colonel—I want those murderers."

Then Sherman promptly proceeded to lay plans to lure the chiefs to the post where Grierson's Negro soldiers would be in hiding, behind doors and window shutters, ready to show themselves the instant their quarry was surrounded. Within minutes the plan was agreed upon and Grierson had his captains prepare their four companies for possible action. The three veterans of the Civil War were congratulating themselves when Grierson's adjutant suddenly appeared at the colonel's door, his face tight, pinched with surprise.

"Col-Colonel Grierson," he announced, pushing only the upper part of his body through the door. Behind him arose a commotion.

"What is it—"

"Colonel . . . one of the chiefs is here—"

The adjutant was suddenly shoved aside as the door itself was flung open by a bare, brown arm. In strode a tall, stout Kiowa dressed in leggings and a red breechclout. Over his shoulder he had slung a shiny bugle. On his left arm hung a rawhide shield, and in that hand he held a tall red medicine lance, his *zebat*.

"Sir, I couldn't stop—"

"It doesn't matter now, Lieutenant," Grierson said, moving halfway across the room toward the visitor.

Sherman looked at Grierson, expectantly enough that the colonel answered on his own.

"General Sherman, you see before you the great chief of the Kiowa—White Bear."

"White Bear?"

"The translation of Satanta."

Sherman nodded slowly in satisfaction. "I'll be bloody damned," he whispered as more commotion was heard from the porch. A civilian in his mid-thirties strode in the door, looked over the soldiers, then moved over to stand with Satanta. "What in blazes brought this red son of a bitch to us, do you suppose?"

"I ain't got a clue," declared the civilian as he inched up to Satanta.

"Who the hell are you, sir?" Sherman inquired.

"He's Horace Jones—my post interpreter, General."

"Then bloody well find out what brings White Bear here," Sherman demanded.

"I was just about to do that for you, General." Jones asked his questions, mostly in Kiowa, some Comanche, but also with a sprinkling of Spanish thrown in. "He says he heard the Big Chief of the white man soldiers was here on a visit. Satanta came to see you for himself . . . since he is the Big Chief of the Kiowa. He came here to . . . to measure you up, General."

"I thought there were other chiefs of the Kiowas," Sherman said.

"There are," Jones explained. "Lone Wolf and Kicking Bird are leaders of their own bands. But Satanta is clearly the war leader of the Kiowa."

Sherman found himself smiling, more satisfied than he had been since moving out of Washington City, so peopled as it was with phony back-slapping, back-stabbing politicians talking out of both sides of their mouths.

"I damn well realize who Satanta is, Jones. Tell

him I know of him—tell him the Big Chief knows
Satanta led the raid on the wagon train."

The room filled with officers fell hushed as Jones
translated. Then Satanta took a step forward and
spoke, pounding his chest at times for emphasis.

"Yes, soldier chief—I am the one who led my hundred warriors down on the wagon train. We killed
seven white men, but we lost three of our own, and
had more wounded. This makes us even."

"Tell this pompous windbag of a butcher that it
would take ten—no! A hundred Kiowas to equal the
life of one innocent white man, Jones!"

As the interpreter began translating, Satanta's eyes
grew wide with the ferocity of the soldier's words.
The chief backed up, his right hand playing at the
butt of the pistol stuffed in the bright red silk sash
tied around his ample waist.

Sherman pointed at the gun. "Don't you dare
touch it, you red bastard!"

Satanta's hand froze. His face grew tight, flint-chip
eyes bouncing off the others in the room. Then something lit by desperation came over his countenance.
"There were more chiefs there when we rode down
on the wagon train," he began to explain, his tone
nowhere near as haughty.

Sherman stood there, slowly crossing his arms as
Satanta explained things, with Jones translating at
his elbow.

"Other chiefs . . . they ordered the young men to
capture the wagons. We . . . they didn't want to kill
the white men. Only take the wagons. The white men
shot at the warriors. Killed three and wounded some
more. None of us could hold the warriors back. I am
not a powerful man to hold them back when their
blood is up. They . . . the warriors killed to revenge
the white men who killed our—"

"Those white men were protecting their property, you son of a bitch!" Sherman roared. "I damned well wish they'd made more of you good Indians that day!"

"I need to go back to my people," Satanta said quietly, his eyes furtive, longing for the door as he started to inch off in that direction, putting himself behind Jones. "To get our presents, I must be there with my wives."

"You stay—"

Satanta was past Jones and out the door, flying off the porch toward his prize pony. He had the rawhide reins in hand just as Grierson's orderly got to the chief, pistol drawn. The chief stared down at the pistol held inches from his belly, then stared at the young soldier's face, and finally up at the faces of those officers squeezing out the door onto the shady porch.

Sherman waited for the interpreter to push his way through the gathering of the curious. "Mr. Jones, tell the chief he is my guest for now. Tell him he must take a seat on the porch. Here. While we wait for the others to come."

He turned to Grierson. "Let's proceed with our plans, Colonel. Put a guard on Satanta here and send Jones to fetch the other guilty leaders from the agency across the creek. I want to secure all the big fish in my net."

When the Kiowa did come over from Tatum's agency, more than the chiefs accompanied the Indian agent to Fort Sill. Like Satanta, they had heard the Big Chief of the Great Father was at the fort and had come to see for themselves.

"Jones," Sherman whispered as the Kiowa streamed onto the post parade, "tell Satanta to keep his mouth shut if he knows what's best for him. Tell him I wouldn't mind killing him myself if he makes a sound."

While the warriors squatted and sat on the ground before Grierson's porch, the women and children clustered behind them in a milling throng, interpreter Jones invited the chiefs to have a seat in the porch shade, joining Satanta as a sign of respect for them.

"Who's missing, Mr. Tatum?" Sherman asked.

The agent said, "Only Big Tree and Eagle Heart."

"Where are they? Still across the creek?"

"No," Jones replied. "I don't know about Eagle Heart, but I saw Big Tree cross the parade, heading for the post sutler's place."

"All right. We'll corner him soon enough." Sherman turned to Grierson. "Are your brunettes in place, Colonel?"

The commander of the Tenth Cavalry glanced over the perimeter of the parade ground. "Appears everything is in order, General."

"Very good. Jones—tell these chiefs that they, like Satanta, are under arrest for the murders of seven white men and the theft of property from Henry Warren's wagon train."

The words were barely off the interpreter's lips when the commotion started: women keening, the chiefs starting to rise, exposing pistols; warriors edging forward muttering their anger and their warcries.

"Captain Carpenter! Lieutenant Pratt!" shouted Grierson.

Down both sides of the excited throng of Kiowas moved two companies of buffalo soldiers, Springfield carbines held at ready. Lieutenant R. H. Pratt's D Company spread front into line at the left of Grierson's headquarters. Captain Louis H. Carpenter and his H Company, rescuers of Forsyth's civilian scouts at Beecher Island back in 1868* loped into line on the right.

Grierson yelled, "Mr. Orleman—now!"

The red crowd surged back on itself, angry and yelling, the women wailing and children crying. At that moment their escape route was snapped shut as Lieutenant L. H. Orleman, also at the rescue of Major Sandy Forsyth's survivors, stepped forward with ten more grim-faced brunettes.

The tension in the air was so thick a man would have to cut it like fleece from buffalo hump-ribs as the warriors surged forward, then back, then suddenly in another direction to attempt to knife through the cordon of black-faced soldiers sweating beneath their kepis in the spring sunshine.

"Jones! Tell the warriors we want no trouble. Only their chiefs. Tell them I'd like to round up every one of their miserable number who had a hand in that raid . . . but I won't," Sherman ordered. "Tell them to take their women and children back to the agency now before something ugly happens."

The chiefs were yelling at their men, the warriors and women hollering back in a confusion of voices and keening cries.

"General, they're demanding to know what's to happen with the chiefs you've taken prisoner," Jones said.

"We're taking them down to Fort Richardson to trial."

"Why Richardson?" asked Tatum.

Sherman grinned. "Because that's the military district where the ghastly murders took place . . . and that's where we'll form a jury."

* The Plainsmen Series, vol. 3, *The Stalkers*

"You mean a lynch-mob, Sherman," Tatum spat, suddenly angry and no longer able to contain it. "That's what you'll find—a bloody lynch-mob!"

"We're giving these red butchers more than they gave those seven dead heroes," Sherman growled. "What trial did they give those seven—"

"General!" shouted Horace Jones, tugging on Sherman's elbow.

"Who the hell is that?" Sherman asked as he turned, seeing an older Kiowa approach on horseback, coming from the direction of the sutler's. The rest of the Kiowas parted for his pony, quieting to some degree. "Is that Big Tree . . . or Eagle Heart —the one we're looking for?"

"No. That's Lone Wolf."

Sherman grinned. "So, that's the one who Custer and Sheridan captured, along with Satanta, back in Indian Territory a month after Custer wiped out Black Kettle's village on the Washita."

"The same," Jones replied.

Lone Wolf's face did not betray any emotion as he kicked a leg over his pony and dropped to the ground, his arms filled with weapons. He stopped at the edge of the porch, slowly sizing up the scene, then handed a bow and quiver of arrows to a warrior. To another Lone Wolf tossed a Spencer repeater. With only a Spencer left to him, the Kiowa chief cocked the hammer and advanced on the tall, graying soldier from Washington City who stood at the center of all those on the porch.

Sherman flung his arms out to stay the soldiers who suddenly threw open the window shutters behind him. "Let's keep everyone calm, fellas," he said quietly.

Lone Wolf's eyes looked over the chiefs as if reading the story as plain as print. Behind him the crowd fell completely silent as the Kiowa chief placed one moccasin on the bottom step. Slowly, Lone Wolf climbed to the second step, bringing up the muzzle of the Spencer to point at Sherman's chest. He stood there a moment longer, then placed a foot on the third step, which would bring him within point-blank range of the soldier chief.

Grierson waited no longer. He lunged from the edge of the crowd on the porch, seizing the muzzle of Lone Wolf's carbine.

"Jones, tell these warriors that bloodshed is no way to save their chiefs! Tell them!" shouted the colonel as he wrestled with Lone Wolf to keep the muzzle pointed at the porch awning.

Angry muttering ran through the crowd as Lone Wolf ceased his struggle and reluctantly let the colonel take the carbine. Completely ringing him stood soldiers, their sidearms drawn and pointed at the old chief. Behind the rest of his people stood more of the buffalo soldiers, while at the windows behind Satanta and Satank waited more, their rifles at the ready.

"Jones, tell one of these warriors to go to the sutler's and fetch Big Tree back here. Send another to search for Eagle Heart. I want them both," Grierson said, watching Sherman nod in approval.

Minutes passed by as Captain Carpenter's men allowed the women and children to pass off the parade and begin filing back to the agency in hopes of quieting the angry warriors.

"We're not waiting any longer, Colonel. Get some men over there to the sutler's place now!" Sherman ordered.

Grierson sent Lieutenants Woodward and Pratt with D Company.

When they reached the post store, there was a small crowd of Kiowa gathered both outside and in as Woodward led a small detail through the door, sending Pratt and the rest to surround the entire building.

Behind the counter stood a young Indian, for the moment busy passing out the goods he was taking from the shelves behind him. He froze when Woodward entered and the buffalo soldiers spread out behind their lieutenant.

Then in the blink of an eye the warrior tore off behind the counter, pulling his blanket over his head as he dove through the window at the back of the store with a crash of glass and wood. The Kiowa were screaming in the building, shouting outside as well when the war-chief rolled onto his feet, abandoned his blanket and took off at a sprint.

"Get him, boys! Catch him alive if you can—catch him alive!" Lieutenant Pratt ordered above the commotion.

At that moment near the trees shading the store, Eagle Heart was himself coming to the army post, answering the summons to see the soldier chief. From the shadows he heard the commotion and saw Big Tree hurl himself through the window, taking off across the field behind the store. Eagle Heart disappeared into the shadows, fleeing before he was discovered.

Big Tree reached the fence and vaulted over it about the time a handful of fleet-footed young soldiers hurdled the rail fence behind him. In a matter of moments there were enough brunettes to have the Kiowa war-chief surrounded. He was ordered to throw up his hands, his pistol and knife taken from his belt before the soldiers escorted him to Grierson's headquarters.

By the time they got back to the parade with their angry prisoner, the women and children were racing across the creek in panic and things had turned ugly, with the warriors spilling across the open ground and between the post buildings. Many of the sub-chiefs stood their ground, however, shouting, urging their men to resist and escape when Colonel Grierson ordered Lieutenant Orleman to stop all who fled.

Two dozen of the warriors wheeled and opened fire with what weapons they had carried to the post: bows and arrows, pistols and a few rifles. With all the madness, however, only one of the brunettes was hit with an arrow in the melee. A solitary warrior dropped, a bullet through his heart. The rest scattered into the timber and were gone, crashing through the brush toward their camps. When they reached their villages, the women and children hastily tore down their lodges, intent on making good their escape to the nearby Wichita Mountains.

From that faint rattle of distant gunfire, those in other camps of Comanche and Kiowa across the creek believed their chiefs were being slaughtered by the soldiers. They too joined in the mass stampede from the country.

"I have what I want in my hands, Colonel," Sherman said proudly to Grierson as the dust settled on the parade. "Put these bastards in irons."

Chapter 5

June 8, 1871

"*I*s everything in order for our march south, Lieutenant?" asked Ranald S. Mackenzie, colonel of the Fourth Cavalry, as he stepped off the headquarter's porch at Fort Sill, I.T.

The young lieutenant, Robert G. Carter, who ofttimes served as Mackenzie's adjutant, replied snappily, "The prisoners should be brought out any time now, Colonel."

At that moment there came a rattle of chains as the first of the three Kiowa chiefs emerged into the bright summer sunlight of these southern plains from the darkness of the guardhouse where they had been held for the past dozen days. Mackenzie, the man who had chased the Kiowa back to their reservation following their brutal attack on the Warren wagon train, was now awarded the duty of escorting the three chiefs down to Fort Richardson for trial. Sentiments in Texas ran strong enough against the Kiowa that, once the three were brought to Richardson, no man among the Fourth Cavalry expected anything less than the end of a rope for Big Tree, Satank and Satanta.

Having graduated at the top of his class at West

Point in 1862 during the first year of the Civil War, Mackenzie went on to participate in many of the war's most famous battles, during which he suffered six wounds. The loss of two fingers from his right hand would, in fact, later cause the Indians of the southern plains to call Mackenzie "Bad Hand." By the time the able soldier participated in the last of the fighting around Appomattox Courthouse, he had earned himself a brevet rank of major general for conspicuous bravery in action.

Despite his stellar war record, it was not until December of 1870 that Mackenzie was appointed to the Fourth Cavalry, the second youngest colonel in the service at that time. It was in fighting and eventually subduing the warrior horsemen who roamed the southern plains across the next twelve years that Ranald Slidell Mackenzie would amass a service record of historic proportions.

He was not new to the country, nor to Texas itself, at this moment in time—having served as colonel in the 41st Infantry in postwar reconstruction duty, commanding a Negro regiment near Brownsville from 1867 to 1870—when he came to the Fourth Cavalry and began acquiring his eventual fame as the man who time and again stung back the mighty Kiowa and Comanche bands.

At Fort Richardson no less than the general of the army himself, William Tecumseh Sherman, had ordered Mackenzie to lead a force of troopers on the trail of those guilty of the raid on Henry Warren's supply train. With 150 soldiers and thirty days' rations, the colonel hurried to the scene. It was there at noon the day following the bloody raid that Mackenzie saw his first mutilations.

He had dismounted and slowly walked among the charred remains of the ten wagons, his boots barely

crunching the corn spilled by the raiders across the
Salt Prairie. A driving rain pelted the soldiers and
their winded mounts after the mad hours in the saddle. Here and there camp equipment and the carcasses of a few dead mules littered the scene of
destruction, arrows with soggy fletching bristling like
porcupine quills from six swollen corpses.

A seventh, who Mackenzie himself identified as a
friend, teamster Samuel Elliott, had been chained
belly-down on a wagon's single-tree and burned over
one of the fires. The extreme heat of the flames had
caused some of the blackened bodies to burst open,
fissures of pink and white erupting with a stench that
no man could stand for long, even in that afternoon's
hard rain.

Having swallowed down his anger, Mackenzie ordered the rest to dismount and stand to horse. It was
a grim silence that surrounded the colonel as he went
from body to body, looking at what was left of the
faces, each one pounded to jelly, to look for any others he might know.

"Captain," he called back when his own tour of the
scene was complete, "let's break out the spades and
get these men buried."

After a few words over the common grave marked
by a small cairn of stones, Mackenzie informed his
men they would be pushing on from here, using every
bit of light left to them that day instead of stopping
for the night. He drove them on, hoping that the
wind-driven rain that was their companion that season had not obliterated every trace of the raiders'
trail.

Mackenzie's determination had been rewarded late
the following day when his advance guard under
Lieutenant Peter M. Boehm had run across four of
the raiding party on the south bank of the Wichita

River where the Kiowas had discovered some buffalo crossing to the north shore. After killing a half-dozen of the shaggy beasts, the four warriors were butchering the buffalo for the rest of the raiding party when Boehm's twenty-five troopers happened upon them.

In a rapid, furious gun battle, the warriors wounded one trooper, and a single Kiowa was killed before the rest swam the Wichita to safety, dashing north for the Red River and their reservation, driving their mules among the small buffalo herd for cover.

The colonel and his Fourth followed that fresh trail straight to Fort Sill and the Kiowa-Comanche Agency, where Mackenzie himself reported his findings to General Sherman and Colonel Grierson, post commander.

Into the first wagon now this early summer morning, the buffalo soldiers of Fort Sill hoisted Satank, the oldest of the prisoners. He was placed between two privates, with a corporal settling in the wagon as well. Big Tree and Satanta were confined in a second wagon with only two guards.

All three of the Kiowas still squinted into the bright summer sunlight. For the past dozen nights, they had been held in a barrack cellar used as a temporary guardhouse, far from the open prairie where the free wind cleansed the stench of offal and sweat.

"Soldier chief," announced an Indian dressed in a white man's civilian clothes as he rode up to Mackenzie, "I want to go south with your soldiers."

"Who are you?" Mackenzie asked, glancing at Horace Jones, post interpreter.

"I am George Washington," he said proudly, his back going rigid.

"He's a Caddo, Colonel Mackenzie," Jones explained, then looked up at the Indian. "You going to help interpret for the colonel?"

His head bobbed up and down eagerly. "Yes. I know Kiowa good."

"This true, Jones?"

"Yes, Colonel."

Mackenzie nodded. "You ride near the two wagons, George Washington. Tell me if the prisoners need anything—or have something to say."

He watched the Caddo rein his pony toward the two wagons, then gave the order, "Let's move this parade south."

The entire procession had barely rumbled away from the stone buildings of Fort Sill, parting long lines of curious, saddened, and angry Kiowa who had come to watch the departure of their chiefs, when George Washington loped to the head of the columns and brought his pony into step with Mackenzie's.

"Satanta, he say to tell his people they might never see him again."

"He say anything else to them?"

"Only to stop raiding into Texas, and give back the mules to the soldiers."

"What about Big Tree?"

"Him say nothing," Washington replied, then looked away like a man who did not want to be caught keeping a tight rein on the whole truth.

"And the old one, Satank?"

The Caddo looked far from happy to answer.

"All right, George Washington," Mackenzie declared sternly. The colonel was far from being an easy man to like—a stern disciplinarian and taskmaster, and he brooked little in the way of a sense of humor. "I'm countermanding my decision to take you along. If you aren't going to do as you're ordered to—"

"The old one—Satank," Washington blurted, "he's singing his death song to the Kiowas on the road."

Mackenzie turned in the saddle and looked back at the first wagon. "I don't see him."

"He have his blanket over his head—singing death song."

"What is that . . . this death song? Translate for me."

> "*O sun, you remain forever,*
> *But we Koitsenko must die.*
> *O earth, you remain forever,*
> *But we Koitsenko must die.*"

"What the devil is this Koitsenko?"

"Kiowa warrior society. Satank is chief. He took vow never to die like a animal. Only as a man—fighting soldiers."

"That what he's telling these Kiowa?" Mackenzie asked, gazing up and down the road at the Indians they were passing.

"Satank has promised his scalp to your Tonkawa tracker up there," Washington said.

"Sounds like he's stirring up as much trouble as he can," said the colonel.

"He say him a warrior and chief—too old to treat him like a child now."

"I'm not treating him like a child," Mackenzie bristled. "I'm treating him like the goddamned murderer that he is."

A mile south of the fort on the Jacksboro road, the road dipped down a gentle slope to the Cache Creek Crossing. It was in descending that slope that Satank pushed back the blanket from his head and called out for George Washington. The Caddo urged his horse up from the second wagon, where he had been talking with Big Tree.

"You, Caddo," Satank said in Kiowa. "See that tree ahead?"

Washington looked down the gentle slope and spotted the tall tree standing much by itself. "I see."

Satank smiled grimly. "I will not go past that tree."

Washington nudged his horse forward without a word, intent on finding the soldier chief. He was nearing the head of the columns when angry, shouting voices erupted behind him. Mackenzie turned in his McClellan, then reined his mount out of formation and loped back toward the commotion.

Satanta and Big Tree were yelling at the same time in Kiowa from their wagon. In confusion, a dozen soldiers rushed past the wagon, bolting for Satank's wagon, where the chief's three guards suddenly flushed like a covey of quail, one of them clutching a hand over a glistening arm wound.

The old chief wheeled on the other troopers closing in on him, yelling out his Koitsenko death song. From one wrist dangled the loose end of the iron shackles. The other wrist had been torn, flesh peeled from bone in ripping the shackles from his hand. Blood streamed onto the Springfield rifle he had wrestled from one of the guards.

Satank shouted in frustration as he worked the bolt, a cartridge already in the chamber, jamming the rifle's action as he brought it to his hip, growling at the soldiers closing on his wagon.

One of the nervous troopers fired. The bullet struck Satank high in the chest. He shrieked in rage, flinging blood over the jammed action of the Springfield as he struggled with the bolt, yanking back on the trigger again and again. Another shot struck the Kiowa chief, then a half-dozen in a staccato volley that knocked Satank over the side of the wagon onto the dusty road that would have taken him to Fort Richardson, Texas.

By the time a stunned Mackenzie had dismounted and hurried to the chief, Satank's eyes were already glazing. Still breathing, blood darkening his cloth shirt in more than a dozen places, the old warrior gritted his teeth in excruciating pain rather than show the white men he was weaker than this excruciating walk into death.

After twenty minutes of refusing water from the soldiers, and staring with glassy eyes at the faces gathered in curiosity around him, Satank breathed his last, raspy, sputtering breath. A bit of pink sputum rolled from his lower lip as his body relaxed.

"I get scalp," said the Tonkawa tracker who stepped up beside Mackenzie.

"Get the hell out of my sight before I scalp you myself!" the colonel snapped.

Trudging off two steps, then wheeling, his shoulders thrown back in a haughty defiance, the Tonkawa tried again. "He told me: I get his scalp—when he die."

The colonel shook with rage, holding his fist beneath the tracker's nose. "This is the last time you'll work for me. And I'll make sure it's the last time you work for the U.S. Army. Now—get out of my sight!"

He trembled for a moment more as he watched the Tonkawa making good his exit, then Mackenzie ordered a sergeant to retrace the mile to Fort Sill and request a wagon of Colonel Benjamin Grierson.

Satank was buried at Fort Sill by the Kiowa and the Negro buffalo soldiers as Colonel Ranald S. Mackenzie once more pushed his columns south for Fort Richardson.

That evening, and for six more following that first, the Fourth Cavalry feared a night attack by the Kiowas attempting to free the other two chiefs. One chief had already been killed by the soldiers while he was their prisoner. Mackenzie analyzed the situation. Chances were the Kiowas would try something to keep the soldiers from killing the last two.

He ordered every precaution to be taken, including pegging Big Tree and Satanta out, spread-eagle with iron picket pins and rawhide, at the site of each night's camp.

"What's that Indian's problem?" asked the colonel as he placed a burning twig over his pipebowl that first evening south of Fort Sill.

"Seems a might restless, don't he, Colonel?" answered a captain.

Mackenzie strolled casually over to the patch of grassy ground where Satanta lay squirming and tossing against his taut rawhide tethers. For a moment the chief ceased his gyrations and stared at the soldier chief, hard-eyed and full of hate. But he was not about to let the white man know of his discomfort.

"Sergeant of the guard," Mackenzie said, not taking his eyes off his prisoner.

"Yes, sir, Colonel?"

"I'm putting you in charge of something. Assign a rotation of men, two to a watch."

"We have guards on the prisoners, sir."

Mackenzie shook his head. "This is something else. Have the soldiers stand watch over Big Tree and Satanta through the night. I want guards swatting mosquitoes off the prisoners."

"Mosquitoes, Colonel?"

"Good God, man! They're eating these Kiowa up alive!"

So it went for the following six nights. Until Mackenzie's Fourth arrived back at the community of Jacksboro on the evening of 14 June, and removed their shackled prisoners from the wagons, lashing the Kiowas to horses and putting a strong guard around the chiefs to protect them from a lynching. Mackenzie had to admit he was anxious about the nasty disposition of the civilians crowding into the small Texas town once word had spread the army was coming in with its prisoners. On the fifteenth, the Fourth Cavalry finally deposited Big Tree and Satanta in the guardhouse at nearby Fort Richardson and prepared to let the civil courts grind out the end to the leaders of the raid on Henry Warren's wagon train.

It was an interesting trial, albeit short and without question when it came to the matter of a verdict. District Attorney S.W.T. Lanham served as chief prosecutor, and in his most fiery summation to the jury of twelve well-armed male citizens of Texas, he pointed at Big Tree and declared, "This beast before you is a tiger-demon who has tasted blood and loves it as his food!"

As strong as that was, Lanham nonetheless saved his strongest denunciations for Satanta. Standing before the table where the sixty-year-old chief sat, the district attorney told the jury, "Before you sits the arch fiend of treachery and blood—the cunning Cataline, the inciter of his fellows to rapine and murder, an abject coward, canting and double-tongued hypocrite!"

By 8 July, Judge Soward was ready to render his sentence on the guilty verdict the jury had no trouble deciding. With the two prisoners standing before his bench, Soward told the two chiefs they now had the chance to make a statement before sentence was passed.

"I know nothing of the white man's court," Satanta explained in his bad, halting Spanish salted with some Kiowa phrases. "I am innocent of a bad heart. I did wrong only because I was led down that bloody path by Lone Wolf, Kicking Bird and Satank. See what became of Satank? I do not want to go the way of that evil wizard!"

"Are you done?" asked Soward.

Satanta hung his head a moment, as if considering more, then replied, "If you let me go back to my people, I will never again make war on Texas. This I promise you." Then the old chief straightened, cocking his head arrogantly for his final parting show of intractability. "But if you kill me . . . all of Texas will run deep in blood."

Soward nodded once to indicate he had understood the translation, then said, "If there is nothing else, this court hereby passes sentence on Big Tree and Satanta—found guilty of theft of government property, and of the murder of seven citizens of Texas. This court finds that on one September of this year, the two prisoners are to be hanged by the neck . . . until dead."

Chapter 6

October 1871

Here in this great solitude of nature we found our deepest study spread out before us, and gathered "sermons from the stones," "books from the running brooks," and "God in everything." In these magnificent temples made with His hands we gathered inspiration and from this self-communion added to that breadth of knowledge and experience which come not in the life of every man, even when travelled, fully educated, and intellectually developed. Hardships, dangers, privations, and sacrifices —quiet conceits—remove selfishness and make all mankind akin.

The young lieutenant, less than a year and a half out of the U.S. Military Academy at West Point, sighed as he kneaded the back of his neck, rereading those last few lines he had just penciled in his journal by the evening meal's firelight. Soon enough Robert Goldthwaithe Carter knew he would have to cash it in and put the leatherbound lap-journal away in his saddlebag. Colonel Ranald Mackenzie would not allow any of these men with the Fourth Cavalry to build the fires higher once full darkness descended upon them here on the Staked Plain.

Carter and the rest of Mackenzie's troopers were again in enemy territory, this time stalking the elusive Comanche.

The muscles along Carter's spine ached from the pounding of the saddle on their endless march across a land hard-baked beneath a relentless sun. So he strained now, hunched over his journal, to capture many of the thoughts he had clambered to remember throughout the long day of following Mackenzie's Tonkawa trackers who led the soldiers a little west of north, out of Fort Concho, on the trail of the Kwahadi warriors who had long scorned the white man and all his gifts and annuities, a band that proudly scorned signing the great treaty made at Medicine Lodge Creek four years before.

The light was going, and still there was so much for him to get down, after brooding through much of the day on religion and God and the profession he had chosen for his life's undertaking.

> It has been said in ecclesiastical circles that soldiers and sailors are neither atheists nor infidels but always cling fast to the hope of the immortality of the soul. Yet, by such close contact with nature, and sleeping perhaps for years under the canopy of heaven, they accept pretty largely the theory of the *God of Nature* and leave the mere theology of religion with all the various beliefs, creeds, etc., etc., to be taken care of by religious quacks and scientists who are lacking in their own service experience.

Rubbing his eyes, Carter put the pencil away in a pocket of his tunic still damp from the day's sweat, now cold against his skin with every insistent nudge of the breeze.

Indeed, the army was the lieutenant's religion.

With God Almighty the Supreme Commander, the President and all the rest were only officers positioned in the chain of command.

Born in Maine and later moved to Massachusetts with his family, Carter volunteered his service to Lincoln's shaken Union as soon as he was old enough. For most of the war, he served with distinction in the 22nd Massachusetts Volunteer Infantry, an outfit possessed of a blood-soaked reputation by the time Lee surrendered at Appomattox. Young Carter celebrated the end of the "Great Rebellion" by informing his family he had chosen to make the military his life, and would be seeking an appointment to West Point.

Following his graduation in June of 1870, Carter married his Massachusetts sweetheart in Boston. By November he and his young bride, Mary, had traveled halfway across the continent to report for duty with the Fourth U.S. Cavalry in the wilderness of west Texas—Fort Concho. The following February of '71, the newly appointed colonel of the Fourth reported for duty at Concho: Colonel Ranald Slidell Mackenzie. A slight, morose man, Mackenzie had much in common with Carter—both ate little, slept even less, and neither cared much for cutting a dashing figure in uniform, as did a few of the gilt-braided and strutting peacocks of that same frontier Army of the West.

Carter and Mackenzie were both true loners. Neither comfortable in the company of their wives, nor in the company of their fellow soldiers.

He thought now a moment on Mary, and those early days back at Fort Concho before Mackenzie moved the regimental headquarters northeast to Fort Richardson, remembering how they both had laid in that canvas tent at night, listening not only to the howling, ever-present Texas wind and the yipping of nearby coyotes lurking close to the slaughter yard, but listening as well to the distant laughter and tin-plated plinking of out-of-tune piano keys across the river in the crude settlement of Saint Angela, that fleshpot so like many others just beyond the fringe of every military reservation on this frontier.

Licking the drops of cold coffee from his thick mustache, Carter shoved a hand through his light-colored hair, listening to the musical snoring of some of the men already asleep in their blankets. Autumn was clearly here, this ninth day of October, and the nights grew cool all too quickly.

Carter turned at the footsteps, recognizing by shape the form of his colonel, even before Mackenzie stepped into the dimming, crimson light of the coals.

"Dawn still comes early this time of the year, Lieutenant," the colonel's voice declared quietly in the starlit darkness. "Especially after I've pushed every man of you so hard today."

Glancing over his shoulder at the thin rind of a moon rising off the purple horizon, Carter nodded. "Yes, sir." Around the sliver of moon clung a wispy haze, a sure sign of a change in the weather. And at this time of the year, a change meant one thing—cold coming.

"Why don't you get into your blankets? It's been a helluva ride we've had us," Mackenzie said, holding his bare hands over the writhing, red coals. "And now the Tonkawas say the Kwahadi aren't all that far ahead of us—camped a ways farther up Blanco Canyon."

"We've got the horses double hobbled, Colonel. If they hit us tonight—they won't get away with much," Carter replied, glancing northwest, toward the route White River took to cut through a hidden part of the Staked Plain.

It was here that Blanco Canyon buried itself from view across this flat, austere tableland. Mackenzie had ordered bivouac made in the narrow defile of the canyon, a camp bordered on one side by the river and on the other by a line of sharply defined bluffs.

They were friends, these two, compatriots of a sort, even though Carter no longer served as Mackenzie's field adjutant this trip out. On this campaign the young lieutenant was back among his fellow fighting men.

"I've ordered out a double picket, Lieutenant. Time to grab some sleep while you can."

"Thank you for the suggestion, Colonel. Good night, sir."

As the wind came up, biting now with the presage of the coming cold, Lieutenant Carter sank against his McClellan saddle and pulled the gray army blanket over his shoulders, his fingers groping into the saddlebag one last time for the reassurance of the leatherbound journal. He smiled, thinking how alike he and Mackenzie were: although they served in the cavalry, both men possessed a passionate distaste for horseback riding. Yet, like the colonel himself, Carter rode well and stayed in the saddle just as long as the job required. And for the past few days, that meant mounting up before the sun came up, along with staying planted in their McClellans until the light began to seep out of this prairie sky at dusk.

It had been much like that for almost as long as Mackenzie had been commander of the Fourth Cavalry—vigorous, soul-hammering campaigns against the elusive horsemen of the Llano Estacado. At least since last May, when Carter had served as field adjutant to the colonel and together they had set off after those Kiowas believed responsible for the deaths of Henry Warren's teamsters. Half a year gone now: all those baked, shimmering alkali flats that burned at a man's eyes, powdery, stinging dust stived up by the horses' hooves, caustic to a man's nostrils and torture to his lungs. Finding graze for the mounts was an ordeal in itself every twilight in these chases—everything gone brown by this late in the year. What hadn't been seared in the oven of a relentless summer on the southern plains was now made brittle by the drying autumn winds that sucked moisture right out of every horse soldier plodding along behind Colonel Ranald S. Mackenzie.

For the better part of a month they followed—drinking water that made them sick, and if not sick then at least the rest sat on a sore, much-abused part of their anatomy. By necessity Mackenzie cut the regiment to half-rations, then quarter-rations, far too little for a man and his mount to go on as they tumbled down one steep ravine and clambered up the rocky side of the next. The heat grew unbearable through the late summer months of tracking Kicking Bird's band, thought to be somewhere out on the Pease River.

Mackenzie never found them.

A fruitless search they made that May—the Kiowa had disappeared, or more likely slinked back onto their reservation to disappear among the others. No one had given any serious thought to the notion that the chiefs would own up to their part in the butchery and slaughter.

And now it was October.

Carter closed his eyes, thinking how he had asked Mackenzie upon making bivouac earlier that evening if they'd ever find the Kwahadi Comanche, or if the warriors would simply disappear like the Kiowa had done the previous May.

Mackenzie had chuckled in that tight, nervous way

of his, a humorless grin crossing his fair face orna-
mented with deep-set, sensitive eyes and a bushy
mustache. "We'll find them, Lieutenant. Or they'll
find us. Either way—I'll have my fight of it."

There was no apprehension in Carter, least of all
anything that could be called fear; fear at the possibility they would run across the most intractable warriors on these southern plains—the Kwahadis. And
like Mackenzie, a serious, businesslike military commander, Carter believed there to be but one way to
stop the Indian raids on Texas settlements and civilians.

"Ride those goddamned warriors into the ground if
we have to," Mackenzie had said time and again,
"and then whip them soundly."

After all, Mackenzie had six hundred troopers with
him this time out, even though the Fourth was on
forbidden, foreign, enemy ground. Less a frontier,
more so a true wilderness populated by wild game
and the equally wild Comanche, the Staked Plain was
a land of centipede, scorpion and hairy tarantula, as
well as a land where under every rock might hide a
diamondback rattler or a wolf spider. Neither the
land nor its people were to be trifled with. Many of
the water courses at this time of the year were dried
up, and what creeks and streams and rivulets sur-
vived this late in the season played host to a multi-
tude of carcasses—testament to those animals that
had become bogged down in the mire of mud, those
carcasses now attracting birds of prey.

As the cold wind with a clear taste of winter to it
shouldered out of the north, Lieutenant Carter let
sleep overtake him, happy for the rich, clean bite of
the air, happy for the company of the other snoring
horse soldiers here on these high plains of West
Texas, happy to have as his commander the tenacious

bulldog of the Fourth Cavalry. Sleep came so deliciously to him that night.

"Turn out! Turn out!"

Thrashing at his blankets, bolting upright into the shockingly cold air while grinding his fists into his sleep-matted eyes, Carter found his Spencer and then his feet.

Everything around him was pure pandemonium: noisy horses, gunshots, screaming men and animals, orders hurled here and there above the commotion. And behind it all was the gallop of pony hooves and the yip-yipping of brown-skinned raiders flapping their blankets and rattling pieces of rawhide to scare off the army's horses and mules.

How Carter's heart leapt with excitement, more so a relief from the tightly wound tension that had controlled him for months now.

We've found the hostiles at last! he thought, racing for the sound of the shooting, where the regiment's herd was picketed.

He watched the backs of the last of the raiders disappear into the darkness after their ponies had kicked sparks from the dying fires with their slashing hooves as they tore through the regiment's encampment.

After those brief moments of sheer panic and confusion, the hammer of those pony hooves quickly faded north into the canyon, leaving the soldiers behind to ascertain the damage. Mackenzie called for report: no casualties . . . but some seventy animals were gone and unaccounted for.

"Colonel Mackenzie," called out the colonel's guide and interpreter, Sharp Grover, "your Tonkawa trackers figure the Comanche content to run off the stock for the time being. They won't be back now that we're on the alert."

"Damn them!" Mackenzie growled, pounding a fist into the bracing air heavy with the frost of men's voices. Then he suddenly whirled on his chief of scouts. "What do the Tonkawas believe the Comanche are going to do now? Shouldn't we trail them back to their village?"

Grover shook his head.

From the lines on that war-map of a face, the scout was a man of middle years, Carter figured, watching Mackenzie's chief of scouts scratching at his salt-flecked beard, perhaps digging for a louse hiding in that knot of coarse hair.

"You won't want your bunch of green recruits following them warriors anywhere in the dark," Grover advised, "not when your outfit can't see where you're going . . . running into some blind ambush or what. No, Colonel—right now them warriors are out there in the dark rounding up what stock they run off from you."

"If they're busy looking for the stolen horses, then we'll go round up those warriors ourselves, Mr. Grover." Mackenzie turned on his officers, who had clustered nearby, shivering in the cold, murky darkness for orders. "Captain Heyl."

"Here, Colonel," replied E. M. Heyl.

"Take Mr. Carter and a dozen men on the first horses you can saddle and mount," Mackenzie explained. "See if you can locate anything out there . . . perhaps a trail those red bastards took running off with our stock."

With his own teeth chattering, Carter followed Heyl, and between them soon had a dozen more soldiers mounted on fourteen of the horses left to Mackenzie's command, all fourteen loping into the gray light of cold, predawn darkness.

"Captain Heyl, I suggest we find out if the Comanches overran any of the outer pickets," said the lieutenant.

Heyl replied, "Very good, Mr. Carter."

Gripping a pistol in his right hand, ready for any ambush that might surprise them, his reins in his left, Carter was relieved to find the farflung pickets still in place and alive. The horse-raiders had simply come upon the camp guards so suddenly, swept by them so quickly that the young soldiers hadn't had a chance to fire a shot into the starlit darkness.

The lieutenant was relieved as well to find the night dark enough that no one could really see the concern etched on his young face. Carter was beginning to wonder now about this enemy who hit and ran, appearing like ghosts out of the darkness. He was being shaken to his core as a young officer in this frontier army—for it seemed the army was being proved wrong about a few things regarding this new bareback enemy.

One of those things the white soldiers had wrong was some unfounded belief that these Indians would never attack at night.

That kind of superstitious thinking had probably lulled far too many outfits like this into a false yet suicidal sense of security, he thought as they pressed into the darkness, riding the circuit of picket posts.

And got some soldiers killed as well.

Four risings of the sun ago, his young scouts had first reported seeing the dust rising above a large column of invaders coming out of the southeast.

Soldiers—a long parade of blue-clad soldiers the young wolves had discovered beneath that spreading dust cloud.

Quanah Parker knew these yellowleg soldiers were coming after his three villages—the bands of Coman-

che who normally came together and camped as one
great village here in the Moon of Leaves Falling so
they could hunt the great antelope herds together.
They were, after all, the "Antelope Eaters"—the
Kwahadi: those who had never signed a treaty with
the white man as far back as elder's memory could
recall.

Instead, for the most part they stayed out here
crisscrossing the mapless expanse of their ancient
homeland where they had been driven many decades
before, here to hunt the buffalo and other game
abounding on the Staked Plain. From here the young
men occasionally raided to the east where the white
man built his settlements.

It was there many, many summers before that his
father, Peta Nocona, had been on one such raid. It
was then that his father captured the young white girl
who would nine years later marry Peta Nocona—the
Comanche chief called "Wanderer"—the woman
with hair like summer-cured grass who would bear
her first child, a boy she had named Quanah, meaning "Fragrant."

Twenty-six winters had come and gone since his
mother had first suckled him at her breast.

But now the son of Wanderer had no father, and no
mother.

In the short-grass spring seven winters gone—
1864, in the reckoning the white man gave to time—
Tonkawa trackers had led a large band of Tehannas
to the Kwahadi village nestled in a tree-shrouded
canyon, standing beside a narrow creek of cool water. And there they recaptured Quanah's mother.

With most of the other warriors, Wanderer and his
son had been away from the village that day—already
gone for many suns on a hunt for buffalo and antelope. When the providers returned, there were many

dead to mourn: women and children and old ones among them.

But there was also the undead to mourn.

A hard thing for Wanderer to accept. Harder still for the young warrior son. For years Quanah had struggled to find his own way to mourn the undead—his missing mother.

To bury this hurt . . . to salve this awful, open wound of her capture, Quanah began raiding the settlements and soldier camps with a vengeance. If he could not find her among the white man's buildings, then he would wreak a terrible revenge upon them.

So it was when the young wolves he had sent out to scout their village's backtrail had returned late one afternoon with the report of soldiers marching from the south. Into the land of the buffalo and the Staked Plain—the land of the Kwahadi Comanche.

"Young men—gather your weapons!" he had told them as the autumn shadows grew long out of the west above their Blanco Canyon campsite. "We will strike these soldiers . . . drive off their horses! They will have to walk back to their forts when the Kwahadi are finished with them!"

Above Quanah the twinkling stars went out one by one by one as storm clouds scudded out of the north across the dark sky, driven on by a stiff wind from the prairies far to the north. It was good—this cold and the coming storm would keep the white man close by his fires this night.

Quanah, the Fragrant One, led his barebacked horsemen down on the camp of Three-Finger Kinzie —leader of the yellowlegs.

Chapter 7

October 1871

*B*eneath the dimmest of cold moonshine in that bone-numbing air of predawn, Carter and Heyl made out what was clearly the hammered trail of the retreating warriors driving off the army's seventy stolen horses and mules, a faint scar on the seared earth of the Staked Plain.

"They're headed up the canyon, Captain."

Heyl nodded. "Looks that way."

"We have one last outpost to check on," Carter said, pointing. "On that hilltop—there, sir."

"But that's in the opposite direction the savages took, Mr. Carter. That outpost was never in any danger. It would only be a waste of time."

"The colonel wanted to know if every outpost was still intact."

"Very well then. Let's find out what we can see from up there," Heyl replied, disgruntled, "even though that hill is in a different theater."

The rounded crest did indeed overlook Mackenzie's bivouac, a scene now of activity throbbing below them as the rest of the regiment broke camp, others heading out to round up what remained of the frightened stock. The far slope of this hill faded into the gray light of early dawn where murky, smeared shadows still betrayed the landscape for as far as the eye was able to see.

Heyl's patrol had no sooner reached the lone picket atop the hill than a single pistol shot split the cold, gray darkness. A sound immediately answered by a yelp of pain.

Hooves hammered out of the distance—another squad of mounted soldiers also on the prowl for the raiders. A sergeant hollered his order, halting his men. They rattled to a stop near Carter and Heyl.

"You see anything down there, Sergeant?" Heyl demanded.

"Injuns, Captain. I shot one," he answered, breathless and clearly excited. "At least—one of 'em yelped real good after I fired."

"Where were they headed?" Carter asked, his breath making heavy hoarfrost like a wreath at his face.

"Away from us—that's for sure, sir," another soldier answered. "Down there."

Every soldier on the crest of that hill could now make out the faintest of shadows smearing themselves across the gray of the prairie: a dozen or more not-too-distant horsemen, driving before them at least that many horses—the stock they had frightened from Mackenzie's herd and were now rounding up from the nearby country.

"There's our quarry, Captain!" shouted Carter. "What say we get our horses back—and some scalps too!"

Heyl led his fourteen men off the hill, streaming down the slope onto the flat plain after the Comanche raiders. As the race stretched farther across the prairie, the more rested army mounts were able to close much of the distance on the weary Indian ponies.

From every nostril, white, red and animal alike, streamed long, gauzy strips of breath-smoke that quickly disappeared into the cold, winter darkness before the coming storm. Ahead of Carter the warriors shouted among themselves, then suddenly rode off at an angle, abandoning the army horses.

The lieutenant looked behind him, finding the sergeant and his squad galloping on their tails, turning off to recapture the army mounts. Now it remained up to him and Heyl and their men to pursue the dozen raiders as they galloped with manes and tails flying down into a coulee and up the far side without breaking stride. It had become a test of horsemanship and wills—a wild race across the prairie which with almost every beat of Carter's hammering heart grew brighter with the coming of day, revealing with each surge of blood pounding in his ears a butte looming ahead in the mid-distance. Its gentle slopes had to be the warriors' destination.

And between the horsemen and that butte—a deep, sharp-sided ravine.

Down into it the warriors plunged, disappearing. Seconds later their ponies reappeared, clawing their way up the far slope, racing ever onward toward the butte.

Without hesitation, Carter and Heyl led their dozen troopers down into the ravine and across its sandy bottom, where the lieutenant and his men found the Comanche horsemen out of sight for a few seconds before they pushed their heaving horses up the far side. If the warriors could ride hell-bent for election across this broken landscape, Carter believed his men could do it every bit as well.

As the first to break the lip of the ravine on the far side, his mount growing more weary with every yard in the pursuit, Carter was the first to discover the grand surprise waiting for the fourteen soldiers.

At the foot of that nearby butte milled a whirling mass of Comanche horsemen who burst into a gallop as soon as the soldiers clambered out of the ravine. There were more warriors racing on a collision course for the soldiers than the lieutenant had ever seen in his life.

Hundreds—against Heyl's fourteen.

In confusion and fear, the soldiers reined up, shouting, their horses prancing and almost done in. Carter checked his mount with a tight rein, gazing at the oncoming warriors in astonishment.

"Just look at those goddamned Indians!" Heyl muttered, his face gone as white as the breath-smoke issuing from his lips.

Beneath him, Carter's horse began to quiver, then sag as it blew in exhaustion. A new and deadly problem, this—chances were the animal would never be able to carry him back to his lines.

"This is the supreme moment in a soldier's life," he said to the captain beside him in the commotion. He then turned to Heyl, finding the officer wide-eyed in fascination at the onrushing warriors. "Captain?" he asked. Then asked it again, much louder. "Captain!"

Still no answer. Carter decided Heyl suffered the sort of shock he had seen others suffer during the war down south a decade before. Paralysis in the face of the enemy.

Their lives might well rest in his own hands now, the lieutenant decided.

Could they make it back to the ravine in a mad dash to safety? Could they hold off the warriors there at the ravine—or would it be suicide to be caught in the bottom? Where else could they go for cover on this flat tableland—with more than three hundred warriors between the soldiers and the high ground?

All his training at the U.S. Military Academy—more so all his experience fighting an enemy dressed in butternut gray—his career and life itself suddenly all came down to this moment. Allowing no time for thought and deliberation. Requiring only the utmost in immediate decision . . . taking action to save the lives of his men until the rest of the regiment could hear the sounds of their gunfire and race to the rescue.

Their only hope . . .

"We have to meet their attack here, Captain!" he shouted, nudging his horse against Heyl's with a jolt.

The captain blinked, as if coming awake.

"We can only hope to retreat in force!" Carter continued.

"Yes!" Heyl said, shaking his head as from a dream. "We must try!"

Carter reined about, shouting to the dozen troopers. "Deploy out on the run, men! Left and right, then dismount and use your horses for cover . . . try to give them the best of your carbines!"

"We'll fall back slowly," Heyl added as the soldiers spread out in a small line of panic. "Slowly. Slowly!"

Heyl went to the far end of the right flank, leaving Carter with the five remaining soldiers on the left as the troopers began laying their first rounds into the rush of Comanche horsemen closing the gap. For a moment the cracks of those Spencer carbines drowned out the nearby war cries of the attackers who spread out in a wide crescent, as if upon some order or direction.

"They'll flank us if we don't get to the ravine before them, Captain!" shouted Carter as he turned in Heyl's direction, where he found the captain leading his seven troopers farther and farther to the right, opening the distance between his squad and the lieutenant's.

"Aim low!" Carter yelled at his five. "Aim for their ponies, goddammit!"

It was enough to break the charge he knew was intended to overrun their position before any reinforcements could arrive. The brown horsemen scattered, hollering in disappointment and rage as their solid phalanx broke ranks. Beyond the Kwahadi waited a single warrior, waving a blanket as if in signal.

The Comanche suddenly reformed, this time bearing down on both groups of soldiers in a single maneuver—intent on ringing in the white men, dropping to the far side of their ponies and firing arrows and rifles and pistols from beneath the necks of their surging, straining animals.

"Retreat a yard at a time!" Carter hollered at his five. "Stay together—together!"

On all sides of him now the Spencers rattled with consistency, if not accuracy. Beyond in the mid-distance, Carter could make out the crack of Heyl's rifles. Farther still, racing around and around them both, Carter listened to the war-cries and the screeches and the hammering of the Comanche guns and the thundering of the unshod pony hooves on the sun-baked ground of the summer-tortured Staked Plain.

Closer, and closer still, the red noose tightened as the soldiers retreated a yard at a time, each man sweating not from the rising sun, but from knowing the great distance left before they would reach the ravine and that hoped-for safety. That pitiful scar of prairie ground where they could make a stand of it.

And as the circle closed in on Carter's men, the

young lieutenant could not help but marvel. He had
been close to Kiowa warriors on the reservation far
to the north—yet nothing had prepared him for this
wild scene of warriors on horseback.

Feathers streaming and fluttering on the cold wind
of dawn. Paint of a dozen hues smeared on faces and
bodies, paint adorning the flanks or necks of their
war ponies. Necklaces of claws and fur and beads,
shiny round conchos of all sizes reflecting the new
light of day—treasures traded or stolen in the land
called Mexico, far away to south. Strips of red or yellow, blue or green cloth, bound up the tails of every
pony, woven into many of the manes flapping on the
wind. Dust raised from every slashing hoof, made
golden by the newborn, slanting light of a cold, winter sun.

Beyond the red noose of horsemen stood a half-
dozen warriors calmly waiting on horseback. From
the waving of the blanket they took their commands,
then passed those orders on to the horsemen by flash-
ing their small, handheld mirrors. Some distance behind the blanket-waver milled women and children,
shouting their encouragement to the young warriors.

"Lieutenant! They're bolting!"

Carter wheeled at the shout from one of his men,
finding two more of his troopers pointing at Heyl's
squad.

Anger boiled in the lieutenant. "Damn him!"

A hundred yards away the captain had remounted
his seven soldiers, reined about and was leading
them away from the fight in a wild retreat toward the
ravine.

Carter joined his five in shouting, pleading, cursing
at the retreating cowards. Their futile voices were as
quickly drowned out by the renewed war-cries of the

warriors who exulted in triumph, seeing that they
now had only six soldiers to rub out.

"We don't have far to go now, men!" Carter yelled
above the deafening noise.

The ravine lay a little less than a hundred yards off.
But with the warriors closing in so quickly—it might
well have been a mile for all it mattered now.

Yet, if the soldiers did not make a race of it now—
in these next few seconds—the renewed strength of
the warriors would easily overrun Carter's squad
with an avalanche of sheer numbers.

"MOUNT!"

Carter did not have to repeat the order a second
time. In a swirl of dust the troopers jammed boots
into the hooded stirrups and rose to their saddles
atop the frightened, snorting animals.

"Spread yourselves out!" he commanded them.
"Lay along the necks of your mounts—and keep firing the best you can. Keep the bastards back from us
as we make a run for it! Don't panic! *KEEP FIR-
ING!"*

When he brought his jaded mount around, closing
the file just as he had learned a good officer should
always do to cover his men, a volley of arrows whispered among the soldiers. Carter's own horse took
one in its lathered rear flank. His mount staggered at
the shock, then reared. Another horse clawed at the
sky, screaming out, humanlike in pain. But neither
spilled their riders as renewed riflefire fell among the
troopers.

A soldier cried out, a quick, stifled yelp—grabbing
his left hand, blood streaming from the gaping flesh
wound. He gritted his teeth and returned the Comanche gunfire as best he could while they strained to
reach the ravine, yard by yard. The man's wound had

begun to freeze already with the falling temperature brought by the coming storm.

The air had a metallic taste of winter to it, so real Carter could sense it on his tongue—a taste every bit like that flavor he had known as a boy in Maine when a downeaster was brewing and set to come inland from out there on the North Atlantic.

Carter realized his men were getting spread apart. The time had come to make a last dash for the edge of the ravine.

"Bunch your shots, men! Pump it into them good—and make a run for your lives!" ordered the lieutenant.

The five responded with courage, flinging a volley, then a second at the closing noose of horsemen. Stung by the sudden fury of soldier bullets, the Comanche fell back momentarily.

"Lieutenant!"

Carter found one of his five had fallen behind, off to the right and separated from the rest.

"My horse is done in!"

The animal was clearly giving out, legs splayed akimbo, shuddering with exhaustion. Half-frozen, slickened mucus seeped from its nostrils. Nearby the red horsemen recognized this opportunity and were closing in for the kill.

"All about!" Carter shouted, halting the ride of the other four troopers. "We must help him before he's overrun!"

The quartet reined about and joined Carter to attempt the suicidal rescue.

"Fire into them—make it heavy! Keep your shots low! And give it to 'em hard!" the lieutenant screamed at his men while the red horsemen surged closer than ever.

Even though two volleys from the soldiers un-
horsed five Comanches, something in the pit of
Carter's gut convinced him these were his last few
moments on earth. Serenely he thought of Mary, of
the children they had talked of raising—saw her now
in that small log and canvas hut of theirs back at Fort
Richardson—each morning she would sweep out another collection of scorpions and tarantulas as
bravely as any Boston girl could face this unforgiving, equalizing wilderness.

He thanked God for the time they had shared together—less than a year and a half. He thanked God
with moist eyes . . . as an unearthly cry clawed at
his attention.

Astride a coal-black pony rode the war-chief who
had been signaling the others with his blanket. The
Comanche worked his animal closer than the others
dared, hammering his heels against the pony's flanks
and firing his pistol when it seemed he had a good
shot. His facepaint furred with yellow dust stived up
from the pony's hooves to give the warrior a savage,
satanic appearance beneath a headdress of eagle
feathers that streamed down his back and off the side
of the black, prancing war pony. Two braids fell beneath the headband adorned with porcupine
quillwork, that gleaming black hair interwoven with
red strips of trade cloth and wrapped with a glossy
strip of fur. Huge brass rings hung from his pierced
ears, glinting with the new day's sunlight. He wore
no shirt, despite the rapidly dropping temperature
. . . only leggings, tiny bells sewn along the fringed
seam, along with a breechclout and moccasins. More
of the sun glinted off the warrior's bridle, decorated
with a dazzling array of round and shiny Mexican
conchos.

In stunned fascination Carter watched the muscular warrior guide his pony toward the private who struggled with his balky mount. The war-chief closed the gap with a lunge and pointed his pistol down at the soldier's face, point-blank. Then pulled the trigger.

A rosy splatter smeared the bright corona of sunrise an instant before the soldier tumbled from the saddle and his horse bolted away from the quivering body. In the next moment the war-chief was on the ground, pulling free his scalping knife as other horsemen surged past him toward the rest of Carter's soldiers.

"Mary—sweet, Mary . . ."

Then as suddenly as the warriors were charging headlong toward them, the Comanches wheeled about as if on some signal, beating a hasty retreat.

His heart still sour in his throat, choking all chance of making even the slightest sound, Lieutenant Robert G. Carter whirled at the realization of distant, pounding hooves. Iron-shod cavalry horses. A half-dozen Tonkawa scouts spearheaded the charge of more than a company of troopers.

"It's Lieutenant Boehm!" hollered one of Carter's five as the other three started to whoop and celebrate their deliverance at the edge of the ravine.

"We're saved! By God, we're saved!" shouted another.

At the rear of Boehm's charge rode Captain Heyl and his seven troopers, each one looking sheepish as could be and unable to meet Carter's thorny gaze as they reined up. Despite Heyl's higher rank, the captain was clearly riding second in command to Lieutenant Peter M. Boehm.

"Sweet Mary," Carter whispered to himself, his

voice raw and more of a croak as he struggled to loosen the taut muscles in his left hand that had imprisoned the reins in a death grip. "I'll . . . I'll be coming home after all."

Chapter 8

October 1871

"Suvate!" Quanah Parker hollered when he learned from his outlying flankers that more soldiers were on their way to rescue the five yellowleg soldiers. "It is finished! We go!"

He had the one poor scalp—tattered, in shreds after the point-blank pistol shot to the soldier's head. Too, Quanah knew he had the tall gray stallion that had been a favorite riding animal of no less than Three Finger Kinzie himself. It had not been a bad day, considering.

Yet the Kwahadi had suffered many wounded, and half a dozen were dead. The rosy glow of victory dimmed quickly for Quanah.

Worst still was the reality that the soldiers were now stalking the Kwahadi.

For so many seasons he had fearlessly led his warriors off the endless wilderness of the Staked Plain to raid the settlements of the Tehannas. Like a cold ball of sour bile, the fear rested in his belly—a fear only for the women and children, for the old ones unable to fight for themselves.

No longer were the white Tehannas content to swat at the troublesome Comanche wasps. Now the white man was sending his soldiers out to hunt down, smoke out, and smite the wasps so they would sting no more.

"Suvate," he told his warriors as they disappeared behind Mount Blanco into the white mouth of the coming storm. The sun had been blotted out in its rising, and to the north the horizon had gone black with the vengeance of Winter Man. "It is finished—for today."

But it was hardly over for Quanah.

As his gray eyes swept the prairie behind him, watching the oncoming yellowleg soldiers, the Kwahadi war-chief knew he would never give up. Just as he and Wanderer had never given up looking for his mother. Until the day Wanderer was killed in a raid he had made to take revenge on the Tonkawas for leading the white Tehan rangers to the Comanche village, seven summers gone now. It was a sixteen-year-old girl—a wife of Placidos, the Tonkawa guide who had sworn vengeance on Wanderer and who himself had led the Tehannas in the recapture of Quanah's white mother—the young girl who fired the fatal pistol shot that killed the old Kwahadi warrior.

His father was dead now. His mother . . .

For three more summers Quanah led his warriors off the Staked Plain and into the realm of the white man—looking, searching, stalking, praying for some clue that might tell him where the white man had taken his mother. Across all that time, he heard her spirit calling out to his heart, pleading with him to come find her, begging him to come take her home to her adopted people and their windswept homeland. It was not until the Moon of Leaves Falling, four winters behind him now, that Quanah learned of the tragic death of Cynthia Ann Parker.

"I must talk to you," said Philip McCusker quietly, standing at Quanah's shoulder.

The Comanche chief, already disdainful of these talks with the white treaty-makers at Medicine Lodge Creek in Kansas Territory, looked into the face of the army interpreter.

"Now, Ma-cus-kuh?"

At the white man's insistence they had walked to a quiet spot away from the soldiers and teamsters, the treaty-talkers and chiefs and the warriors and onlookers. Down in the willow and creeper beside the creek itself, Ma-cus-kuh made him sit in the tall grass gone yellow with the passing of the season, foretelling the coming of winter.

McCusker's news was like winter ice on Quanah's heart.

"My spirit is not happy to tell you this," explained the interpreter. "But you are a man I respect. I may lead the army against you, and my skin is white—as my own heart always will be. But I still respect you for the way you have loved your mother and have never given up your hunt for her."

"I never will," Quanah had told him. "Until I find her—I will continue—"

"Your mother is dead, Quanah."

The words had stung like nothing before, or ever since. With a pain that had diminished little since that terrible moment beside Medicine Lodge Creek.

"My sister—Prairie Flower?"

The interpreter explained how the infant had contracted some illness after her mother was recaptured by the Texas Rangers led by Placidos and his Tonkawas. "She began the long journey to the Other Side before your mother."

"How?" he had choked free of his lips.

Ma-cus-kuh had stared at the slow-moving stream

near their feet. "Your mother died of a broken heart —yearning to return to her husband, Peta Nocona— and you. To the Staked Plain. Cynthia Ann Parker was never the same after she came back to her white family . . . always sitting, never speaking, staring into the west with those sad eyes of hers."

Quanah had attempted the sounds of his mother's white name.

"Among our people," Ma-cus-kuh had explained its significance to him, "we have a first and a last name."

"My mother's last name was Pah-kuh?"

"Yes, Parker."

Knowing his eyes were growing moist, already stinging at the deepening pain that even then he knew would have no end, Quanah had stood, shaking hands with the interpreter. It was something the white man put great importance on, this shaking hands.

"Ma-cus-kuh, I will take my mother's name. In memory of the life she gave to me, not only will I never live captive on a reservation . . . but from this day on, I will be called Quanah Pah-kuh."

Looking behind him one last time now as he pushed his warriors before him, sheltering the women and children who were fleeing the oncoming soldiers of Three Finger Kinzie into the fury of the winter storm, Quanah Parker again swore he would never give up this free-roaming life as long as there was breath in his body, and his mother's blood in his veins.

When Lieutenant Peter M. Boehm led that rescue of Carter and his four surviving troopers, they were riding the advance of Colonel Ranald Mackenzie's assault on the Comanche.

The colonel had seen to it that every soldier he could mount was in the saddle within minutes of the Kwahadi attack. Leaving behind those who were without horses to protect their supply train, Mackenzie led some five hundred troopers north toward the sound of the gunfire—just as Lieutenant Robert G. Carter had hoped they would.

And just as he had prayed in those last moments before he was rescued. Now Carter joined Boehm's advance as they pursued the Comanche horsemen who moments before had been close to claiming the young officer's hair. With flankers out left and right, Mackenzie plunged his five hundred ahead, up the canyon and on a course for Mount Blanco where the Comanche village was fleeing. Northward—into the jaws of the first winter storm to attack the southern plains.

Little more than a mile ahead Carter began to see the first signs of the enemy in the dimming light as the rising sun was snuffed out beneath a blackening, winter sky. Women and children hurried to load ponies with their possessions and lodges. Those too young or too old to walk were hoisted onto the backs of ponies or settled on travois before the wild flight bolted for the slopes of Mount Blanco. It wasn't long before the sound of their screams and warnings came to his ears, carried on the cold wind out of the north, blowing so strong in Carter's face that it whipped tears from the corners of his eyes.

Between Mackenzie's advance and those women and children milled the angry wasps, shouting their war songs, working one another up for the coming fight, daring the soldiers to come on and fight them on equal footing. For the moment, they would cover the retreat of their families into the first, icy flakes of the storm and the darkening shadows of that tall

ridge called Mount Blanco. Near the bottom where
the women were now pushing the ponies and mules,
the slope was gentle, covered with some waving, yellowed grass and scrub. But farther up, the climb
grew much steeper.

And what the Comanche were going to climb—
Mackenzie's five hundred would have to climb as
well.

Yard by yard the warriors dropped back as the blue
wave came on. With their families safely climbing the
slopes above them, the Comanche melted into the
rocks and fissures of the ridge, most dismounting to
turn and fire back at the approaching yellowlegs.

Bullets whined overhead, smacking into the rocks
around the soldiers, kicking up spouts of dirt all
around them. Unlike many of the plains tribes,
among the Comanche were many marksmen. They
had long had the white man's weapons. Among Mackenzie's Fourth Cavalry that winter day were more
than his share of green recruits asked now to fire
back into the jaws of those screaming, painted hellions protecting their families climbing higher still
the slopes above the prairie floor.

"Carter!"

The lieutenant turned to find Boehm skidding to a
halt behind the rock Carter was using for a shield.
"Peter!"

"We'll have the whole advance pinned down here
if we don't knock out the sharpshooters up there,"
Boehm said, pointing up the slope with his pistol.

"Let's get some volunteers who'll make the ride
with us," Carter replied. "We can clear that nest ourselves!"

With seven soldiers, the two lieutenants remounted, reined about and with a shout burst from
the rocks, kicking their horses into a fury up the

slope. Yard by yard at first, then foot by foot as the pace slowed, the Comanche rained down a furious hail on the nine yellowlegs following a narrow, winding trail up the stony ridge.

So intent was he on watching up the slope for the puffs of rifle smoke he aimed his own shots at, that Carter did not see a sharp rock jutting out into the trail before it was too late. He sawed the reins hard to the right as his horse tore by the stony outcrop with a sound like the crack of a pistol shot.

The collision nearly lifted the lieutenant out of the saddle as the icy shards of pain made him grow woozy instantly. In panic he clutched the saddle pommel, afraid of losing consciousness and falling where the Comanche could finish him off. Blinking rapidly as the darkness seeped down over his fevered eyes, Carter swallowed repeatedly to hold down the bile at the back of his throat—afraid he would throw up what was left in his empty belly.

As the thick blackness enveloped him, Carter sank forward, grasping with his last bit of resolve to clutch his arms around the horse's neck. He was now nothing more than dead weight on an animal he had required so much of in the last few hours.

On the foggy periphery of his awareness, the lieutenant heard the wild yelps of the Comanche quickly fading from his ears, as the wild yells of his white compatriots grew stronger. Surely, he thought in some part of himself still struggling to maintain consciousness, Mackenzie's men must be coming now.

"Get him down from there, dammit!"

"Here—let him fall into our arms."

Voices prodded him, but still Carter could not open his eyes. The insistent cold wind and a few icy snowflakes stung his cheek as he felt himself gently pulled from the staggering horse.

"Pull his damned arms loose, soldier!"

Then he felt himself on the rocky ground, someone attempting to cradle his left leg as best they could.

"Gimme your canteen. There—off that horse."

He was trying to place the voice when a cold splash of water slapped his face. Carter came to with a start, fighting those who held him. The movement brought a sharp stab of overwhelming pain to the left leg.

"That's it," said an old sergeant, his breath thick with fragrant chew, "just settle down till the surgeon gets here, son. Er, sorry, Lieutenant. That ol' sawbones look at your leg and fix 'er up for you."

With trepidation Carter looked down at the leg. Just above the top of his boot his britches gaped open, torn crudely, blood still seeping from the wound into a bandanna a second soldier, a young private, held against the leg.

"Is . . . is it broke?" Carter asked as a wave of pain passed over him.

"You get that whiskey I sent you for, Corporal?" asked the old sergeant before he looked back down at Carter. "Most likely it is broke, Lieutenant."

"Here, Sarge," the young corporal replied. "Found it in your bags, like you said it'd be."

"You won't tell the old man, will you, Lieutenant?" asked the sergeant with a wry grin.

"The whiskey?" was all Carter could force out between his clenched teeth as a wave of pain washed over him.

Beyond them, fading down the far slope of Mount Blanco, were the assorted sounds of the chase: gunfire and war-cries, the screams of women and children and horses and ponies, the pounding of hooves and the tumbling of rocks spilled loose.

"Yeah," the old sergeant replied as he worried the fragrant cork from the bottle's neck. "I keep it for just such occasions as this. You need some, Lieutenant—in the worst way. Here," he said as he and another propped Carter's head up, "drink some while we wait on the surgeon."

It didn't take as long as he thought it would until the surgeon got to his side, grumbling and cursing about the climb.

"I'm too goddamned old for this, you know—being a contract surgeon out here in this wilderness," he growled as he tromped to a halt and knelt beside Carter.

"Broke leg, Doc," explained the sergeant.

"Since when did you go to medical school, soldier?" snapped the surgeon.

"Since I seen it with my own goddamned eyes, that's what," growled the other old man.

The surgeon chuckled, nodding at the graying sergeant, then peered down at Carter's face. "At least you're making a better patient of yourself than Mackenzie himself is."

"The general's shot?" asked one of the younger soldiers gathered in a tight, shivering knot as the snow began to lance down with a whining fury out of the lowering, gray underbelly of the sky.

"Take 'er easy, son," coaxed the surgeon. "Just had to pull a arrow out of his leg is all. He don't take to sitting still much, you know. And he sure made the job a hard one on me—pulling that barbed son of a bitch out of that bloody meat . . . my hands shaking to beat the band. Damn, but it's cold!" He sighed and sank back on his haunches.

"Bad news, Doc?" asked the sergeant.

With a shake of his head the surgeon reached for the whiskey bottle the old soldier held. "Gimme some of that. Damn, I ain't been this cold in . . . no—it ain't bad news at all. In fact, the lieutenant's leg ain't broke. But we're gonna have to splint it up and splint it good to get him down off this goddamned mountainside."

"You boys there," the sergeant called. "Cut me some stout limbs off that mesquite bush yonder. Gimme four long ones for the lieutenant's leg."

Between gasping, throat-numbing draws on the sergeant's whiskey bottle, the surgeon dressed the gaping, bloody wound and splinted the leg so Carter could not bend it, between promises to repay the old sergeant for the whiskey the old surgeon was greedily lapping up as the first storm of the winter bore down on Blanco Canyon with a vengeance.

"You'll pay me back soon's we get back to Richardson, won't you, Doc?"

"I will—but the way Mackenzie's going at it, growling like a bear with the mange—we won't see Richardson for some time."

The old sergeant chuckled heartily. "You ain't no soldier, Doc. Won't be long before we head on the backtrail to home and you can repay me my whiskey. Winter's come," he said, scooping up a little of the icy snow from Carter's chest. "And that means Mackenzie will be forced to give up the chase and let the Comanche go until spring."

"That too tight, son?" asked the surgeon as he cinched a knot in the bandage.

"Yes, dammit. It's real tight," Carter complained.

"Good," replied the surgeon curtly. "Then it's on just right. Here, let me have the last of that whiskey. Mackenzie's turning this outfit back out of this storm. Damn, but ain't it cold?"

It was, and a lot of that cold was seeping down into the young lieutenant's bones. But not where the thoughts of Mary rested. There it was warm.

Carter knew he would soon be turning around and

heading back to Mary at Fort Richardson. And for a moment he looked north into the swirling fury of that snowstorm come to batter these southern plains, a snowstorm the army itself would not buck—wondering on the wild people they had been tracking and fought, marveling that without a word of complaint, that band of wild people was marching into the jaws of a prairie blizzard.

Chapter 9

*T*he sun hung halfway into the western sky, off the left shoulder of Colonel Ranald S. Mackenzie this late September day.

He hated this waiting. Almost anything would be better than waiting.

For a proven, blooded warrior experienced in fighting Confederates, the past twenty months had been something altogether different. Since December of 1870 he and his Fourth Cavalry had never been given anything to really sink their teeth into here on the plains of west Texas. Instead, they had only suffered through two long-ranging expeditions stalking after the warrior bands who repeatedly struck east from the long-held security of the Staked Plain.

That's the way it had been when Mackenzie went stalking after the bunch who had jumped Henry Warren's supply train out of Weatherford, Texas, in May of '71. Then just this past May of '73, the commander of the Department of Texas, General C. C. Augur, had ordered the Fourth back into the field to make an attempt at breaking up the Indian-Mexican trade long ago established but of late making new inroads into relieving Texas settlers of both horse and cattle herds.

For some time the Mexicans west of the forbidding and austere Staked Plain supplied powder, bullets, guns and whiskey to the Indians, in exchange for those horses and cattle stolen from the white man's ranches.

Just the past spring, the army had stumbled onto a small group of the Mexican traders before they could recross the Staked Plain, their Llano Estacado, with their ill-won booty. In a running battle, one of the wounded Mexicans had been captured. Upon reaching Fort Richardson, the prisoner had decided to talk not only about his wealthy employer, but the various trading stations along the lengthy route home, and the trading operation as a whole.

Mackenzie, as well as the rest of those who interrogated the Mexican, was astounded to learn there was not only a trail across what the army believed was a trackless region, but there was in fact a well-established wagon road, with good grass and water for every night's stop made with the stock stolen from Texans' ranches. What a scheme it had been, Mackenzie brooded: bringing in huge profits for the wealthy Mexicans who hired their own private armies to bribe the warrior bands into stealing the cattle and horses. Yet it was something the Kiowa and Comanche themselves did gladly. Besides the whiskey and weapons, there was always the added lure of lifting white scalps during the raids.

For too long now the army had turned what amounted to be a deaf ear to the complaints of the Texas stockmen. Up until now, post commanders had believed the reports were exaggerated. No one could take that many animals across that hostile a piece of country and survive, season after season.

But suddenly, with the admissions of the Mexican thief, the army had decided it would do what it could to strike back at the raiders. After all, the soldiers had been stationed here to protect the Texas frontier. It was time, General Augur had decided, to do some protecting.

Yet what had started as an auspicious undertaking last May turned out to be another frustrating goose chase for the Fourth Cavalry. Out of rations, adrift on the trackless tableland of the Staked Plain, Mackenzie found himself forced to turn back. While he did not locate the Comanches and Kiowas adrift in that great sea of grass, Mackenzie nonetheless did go a long way to dispelling the belief that the Llano Estacado was completely uninhabitable. The colonel and his campaigners had in fact laid eyes on the headwaters of the three important water sources of those prairie raiders: the Brazos, the Pease and the Wichita.

It was now clear to Ranald S. Mackenzie that these horsemen and their families had never simply vanished into the clean, thin air of the Llano Estacado. Instead, the colonel had discovered that the raiders could indeed push into the hostile stretches of the Staked Plain and there find enough water, grass and game on which to survive until such time they chose to venture east, once more to raid the cattlemen and settlers of Texas when it suited them best.

Now it was late September, and Mackenzie was back in the field with his Fourth Cavalry. Sitting here, waiting in the autumn sun for—

"Trackers coming in, Colonel."

Mackenzie snapped to, watching the two Tonkawa scouts loping in at a good clip, all eight hooves kicking up spurts of dust as the animals carried their riders across the rolling tableland blanketed with waving grass. He tried to wait patiently while the two Indians jabbered with the white civilian scout, speaking with their moving hands.

"They say they've found you something, Colonel," said the white scout who was past his middle-age and nudging into his fifties.

"For God's sake, Grover—spit it out. I didn't hire you to—"

"I made it clear from the start, Mackenzie: I didn't wanna come along on this little soldier parade of yours. Not last May when we ran ourselves out of water and one time had to open our own veins up for something wet to drink. And now . . . here you are, dragging me back into another goddamned war."

Mackenzie sympathized, yet glared at the civilian all the same. "I had no one else and you damn well know that, Grover. No one, that is, who could use enough sign to understand these Tonkawas."

Sharp Grover shuddered, glancing at the two trackers. "Bloody cannibals is what them Tonkawas are. Only Injuns I ever knowed what would eat human flesh."

Mackenzie squinted into the sun, then put his eyes squarely on the civilian. "We have a problem with time today, Mr. Grover." Then he sighed, sensing the scout bristle. "Yes, I agree about the Tonkawas. But they are our trackers—and there is no love lost between them and the Comanche or the Kiowa. What have they found?"

"A big village."

"What are they?"

"From the looks of things, the Tonkawas say they're Kwahadi."

"Comanches," Mackenzie whispered, his eyes smarting as he once more looked at the sun dipping out of mid-heaven. "Do we have time?"

"Ain't that far ahead, Colonel," Grover replied. "Up on McClellan's Creek. Just . . . one thing."

"What's that?" he asked, watching the scout gaze back along Mackenzie's dusty columns, only four companies strong.

"It's a damned big village."

"How big?"

"We counted at least two hundred fifty lodges. There're more'n that though."

"How many warriors that make it?"

"At least five hundred of fighting age."

"I see." Mackenzie leaned back on the cantle of his saddle and stretched as he considered it: taking some 280 weary men into battle against twice their number. "All right," he said, turning to his adjutant, "pass the word back that we're closing on a hostile village. Put out flankers, left and right. I plan on engaging the enemy well before sunset."

"We best be getting on, Colonel," the civilian said.

"Lead on, Mr. Grover. Lead on."

He didn't look like the rest of the Kwahadi Comanche who were his people. A little taller than most, his skin a shade lighter.

His mother, captured from a stockade of white Tehannas when she was a child, had grown into a fair-skinned, blond-haired young woman who became the wife of a fearless Comanche warrior named Wanderer. Cynthia Ann Parker grew to be every inch a Kwahadi—as was her son, Quanah.

Almost ten years ago now she had died. Quanah had not been with her. Cynthia Ann Parker had been recaptured by the white man and returned to her people.

That had always made him laugh, this half-breed son of Wanderer's. From the lips of a white man

Quanah had heard that his mother had refused to become white again, refused to talk, to eat, to do nothing but stare west into the distance of her mind, squeezing shut on the memories.

Until she died of a broken heart, ten years ago.

Now Cynthia Ann Parker's son was a war leader in Mowi's band camped here in the sheltering timber along a creek east of the Staked Plain. The hunting this fall promised to be as good as ever. Few white hide hunters had ventured south of the Arkansas River, fewer still had ventured near the Llano Estacado where the great herds were retreating from the pressure of the hunters' big guns to the north.

It was here that few white men ventured anyway. Here the Comanche was a feudal lord, with no tribe strong enough to challenge them for over 150 years. Almost two hundred years before, the Shoshonean ancestors of the Comanche bands had migrated out of the land now called Wyoming Territory. In sign language the tribe's symbol for themselves is a gesture made by putting the right arm in front of the body, palm downward, wriggling it back and forth— in the sign of the snake. Another clear indication that the tribe was an offshoot of Shoshonean stock.

Pressure from the great warrior bands of the Blackfoot confederation and the westward encroaching Lakota warrior societies pushed the Comanche into what became eastern Colorado and western Kansas territories in the 1700s. By the turn of the century the five bands were roaming far and wide, in command of the country from the Arkansas on the north to the Brazos on the south. In fact, in time the Comanche tongue became the language of trade among the various bands that traded horses and robes across the central and southern plains.

To win this land the newcomers had to drive off not

only the Osage, Tonkawa, Apache and Navajo, but the Mexican and white Tehannas as well. All were lesser men to the Comanche, for the tribe called themselves "The People," and more often referred to themselves as "The Human Beings."

Yet it was not the sign language, or the Comanches' own name for themselves, that proved most notable in their contact with the white man. Instead, it proved the Ute tribe's name for their fearsome enemies to the south that came into general usage. Simply put, Comanche meant "enemy." More specifically, the Ute word *komantcia* meant "enemy who fights me all the time."

The war-loving lords of the southern plains: these Comanche.

By the time the Tehannas won independence from Mexico, the tribes ruled west Texas and beyond, from the Arkansas on the north to the northern provinces of Mexico across the Rio Grande. For more than a century the bands absorbed countless Mexican captives into their bloodline. Make no mistake: this was their land, shared at will with the Kiowas, and God bless the white man who dared enter this wild domain of the intractable spear hunters.

Some thirty years later, at the end of the white man's Civil War far to the east, the dozen Comanche bands had confederated themselves into five warrior bands: the Penatekas or "honey eaters"; the Yapparikas or "root eaters"; the Kotsotekas or "buffalo eaters"; the Nokoni or "wanderers"; and the Kwahadi or "antelope eaters."

These Kwahadi had never been party to any treaty with the white man, anywhere, at any time. They seldom went near the white man except to steal what was there for the taking, and they most assuredly never ventured onto a reservation and never did take the white man's handouts and annuities. Most of the time, in fact, the Kwahadi had little to do with the other four bands, preferring instead to stay in their ancient haunts on this grassy prairie of the Staked Plain. They were a people of honor and dignity, preferring to care for themselves as they always had— with gallantry in war, and honor when peace was made with an old enemy.

In 1865 the old chief Ten Bears and a few others had journeyed east to the city of the Great White Father. And two years later ten of the Comanche chiefs touched the pen to the white man's peace treaty at Medicine Lodge Creek. Nonetheless, the Kotsotekas and Kwahadi refused to sign and left Kansas without their presents.

While most of the Comanche did move onto the new reservation carved out of lands ceded from the Choctaws and Chickasaws near Fort Sill in 1867, the Kwahadi remained free on the Staked Plain. But even those who had chosen to live on the reservation by the rules laid down by the white man found they were not safe from the yellowlegs. On Christmas Day 1868, a large band of Comanche waiting for the distribution of the first annuities following the Medicine Lodge Treaty was attacked by Evans's column of soldiers campaigning out of Fort Union in New Mexico.

Very little of the annuities were distributed to the reservation Comanche in 1869, in part to recoup losses due to depredations by the free-roaming bands. The policy went a long way to convincing the reservation Indians that it was far better to raid and steal. Only then would the white man be eager to make a new treaty with the warrior bands, and a new treaty meant many new presents. And besides, the white man's practice of giving a one hundred dollar reward for the return of any white captive only encouraged the Comanche raiders to steal more victims.

So those who waited on the reservation for help would do just that—wait.

Quanah Parker would remain here where he continued to live the old life his father had lived, and his father before him.

All but the Kwahadi came in for rations at Fort Sill Agency in the brutal winter of 1871–72. As soon as the grass turned green on the rolling prairie, the young men and families of the reservation bands slipped away anyway, joining Mowi's Kwahadi. In fact, some of the young warriors struck the government corral at Fort Sill in a parting gesture, relieving the army of every one of its fifty-four horses and mules.

The newcomers to the nomadic villages told the Kwahadis of a council the Indian agent had just held at Fort Sill, led by representatives of the five civilized tribes in Indian Territory. They urged the Comanche and free-roaming Kiowa to take up the white man's road before they would starve, unable to survive on the dwindling buffalo herds.

Quanah laughed, scornful of such foolishness.

The buffalo disappear?

Never. Surely, he had to admit, there were fewer buffalo this summer than before, but nothing to show that the buffalo were disappearing. Besides, the Kwahadi had decided on their own already to take fewer of the shaggy animals this year and next, allowing the buffalo to repopulate in its great numbers. The Comanche, Quanah Parker told the disbelievers, would continue to live in harmony with their brother buffalo, into generations as yet unborn.

So it was that the war-chief was securing iron arrow points to the rosewood shafts with long, thin strips of sinew Quanah held in his mouth to soften. Each shaft he had deeply and painstakingly grooved so that it would bleed its intended victim—buffalo bull, Tehan settler, or yellowleg soldier.

At the same time, he watched his young son play on the buffalo hide outside the lodge this warm autumn day when the first stirrings of alarm shot through camp.

"Soldiers!"

Quanah bolted to his feet, scattering the arrow shafts and iron tips and sinew and owl feathers he used as fletching because owl feathers kept their shape even dipped in blood. He pushed his infant son into his wife's hands, ordering her to flee. In one easy movement he lifted them both to the back of the war pony he always kept tethered at the side of their lodge, grazing close at hand. In an instant he was into the lodge, then back again, handing his woman a small rawhide satchel filled with dried meat for their trip.

She looked down at him, tears coming to her eyes. He did not want her to speak.

Quanah tried to smile. To make her brave. She must be brave, for she was the wife of a war-chief and the mother of his son.

"I will see you both again, very soon. It may be with the coming of the new sun. Maybe two suns. But we will be together again. You must believe . . . and now you must ride!"

He slapped the spotted pony's rump, causing it to jump to the side as the woman pulled hard on the buffalo-hair rein.

After seeing her disappear into the tangle of women and children fleeing from the far side of the village in a noisy cacophony of keening, crying, pony-neighing clamor, Quanah wheeled and snatched up his bow and quiver of arrows, then found a place in his hand for the brass-studded Winchester repeater he had stolen from a white man he scalped along the Pease River.

The distant gunfire was growing in volume now. And he could see that the white soldiers were led by the Tonkawas. Quanah Parker cursed them—these savages who ate the flesh of other people. Surely these Tonkawas were not human beings.

Were the white men who followed the Tonkawas not human beings as well?

Levering the first cartridge into the breech, Quanah squeezed the recurring thought out of his mind—much too painful, for he was half white himself.

Chapter 10

September 28, 1872

Sharp Grover felt too old for all this.

He waited as his heartbeat slowed, now that the gunfire had died off and the excitement passed in the prairie darkness, like the leave-taking of a prairie thunderstorm here seven miles from the north fork of the Red River. There hadn't been much fighting to speak of there beneath the starshine. Only a lot of shouting and noise and confusion when the Comanche came screeching in to reclaim their pony herd from the soldiers who had attacked the Kwahadi village.

His chest had burned with some mysterious fire, hurting him from the moment the Tonkawa trackers had returned with the news that they had located the village on McClellan Creek, near the mouth of Blanco Canyon, that autumn afternoon. Now there were stars twinkling brightly overhead and the sound of hoofbeats and gunfire fading into the distance.

Sweeping in out of the blackness, the Kwahadi Comanche had come back for their ponies.

During the short, furious battle earlier that afternoon, Colonel Ranald S. Mackenzie ordered three of his companies to bear the brunt of the attack. Grover knew the colonel was planning on holding his fourth company in reserve at the point of attack, but when the charge began and Sharp saw that the young Comanche herders were hurrying the ponies toward the village so the warriors could fight off the assault mounted, Grover advised Mackenzie to send that last company out to cut off the herd. They and the Tonkawas were directed to capture the enemy's greatest wealth—those ponies.

"Left front—oblique!" Mackenzie shouted into the arid, crackling prairie air astir with dust.

Up and down the line of rattling bit-chains and squeaking leather, clattering carbines and nervous, snorting horses, the order was echoed above the remaining three companies. Most of those troopers had only glanced at the company of soldiers riding after the pony herd, for their attention was captured by the screeching, enraged warriors preparing to cover the retreat of their families.

"We've gone and stuck a big stick in this hornets' nest, Colonel," Grover had whispered.

"Now that they're stirred up, I've got no other choice but to swat them!" Mackenzie had replied grimly, then turned to his staff. "Order the charge!"

His adjutant twisted in the saddle, finding the color bearer and the bugler waiting expectantly. "Bugler—sound the advance . . . charge!"

On the dry, autumn wind their red, white and blue guidons snapped furiously as the entire line bolted into motion like a surging ocean tide racing headlong for the shore. And by the time the troopers reached the outskirts of the village, the warriors were pulling back. Mackenzie ordered one of his companies sharply to the right flank to cut off any escape through a narrow cut in the grass-covered hills, the maneuver coming quickly enough to entrap 124 women and children. For the rest of the Kwahadis, the back door had slammed shut after the quarry had flown.

Their women and children either captured or already racing into the hills, the Comanche fought only long enough to cover the retreat of the rest, then dissipated onto the prairie like ground fog warmed by a spring sun.

In thirty minutes of furious action, twenty-three Comanche were dead, most of them warriors who had turned back to fight. As the first of the regiment's supper fires began to glow at twilight, the colonel had his report: three troopers killed, another seven wounded, two seriously enough that in all likelihood the surgeon figured they would not make it through till morning.

And just before moonrise, in the blackest part of night, the Comanche warriors swept down upon the weary, overconfident bivouac, driving off the regiment's horses and those of the Tonkawas.

"I'd always been told Indians didn't attack at night," the handsome Mackenzie said grumpily, looming out of the darkness toward Grover's cookfire. He settled on a cottonwood stump.

"I never told you that, Colonel. Better you never gamble on what Injuns will do. Soon as you think you got a Injun figured out, he'll prove you wrong."

The soldier regarded his chief of scouts for this expedition. "No, you didn't, Grover."

After several minutes of silence between them, Mackenzie asked, "You really didn't want to come on this campaign, did you?"

"Not from the start. I've had enough of scouting to fill my craw."

"You're the best I've got for now, Grover. The others are just buffalo hunters—nothing like the experience you have. And besides, the money is good, isn't it?''

"I'm just a settler now."

Mackenzie smiled. "What, you? Raising some corn, maybe a few cows? Waiting for the Comanche to ride down on your place? C'mon, Grover—save your breath and try to convince someone else."

"I'm serious. That's why I came down here, to get away from the army and Injuns up in Kansas. All I figured to do was make a place for myself just across the Red River from I.T.''

"You made the mistake of choosing to settle down in Jacksboro, Mr. Grover."

Sharp studied the handsome officer's smile beneath that droopy mustache. He liked Mackenzie. "I suppose you're right, Colonel. Jacksboro is a might close to Fort Richardson, ain't it now?"

"And a man with your reputation can't stay hidden for long, can he?"

"So, what you figure to do now, since this outfit hasn't got a single animal left for your cavalry to ride after the Kwahadi run off their ponies, and your horses to boot?''

Mackenzie slung the dregs of his coffee into the grass at his feet. "We do have one left, a damned burro—twelve years old and sore-backed as well. That bloody Quanah Parker and his Comanche didn't get everything!"

They laughed together, a sudden, furious joy shared between them beneath the starshine. There wasn't anything else men like them could do but laugh, here in the middle of this grassland kingdom of the enemy, set afoot of a sudden. At first the other officers and nearby soldiers did not know what to make of it—how their regimental commander and chief of scouts could be laughing in the face of such adversity. But then, one by one, the rest joined in.

Lord, did the laughter help that night.

Mackenzie assigned two of his companies to escort the Comanche captives all the way due south to Fort Concho. That seemed to be the best idea—getting the prisoners that far from their menfolk.

On their own long walk back to Fort Richardson, Sharp Grover had a lot of time to think on things again, just as he'd had those nine hot, September days to brood on that sandy scut of island in the middle of the Arickaree Fork of the Republican back in '68.* Never again, he had promised himself, would he go riding out with civilians just looking to stir up some trouble. Major Sandy Forsyth had stalked the Cheyenne of Roman Nose until they found him. And then it had come down to the nut-cutting.

Things were a lot different now with the Kiowas, who by and large had settled down. There were reports here and there of bands of the young men and their war-chiefs slipping off the reservation and crossing the Red River into Texas. In fact, last summer down at Howard's Wells in nearby Crockett Country some wild-eyed Kiowas had found an unescorted government contractor's wagon train camped and swarmed over the Mexican and gringo teamsters. Every man jack of them was killed. And the one woman along, a teamster's wife, the Kiowas had allowed to live—Marcella Sera.

There would be times, Grover supposed, that the woman would wish she had not lived, having now to go through each day a prisoner of that memory of what she had witnessed. Remembering the screams of her husband and infant son, the agonized terror

* The Plainsmen Series, vol. 3, *The Stalkers*

given voice by the other eight teamsters as they were tied to the wheels of their freight wagons and consumed by leaping flames.

By the fall of 1872 most of the Kwahadis came into the reservation at Fort Sill, bringing with them a few white captives to exchange for their women and children who had been held ever since the Fourth Cavalry's attack on their Blanco Canyon camp.

Now there sprang some new hope eternal among most on the Texas frontier that Mackenzie had indeed struck the Kwahadi a harsh blow. The early part of the summer had been unusually wet, with the prairie grasses growing taller and richer than ever before, feeding the Indian ponies and buffalo and the white man's cattle at the same time. Then the dry winds of August had come to sear the prairie and turn the land golden before Mackenzie's raid on Mowi's Comanche village.

But autumn always came, and with it the touch of gold to the cottonwood and the red-tinged alder like crimson fire in the draws and down in the watercourses. Swamp willow turned with the season, bloodlike **arro**wpoint leaves tangled in a mat of blazing color. **Ind**ian summer arrived like a peaceful benediction for the land and Sharp Grover both. And still he wondered if ever he would see Jack Stillwell, ever lay eyes again on the tall Irishman.

A life full of memories made his old eyes sting at this moment as the wind shifted out of the north— what with this thinking back to how close he had been to Seamus Donegan's uncle, Liam O'Roarke. How both he and Seamus had been forced to watch Liam lay there at the bottom of a sandy riflepit, the side of his head turned to maggot fodder on some nameless river on the high plains. And in his own way, Sharp Grover prayed his letter and the other would get to Seamus through Jack Stillwell, no longer a young nineteen-year-old scout, as he had been when he heroically crossed a hundred miles of prairie wilderness back in '68 to carry Major Forsyth's desperate plea for rescue—but now an able and proven frontiersman carrying on where Sharp had cashed in his cards.

The air smelled of cold, Sharp thought as he poked the top button of his coat through its hole and turned up the collar.

"Why don't you come in, Sharp?"

He turned, smiling the way that crinkled the corners of his farseeing, plainsmen eyes, and blew his wife a kiss. "I'll be in. Just a little while longer now."

Sharp felt it in his bones, in his blood, that change in the wind. Knowing the old buffalo did as well, how they read the seasons with their noses if nothing else, turning south when the wind shifted out of the north. Natural that the old buffalo hunters so readily became like their prey, he figured. Practiced in their habits after so many years of following the herds, coming in the wake of those nomadic bands that followed the herds as well.

Sharp turned back to the little cabin he had built her. Got halfway there, then stopped as the gale picked up intensity in the yard. Dry leaves scattered before him, whispering with names and faces and times gone before and never to hold again in his hands. Sweet Jesus and Mary, he hoped he was doing the right thing in sending word out for Seamus Donegan.

The whispers of that very winter Sharp Grover was the first to hear turned into the killing blizzard of '72. In west Texas, with nothing to stop the snow and wind roaring out of the west and tumbling the cold straight down from the arctic north, the drifts rose hour by hour, day by day. At forty below zero a man could not stay long outside in the wind. There wasn't much a fella found need of doing outside anyway, as long as the wood box was filled and he kept a pathway tromped down to the tall lean-to he used as a barn for their horses.

Up north along the Kansas Pacific and the Smoky Hill, a train had tried to plow its way west into the brunt of the blizzard and impaled itself in a monstrous drift, unable to grind its way backward to free itself. Inside, the crew and passengers settled in to get through the storm, then send word out once the blizzard had passed.

But then a faint, rumbling roar was heard coming across the rolling, white tableland aswirl with icy buckshot. The thunder grew louder and louder out of the north when suddenly the first loud thump collided with the side of a passenger car. Then another, and another. Until up and down the entire length of that train, the ice-shrouded black beasts were hammering against the cars, more thousands upon thousands coming behind, pushing against the first, migrating south blindly through the blizzard. Most of the animals ended up crossing the tracks in front of and behind the train. But those buffalo that could not move merely waited with the patience taught their kind across the ages, huddling here out of the lee of the wind that drove the icy snow in brutal, horizontal gusts.

Most of those beasts died there where they stood, frozen in death beside the windows where they were butchered and the passengers lived on their meat for eight days until a rescue train arrived from the east to pull the missing train out. The wide cut through the snowdrifts was packed solid with huge, black, furry carcasses, frozen in time along the Smoky Hill Route of the Kansas Pacific Railroad.

Death would not be a long time coming for the rest of the great Arkansas herd.

The blizzard had put a lot of men out of work, more men set adrift and aimless than ever before come freeze-up for the railroad gangs. Construction on the Santa Fe Railroad had made it to the border of Colorado and stopped. By New Year's Day there were more men in Granada, Colorado, and back in Dodge City, Kansas, than anyone had thought possible: Irish, German, and Scandinavian too. Along with the ones who still had no home to go home to some seven years after the war. Still wandering.

All of them in their own way talking about spring and throwing in together and buying a wagon and an outfit to punch into the buffalo herds. Still, there were a number of them who weren't waiting for spring green-up to get started after the beasts. On a quiet morning in the middle of Dodge City's main street, a man could stand and listen, and in all likelihood hear a distant booming of the big rifles not that far from the town itself. In fact, by spring a man could travel west from Dodge to Granada without ever being out of sight of one buffalo hunters' camp or another.

But what with the buffalo hunters still staying well north of the Cimarron, and the fact that Mackenzie's Fourth Cavalry had enough hostages to keep the Kwahadis quiet, along with the Kiowas, subdued now that their chiefs were serving terms down in Huntsville prison—all made for a fairly quiet winter of it on the southern plains.

More quiet than young Billy Dixon could say he had known out here.

Four years ago he had freighted for Custer's Washita expedition that had charged in and wiped out old Black Kettle's Southern Cheyenne. And later that winter Billy had stayed on to teamster for Custer's Sweetwater campaign while the Seventh Cavalry stalked the Kiowa and the other bands of fighting Cheyenne. Dixon recalled how Yellow Hair Custer had gone out to parley with the Kiowa chiefs, Satanta and Lone Wolf, then turned around, making the chiefs his prisoners. What a dangerous gamble that had been, holding the two as hostage to assure that the Kiowas would indeed come back to their reservation and live in peace at the new post the Tenth Cavalry was building at Medicine Bluff—Fort Sill.

And this spring of '73 had brought changes there as well.

No longer did Colonel Benjamin Grierson command the Tenth. When he was ordered east on a recruitment detail, his lieutenant colonel, John W. Davidson, was placed in temporary command at Sill.

West of the post across Cache Creek, at the Kiowa-Comanche agency, Lawrie Tatum had himself enough and resigned with plans to return to his Iowa farm. He was replaced by another eager Quaker, James Haworth, who still believed the tribes could be pacified without the might of the army being brought into play.

Hell, Dixon thought—back to that winter campaign down in Indian Territory, Sheridan had proved to everyone the only thing that Injuns respected: force. He had Satanta and Lone Wolf strung up and ready to hang if the tribes didn't come in.

And the time would come, Dixon believed, that Sheridan would rue the day he hadn't hung those two murdering bastards from a tall tree beside Rainy Mountain Creek.

If they'd only keep whiskey and guns out of their hands, Billy thought, there'd be no problem with the Injuns, and a man could make his living hunting buffalo.

But there was those who wanted easy money, not wanting to have a thing to do with the smelly, bloody carcasses that were the refuse of the hide trade. Their kind set up tent camps just north of the reservation boundary and from there sold their whiskey to the Indians for hides and ponies and squaws. Cheyenne agent John D. Miles finally had himself enough of the whiskey peddlers late that winter and prodded Lieutenant Colonel Davidson to take some action. Lieutenant R. H. Pratt was dispatched with twenty troopers from D Company of the Tenth Negro Cavalry to break up some of the "whiskey ranches."

The cold had settled on the land and made it a miserable march north from Fort Sill, but the same storm had also caused the whiskey peddlers to hunker down until the weather broke. Pratt arrested fifteen of them, destroyed hundreds of gallons of gut-wrenching liquor, besides confiscating a large supply of weapons and powder, sugar, flour, coffee and bacon. In storage ricks behind their crude cabins, the peddlers had stacks of buffalo robes, as well as a sizable herd of cattle given to the tribes by the government as part of their annuities. The warriors had been trading off anything and just about everything, including wives and daughters, to get their hands on the mind-numbing whiskey.

Prisoners, trade goods and cattle were all pushed on to Camp Supply in the northern part of Indian Territory, but not without some casualties. Thirteen of Pratt's twenty troopers sought out the surgeon at Camp Supply upon returning from their police duties. Most lost fingers or toes to frostbite that brutal winter on the central plains.

Dixon wondered if the army thought it was worth all the trouble those brunettes went to, losing those fingers and toes and riding off into a prairie snowstorm to capture those fifteen lazy whiskey peddlers when all that happened after the white men were delivered to a court in Topeka was that they were each fined ten dollars apiece and sentenced to thirty days in jail.

The young buffalo hunter shook his head, his long, black hair brushing his shoulders as he rose to the saddle. Billy Dixon was fixing on heading south for the Cimarron to see what the herds looked like down there. Funny, he thought, how the government never did nothing the same way twice.

Seemed like the army and the government fellas just wanted the Indians to cause trouble.

Maybe that was it, Billy decided. If the warrior bands stirred up a bunch of shit, then the army would have reason to go in and squash 'em.

It almost made him laugh on this bright spring morning, heading south into buffalo country. Almost . . . if it hadn't been so damned scary too.

Yes, indeed: old Phil Sheridan himself would likely rue the day he didn't string up them Kiowa butchers from a tall tree standing beside Rainy Mountain Creek.

Chapter 11

Spring 1873

$\mathcal{D}$amn, but the air smelled good.

Billy Dixon stood stretching the kinks out of his body, wiggling his toes before he stuffed his sweat-stiffened stockings down the tubes of his tall boots. Morning like this, with the frost ablaze like sparkling pink diamonds as the sun rose out of the east, a man wondered why anyone would ever sleep a night with a roof over his head.

The five skinners he had hired to come along were beginning to stir. Even red-headed Mike McCabe relished every last minute of sleep, his head buried beneath his blankets and canvas bedroll.

Dixon wanted coffee.

From the creek he pulled a pot of water. Beneath the trees he found enough squaw wood to rekindle the coals from last night's fire. Then he stretched out on his bedroll once more and waited for the water to come to a boil as the others rousted, stomped onto the prairie and sprayed the ground in their morning ritual.

Dixon pushed a small quid of tobacco inside his cheek and lay back, his head pillowed on the crook of his arm, as contented as any man could be here

across the Arkansas River, south of the "dead line."
He had brought his outfit into territory expressly
given by treaty to the Indians for their own hunting.
If soldiers caught a hide hunter down here, it would
be trouble with the army. If on the other hand a wandering party of warriors ran across a hide outfit like
Billy's south of the Arkansas . . . there might be
nothing left but some blackened, bloating carcasses
sprouting arrows beside the smoking char of what
had been their wagons.

Ever since the treaty at Medicine Lodge Creek had
spelled out the buffalo hunting ground for the southern tribes back in '67, the warriors had become all
the more steadfast in their vigilance to keep the white
man out of this country. Billy had seen what the
young bucks could do with a man tied to a wagon
wheel, the whole thing ablaze . . . or a teamster
would be lashed to a single-tree and slowly roasted
like a pig on a spit, until his skin turned black and his
gut burst open with the intense heat—

He shook the thought off, knowing it did no good to
brood on the danger. Dixon had never shirked a challenge. And now, with the big herds north of the Arkansas killed off, the challenge lay south of the "dead
line." South of there was Indian country, where a
white man dared go only if he was stupid, or had
fifty-caliber balls.

To go there—south across the "dead line" to the
gentle, rolling southern plains, which served as both
the arena for the coming struggle and the reward itself for their beauty stretched away from Billy in every direction—satisfied Dixon's soul. And in any
direction he cared to look, all was peace. Up north
among the soldiers at Fort Dodge, word had it that
there was an Indian war going on with the Modocs
out west in Oregon. Up north the Sioux and Chey-

enne were said to be causing trouble. Back east . . . well, Dixon just smiled, those starched-collar fellas made their own problems for themselves.

Out here though, a man could lose himself. With some hope, maybe even find himself again.

From the wide and mighty Platte River beside the well-tracked Emigrant Road that had carried countless thousands west to Oregon and California or down to Salt Lake City of the Mormons, from there all the way south to the Rio Grande River, the southern great plains rolled on and on to the horizon. Sloping gently all the way from the Rocky Mountains down to the ninety-eighth meridian, this tableland was for the most part level and semiarid, covered with a thick carpet of tangled root grasses, making this land one of the most ideal natural grazing pastures in the entire world.

Most of the year the southern plains suffered from a lack of moisture, constantly buffeted by drying winds; it could very well be called the "Great American Desert." Yet in April, May and June, this great pasture received the blessing of rain which immediately turned the land green before the arrival of the drying winds of July and August came along to sear the plains and force the grass to seed in an endless cycle of life and death and rebirth once more.

From autumn to spring, for three seasons of the year, a man had to be wary of the dark horizon and any shift in the wind. A norther could blow in over a matter of an hour, catching man and beast unprepared for the onslaught of arctic cold driven before a furious gale. It was not uncommon on the high plains for the temperature to drop more than fifty degrees in that hour that it took the wind to shift out of the north, bringing the maw of the arctic itself to a land so recently a parched furnace.

To the east of the great flatlands, the southern plains began to bunch and roll themselves into the hill country, and even mountains like the Wichitas, cut with numerous streams and dressed in thick hardwood forests. Just west of the southern plains, however, the land became much more austere, cut crudely with breaks and badlands and buttes as it rose to the most severe piece of real estate of all: the Llano Estacado, the Staked Plain. A few rivers bravely cross the land between these two extremes, rivers that rose like a ladder that would take the migrating buffalo herds north from the Pecos, Colorado, Brazos, Pease, Red, Washita, Canadian, Cimarron and the Arkansas. Most of these were typically bordered with low, sandy banks, filled with gypsum and enough other salts to make them unfit for drinking.

Growing in abundance along the western streams was a profusion of plum and grape and mesquite, while to the east grew pecan and walnut trees and the sweet, juicy persimmon. If a man camped along a watercourse, firewood proved no problem: cedar, scrub oak, hackberry, cottonwood, chinaberry, elm, redbud and ash.

Elk, turkey, deer, pheasant, antelope—they all abounded and made a place for themselves in this wild and unforgiving country. And of course the buffalo. No one knew how long they had been here. But as soon as the white man had seen them back when the century was but an infant, the days of the buffalo were numbered.

Still, the land at that time was fit only for a few fur trappers and the Indian, who was considered a red prince of the wilderness, a creature who was eagerly studied and painted by the nobility throughout the rest of the world. So it was there, to the great plains of that time when the new nation began stretching its arms, that the white man shipped the eastern tribes when the government needed to move them out of the way of progress. For resettlement they were given permanent homes in Kansas Territory.

But by 1854 the white man was back, telling the tribes they would have to move once more, this time south to a place he was calling Indian Territory. Settlers, farmers, and the railroads wanted the land. No longer was the red man a noble savage. Now he was simply a savage who had placed himself squarely in the middle of the road to progress.

It did not take long for the white man to realize that both the Indian and the buffalo would have to go if the land was to be tamed and subdued and made fruitful, if not for the glory of God, then most certainly for the almighty dollar. The men who controlled more dollars than most were the powerful railroad barons, like Jay Cooke. It was by squeezing dollars out of the government and by their own courageous pluck that men like Cooke pushed the railroads west after the Civil War whimpered to a close. The costs were enormous—yet the rewards promised to dwarf any of the costs along the way west.

Land.

The government gave it away to the railroad barons. And the barons would sell it to the settlers who would be coming west. But first the folks back east had to hear what a Garden of Eden was these Great Plains. The railroads saw to it that the eastern papers always headlined stories of the rich prairieland populated by an endless supply of buffalo. In fact, a 120-mile trip taken by one journalist from Ellsworth to Sheridan, Kansas, was made through a continuous herd so thick the engineer was compelled to stop over a dozen times, since the beasts refused to budge from the tracks despite the whistling, smoke-belching monster on rails.

Black-bordered advertisements proclaiming "Grand Railway Excursion to the Land of the Bison!" and "Buffalo Hunt on the Plains!" were in every newspaper, promoted by the Kansas Pacific.

Customers from all points east were routed west to Phil Sheridan Station, Kansas—near the site where Forsyth's fifty civilians stood off five hundred Cheyenne for nine days. Make no mistake, the conductors told their passengers as the railway employees buckled on their sidearms once past the Ellsworth Station —this was the Great Plains, home to the savage red man. Details of buffalo soldiers were assigned to protect the watering and refueling stops like the one at Buffalo Tank. But by the time they reached Sheridan, the eastern dudes come to shoot a shaggy buffalo got their money's worth.

There among a collection of dingy sod hovels and hillside dugouts, the owners of watering holes and saloons and whorehouses plied their trade. Here too flocked the gamblers ready to fleece those newly arrived from the east of their easy money. And surrounding the tiny, stinking town for miles around were thousands of buffalo hides, pegged out and drying, ready for shipment to the tanneries back beyond the great Missouri River.

While most of his kind swirled as headily as nectar-sucking hummingbirds around such places as Sheridan and Dodge City, Billy Dixon had always done his best to steer clear of such fleshpots. It was out here to the prairie that men like him came to reclaim a big piece of themselves.

The winter drifts were staying long this year, Billy had noted as he had ambled south from Dodge, already a growing, rowdy and raucous new town. But with the persistence of the spring sun, the drifts were shrinking at last. Each one a murky gray by now, windblown and carved in sharp relief, the final sprigs of snow gave way to the onslaught of spring. Snowmelt seeped into the ground, trickled into every arroyo and coulee, roared down every creek and stream toward the Mississippi and the Gulf of Mexico.

Soon enough the buffalo would be coming north once again in their annual dance of mating and mauling, snorting and grazing with their noses always into the wind.

And when they did turn north, the hide hunters would be there to greet them, in numbers never before seen on the southern plains.

Billy Dixon had wondered on it, watching the throngs of men coming into Dodge, some with their own outfits, others having to count on getting outfitted right there in the buffalo country. A team, a wagon, blankets and knives, and a big-bore gun . . . why, anybody's cousin could call himself a buffalo hunter.

Dixon snorted as he savored the aroma of the coffee grounds he had just dumped into the roiling water, then pulled the old kettle to the side of his small fire. He leaned back to let the coffee brew while he tore at the venison he had jerked two days before.

Anybody and everybody was coming to the southern plains this year, in numbers never seen since the rush to the California gold fields in '49. Out-of-work railroad laborers, burnt-out settlers needing a new stake in life, men with failed business back east, fortune hunters looking for the next mother lode, each of them with his own story and his own reason for being here in buffalo country with a rifle and skinning knife, their eyes straining at the horizon, waiting for the first of the herds to come in sight now that winter had fled the land.

Back some five summers ago, when Dixon had first come to this country driving wagons for Custer's Seventh Cavalry, the dim-sighted buffalo were so unconcerned and unafraid of man they had to be shooed aside from the path the regiment and wagon train was taking. The country was a paradise, like a hive. And hunters such as Billy Dixon were the bees. One day the white men would be swarming south of the "dead line." For now, Dixon and his five were alone.

At this camp, they had busied themselves the first two days cutting the tall grass and stacking it so the stock would have proper graze without having to let the animals forage far from camp, where warriors on fleet ponies could run off the horses and wagon mules. This morning was the day Billy had chosen to take one last look south of their camp. McCabe rode horseback beside him, and with them came one of the old skinners in the lightest wagon, hitched to a tandem of mules.

If trouble raised its head, Dixon wanted his bunch to move and move quickly.

From the day they had crossed the Arkansas and pushed south into Indian country, Billy's outfit had spotted small war-parties in the distance. For the most part, that's where the warriors had stayed, never venturing too close, firing only from long-range at the intruders, respectful of the hunters' big-bore, far-shooting guns. They seemed content for the time just trying to push the white men north, back across the river and out of buffalo country.

"Jesus, Mary and Joseph!" Dixon cried, reining up suddenly on the slope leading down to Crooked Creek.

The other two with him had no trouble seeing the

war-party across the creek, each warrior painted and
feathered, milling and talking among themselves.

"It won't be too long they'll figure out there's only
three of us, by gor!" McCabe cursed.

"Let's fort up!" suggested the old skinner as he
lashed reins to the brake and hopped to the ground.
He dragged his own rifle from beneath the seat and
found himself a spot in the shade of the wagon.

One of the warriors came to the middle of the
stream and waved his arm, signaling the white man
to go back. To return north. Behind him a dozen
younger ones milled and shouted their challenges to
the outnumbered white men.

"I'll knock him down, you want me to," offered the
old skinner.

"I don't figure they want to draw any blood today,"
Billy replied. "Else't they'd roared across the creek
and been done with us."

"Day ain't over yet, Dixon," McCabe growled.
"They're standing their ground where they are because of our guns. If we start rolling back now—
they'll sweep down on us and make easy pickin's."

A shot whined overhead, causing the three white
men to duck. Down at the stream, the older warrior
had turned about and was shouting at the younger
men smeared with ocher and red earth and bright
yellow pigment. Then another of the hot-blooded
bucks fired his rifle at the wagon. Lead slapped
through the sidewall.

"Goddamn 'em!" snarled the old skinner. "Let's
fight the red bastards, Dixon!"

"This is still my outfit, and if I say stand—we'll
stand."

"I didn't join up with you to get my scalp raised,
Dixon," spat McCabe.

"Who'd want red hair like yours?" Billy asked, smiling.

"Just let me show 'em we're not to be trifled with," McCabe pleaded.

"Over their heads," Dixon agreed. "Let's see if we can shoo them off, like flies off a fresh hide."

The two others began firing over the warriors. The Indians stirred, their horses prancing, splashing in the stream then easing back to the far bank, continuing to shout their own brand of obscenities.

But the old man in the creek stood his ground, shouting something after each shot fired between the two groups. He had a single feather tied beneath his left ear, where it fluttered beneath the old warrior's jawbone as he harangued the white men.

Finally Billy tired of the long-distance gun battle and waved his arms, signaling that he and the others were withdrawing—to the north. The war-chief nodded in no little satisfaction, then turned his pony out of the creek and waved his painted warriors away from the scene. Their job done, the white men turned back to where they belonged.

"My ass was puckering like a whiskey keg bung-hole," said the old man.

"What you think they were?" McCabe asked.

"Cheyenne, most likely," Billy answered.

"Chances are you're right—still far enough north for Cheyenne."

"Man's gotta push far down on the far side of the Cimarron to bump into Kiowa, don't he?" Dixon asked.

"Them, or the godblamed Comanche," said the skinner.

"You like hunting on the other side of the Arkansas, boys?"

They both eyed him, not sure just what he was asking.

"I like keeping my hair, red or no," McCabe answered.

"How 'bout making money."

McCabe looked at the skinner. "That too."

"Then we ain't leaving," Dixon said. "We'll just go back to camp, pull up stakes and make it look like we're pulling out."

"We ain't gonna make it back to camp afore dark," the skinner declared as the empty wagon rattled and bounced over the grassy prairie.

"Then we'll ride till it's slap-dark," Dixon told them. "And bed down where night finds us."

"Night finds us," McCabe repeated. "Night . . . or them murdering Cheyenne do."

Chapter 12

July 1873

*W*ith a nerve-rattling screech of iron upon iron, the great hissing weight of the eastbound freight was eased into the station at Hays City, Kansas, beside the Smoky Hill River.

It was almost as if the great black monster sighed as it settled itself there this early evening beside the battered platform that had seen countless thousands of boots and moccasin soles over all those years it had stood here beside the Kansas-Pacific. To most who found themselves meeting this train at twilight, this appeared to be just another eastbound chain of freight cars and passenger wagons shuddering to a stop behind the wheezing engine as it hissed its first of many spouts of steam among the legs of those gathered in the fading summer sunlight on that scuffed platform of cottonwood planks.

Seamus Donegan rose slowly from his horsehair, leather-covered seat beside the window on the far side of the train, away from the station platform. He was in no real hurry, he figured, time enough to let the other passengers scurry down the aisle in their rush, down the iron steps and into another life than the smoky, dusty, confined life they had all shared for what time they gave themselves over to this black snorting monster that had pulled the Irishman here all the way from Redding, California, and the land his uncle Ian O'Roarke had come to call his own.

Seamus was moving east, heading back to the only place he could ever admit to feeling was home. Ireland.

With a sense of some completeness now fully a part of him, the tall Irishman set the battered brown slouch hat atop his shoulder-length curls then tugged the heavy canvas mackinaw onto his arms. The sun had just settled at the edge of the far prairie, giving a pink tint to the underbellies of the summer flecks of clouds overhead. The air would be growing cool soon enough.

Seamus had been a long time returning to these plains, gone to the edge of the western world, tracking down Uncle Ian and fighting Modocs in the devil's playground called the Lava Beds.* And he had spent more nights than he cared to now remember wrapped in his bedroll at the edge of this endless prairie wilderness.

The plaintive howls of wolf and coyote, the whisper of wind and the hammering hoofbeats of summer thunderstorm on his gum poncho, the minute cry of insects at work in the dark, a sound almost lost against the aching immensity of the whirring of the faraway stars a man could almost make out coming from that great black velvet canopy overhead. A great, arching skyscape just out of reach above the bed he made in that lonely land of the high plains that only a true, wandering soul could learn to love.

"This land will bake your brains in the summer

* The Plainsmen Series, vol. 5, *Devil's Backbone*

. . . freeze your balls in the winter. Nothing like the high plains, Seamus."

He snagged the worn leather of his holster belt, slung it over his shoulder as he recalled those words of Abner Grover, the prairie scout who had for a time shared a riflepit on a stinking island in the middle of a nameless river bottom somewhere up high on the Colorado plains.

Pulling up the scarred remains of his trail-weary saddlebags, he hefted the saddle that had cradled his ass for so many miles, and half that many years. With his free hand Seamus retrieved that last item of his belongings wedged into the narrow seat: the brass-mounted, blue-barreled .44-caliber Henry repeater. Much as if the rifle were coming home, he swept his huge paw around the action, his hand cupped in a made-to-order groove ready to receive the weapon.

He was alone in the car. The noise was all outside now: the calls of friends and family to those who had stepped off the wheezing monster. Stevedores hustled, shouldered back the huge doors and disappeared into baggage cars to retrieve luggage and trunks and freight bound for off-loading at this stop on the central plains. A clanging of bells, a rush of pouring water from the railside tank and another loud exhaust of steam greeted the Irishman's ears as he turned his bulk sideways and eased down the aisle for the narrow door at the end of the passenger car.

Three steps and his tall, mule-eared boots clattered to a halt on the platform. He glanced up, then down, and found a uniformed station man hurrying past with papers rolled beneath his arm. Seamus held out the Henry rifle like a man who required a toll to be paid before passing.

"Where might I get my animals?"

"What sort of animals, mister?" the man asked, irritated.

"Horses."

"You bring with you in from Denver City?"

"Aye. Farther still. California."

The harried man pointed back down the track. "Likely they were loaded in the last few cars. There ain't another platform, but they run a ramp up to the cars and put 'em down in the corrals."

Seamus looked downtrack then turned around to utter his thanks but found the small man hurrying on to other duties at the far end of the passenger platform.

In the fading light of this early summer's eve, every form took on a unique texture of its own here in the clear air of the central plains. Ever since the iron rails had catapulted him over the California mountains and onto the plains, his nose had reveled in that special quality to the air that bespoke this high land yearning against and for the endless sky. Not that the land hugging the boundary of California and Oregon wasn't pretty. It just wasn't country for him.

But, saints almighty, if that hadn't been land that reminded every fiber within him of his native soil so far from his boot soles now. The air of that Oregon-California borderland smelled of the same high, chilling dampness of County Kilkenny. That same rugged blending of rock and turf and those brittle plants that clung tenaciously, resisting a brutal environment. And in passing up the western slope of those California mountains, looking down one last time into the land his uncle had adopted, Seamus finally and fully understood why Ian O'Roarke had chosen that rainy land as the spot where he would send down his roots and raise up a family with his sweet Dimity.

That far land had reminded Ian of all that he had

once had back in Ireland, before so many started slowly dying off from hunger and disease, or from nothing more complicated than simple despair.

Seamus started for the far end of the platform, hoping the green land of his birth had come on better times in all the years he had been gone from Town Callan. Were that those better times would not be too much to hope . . .

He was nearing the edge of the platform, having just found the steps that would take him down into the dust and the dung that lay stretched clear to the corrals hugging the tracks run endlessly back across the flats of western Kansas and into Colorado Territory—where twice already he had fought the Cheyenne: once beside Sharp Grover at Beecher Island, and a year later helping Major Eugene Asa Carr's Fifth Cavalry scatter the mighty Dog Soldiers plundering the high plains under chief Tall Bull.*

So deep in thought was he of those places and the weeping scars they had left upon his soul that the Irishman really did not hear the voice call out his name the first time. It came more like an unsettling part of the damning recollections he carried with him in his waking hours. Yet, too, ringing with every bit as much stark terror and physical pain as the dreams he suffered when he closed his eyes each night. Alone.

"Seamus? Is that you?"

But this was a real voice, not one of those that haunted the unplumbed depths of his solitude. Donegan turned.

A figure moved toward him from the shadows cast beneath the rail station awning. Then the dark shadow halted.

* The Plainsmen Series, vol. 4, *Black Sun*

"Lord, Seamus—it is you!"

He strained his eyes, inching the finger into the guard, encircling the trigger of his Henry, a cold prickling at the back of his neck as the stranger swept out of the shadows, wearing the flaring drape of a long coat that nearly reached the platform etched with the inky clomp of the thin man's boot heels.

But the stranger stopped as Seamus brought up the Henry.

"Seamus—it's me—don't mean you no harm."

The thin man raised his arms out in a way that reminded the Irishman of the crucifix hung over the head of his bed, where he slept as a boy in Town Callan, listening to the lonely sobbing of his mother on the far side of the thin wall, crying herself to sleep each night for want of the return of her husband— now dead and buried beneath the loamy soil of Eire so stingy and refusing to give back life to its own.

"It's Jack. Jack Stillwell, Seamus."

"Jack . . . young Stillwell, is it?"

The stranger stepped fully into the last pink light of the sun as it eased off into the far side of the prairie behind the Rocky Mountains, days away in Colorado Territory.

"Damn, but I don't believe it's you, young Jack!" He dropped pistol belt and saddle and bags in a mad rush at the tall, thin man, sweeping Stillwell against him in a crushing embrace.

They pounded one another on the back until weary in a close-cropped dance of glee that hammered the cottonwood platform. Then Seamus stepped back, moistness at his eyes and a lump come again to his throat.

"Good to see you, young Jack."

"It's been five years, Seamus," Stillwell said, gone serious. "None of us so young now as we was then.

On that bloody island where Lieutenant Beecher fell."

"Aye," he answered softly, the sting come again to his eyes. "But were it not for the grit of a likely lad by the name of Stillwell, who went to fetch us relief from Fort Wallace, likely that island would have proved a grave for Major Forsyth and the rest of us what rode after Roman Nose."

"Then you know . . . it was Roman Nose you killed in that first charge?"

"If it weren't me—likely it was Liam."

"Everyone here on the plains talks of you being the one who brought that red bastard down."

"They do?"

"It's a story makes the round of every barrack and barroom that I know of."

"And what would Jack Stillwell be knowing of barracks and barrooms. You ain't gone and become wolf on me, have you?"

"No—ain't likely. But I enjoy army food—and two squares of it a day, as a matter of fact. Gotten used to it."

"You still scouting for them out here?"

"I am, Seamus. In fact," he said, craning his neck, "I'm here to pick up two gentlemen the army's hired me to guide down into the southern part of Indian Territory with an army escort from Fort Dodge."

"Sounds like it might be a dangerous ride."

"Naw. Ever since Custer and his Seventh settled things back to 'sixty-nine—been mostly quiet down there. Look, I think I see them two off the train and looking for someone who's supposed to be waiting for them. So, here," Stillwell said, as he stuffed a hand into the inside pocket of his long trail coat. He brought out a small, folded bundle, none too thick and about six inches square, tied up in brown baling twine. He dusted off the flat package, much rumpled, wrinkled and trail-worn.

"Damn my soul if I walk off from you and didn't give you this."

"What is this?" he asked, staring down at the bundle.

"Letters," Stillwell answered, as if it were the most normal thing in the world to hand such a thing over to a friend one has not seen in the span of five years.

"How long you—"

"Been carrying 'em for Sharp Grover. He toted 'em around for you for two year. Listen—I gotta be getting, Seamus. Those two fancy fellas getting nervous. Meet me later in town. Where you gonna stay?"

"You tell me."

"Henshaw's place. I'll find you there tonight, Irishman." Stillwell held out his hand. They shook. "Damn but I'm glad to bump into you. And finally get shet of those letters Sharp's had me lugging around for you the last three years—hoping I'd run onto word of you somewhere after you quit scouting for Bill Cody and the Fifth."

"That's a story we'll share over some whiskey tonight."

"Damn right we will, Irishman. I figure we got a lot of tales to share."

"Five years' worth, Jack."

"I'll see you to Henshaw's after I get these two gentlemen with their paper collars tucked in for the night."

"Watch your backside, Stillwell."

"I'll watch yours as well, Seamus!"

As the young scout disappeared into the twilight of that station platform, oily, yellow light beginning to spill from the multipaned windows, Donegan stared down into the package suddenly going heavy in his hand. With nervous fingers he tore apart the twine knot and unwrapped the coarse, browned paper that enclosed two envelopes.

After dragging his trail gear into the splash of saffron lamplight pouring from a window, Seamus spread the wrinkled brown paper with his fingers and began reading what appeared to be the unfamiliar handwriting of a woman.

Dear Irishman,

If you are reading this, then you are alive. I've carried these two letters with me for close to two years now, but am fixing to move on south and do something new with my life. My woman's had enough of Kansas and hears good things from her family gone to Texas. That's where I'm going, south across the Red River. So I'm giving these two letters over to Jack Stillwell.

Lord, has that fella growed. But as I give them over to him for safekeeping for you to show back up, I'm having the wife of a storekeeper in Sheridan write this letter for me since I can't make no word on paper but my name.

Want you to think about coming south with me, Seamus. Plenty of ranching land for a man down there. Good timber and water. We can make a go of it and live out our days as peaceful country gents. Something me and Liam always talked about. It does still give me pain to think on Liam now—how he talked so on one day settling down with me and we could run some cattle and raise some fine-strutting horses.

Won't you come look me up? Jack will always know where I end up roosting. I'll let him know how you can track me down.

Don't blame this on the woman, Seamus. I gave the army my best years, and owe that woman the rest of what I got left in me. Come on down to

Texas, put your boots up on the rail with mine for a change. Neither one of us meant to be a Injun fighter the rest of our natural days.

Abner Grover

There was a trembling of emotion that threatened to spill over as he stared down at that name illuminated by the lamplight on that Hays City station platform. "You always hated that name, Sharp. Thank you, Abner—but I don't figure I got any business coming south to Texas, when I've got something stronger still tugging me back to Ireland."

Stuffing the brown paper in the pocket of his mackinaw, Seamus stared at the top letter, much wrinkled as well, addresses crossed out and new ones squeezed into what blank space was left on the folded envelope. A litany of posts and forts and towns up and down the Platte River Road and on up the Bozeman Road. It had been better than seven years now since he had started up that bloody trail into Red Cloud's country, looking for yellow gold but finding instead an unrelenting red wall.*

Unfolding the envelope, Seamus found it hard to believe his eyes.

Dear son,

I am writing this at the old table where we all used to sit for what meals I could place before my family. It brings back so many memories of you now. Gone so long from this place. How I would love to see your face come past the window one more time.

Ian has written me. From someplace on the far side of America. Calls the place Linkville Town. Oregon must be the county he's settled in from the

---

* The Plainsmen Series, vol. 1, *Sioux Dawn*

sounds of it. Happy he is too. God bless him now
that Liam's gone. Your letter telling me how Liam
died reached me here several months ago. How
scared I am for you still.

Come on home now. Liam has gone on to stay
with God and Ian is putting down deep roots with
his family in that new land. He writes like I remember him as a boy, not like the hard man he became
before leaving Eire. But now full of hopes and
dreams once more, like our papa, like your papa
too, had dreams for you living close to the earth. Ian
has that now, and a good woman to love him and
stand by him.

Come home now so you too can be far, far away
from those savages who have claimed your uncle
and nearly took your life too. I wait every day
watching for your face at the window, to hear your
steps on the stones at the stoop before you open the
door.

Your mother loves you, Seamus.

For a moment he held the letter against his breast,
almost as if the warmth of her hand were still there
upon the page despite the years and the miles and the
aching loneliness that had separated them for so
long.

"I'm coming home, Mother."

Carefully folding her letter, Seamus put it in the
pocket with Grover's, then glanced at the last letter,
nothing more really than a twice-folded page, addressed much as the first had been. And from Town
Callan in Ireland as well.

Dear Seamus Donegan,

You will not remember me, nor know me. I came
to the parish several months after you were bound
over to America, as your mother told me of you on
so many occasions. I was her priest all these years.

She became a friend to me, one of the few I could count on in this land and a time of little to count on.

It is not easy when anyone dies, but especially a friend. So it is that I hope you can feel my remorse and pain in losing your mother. We share that loss together.

He blinked his eyes, smarting with the sudden tears, straining at the words swimming now in that smear of lamplight splashing from the window where he stood. Then slowly, ever slowly, he sank to his knees, sobbing silently, falling back against the clapboards beneath the station window.

Seamus ground a fist into both eyes angrily and read on.

She died peacefully, after a hard illness, Seamus. And she died with the love of God in her heart and a smile on her face. But, I am writing you since she asked me to, just before she breathed her last, and to tell you that in those final moments, your mother prayed for your welfare in a far and savage land, at the hands of strangers, and not among the bosom of your family.

She is laid in a small spot beside your father, as she wanted. Your brothers and sisters come to the grave often these past two weeks, for I always find fresh sprigs of this or that on her resting place. You would be settled to see it for yourself some day.

My prayers are for you, as your mother asked me to ask God to watch over you now that she can't pray for you. But, I feel she is watching still, Seamus. Now much closer to you than she was in her last days here in Eire. Her spirit is with you, and her love as well.

Father Colin Mulvaney

The moon rose full on the horizon and climbed toward mid-sky before Seamus felt capable of arising without shaking. He folded the last letter neatly and found a place for all three at the inside pocket of his mackinaw.

Dragging a hand beneath his nose while the summer night cooled the Kansas tableland, the Irishman dragged his saddle and gear to his shoulder then stepped off the platform.

He was moving into Hays City now, to Henshaw's place. To find Jack Stillwell.

Ireland lay behind him now.

He would ride south through Indian Territory with Stillwell's government men and army escort to find Sharp Grover. Seamus Donegan was heading south for the Red River country of Texas.

Chapter 13

July 1873

"*A*s things turned out," Jack Stillwell explained to his gray-eyed drinking partner at Drum's Saloon in Hays City, "those two Kiowa butchers never was hung."

"By the saints!" exclaimed Seamus Donegan, swiping whiskey from his mustache with the back of his hand.

"Seems some folks back east grabbed the ear of the President, so Grant put the arm on Governor Davis of Texas."

"Grant made the governor change his mind about hanging them Kiowa, is it?"

Stillwell nodded. "Instead, the governor sent the two chiefs to prison for life."

Donegan shook his head. "Why is it I've got the sneaking idea what you haven't told me is that those two won't be spending the rest of their miserable lives in prison?"

Stillwell did not attempt to hide the sheepish look on his face. "They was scheduled to be released back to the Kiowas last March."

"I take it the chiefs are still down in a Texas prison?"

"For now."

"So what's to come of it?"

"I think Governor Davis has gone and promised the tribe they'll have their chiefs back by October."

Seamus stared into his murky reflection in the brown whiskey. "Sounds like you've got me riding south into Texas to find Sharp Grover just about the time the Kiowas are due to get their bloodthirsty chiefs back."

Stillwell pursed his lips. "You're due, Seamus. Got a right to know."

"What else, Jack?"

"Them two I been hired to guide down through Injun Territory—they know all about Satanta and Lone Wolf. In fact, they said they've been given permission to talk to those two chiefs when we're down at Fort Sill."

"You're telling me now that we're going to be around when those two Kiowa are released?"

"You don't wanna go, you don't have to."

Donegan brooded into his whiskey. He finally gave Stillwell half a grin. "I haven't seen Sharp Grover in a long time, Jack. And, I figure you and me been through enough together that something like this ought not to scare me. I've heard nothing yet that makes me change me mind." Then he glowered at the scout. "Unless you've got something else up your sleeve you're not telling me about."

Relieved, Jack sat back, a grin on his face. "No—nothing, Seamus. I'm telling you everything."

"We leaving tomorrow?"

"Day after, I'm told."

"I suppose that gives me time, Jack."

"Time . . . for what, Seamus?"

He hoisted his glass. "To get meself in trouble before you take us south to get me scalped!"

* * *

Last spring, Billy Dixon's three-man outfit didn't sleep much that long, anxious night out on the prairie, deep in the buffalo country of the Cheyenne.

With every crunch of grass by the horses or every faint call of a bird swooping near their fireless camp, with every sigh of the wind that brought the rumor of hostile warriors to their ears, the trio bolted out of their bedrolls. No man could really sleep in country like this. He might only close his eyes because they burned from the long day's ride, or from the sun and grit and pure weariness. But no man really slept.

When dawn spread a murky gray the color of backwater in a buffalo wallow out of the east, Dixon had the old skinner and McCabe on the move. They were back among the other three skinners before dawn gave the rolling grassland a red glow.

"Sorry to scare you boys," Dixon apologized to the trio, who themselves had spent a fitful night in camp, fearing the others had been set upon and wiped out by hostiles. "I just plain missed my bearings when it got dark last night."

"We was worried—'cause we knew we'd be next," one of the skinners explained.

"We're clearing out this morning," Dixon went on.

"Where to?" McCabe asked.

He shook his head. "All I know is, this country isn't healthy for us. We'll spend too damned much time watching for Injuns . . . time we should be hunting buffalo."

"Can't say as I don't disagree with you, Billy," said the redheaded McCabe as he strode off a ways, turned his back on the others and unbuttoned his fly.

"We'll spend too much time fighting and losing sleep," Dixon went on to explain. "I figure we'd have to stand watch in rotation—"

"Billy!"

They all turned at McCabe's call.

"C'mere!" he shouted, wagging his arm to the others, still holding his limp flesh with the other hand. As they drew near to him, McCabe said, "Listen. Now shuddup, and listen."

Dixon, like the other men, put his ear to the spring wind, straining—at first only hearing the sound of the breeze and the faint thumping of his heartbeat. It wasn't like he didn't want to hear the distant lowing, and snorting and bellowing.

"By God!" one of them shouted.

"I hear it!" exclaimed another.

"Jesus, Mary and Joseph," Dixon whispered. "If that ain't buffalo, then Mother Dixon raised a rock-headed idjit!"

At a lope he swept up his Sharps rifle and snagged up the reins to the horse he had just ridden into camp.

"I'm going to find out for myself, boys," he told them once he was in the saddle, tightening up on the rein. "Get your knives sharpened—I got a feeling we'll be working hides before the day's half old!"

What he saw less than five miles off was a sight that could bring tears to the eyes of a buffalo hunter. The herd was moving north at its own slow, time-honored pace. Grazing and browsing, flocks of the tiny black birds sweeping over the black carpet stretched between the hills in its slow, undulating migration. The little yellow ones were frisking beside their mothers at the head of the grand march. Young bulls and old were relegated to the rear, kept to the fringes of the procession.

Whooping, Dixon wheeled his horse and raced back to the skinners' camp, where he confirmed the good news.

"How long you figure we can chance staying?" Dixon asked the old skinner.

He ran a tongue through the gap in his mouth where three rotten teeth had been yanked with ramrod pliers in years gone by. "Three, maybe four days, Billy."

"That herd will bring in the hunters, won't it?"

The old man nodded. "And we ain't talking about white hunters neither. Don't push your luck, and when we pull out—we best not spare the mules making it for the river, Billy."

"All right, boys," Dixon replied. "You heard it. I plan on this outfit hanging on here and working hides while we can—for four days."

That afternoon the five skinners were put to work. Not a one complained, for this was the only way a hide-man made his money. And besides, they hadn't seen a hint of a feather in any direction. Perhaps the buffalo gods had finally smiled on Billy Dixon after all.

So successful were they that not one of them really kept track of the passing days, not even the old skinner. The hides piled up from sunup to sundown, and at night Billy Dixon cast bullets for the next day's go at the passing herd. For hundreds of yards in all directions around their camp, green, heavy hides were pegged, still much too heavy to haul north.

For weeks now McCabe had served as chief camp cook each morning and evening in return for a bigger share of the outfit's profits. One starlit evening it was the redheaded skinner who told Billy they needed some fresh meat from the next day's hunt for the larder.

"Boss ribs, it is, McCabe," Dixon declared.

"Come to think on it—anyone know how long we been here?" asked the old skinner.

"I got a idea it's more'n a week," replied one of the others.

"On the order of ten days, by my count," Dixon answered. Then it struck him as he turned to the old skinner. "Something wrong?"

"Just hope we didn't overstay our welcome, Dixon."

"Damn, if that ain't the story, boys. Unless we wait till they're cured, how we gonna haul these green hides too heavy for the wagon? And if we wait on the hides to cure—why not hunt for more instead of sitting on our thumbs?"

"It don't really make sense sitting on your thumbs," the old skinner replied. "But it don't please me losing my hair waiting for a single hide to dry neither."

"All right. Two more days won't hurt," Dixon decided. "I'll go out early tomorrow and make meat to last us till we get north of the Arkansas. And we'll pull hides till we pull out, fellas. Each one of these damned hides is worth too much for me to leave it behind."

That seemed to settle it, without much grumbling from the skinners. At least any grumbling that Billy overheard. The next morning after a scalding cup of McCabe's coffee, Dixon was gone into the herd roaming and feeding as little as two miles to the west of their camp. What he ran into was mostly younger cows and some young bulls along for the march. And for the most part the whole bunch of them acted as if they'd been chivvied of late, stirred up and restless. Downright spooky and ready to bolt at any sudden change in the breeze.

If he didn't know better, Dixon would have figured the herd had been chivvied by Indians. But he was here to make meat, and hides too, if he got a good stand out of it, so he dismounted and rein-hobbled his horse.

Near the top of a low hill he went to his belly and crawled to the crest. Down below, the herd milled as if ready to make the jump, tails high and noses into the wind. Dixon chose a young bull and eased the barrel of the big Sharps down on the crossed sticks he had jammed in the ground to steady his aim. The gun roared.

As the stinging, gray smoke cleared, Dixon could see not only that the young bull had dropped, but that the rest of the herd was whirling away in a blinding cloud of dust, spooked by the gunshot and blood. He rammed home another cartridge, fired. Chambered another and fired as fast as he could. One after another Dixon aimed by feel into the blinding cloud of dust raised by the herd lumbering past the slope of the hill. If they were running off, then Billy Dixon was going to take as many as he could right here and now before they got out of range of his big gun.

When the thundering noise of their passing had faded and the dust cloud hung far down the valley hemmed with rolling hills, Billy rose and surveyed the scene. He tapped a finger on the Sharps barrel, searing his flesh. At least there were a dozen, perhaps more, down there for the others to skin. A good start on the day's work, he decided.

At that moment back in camp, McCabe and the others had heard the first shot, then the second and all the rest rumbling in from the prairie in rapid succession.

"He's pinned down," declared the old skinner.

"We best get," suggested another.

"I ain't leaving Billy!" McCabe growled.

"Lookit!" one of the others shouted, pointing at a distant hill, in the general direction of the gunfire.

Silhouetted on the crest of the knoll were several dark forms that to the eyes of the skinners appeared to be mounted warriors adorned with feathers in their hair. Instead of being a war-party of Comanche, a small band of some two dozen antelope had been driven toward the skinners' camp by the stampeding buffalo. Those shadowy outlines of the confused, frightened antelope was all it took to light a fire under the hide-men.

"We're next, by God!"

"They got Dixon—and now red bastards coming for us!"

"Get ready to fight for your scalps, boys!" the old skinner exhorted them. "We'll try for the river if we can."

"We're staying here—and waiting to find out what happened to Billy!" McCabe yelled at them.

The old skinner stepped up to the redheaded young man. "We're going to the river to save our own hides." He whirled on the other, younger men. "Now, the rest of you—round up the stock and let's get loaded. Maybeso we can reach the Arkansas afore they kill us all."

They had the wagons hitched and the horses saddled, leaving the hides, both dry and green, where they dotted the surrounding prairie . . . when of a sudden one of them spotted a lone figure appear on the far hilltop.

"There's one of the bastards," he said.

The old skinner pushed forward through the muttering, frightened men. "He's probably come in to show us Dixon's scalp and tell us we better push north, we know what's good for us."

"Don't shoot," McCabe begged them. "Let's find out what happened to Billy first."

They watched the rider come in at an easy lope,

with something shadowy and dark slung over the front flanks of the horse as the rider came out of the west. After a moment McCabe rose behind the wagon where he had taken refuge, ready to sell his life dearly.

"Glory! Glory be! Howdeedo, Billy!"

"Halloo, the camp!" Dixon hollered back. "Made meat, fellas." He rode into their midst, looking over the hitched teams and loaded wagons. "Didn't mean to starve you to the point you'd just up and take off on me."

"They was fixing to light out for the river, Billy," McCabe explained.

He gazed at the old skinner, then the rest. "That right?"

"We heard all the shooting," one of them explained sheepishly. "Figured you'd made a fight of it and was a goner."

"Then we saw some Injuns on the hill over yonder," another skinner jumped in to declare.

"Injuns?" Billy asked, turning in the saddle. "I ain't seen nothing but some antelope on my way in."

The rest looked at one another.

"Antelope?" McCabe asked. "So what you got for my stew kettle, Billy?"

Dixon glanced down at the bloody, fresh chunk of meat he had slung in front of him for the ride in. He eased the heavy load down to McCabe's arms. "I promised you boss ribs . . . so boss ribs it'll be."

"I wasn't gonna leave you, Billy," said the fiery redbeard as he juggled his load of buffalo meat. "The rest was set to pull up stakes."

Dixon's eyes touched them all, not finding any that would hold his for very long. "That true? You was ready to pull out and not even come back and claim my body?"

"You wasn't killed, Dixon," said the old skinner.

"What if I was—you'd just leave me for the wolves and the buzzards?"

"Shit no," the old man answered, his arm sweeping an arc across the surrounding prairie. "No wolf or buzzard I know would chew on your carcass . . . not when we've left the carcasses of more'n enough good buffalo out there for 'em to eat!"

After selling what he had in the way of hides back in Dodge City to the Mooar brothers that spring, Billy had ventured south once more with a new outfit and a new bunch of skinners. This time they pushed past Crooked Creek and the Cimarron. On to Coldwater and Palo Duro Creeks. Farther south than any of them had ever been, or dared push into Indian country. They were past the land of the Cheyenne, pressing into the haunts of the Kwahadi and Kiowa. For certain this was not a white man's land.

Dixon found piles of old bones where the Indians and Mexicans had once hunted these austere plains. Those bones and a prairie dotted with buffalo chips were the only evidence that the herds had been here of a time.

But there were no buffalo.

One thing was coming clear in his mind: if a man was to keep making money at this hide business, he would have to dare to ride farther and farther south each season. And if he wanted to make his fortune in buffalo, then a man had to say to hell with the red devils.

To hell with the Kwahadi of Quanah Parker. And to hell with the Kiowa of Satanta and Lone Wolf.

Chapter 14

August 1873

"$\mathcal{E}$xcuse me, fellas," the stranger said as he rose from his chair and eased over to the table where Seamus Donegan and Jack Stillwell sat. "Did I hear one of you say the name Sharp Grover?"

Here in this smoky watering hole in Dodge City, Murray & Waters Saloon, the Irishman glanced at Jack, then looked up at the young man's face. An open, friendly and well-groomed face with a waxed mustache beneath the handsome nose. Black hair hung to his shoulders.

"We did," Seamus answered. "You know him?"

"I might have—if it was the same Sharp Grover who worked for Silas Pepoon in the winter of 'sixty-eight."

"Pepoon?" Donegan asked.

"Chief of scouts for Custer's campaign against the Washita tribes," Jack Stillwell explained. He looked up at the stranger. "Yeah—so it must be the same Sharp Grover."

"I was hoping there wasn't two of them. The man was like a father to me back then. Jesus, Mary and Joseph—but it's been five years already, ain't it?" His large, callused hands grew nervous. "May I join you fellas for a drink—bringing my own?" He hoisted the nearly full bottle.

"Have a seat," Seamus said. "Never turn down a man who wants to bathe strangers in whiskey."

"I figure friends of Sharp Grover's will be friends of mine soon enough," he replied, holding his hand out to the Irishman. "Billy Dixon's my name."

They introduced themselves then watched Dixon pour a round.

"You made some money I take it?" Seamus inquired, throwing a thumb over his shoulder at the gaming tables.

Dixon smiled. "Never was one to have much luck at that. No, Mr. Donegan. Made my money bringing in some hides that are already on their way back to a tannery in New York."

"Buffalo man, eh?" Stillwell said. "You can't be much older'n me. How long you been doing that?"

"I'll turn twenty-three on the twenty-fifth of next month—September," Dixon replied proudly. "Been a hide hunter for the past few seasons—since the spring of 'seventy. First laid eyes on the herds when I was a teamster for Custer's Seventh Cavalry down to the Washita. We herded the Kiowa into Fort Cobb then went chasing after the rest of the Cheyenne, clear west to the Sweetwater in 'sixty-nine."

"That's how you met Sharp?"

"He showed me things—taught me some tricks to get along out here. Truth of it—I'll never be able to repay Sharp Grover for his friendship that winter down in Indian Territory."

Stillwell nodded, gazing down at his glass. "Sharp took a lot of us young ones under his wing, Billy. I only got a year on you myself."

"By the saints! Don't you two young'uns know how to make a man feel his age?" Seamus grumbled, a smile cracking the side of his face. "I got ten years, couple thousand miles, and more than my share of scars on both of you young hellions. So, here—let's drink a toast to a grand old man: Sharp Grover!"

"Here, here!" Stillwell replied as he hoisted his glass.

"To Sharp Grover it is!" Dixon agreed.

Less than two years before, trader Charlie Myers had parked his hide wagons beneath a lone cotton-wood tree and erected his little sod trading house right here on the road west from Fort Dodge. The following spring of 1872, the construction gangs laying track for the Santa Fe Railroad raised their own tents nearby and the little settlement of Buffalo City was born. There was no shortage of customers for Myers, and soon enough a man named Hoover, who became the biggest trader in whiskey, was selling out of his wagon with its hinged sidewalls that allowed the buffalo hunters to walk up the planks right into the wagonbed.

Card players and whores weren't long in arriving either. One outfit called it quits on a too-quiet Hays City and moved out, packing bar, bottles and beds in ten wagons for the trip west. Those half-dozen girls who unashamedly showed their assets as they rode into Buffalo City, accompanied by the cheers and hoots of a joyous throng of stinking buffalo men, were sure to make a living bringing progress to the plains. Before there was a bank, a postal office or a sheriff, the fleshpots were open for business and promising a brisk trade.

The hide hunters came to this country, for here in southwestern Kansas roamed the immense Arkansas herd. So to southwestern Kansas flocked a thousand hide hunters.

By August, Buffalo City had come of age as a wild

and woolly gathering place for all the best and the worst of mankind streaming onto the central plains. More and more newcomers burrowed dugouts or shoveled sod loose to build their earthen shanties on neatly platted town lots, measured and staked out by Charlie Myers using only a length of rope. Now the main street measured two blocks long, with two general stores among the watering holes and whores' cribs. Old Mexican Mary still persisted in plying her trade, as she had from the earliest days of Buffalo City—entertaining her customers on a pallet of blankets she laid on the floor of her dugout carved out of a creekbank near the Arkansas.

Old Maria laughed when she learned of the death of one of those six fancy whores recently come to town and working out of an honest-to-goodness featherbed—a whore who died of "galloping consumption." Maria laughed till she cried when she heard another had poisoned herself when, drunk and curious, she had tasted the vial of wolf poison she found in a hide hunter's coat pocket before she could be stopped.

Between the hunters and the railroad construction gangs, the girls didn't lack for customers, night and day, working their cribs in nonstop shifts. And when the buffalo men pulled out for the prairie, the Irish and German laborers took up the slack. They had already seen to it that their track reached the sod-and-pole corrals where stood immense piles of flattened buffalo hides and huge ricks of bleaching bones, waiting for shipment east to the tanneries and fertilizer factories.

It was a wild place, in every sense of the word—where the only law was a man's pistol and his Sharps rifle, and perhaps the well-honed skinning knife he might have to use to carve up a bothersome antagonist. Arguments and fights and brawls and gun battles occurred with such regularity in those early days that no one really grew concerned enough to call for a badge. The only law was in the weight of the weapons a man packed, like those old fukes kept handy beneath the crude bars in every saloon. Both barrels sawed off short, loaded with buck or ball, these ready shotguns settled more than one argument and quieted more than one rowdy, overzealous railhand.

Like the ever-wandering frontier and the ever-nomadic buffalo themselves, Buffalo City did not last long—at least as a name for the town. When the federal government refused to approve the name for a postal drop, stating that Kansas already had a Buffalo and a Buffalo City both, it suggested the town assume the name of the nearby fort.

It was to this newly christened Dodge City that Seamus and Jack bid farewell that late summer, farewell as well to Billy Dixon. Although the sun was only then creeping over the horizon as they mounted their horses to ride to the fort to pick up their civilians and army escort, the music from out-of-tune pianos still punctured the quiet of the morning, as well as the raucous, discordant shouting of men too long without sleep and filled with a bellyful of puggle.

On the afternoon of the sixth day out from Dodge, Jack Stillwell led the fifteen others into Camp Supply after a hundred monotonous miles of trail south from Kansas. Here in the vee of land formed by the mouth of Wolf Creek, dumping itself into the North Canadian, the troops of George Armstrong Custer's winter campaign had built Camp Supply back in '68. And here almost five years later a permanent stockade of log and sod had replaced canvas tents. Ten-foot-high walls complete with loopholes, a blockhouse at each corner, and eighty-foot-long barracks housed the troops of the Tenth Cavalry beneath sod roofs that leaked in the rainy months, spilled dust the rest of the year.

A dispensary, a hospital with three wards, along with a large mess hall and a separate kitchen and bakery, joined the quartermaster stores, stables and headquarter's offices inside the palisade walls guarded by sentries.

Officers and married soldiers were given small log cabins just outside the stockade walls. Because the floors were always more damp than dry, and because of the lack of glass which dictated a lack of windows for the cabins, the laundress wives of the enlisted men and officers alike found themselves harvesting a crop of toadstools each morning as a part of their housekeeping routine.

"This is where Sharp and Dixon met, back to the winter of 'sixty-eight," Stillwell reminded Donegan as they dismounted.

Seamus watched the two easterners Stillwell was escorting climb down from their army mounts, unabashedly rubbing their saddle galls, and with a bow-legged gait walk up the four steps to the post commander's office to report their arrival.

"We'll be ready to leave after breakfast in the morning, Mr. Stillwell," said the lieutenant in charge of the escort detail.

"Can't get you to calling me Jack, can I?" Stillwell said to the older man.

"All right . . . Jack." The officer smiled. "We'll see what we can do about that."

"That's better, Lieutenant Marston," Stillwell replied. "We're gonna be spending a whole lot more time together. All the way down to Fort Richardson before you and your soldiers can turn back north."

Ben Marston nodded. "That's a bit of a journey in itself."

"I'll bet your men can't wait to get back to Fort Hays."

"Actually," Marston whispered, leaning in close to Stillwell and Donegan, "all my men have been thinking about lately is Dodge City and its attractions . . . and getting back there as soon as they can get you dropped off and turned around."

Seamus grinned. "You don't really blame those boys, do you, Lieutenant?"

Marston laughed easily at that and nodded. "Can't blame a young man a bit for wanting to horn up the prairie like a young bull in the rut. Ah, we were all young of a time."

Donegan snorted, looking at young Stillwell. "By the saints but there's more talk of me getting to be an old man! What've I done to deserve this hacking, pray tell?"

"One day you won't mind wearing your age, Mr. Donegan," Marston said. "The wrinkles and the gray hair. But for now, fight it with all that you've got."

"I plan on it, Lieutenant. I didn't survive Lodge Trail Ridge and the hayfield fight* not to wear my scars proudly. There were times at Beecher Island and out to the Modoc's Lava Beds† where I caught myself wondering if I'd see another winter come and go."

"And look at you now," Stillwell piped up. "Riding down into Kiowa and Comanche country—just like you know you're going to die an old man."

Marston chuckled, then waved as he strode away.

---

* The Plainsmen Series, vol. 2, *Red Cloud's Revenge*
† The Plainsmen Series, vol. 5, *Devil's Backbone*

"After breakfast, we'll meet you and the bureau men right here."

They watched the lieutenant lead his eleven soldiers toward the stables before Seamus spoke quietly.

"Did I hear the lieutenant right, Jack—did he say *bureau* men?"

Stillwell gazed at Donegan a moment, a quizzical look crossing his face. "He did, didn't he?"

Now it was Donegan's turn to be confused. "Wait a minute. I thought you knew who those two were, Jack. Here you're asked to guide them down here—"

"I never said I knew who they were or what they were up to," Stillwell protested.

"*Bureau*." Seamus repeated the word. "Sounds like only one thing to me."

"What's that?"

"How many bureaus you know of in the government?"

Stillwell held up his hands in a helpless gesture. "I don't know a thing about none of that government folderol, Seamus."

Donegan stared for a moment at the nearby headquarters' office where the two had disappeared minutes ago. "Only one I've heard tell of is the Indian Bureau. So maybe this had something to do with those two Kiowa chiefs you were telling me about."

Stillwell shook his head. "I don't tally it that way, Seamus. Those two fellas aren't going down to Texas to see some old Kiowa chiefs now. They could do that right here. C'mon, the Indian Bureau has agents and sub-agents all over the place in Indian Territory. They don't need to send two soft-assed dudes from back east out here to talk with Satanta and Big Tree . . . now, do they?"

With a shrug, Seamus breathed in the late afternoon air. "Be suppertime soon, Jack, me lad. I can't make no sense of it—but things just ain't fitting together with those two bureau men. And when me own mind can't make things fit like they should, Seamus Donegan looks for him a place to find a bottle of whiskey and someone to share it with. C'mon, Jack—you'll do to share my whiskey!"

The next morning Donegan's head ached some as he strode into the late summer sun of a new day. Not so much from the whiskey he had punished the night before, as much as it was the grappling he had done to force incomplete pieces of a puzzle to fit together. The worst part of it was he didn't know why it mattered, why it bothered him, this not knowing.

Another six days' ride through the rolling hills at the edge of these western plains brought them closer to the Kiowa-Comanche reservation. Traffic of all kinds picked up on the roads now, but mostly the freight-hauling business.

"They need a rail line in here bad," Seamus commented one afternoon. "Can't be cheap for the government to haul everything in here by wagon."

"It's coming, Irishman."

Stillwell spoke the truth well enough. Soon the lines would be laid and supplies would come in from the north and up from the south into the Nations, bringing the white man's wealth to the varied tribes, both civilized and war-loving. Down in Texas it was the same thing: supplies too were freighted to the outlying posts in west Texas, until the Houston & Texas Central Railroad got its track laid west of Dallas.

Work was proceeding all too slowly on that account—but what was the railroad construction operation to do? It had to contend with cheap labor, provided by Texas prisons for the grueling dawn to dusk shovel and pick work of laying the white man's rails, tracks like an iron arrowpoint aimed to pierce the very heart of the Indian's buffalo ground.

Chapter 15

Early September 1873

With a day lost at the Cheyenne Agency, I.T., to reshoe a couple of the horses, Seamus Donegan followed Jack Stillwell and the rest away from the small settlement of buffalo-hide lodges, dugouts, lean-tos, tents and log shanties where a few hardy white men carried on a trade into the Indian Nations. The afternoon of the seventh day of travel brought the party to the hills surrounding Medicine Bluff and Cache Creek.

It was a country abounding in wild turkey and pheasant, deer and a few antelope who turned their tails like rounded, white flags and went bounding off without the slightest bit of curiosity in the short column of horsemen. Quail whirred up from the hackberry brush, noisily taking to the wing, much of the time startling horse and rider both whenever the birds flushed from their hiding places in the tall, weathered grasses and the shade of yellow-leafed alder.

Seamus found himself surprised at the extent of Fort Sill, the log and stone buildings, the granary and sawmill, the neatly manicured lawns and graveled walks cared for by the Negro soldiers of the Tenth

U.S. Cavalry under Lieutenant Colonel John W. Davidson. Donegan knew well enough of the Tenth, of their rescue of some forty-five desperate white men hunkered down on a sandy piece of island amid the bodies of their dead comrades and the stinking carcasses of their horses, in the middle of the Arickaree Fork of the Republican River.* Indeed, Seamus Donegan knew something of the Tenth Cavalry and Captain Louis H. Carpenter's Company H. At least he had back five years ago, for nine long days in late September, '68.

Most of the faces, black, white and those numerous, curious red faces wherever a man would turn, watched the small procession as it crossed the creek after skirting the agency buildings themselves and climbed from the Cache Creek ford onto the military reservation. This was no small curiosity: a lieutenant and eleven soldiers escorting four civilians. And not a one of those civilians had irons around ankles or wrists or wore prison stripes. Not much reason for a white man to be coming down here to Fort Sill, Seamus imagined, unless he had business to conduct with the army, or the tribes, or was himself a contractor for the government.

"Seamus?"

Donegan turned at the sound of his name coming from a small knot of Negro soldiers who stood in the porch shade as the horsemen moved slowly by.

"Seamus Donegan?" the soldier repeated.

The Negro soldier stepped into the sunlight, shading his eyes with a hand. Donegan could not really be sure. It had been so long—

"Sweet Jesus! It is you!"

"Mother of God, is that you, Reuben Waller?"

* The Plainsmen Series, vol. 3, *The Stalkers*

His ebony face beamed, glistening with sweat, teeth gleaming as a smile seemed to fill the whole bottom half of it. "Why . . . I never thought I'd seen you again in what days I've got left!"

Seamus waved. "Jack!" he called out. "Goddammit, Jack—c'mon back here!" Then he was kicking his right leg over the saddle horn and dropping to the ground, taking all of three steps before he and the buffalo soldier collided on the graveled walk of Fort Sill, embracing, pounding, then hugging again as they blubbered their greetings of those too-long parted and not knowing quite what to say.

The shadow came over them both, causing Donegan to look up into the late afternoon sun. "Jack, get down here and say you halloo to Reuben Waller."

"We met, Corporal," Jack said as he dropped to one stirrup and down.

"That's right, we did, Mr. Stillwell," Waller said, smiling, his kepi in his left hand as they shook.

"I asked you back then—call me Jack."

"All right . . . Jack. I 'member when we met—it was the afternoon you come riding in, guiding Colonel Bankhead to the place where Seamus . . . him and the rest . . ."

Donegan could tell Waller was having trouble finding the words, his throat tightening with the memory of that stinking, Cheyenne-made hell.

"Where Major Forsyth decided he'd have us all hunker down and kill some Cheyenne for nine days," Seamus said, putting his arm around the buffalo soldier.

Reuben grinned up at the taller man, his face shiny with the gratitude, his eyes misting with the remembrance of the time the hard-muscled Irishman had pulled a squad of white soldiers from the Seventh Cavalry off him at Fort Wallace. Long before the fight and rescue at Beecher Island on the high plains of Colorado Territory.

"C'mon over here, fellas!" Reuben called out, turning to the half dozen or so other brunettes who were gathered in the shade, watching with interest this reunion. Waller introduced the two white men all around with a general shaking of hands.

"I remember you, Mr. Stillwell," one of the soldiers said quietly, almost reverently, as he stood before the young scout.

"Were you on the trail out of Wallace?" Jack asked. "Carrying dispatches to Carpenter?"

He nodded, grin growing into a full-blown smile. "You do remember me!"

Jack's eyes grew a little misty. "I'll never forget how good it was for this nineteen-year-old boy to find you on that road to Wallace—and to discover you could carry that map to Captain Carpenter himself for me."

"Mr. Stillwell here—" and Reuben caught himself, "Jack here was the first to sneak off the island the first night."

"I had someone else go with me, Reuben," Stillwell replied, somewhat embarrassed by the admiration in the bright, eager eyes of the brunettes.

"I told 'em all about you, Jack. How you and the old man sneaked across the plains on foot, running onto that Injun village and hiding in the buffalo carcass when a war-party catched you out in the middle of nowhere," Waller gushed. "Told 'em how you made it almost all the way in to Fort Wallace and bumped into Rufus, who was riding dispatches to the captain."

"There a place around here where we can buy you men a drink?" Seamus asked.

Waller pointed. "Trader's place over yonder. He sells whiskey a'times to white men."

"He won't sell to you fellas?" Jack asked.

Waller chuckled. "Oh, he will—if he wants to make money on his whiskey. What I mean is . . . he don't sell to the Injuns."

"And a damned good thing he doesn't," Donegan replied.

"Right, 'cause it'd just make 'em that much harder to deal with," Waller agreed.

"No," Seamus said, patting the soldier on the back, "because it would just mean that much less in the way of whiskey for you and me! C'mon, Reuben. We've old times to talk over and not much time to do it. Jack's driving us a mad pace to get down to Texas."

"You're here just for the night?"

Stillwell nodded. "Head out in the morning. Government work."

"But surely you'll be coming back through on your way north, won't you?"

"As sure as sun, Reuben," Stillwell said. "Be back before you know it, once these two government stuffed shirts are dropped off at Richardson."

"That's Mackenzie's outfit—the Fourth Cavalry," Waller said with an envious glint to his eye. "He's had a chance to raise a sweat chasing after the Comanche and Kiowa."

"I was wrong to think things were pretty quiet down here now?" Jack inquired.

"Have been, for the most part. Since the Kiowa got their war-chiefs locked up down in Texas and Mackenzie's holding over a hundred Comanche women and children hostage—everybody's behaving right smart. But there'll always be a few of them bucks who get to wearing the wild feather and get their tails up behind to go scalp a white man."

"So you're stationed here at Fort Sill?" Seamus asked.

"Yes."

"Captain Carpenter still your company commander?"

"Right on the second account—H Company wouldn't know what to do with itself if Carpenter weren't our captain."

"He here at the post now?"

"Sure is, Seamus. Fact is, I'd be pleased to be the one to tell the captain there's two veterans of Beecher Island come in to see him. You want me give him word you'll be over to the trader's place?"

"If that's where a man can find the whiskey," Donegan answered, "that's where I'll be pointing my nose."

"And that's where Captain Carpenter will find you two fellas," Waller said. "Damn, but ain't this a fine day? A fine, fine day indeed! You both looking so good to my eyes."

"You need go and tell these gentlemen about your stripes, Reuben," said the dispatch courier.

"What?" Seamus asked with a growing grin. "You going to get another stripe and didn't tell us?"

Waller smiled in the bright sunlight. "It ain't official yet. Lieutenant Colonel Davidson gonna approve it or not—only question is if I can stay with the captain. I don't wanna serve in no other company but with Captain Carpenter."

"Well, now—congratulations are in order, I'd say," Seamus cheered, shaking Waller's hand again. "And you're due a drink on me and one on Jack Stillwell. Fact is, we both owe you more than one . . . so plan on drinking your fill tonight."

"I don't take to whiskey all that much," Reuben replied. "But I won't mind having me one or two, especially if Captain Carpenter comes 'round to talk old memories with you gentlemen."

"Then go fetch that soldier," Donegan said. "I've got a thirst that won't wait!"

As far as he knew, it was the Moon of Plums Ripening. This time of late summer, early fall.

But for Satanta it was difficult to be certain, still a prisoner here in Tehas among the white Tehannas.

He was number 2107. One of the others had explained the marks on his striped shirt to him more than a year ago when Satanta and Big Tree were first taken to Huntsville Prison far to the south of Kiowa country. With practice he could say his number as well as any Tehanna. And he was getting better at understanding English as well. For years already the chief had understood a good deal of the white man's tongue—refusing still to speak it, for his own reasons. Nonetheless, he did understand it, and now he knew more than the other hundred prisoners who had been freighted west from Huntsville to Houston to work for the Houston & Texas Central Railroad, grading roadbed, laying track from dawn to dusk.

This had to be the most bitter of punishments to the two Kiowa chiefs: forced to aid and abet in bringing the railroad to Kiowa country. More times than he cared to, Satanta remembered in the years past how he had sworn with his own blood he would prevent the coming of the white man's smoking wagon to the buffalo country ruled by Kiowa and Comanche horsemen.

Building a railroad that would split the heart of his homeland. Pick and shovel work, hard on an old man of more than sixty winters. Still, the work kept his body firm, and not a fleck of snow betrayed his black hair. Satanta swore he would keep up with the young chief, Big Tree, and the rest of the construction crew of a hundred murderers and thieves who dragged their ankle irons and chains up and down the road-bed, laying track for the white man, pointing their noses north to Dall-ass.

There were all kinds who sweated and groaned under the watchful eyes of the white guards loaded down with guns, some on horseback, some with evil-tempered dogs on short leather leashes. On either side of Satanta worked men guilty of all kinds of crime: white and Mexican and Negro, accused and found guilty of everything from stealing a melon from a field to raping a white woman to killing an old girl-friend and her new lover. To Satanta that was always amusing—to see how the two other races thought most about its stomach and its groin.

If indeed it were the first days of the Moon of Plums Ripening, then almost a year had passed since he and Big Tree had been taken east by the white man to see the other chiefs.

Without explanation last autumn, they were told a messenger had arrived, and they had been ordered to go with the guards. From the roadbed work they were walked four miles back down the track to where an army ambulance awaited them. From there they were taken north for five days until they arrived at the place called Dall-ass.

Without speaking a word, he and Big Tree had looked at one another during those five days, wondering if at last the white man had decided to kill them and was taking them to the place of their death. He had himself decided it did not matter. He had lived a long life, a good life filled with juicy buffalo fat and moist, warm-skinned women. But lately, with these heavy iron shackles he wore on his ankles and wrists, with the white man's bad food so filled with weevils and dust, and the warm water dipped from mossy kegs, along with the beatings he had to endure at the hand of the white Tehannas guards, Satanta didn't really want to live any longer. If the white man chose to hang him now, so be it.

To die would be immeasurably better than being forced to endure the indignity of working as a slave for the white man, forced to build the white man's railroad—a smoking monster that was destroying not only the buffalo herds and the buffalo country, but the land of the Kiowa as well.

But instead of hanging at the end of the white man's rope at Dall-ass, he and Big Tree had been put on a rocking stage to continue their trip north. From the windows of that stage, the chiefs had looked beyond the cordon of their armed escort to the banks of the Red River, familiar like the face of an old friend. For the space of a few heartbeats their spirits had soared like the bounding leaps of a little yellow buffalo calf, playful and happy, for they both had believed they were heading home to their people.

But on the north bank of the river there was a short stop while a second group of soldiers took over for the first, who themselves turned back across the Red River and headed south to Dall-ass with the empty stage. Among the shade of the trees on the riverbank, the chiefs had their heavy ankle and wrist shackles removed, then were shown to remove their striped prison uniforms and were given the white man's civilian clothing in its place.

Instead of heading northwest to the reservation, Satanta and Big Tree were taken northeast, once dressed and mounted on horseback. For another three days they rode, handcuffed only but still sur-

rounded by their new escort. On the third they arrived at a small settlement on the Choctaw
reservation. There at Atoka the chiefs were placed on
board one of the smoking horses at last. Still not told
where they were heading and why, Satanta knew
only that they were going east. Farther and farther
into the land of the white man. Farther and farther
from the land of his birth.

How cruel it would be, he had thought, to be taken
so far from one's homeland to die. Where your bones
would have to lie among the bones of strangers.

Then on the twenty-eighth of September, the two
chiefs were secreted from a railroad station, through
the streets of a large city, to a hotel where they spent
the night sleeping on the floor of their room, refusing
to lie on the white man's too-soft bed.

And that next morning came the biggest surprise of
all: they were ushered into a large room of that fancy
building called the Everette House in St. Louis, there
to be greeted by a dozen of their fellow chiefs and
head men who had brought along clothing for Satanta and Big Tree to wear during the two-day reunion visit. Such joy was this! All was hugs and
happiness, tears and the singing of chants for the surprise occasion. Many times the pipe was smoked
among the old friends brought all the way here from
the reservation, all this way east to visit with the two
prisoners.

From here the others were to continue on east farther still to meet with the Great White Father himself.
But for some reason, the white man had decided to
allow this special visit between the two chiefs and
their friends. The chiefs sang and smoked, took their
meals seated on the carpeted floor and slept rolled in
their blankets among the parlor furniture. The second day, the whole delegation was given a scenic tour

of the great city, where the curious faces stared back
from the sides of the roads and the fronts of the white
man's tall, stone buildings.

It was meant to impress him, Satanta knew—this
transparent show of the white man's wealth and
strength of numbers. Yet it made him only crave his
homeland all the more. Far better the prairie and rivers, the buttes and bluffs and high plains of his home.
Better the wild game of Kiowa country than all this
cobblestone and granite and coal-smoke that made
him cough and his eyes burn. He would in no way
give up what had been his the day he was born a free
man, in return for all that the white man had to offer
in the way of material wealth.

Oh, for the clean, free wind of the open prairie!

Again and again those two days, as he peered into
the faces of his old friends, Satanta harkened for the
old days. So afraid they were now gone and never to
be again.

And then that last night, the chiefs discussed the
serious matter of the white man's anger aroused each
time the young men rode away from the reservation
for raids into Texas. Each one understood that Satanta and Big Tree would never be freed as long as
Kiowa warriors continued crossing the Red River
into the land of the Tehannas. So it was decided by
that council that upon the arrival of the head men
back home, both Lone Wolf and Kicking Bird would
form a police society to patrol the fringes of the reservation both day and night, to prevent any young hot-
blood from riding south for scalps and horses.

Coming all too quickly, the third morning dawned
with immense sadness. Again the hugs and chants in
parting as the others went east to meet with the Great
White Father, while Satanta and Big Tree were taken
back to the terrible, degrading labor on their chain

gang, once again wearing the striped clothes and the heavy iron shackles.

Back again into the land of the hated Tehannas, forced to build the railroad that would be not only the death of the buffalo, but the death of the Kiowa who hunted them as well.

Chapter 16

September 1873

"We'll see you when you ride back here next month," said Reuben Waller as he waved to them both.

"Till then, Sergeant!" shouted Seamus Donegan as he followed Jack Stillwell, the two civilians and their military escort south from Fort Sill, I.T.

Seeing Captain Louis Carpenter again confirmed for Seamus that there were and always would be good officers in the army—as much as meeting Lieutenant Colonel John W. Davidson had convinced the Irishman there were and always would be small, petty and mean-spirited officers in that same Army of the West.

Given the task of commanding Fort Sill and the Tenth Negro Cavalry while Colonel Grierson was on temporary assignment back east, Davidson had quickly proved himself a martinet. Becoming a leader of men brought out the good in some, the very worst in others.

So it had been for the new commander of Fort Sill, a man clearly not popular among his white officers, and especially among the Negro enlisted who served on this Indian frontier. To attempt a sure-handed control of his subordinate officers, Davidson had tried through transfer and outright removal to oust most of Grierson's handpicked officers. And among the rank and file, the lieutenant colonel became quickly unpopular with his harsh and capricious rulings against gambling and restrictions against alcohol on the military reservation.

Not long after the winter campaigns led by Custer and Evans against the hostile tribes, the Tenth Cavalry had been transferred from Kansas Territory to Camp Wichita, soon thereafter to the new post General Philip H. Sheridan himself had named for an old friend of his killed in the war, Joshua Sill. Four companies of the Tenth were assigned to garrison the new post, while two would garrison Camp Supply to the north on the Southern Cheyenne reservation. The six troops of Negro cavalrymen were now expected to keep corraled thousands of free-roaming buffalo-hunting nomads, in addition to running herd on white interlopers and whiskey peddlers, as well as provide escorts along stage routes and for the frequent trains of freight contractors.

On top of that, the Tenth still eked out time to build Fort Sill from the ground up once an old sawmill was dismantled and brought in from old Fort Arbuckle. In the nearby Wichita Mountains, labor gangs of black soldiers cut and dressed stone from the quarries they worked, slowly erecting the buildings that would stand near the clear, sparkling streams called the Cache and the Medicine Bluff.

But even more than all the overwhelming evidence clearly showing Seamus that the regiment had poured its sweat into this outpost in the very heart of Indian Territory, a regiment still troubled by more than what were considered normal conditions in the frontier army—it was more the state of readiness among the Tenth Cavalry that astounded the thirty-three-year-old veteran of the Army of the Potomac and Sheridan's Army of the Shenandoah.

That these Negro soldiers should be asked to do so much, given so little, and to come through guarding the Texas frontier as effectively as they had, was no small miracle to the Irishman.

Down in the stables, a proud Reuben Waller had given a dollar tour to his old friends from the siege on the Arickaree. As brushed and curried as those mounts were, Seamus could tell the horses were the hand-me-downs of the Army of the West. Saddles, bits, cruppers, everything here was secondhand and passed down from white regiments when it was too old or worn or no longer serviceable for those outfits. Instead of spending the money for new equipment on the Negro regiments, the Ninth and Tenth cavalries were instead given the dregs and ordered to make it once more serviceable.

For the most part, Colonel Grierson's Tenth Cavalry had done just that. Passed down a motley collection of nags good only for glue from white units, the Tenth had nursed the last ounce of strength and use from horses who had seen service in the War of the Rebellion.

"That's more than thirteen, maybe fourteen years these horses been used hard," Seamus had muttered angrily, inspecting the teeth of some of the better-looking stock. "And these are your best, Reuben."

"We do what we can, Seamus—with what the army give us."

It had stung the Irishman's soul to have to look into that newly-striped sergeant's black face, reading there the clear and evident pride of accomplishment made against great odds, and not be able to tell Waller what he thought of this continuing injustice to the former slaves and freed men, many of whom had served themselves during the war, men who now served their country in this foreign land, protecting white citizens and settlers from a hostile red race.

"These saddles aren't fit to go on the back of any animal," Seamus had declared there in the shadows of the stables. "They'll likely damage a mount forced to carry a sojur in one of these. These riggings ought to be thrown out—good for nothing more than the wolves to chew on the rawhide trees!"

"We expecting some better ones soon," Waller had explained. "General Augur's inspector come through here a couple months back and saw what a state we was in. The department commander's ordered us to get replacements soon as the army can find some to send us."

"More bleeming hand-me-downs, Sergeant Waller!"

"We'll take what we get, and do with it what we can—like I told you."

Damn, but if that didn't make Seamus proud of Waller, his Captain Carpenter and the whole of the Tenth U.S. Negro Cavalry, forced to fight not only the bloodthirsty Kiowa and Kwahadi Comanche, but forced to struggle for a decent saddle to strap atop a decent horse that could carry a man into battle and back out again.

"Your men any good with your weapons?" Seamus had asked, then found Waller could only look at the earth floor in the stable.

He did not meet the Irishman's eyes directly when he answered, "We don't get a chance to shoot our weapons much."

"You low on ammunition?"

Waller nodded. "When we got it, and our rifles work, we might get in a little practice."

Donegan gazed from the shadows of the stable into the sunshine of the Fort Sill parade where the regimental standard fluttered in the late-summer breeze. It was clearly tattered and badly in need of repair, faded as it hung beside the stars and stripes. Below the proud banner, Waller had stopped them on their way to the stables and proudly declared that some of the men in his H Company had sewn this, their only regimental standard, from cloth begged off some white officers' wives.

"The Tenth wasn't issued the regulation silk-embroidered standard?"

Reuben had shaken his head, eyes glistening. "Never. So we made our own—proud as we are to be soldiers, Seamus. Proud as we are."

"By glory—your men are fighting more than one enemy out here, Sergeant."

"We proud of our record, Seamus. The Tenth Cavalry got the lowest rate of desertion for any regiment, white or black, foot or horse—in the whole goddamned army. And we proud because we got the lowest courts-martial for drunkenness and unseemly behavior."

Donegan shook his head and embraced the Negro soldier, proud to call a man like Waller friend. "By the saints, you black orphans done right well. The Tenth Cavalry gives sojuring a good name, Sergeant. A good . . . and honorable name."

In leaving Fort Sill, Stillwell pointed them almost due south for the Red River, a wide and lazy thing this time of the year, wild and crazed during the turbulent springs come to the southern plains. It was still the shank of the summer in this country, with only the faintest hint of autumn come to the evening air.

"This is the new home of Sharp Grover," Jack said

as they splashed up the south bank of the Red River. "Texas."

"That old man really settled down?"

Stillwell grinned. "I suppose Sharp hasn't told you about the power of a good woman over a man, has he?"

With that said, Donegan grinned. "I see. You suppose she keeps him hobbled good and nosed on a tight rein?"

"Old or not, Sharp Grover would be a handful for any woman to keep a tight rein on, Seamus. Almost . . . almost as much a handful as you're likely to be one day soon."

"What's any of that claptrap of these railroads failing back east got to do with us out here?" Jack Stillwell asked Sharp Grover after they had pulled chairs up to a lopsided table in a sunlit corner of Jimmy Nolan's Dance House in Jacksboro, Texas, the settlement built near the outskirts of Fort Richardson.

Grover shrugged. "All I know is when these railroad fellas get sour-faced and down in their brew about something—it can't be good tidings for us out here."

Upon depositing the two government men and their escort out at Fort Richardson, Jack Stillwell had led the Irishman into the little frontier town of Jacksboro. Like so many other wild and woolly places on the fringe of the white man's civilization, Jacksboro had remained relatively small, populated by no more than two hundred at any one time, mostly by those who followed the fortunes of the frontier army: whiskey peddlers, drummers, snake-oil and love-potion salesmen, gamblers and bummers, along with the women who plied their trade in the stinking cribs at the back of some twenty-seven saloons—the Gem, the Emerald, Island Home and more.

The past spring, Mackenzie's Fourth Cavalry had their share of troubles in town, nothing really that different from the love-hate relationship most fortside settlements had all across the extent of the frontier west. But Company B saw things in a different light when one of their own was killed in a mysterious way, by a mysterious murderer, in the back rooms of a whorehouse in Jacksboro. When no witnesses stepped forward and it appeared army investigators had come nose-up against a brick wall, Troop B rode into town en masse and burned the building to the ground, standing around boldly as the employees and clientele came pouring out of the smoking, fiery clapboard whorehouse.

There was only the briefest of inquests held by the army in a formal setting at Jimmy Nolan's Dance House, with nothing definite noted about the murder, nor nothing done about the men who had set the fire.

"What would the collapse of those fat railroad barons' financial empires have to do with Texas anyway?" Seamus inquired.

"It's their money builds the railroads, Irishman. Simple as that. And when that money dries up and the railroad pulls out of Texas—stockmen and settlers like me get more'n a little nervous."

"That what you're worried about, old man? The railroad not getting finished?"

Grover nodded. "I figure it means this part of the territory ain't gonna get itself settled so quickly like some of us were hoping. With no railroad, means more folks won't be moving in as fast as we'd planned."

"Will you listen to this now?" Seamus asked Stillwell, a wry grin creasing his face. "The once-home-less nomad, Sharp Grover, is now a knee-deep sodbuster!"

Grover shot him a disapproving glare. "And that's such a bad thing for a man getting on in his years and tired of fighting Injuns for a living?"

"So, you're really trying out a new line of work?" Seamus asked, nudging Stillwell with an elbow.

"Try as I do just to raise quality horseflesh, the army keeps sweet-talking me back a'times," Grover admitted.

"Thought it was a woman who sweet-talked you down here in the first place," Seamus asked, trying less now to kid the older man.

He nodded. "It was. I mean, she did. Oh, hell—yes . . . we come down here to give it a try anyway."

"You told me your wife's sister is down here," Stillwell said.

"She came down here with us, the truth be known. I ain't sure why she left Kansas—a handsome woman she is, Seamus."

"Watch out—here it comes, Irishman!" Stillwell warned.

"Sounds to me like Sharp's trying to marry off his sister-in-law in the worst way."

Grover grew indignant at the ribbing. "She's a good woman, in a lot of ways every bit the equal of my Rebecca—and in a few, better than my wife."

"Just one thing bothers me now, Sharp—why ain't the woman found herself a man?"

"Why should she, Seamus? Just to settle on any man?"

"Well, from the sounds of it, your sister-in-law is getting on in years. It's one thing for a man to have thirty-three winters behind him like me. But I think it's another thing entirely to find a woman who hasn't corraled herself a man by that age."

"So where'd you ever get the idea Samantha Pike was as old as you, Irishman?" Grover prodded, the grin now back on his face as quickly as it faded from Donegan's.

"Well . . . I just assumed . . . what with you being older—and Rebecca all likely being older too . . . them two being sisters—"

"That's where you made your first big mistake—is thinking, you dumb mick! Just like your dear departed Uncle Liam, God rest his soul. Samantha is Rebecca's half sister, and she's ain't been of marrying age all that long."

"Oh," Jack Stillwell said, some sudden and sincere interest pricking his voice. "Just how old . . . or young is Samantha?"

"She's twenty-two, Jack."

Stillwell looked at Donegan and winked. "Sounds to me like she might care for a younger man, Seamus."

The Irishman shook his head. "Beware, Jack. Something wrong with a woman who couldn't find a husband in Kansas. Best we both stay out of her way."

Grover wagged his head. "Hard for me to believe I'm hearing you boys say such things. You ever look around you at the quality of fellas coming out to Kansas?"

"Never was much a one for watching the boys— was you, Jack?" Donegan asked. He and Stillwell laughed heartily.

"Them that wasn't married and had a wife and passel of young'uns already was surely a hard lot— not the sort for the likes of Rebecca or Samantha."

"So, did Rebecca really look over the crop before she decided on you, Sharp?" Seamus asked.

"I suppose she did, and that's why she chose me. The rest was real hard cases—buffalo hunters mostly. Those what was coming in to the western part of the territory to whittle away what they could of the Republican herd."

"Hide hunters," Stillwell repeated. "That ain't the sort who's made to settle down with a wife and make a family out of things."

"Say, Sharp—did we mention we ran onto a hide hunter who knew of you?" Donegan inquired.

"No, you didn't. Who was he and where'd you run onto him?"

"Handsome young fella. 'Bout my age," Stillwell replied. "Almost as good-looking as me too, come to think of it."

"C'mon, now—who was he?"

"Name of Dixon."

"Billy Dixon?"

"That's right," Stillwell answered. "Met him up at Dodge City."

"So they ended up having to change the name of the town after all, did they?" Sharp asked. "Yeah, I knew Dixon back to the winter we went marching off with Custer down into Indian Territory." He looked at Donegan, "When you went off with Carr's Fifth Cavalry and Buffalo Bill Cody, Irishman."*

"That's what Dixon told us," Seamus added. "The young fella thinks the world of you for what you taught him that winter."

"What I taught him? Hell, I was nothing more'n just a scout riding with Pepoon, under Joe Milner and Jack Corbin, nothing special. And the lad was a teamster. Eager and bright, as I remember him—eager to learn."

* The Plainsmen Series, vol. 4, *Black Sun*

"But he's one of them hide hunters you said wasn't good enough for Samantha," Donegan said with a smile.

"Oh, but Dixon struck me as being a different sort."

"No, he didn't smell gamey to me, if that's what you mean," Jack said, grinning.

"More'n that—it seemed he had something in the way of good horse sense about him, and cared a bit about himself," Seamus added.

"That does sound like the Billy Dixon I knew who teamstered for Lieutenant Bell of the Seventh Cavalry. Besides hanging out in a saloon in Dodge City and running onto the likes of you two rummies— what else is the lad up to now?"

"I suppose he's waiting to hunt more buffalo," Stillwell answered. "Said he'd just come in with some hides he'd taken south of the dead line."

Grover's eyes narrowed. "Billy Dixon's rode south of the dead line to take buffalo?"

"What he told us."

The old scout wagged his head. "And I just gave Dixon more credit for having good horse sense. Damn. That's suicide work down there across the dead line."

"The army shoot a man for crossing into Indian Territory for no good reason?" Seamus asked suspiciously.

"No, not the army," Grover replied. "That country out west of here is the last buffalo ground south of the Niobrara on the whole of the central and southern plains. The very, goddamned *last*, you understand. And now the Kiowa and those bloodthirsty Comanche are dead set on keeping it that way: out of the hands of the white buffalo hunters."

"Then Billy Dixon's scalp ain't worth much," Stillwell said quietly.

"No man's is," Grover replied, "he goes hunting buffalo south of the dead line."

Chapter 17

October 1873

*A*s much as Seamus might not want Sharp Grover to know, he had to admit, Samantha Pike was a good-looking woman.

In many ways she reminded him of Jennifer Wheatley,* although the memories of her were fading.

Samantha was a bit heavier, bigger boned, and most definitely fleshy in all the right places. At least in all those places Seamus Donegan found himself staring when he didn't find Miss Pike staring back at him. The full promise of hips and the curve of her rounded rump molding into the top of her thighs. And those breasts, amply snuggled into a deep cleavage. He imagined how they must be straining against their buttons, as he dreamed of how those breasts might taste. What sheer delights, he considered, getting his hands on their soft, creamy flesh, kissing and burying his face between them as she arched her back to him, commanding him to take her—

Donegan decided he had clearly been too long

---

* The Plainsmen Series, vol. 1, *Sioux Dawn*, and vol. 2, *Red Cloud's Revenge*

without a woman, and had determined he would see to that concern once he and Jack rode back through Jacksboro, heading north for the Red River and the Kiowa-Comanche reservation at Medicine Bluff. But as things turned out, Seamus did not find himself with an occasion to slip back to one of Jacksboro's notorious houses of prostitution. One evening at supper instead, he had been told that Jack and Sharp had decided to push north the next morning. So a much embarrassed Seamus was left to try to explain why he was eager to ride into Jacksboro for that last night, a ticklish proposition, what with Rebecca Grover and her young sister in the room as Donegan stammered and stuttered and finally gave up trying to explain.

Especially those eyes, he thought again now, looking back. And the way Samantha used them to bounce from Jack Stillwell to the Irishman and back again. As if measuring them both for a wedding suit, Seamus thought. There weren't many who could even make him think such things—but then, Samantha Pike was altogether a different sort of woman. Much like Jennie had been . . . almost eight years gone now since last he had seen the fire in her hair high on the Montana Road.

"She's likely long married now and got at least two more children, Seamus," he told himself that night after the sun had sunk on the far side of the Staked Plains and he sat alone on Sharp's porch, stuffing tobacco into his corncob pipe. It brought him fond remembrance of trader McDonald at Fort McPherson, Nebraska . . . and Bill Cody. Married himself, to that beauty Louisa. A daughter, Arta—who must be all of eight years old now.*

* The Plainsmen Series, vol. 4, *Black Sun*

Somehow, those thoughts of women and children tugged at a secret, well-hidden place within him, and brought to the rippled surface of his need the lines of verse writ by Irish poets:

> *A heart made full of thought*
> *   I had, before you left.*
> *What man, however prideful,*
> *   But lost his perfect love?*

> *Grief like the growing vine*
> *   Came with time upon me.*
> *Yet it is not through despair*
> *   I see your image still.*

> *A bird lifting from clear water,*
> *   A bright sun put out*
> *—such my parting, in troubled tiredness,*
> *   From the partner of my heart.*

"Do you wish to be alone?"

Seamus turned in the darkness, his face gone hot with embarrassment as he found her shadow at the twilit corner of the porch.

"No," he finally answered, stuffing the pipe back into his mouth. "I mean—it's all right."

"I just heard you whispering out here a minute ago," Samantha said. "I thought you were talking to someone."

"No one else here," he admitted the obvious.

She came close, no sign of nervousness to her. "You talk to yourself often, Mister . . . I'm sorry. Seamus."

"No," and he drew angrily on the pipe stem. Ashamed of himself for feeling this way around a woman. A man so assured of himself most of the time, easily moving in the company of hard men and sharp-edged circumstances—made so suddenly uncomfortable around Jennie Wheatley . . . and now Samantha Pike. She swept behind him on the edge of the porch, the air awash with the smell of lye soap and freshly laundered petticoats hung to dry on the line out back. In private Seamus savored it in spite of himself, then listened as she settled herself at the edge of the porch, a judicious distance from him.

"It's . . . I was just repeating some poetry I know," he admitted, then felt the fool for saying it. Why he had babbled that to her, he did not know.

"Poetry," she said as if trying out the word.

"Yes," he replied a little too curtly. "Jack and Sharp inside?" Donegan asked, trying to change the subject, embarrassed that he had admitted he recited poetry.

"They're helping Rebecca with the dishes and banking the fire for the night."

"Sounds like they're going to bed early."

"Sharp wants an early start in the morning—this trip of yours north to Fort Sill," she answered.

"It's a good idea, I suppose. Should be finding my blankets meself."

"Stay," she said suddenly, a little strongly, then looked away at the night sky.

He was filled at that same instant with a sudden wonder of her, and believed he saw her blush there beneath the pale moonlight of north Texas.

"I mean—" and she stopped cold, her eyes imploring his for understanding. "It's early . . . and I get . . . well, there's not many people to talk to around here. I'd like you to stay up and talk to me, Seamus. If you would."

"By the saints, but you've probably got a lot of young suitors paying you court, Samantha—a pretty girl like you."

"You really think so?" she asked in a gush. "Really think I'm that pretty that men would want to court me?"

He smiled, more at ease now, warmed by her openness. "I'm certain of you being pretty—one of the prettiest women these eyes have seen in all my days. I find it hard to believe if you're going to tell me you don't have suitors from Jacksboro banging down your door here."

She stared down at her slim hands she was kneading in her lap. "There have been some. But Rebecca helps me send them away."

"Why, none of them good enough for you?"

The way her eyes shot up and held his made him realize he had made a mistake in this crude attempt to prod her sense of humor. Instead, his thoughtless question had pricked her stiff-backed pride. Those eyes that looked back at him betrayed a deeply wounded and vulnerable woman hiding behind them at that moment.

"I so want to find a man who . . . who doesn't have dirt under his fingernails, Seamus. A man who doesn't have to grub in this soil or raise cattle for his livelihood. But that's the only kind of man that's here." She ground a handful of her cotton skirt between her palms. "How I wish I could go east—to a . . . *city*."

He heard the magic inflection put on that last word. "You've never been to a big city?"

She turned to him in a rush and rustle of petticoats. "I'll bet you've been—I mean, coming from Ireland, you had to. Tell me about them, Seamus. Tell me about the cities back east. What the people wear and what they eat. How they ride around on the paved streets in their fine carriages . . . going off to plays and operas every night after dining on oysters and fish from the great oceans, even fish eggs."

"Seems you know quite a lot about cities back east for so young a woman."

Samantha Pike stared at the dark, north Texas sky for a long time before she answered. "I can imagine. That's all," she finally said. "I hear something now and then about the busy, glorious life of folks on the East Coast. Never have I heard much about California."

"What I saw of it wasn't all that different than Denver City."

"So you've been to California too?" she asked like a wistful child, her face flush with excitement in the starshine.

"Yes—"

"San Francisco?"

He wagged his head. "Never made it that far.* Not to the ocean."

"Oh," she sighed. "You are so lucky—able to travel at your own whim. Where and when you want to go. A man can do . . . well, a woman just can't do that."

"Saints preserve, Samantha—this is still a dangerous land for anyone. Especially a woman."

"That's why I want so to go back east."

"Truth be, the city streets are as unsafe as that open prairie out there." He used the stem of his pipe to jab home his point. "And at least on that prairie you have a chance of hiding from the hostiles. In the cities, like Boston—you can't hide from the thieves and . . . the sort who would do a woman harm."

"I can't believe you about that," she replied, instantly haughty.

It struck him as strange, that she would change

* The Plainsmen Series, vol. 5, *Devil's Backbone*

from woman to woman to woman in a matter of a few minutes before his eyes. Here so harshly defiant when moments ago she was a child filled with wonder, then a vulnerable young woman.

"Better that I don't tell you what I think of those cities back east then," he replied, staring off into the night sky, refusing to look at the deadly mix of deep beauty and haughty fire that lit her eyes.

He listened to her sigh near him, a rustle of layers of cloth as she stood. When Seamus gazed up, Samantha was leaning back against a porch post, her hands behind her, staring longingly off into the distance.

"Will you tell me some more of your poetry, Seamus?"

"I'm not sure what I know is the kind of thing—"

"Do you know any love poetry, Seamus?" she interrupted him in a gush, swirling back down to settle beside him like a fluffy bird come to roost, bringing with her the heady rush of clean linen and lye soap, as much a perfume as any woman had used to overpower him.

He swallowed deeply, glancing only briefly at the heavy rise and fall of her breasts beneath the tight blouse. "Yes . . . I know—"

"Say it for me, please!" she begged, then did something surprising to them both in reaching without thought and took one of his hands in hers. "Please."

In wide-eyed wonder he gazed down at her hands clutching his. Only then did she realize what she had done and quickly withdrew them.

"I got . . . a little, eager. I'm sorry."

He smiled then, surprised himself as he reached out and caressed the back of her hand with his fingertips and said, "I liked it, Samantha. Liked your touch a lot."

Staring at the big moon fully risen over the tree-tops, Seamus began his favorite James Clarence Mangan poem, an Irishman who lived the first half of this, the nineteenth century.

"This one's called: 'The Nameless One.'

Roll forth my son, like the rushing rive,
*   That sweeps along to the mighty sea;*
God will inspire me while I deliver
*   My soul of thee!*

Tell thou the world when my bones lie whitening
*   Amid the last homes of youth and eld,*
That there was once one who veins ran lightening
*   No eye beheld.*

Tell how his boyhood was one drear night-hour,
*   How shone for him, through his griefs and*
glooms,
No star of all heaven sends to light our
*   Path to the tomb.*

Roll on, my song, and to after ages
*   Tell how, disdaining all earth can give,*
He would have taught men, from wisdom's pages,
*   The way to live.*

And tell how trampled, derided, hated,
*   And worn by weakness, disease, and wrong,*
He fled for shelter to God, who mated
*   His soul with song—*

Tell how this Nameless, condemned for years long
*   To herd with demons from hell beneath,*
Saw things that made him, with groans and tears,
long
*   For even death.*

Go on to tell how, with genius wasted,
  Betrayed in friendship, befooled in love,
With spirit shipwrecked, and young hopes blasted,
  He still, still strove.

Him grant a grave to, ye pitying noble,
  Deep in your bosoms! There let him dwell!
He, too, had tears for all souls in trouble,
  Here, and in hell."

For long moments after he finished, she said nothing to disturb the heavy silence between them. Seamus finally turned to look at her and found her pretty, full mouth open in amazement. She blinked a few times, as if coming to after a lapse of consciousness.

"I never . . . never would have expected you to know such beautiful, powerful words. Words I'm sure you meant to stir my soul, Seamus."

He felt uncomfortable at her praise, at her sudden declaration. "It is just a poem I like, and memorized many years ago to help fill some of the pain of my own—"

Seamus didn't finish. He could not, finding her suddenly at him—her soft, wet lips crushing his, her hands and arms encircling him savagely, pulling him against her.

When she withdrew slightly, Samantha was gasping as if starved for air.

"I've always wanted to do that to a man," she announced. "To do that when I wanted to be kissed—not having to wait for a man to figure I need a kiss. I grew so tired of waiting for you to kiss me, Seamus."

He ran the tip of his tongue across his lips, tasting her again before he said, "If I had known it would be so . . . such a treat—I would have done it long ago, Samantha."

"Then—we're both happy," she said, suddenly pressing herself into him again with a second embrace and a much longer, lingering kiss.

When she pulled away this time, Seamus was no longer suffering merely surprise, but intense arousal. The scent of her, the taste of her, the warmth of her full lower lip, which seemed to dominate the way she opened her warm, fleshy mouth to him. And the press of the firm, fleshy mounds against him. He glanced at them, almost unable to take his eyes off the way her chest heaved, rising and falling.

"You . . . you want to touch them—don't you, Seamus?" she asked in that haughty, husky voice of hers.

Her frankness startled him. Then his eyes found hers, and he realized she did not really know what she was asking of him, what she would be demanding of them both.

"As much as I would—I better not. Sharp's a friend and—"

"He's only my brother-in-law and has nothing to do with this," she replied, flicking only a cautionary glance at the cabin window. "They've likely all gone to bed," and she reached up to slip free the top button at her neck. A second came free as he watched her fingers at work, becoming aroused with the slow, sensuous movement of them on the bone buttons.

"We—we better not." He swallowed hard.

"Yes—take me, Seamus. I've yearned for a man to be my first. Not a dirt-grubbing farmer. Not a crude, smelly buffalo hunter. But a man like you—one who would take my flesh this very first time—making us both crazy with desire."

She pressed boldly into him again, there on Sharp

Grover's porch beneath the Texas moonlight, kissing him fiercely, her breathing become shallow and rapid. His own grew difficult to catch with the sudden rise of heat from the core of him. Blood rushed, pounding at his ears when she took one of his hands and guided it inside her blouse.

As she let her head slip back, eyes half closed, Samantha Pike moaned low in her throat.

For Seamus it had been so, so long.

And he had never been more hungry.

Chapter 18

Moon of Leaves Falling, 1873

*I*t had been a little more than a year since he and Big Tree had been taken north to Dall-ass and from there to stage and smoking horse and on to the white man's city in the east where they spent three happy days among their friends.

And now Satanta and Big Tree were again being told to lay down their shovels and drag their heavy chains across the broken ground, trudging down off the roadbed that would one day soon carry the white man's belching black monster of a train. The guards watched the Kiowa chiefs warily as the pair climbed slowly over the rear gate of an open wagon and squatted uncomfortably only a heartbeat before an impatient prison guard slapped his reins down on the rumps of two mules and the wagon lurched away into the unknown.

His chains rattled as the iron-mounted tires and springless wagon trembled over the rough ground. Three armed guards on horseback inched up on each side of the wagon, staying far enough away so they rode out of the dust kicked up by the wheels spinning the fine gold into the mid-morning sunshine this autumn. Down the ruts of the construction road, between the stands of frost-kissed trees, dressed in new colors for this brief dance of suspense before the coming of winter to the southern plains.

It was not long when he heard the driver calling out to the mules. Satanta turned laboriously in his shackles to look up the construction road at the intersection it made with another. There, sat an army ambulance and at least fifteen soldiers in dark blue tunics, rifles across their thighs or standing vertically plugged on a hip.

In a fevered rush of motion, the chiefs were pulled down from the wagon and hurried over to the ambulance without explanation. Satanta and Big Tree did not say a word, exchanging only glances again that said while they hoped this might be another meeting with the chiefs about progress made on gaining their release, there might be another reason for this journey.

Satanta saw in the eyes of the younger war-chief a doubt more than a fear—something that tugged at the heart of Satanta.

Perhaps they would not come back here. Perhaps they would not see their friends. Perhaps this was the time the white man chose to hang them.

With a hollow thud the ambulance door slammed shut and a white man called out to the rest. The driver set his wagon in motion as the soldiers once more formed their two columns. As the ambulance came around, Satanta saw the prison guards peeling off, escorting the empty construction wagon back down the road. Heading south to where the white man laid the track for his smoking horse.

"Do we see our friends this time?" Big Tree whispered later, miles down the road.

With a wag of his head, Satanta admitted he did not know. "If we are going to die—the white man has played a cruel trick on us: forcing us to work so hard."

"Yes," Big Tree answered quietly, aware as well of the need for quiet, and not wanting his voice to carry. "A man is not meant to work like this—at least not a Kiowa. If the white man wishes to dig at the earth with his iron tools, let him. But a Kiowa man is meant for the hunt and the chase, and to sit in the shade and tell stories."

"And dream of soft-skinned women," Satanta added, smiling with the thought of warm flesh beneath him. It would be so good to have a single night with one of the women who awaited him all this time on the reservation.

Big Tree leaned back against the padded leather seat. "Yes. I have been dreaming much of women, Satanta. You have been thinking of your wife?"

He smiled. "Her—and others. Any woman, Big Tree. I am so hungry now . . . it could be any woman."

"Even a white woman?" Big Tree asked, a crooked grin on his face.

"Yes, perhaps that would be better. Especially a white woman—now."

They were quiet after that. Each man somehow deeply content in his own thoughts as the ambulance rumbled along, the hooves pounding the hardened road surface outside, the driver calling out to his four-horse team, and the escort commander calling out to his cavalry. Satanta did not recognize these white men, nor the symbol on their clothing. These riders were so different from the buffalo soldiers with dark skins and short, coarse hair who patrolled the Kiowa-Comanche reservation.

Late that afternoon, the pair arrived at the busy place the white man called Dall-ass. The chiefs were taken to the local jail, where they spent the night behind the iron bars of a second-story cell. Most of the evening a lot of noise drifted up from the street below, even while they ate and tried to sleep—once the sun no longer shined through the open, barred window.

From time to time Satanta peered down at the white men clustered beneath the hazy glow of the yellow streetlamps. They always hollered louder and shook their fists when he or Big Tree came to the window. Here, in the deepening twilight of this stinking place where the air did not blow free, he felt like nothing more than a shadow imprisoned behind these bars. Sadly he realized he was still of enough substance that he could not float free from the windowsill and fly off, taking wing for his faraway and much beloved prairie.

That night passed as so many before it, and the next morning the soldiers came for the two. After the chiefs were allowed to relieve themselves in a small wooden house outside, then fed and given steamy coffee while the sun rose full in the east, they were herded out the back door to the waiting ambulance. Sitting among the horse-mounted soldiers were three men—civilians. New faces to Satanta.

"You see them before?" Big Tree asked in a hushed whisper as the ambulance jerked into motion.

He nodded. "The older one—yes. I remember. He was with Yellow Hair five winters ago."

"A scout for Custer and the soldier chief Sheridan when they captured you and Lone Wolf?"

"Yes," Satanta answered. "The other two, I've never seen. Perhaps they work for the older one."

"I cannot tell the difference really. All three look alike, Satanta."

"White men are that way, don't you know, my

friend?" Satanta laughed harshly. "After all this time, after knowing so many white men—I can say very few look different."

"A young one—he learns how to scout from the old man?"

"Yes," Satanta replied. "And the other, with the little beard on his chin and those gray eyes of his. He is a big, big man."

"I have rarely seen someone so tall before," Big Tree added.

"His scalp would look good on your medicine pole —no?"

Big Tree grinned. "If I have the chance, Satanta. Any white man's scalp would look good on my medicine pole."

"No, Big Tree. When you have the chance, study the tall one with the gray eyes. His hair would be a great prize."

"If you think so much of it, I will leave his scalp for you . . . when the time comes."

Satanta grinned slightly, gazing out the ambulance window for a glimpse of the three civilians who rode along with the army escort. "When the time comes, this old warrior wants that white man's scalp for himself."

After nearly a week of travel the two chiefs stared in amazement from the ambulance windows one mid-afternoon, recognizing not only some of the country, but some of the buildings as well as they drew closer to the Fort Sill military reservation. In a rush of emotion the two men silently embraced, eyes moistening as they realized they were once more among their people. Suspended above and among the trees in the distance, there across Cache Creek, Satanta could see the low-hanging smoke of many fires surrounding the agency.

This was the prison country of his people.

Their home and hearts lay far to the south and west.

Yet there were still small victories to celebrate. And this homecoming was one of the sweetest he could remember.

No less sweet than that terrible time five winters gone when the Yellow Hair Custer had held both he and Lone Wolf prisoner, threatening to hang them if the Kiowa bands did not come in to the Fort Cobb reservation as the soldiers demanded. Satanta would never forget that winter, nor that great humiliation heaped on his shoulders—forced to watch the white soldier chief's hanging ropes swinging in the winter wind from a tall oak tree.

When the ambulance rattled to a halt, one of the white men barked orders while others hurried forward and one soldier pulled open the door. A long gauntlet had been formed by the black-faced buffalo soldiers, a tunnel the prisoners would have to walk from the ambulance into the very same stone building where they had been captured and held more than two winters before.

White soldiers in clean blue uniforms awaited the chiefs on the porch, where they turned and showed the Kiowas into the interior of the buildings. Two more black-faced soldiers stood on either side of a narrow door filled with darkness. A third black soldier held a lamp in his hand, its flame wavering only slightly beneath the smudgy globe.

One of the white soldiers turned to say something to the civilian at his side. Satanta thought he remembered the clean-shaven civilian from the short-grass time he was captured at this place, but then he could not be certain.

"White Bear . . . you and Big Tree are ordered to

go down the steps," Philip McCusker, post and agency interpreter, explained as he pointed to the narrow doorway.

"That is the bad-smelling place where the soldiers kept me prisoner the first time I was put in chains!" Satanta snapped.

"Yes, it is."

"We will not go!" Satanta peered at the soldiers, uneasy with their pistols drawn. He knew it would take a little foolish act on his part and one of them would shoot him.

"You must," McCusker pleaded. "It will only be for a few sunrises. Then the leader of the white men in Texas will be here."

"Why does he come?"

McCusker appeared to search for an answer. "He comes to talk with the soldiers about the terms of your release."

Satanta was suspicious. He glanced at Big Tree's open, expectant face, then glowered at McCusker once more. "I do not believe we are here to be freed of our chains." He held up the wrist shackles, rattling the chain connecting them. "This must be more of the white man's trickery."

"No," McCusker replied. "The leader of Texas is coming here in a few days to talk to you and your chiefs about freeing you. Go do what the soldiers want. Stay down those stairs and sleep and eat until you can once again see your wives and children."

Satanta turned to Big Tree. "Will you go down the stairs into that hole with me . . . for a few sunrises —until the white man will take these irons from our bodies?"

"I will," Big Tree replied. "I am home—at least among my people."

"This is nothing more than a stinking hole in the

ground," Satanta said as he turned back to Mc-Cusker, both cuffed hands indicating the door to the basement.

"You will have food and water and blankets for the short time you are there. Go now," McCusker said. "Before the soldiers get more nervous and there is trouble."

Satanta turned without a word, leading Big Tree to the doorway. The black soldiers inched aside and allowed the Kiowas to descend the narrow stairwell behind the soldier holding the oil lamp.

The place smelled of dust and old water, just as he had remembered it. It was not the smell of the open prairie he hungered for so.

No, this place was like descending into the bowels of some rotting carrion left on the plains by the white hunters come only for the hides and the tongues, leaving the rest to make a great stench that filled the air.

Satanta walked slowly, carefully, dragging his heavy chains down one step at a time into the darkness, following the flickering yellow lamplight, certain he had been swallowed by this belly of some great, stinking monster the white man appeased by feeding Indians to it.

He nursed his bitter hatred, brooding on the gray-eyed one with the long, curly hair Satanta wanted to adorn his medicine shield.

"You know any of that bunch, Sharp?" Seamus Donegan asked as they both looked over the gathering of civilians clustered along the crude tables in the Fort Sill mess hall.

"That big one's supposed to be Davis himself."

"Governor of Texas?"

Grover nodded. "I figure the one who's never far

from his side is the governor's aide. Don't know who
the rest of 'em are."

"Texas ranchmen," announced Jack Stillwell as he
walked up to the two men.

"Where you find out?" Grover asked.

"Just need to ask the right people."

"And that was?"

"Sergeant Waller," Stillwell answered with a grin.

"Then it must be so," Donegan replied. "What they
come up here with Davis for?"

"Came with the governor and his secretary hoping
to recover some of their stock lost to the Kiowas and
Comanches on the reservation."

"How they gonna do that?"

"I suppose they'll inspect the brands," Sharp replied.

"Dangerous snooping, I'd say," Seamus added.
"Those Injin bucks won't let white men near their
cattle, will they?"

"I doubt it. Could bring the kettle to a boil."

Governor Edmund J. Davis had arrived at Fort Sill
with his party of state officials and private citizens on
Friday, October third. The next day, the agent to the
Southern Cheyenne, John D. Miles, rode in, leading
two officials of the Indian Bureau: Commissioner E.
P. Smith, and Enoch Hoag, superintendent of the
Central Superintendency that oversaw the southern
plains.

On that Sunday, 5 October, Davis and the Indian
Bureau officials held a brief and acrimonious prelim-
inary hearing with the Kiowas and Comanches to
find agreement on a time and place for "the grand
council." The white men wanted the conference held
on the parade ground at Fort Sill, where there would
be no question as to the security of the proceedings.

And for that same reason, the Indians protested

that they would not attend such a council held inside the walls of the white man's fort where Indian blood had been spilled and some of their people had died when the soldiers arrested both Satanta and Big Tree.

"Our hearts will be cold and our thoughts will be poisoned by such an evil place as this fort of yours," explained Kicking Bird to the sour-faced Tehanna chief.

Davis was grim indeed. He and the rest were hearing nothing of the Indians' complaints. "We will hold our talks on the open parade of Fort Sill," the governor told interpreter Philip McCusker to explain to the chiefs, "or . . . I will ride back to Texas and we will hold no talks about the release at all."

Grudgingly the angry chiefs agreed to meet with the Indian officials and the hated Tehannas on the following day, Monday, 6 October—on the parade at Fort Sill, I.T.

Chapter 19

October 6, 1873

"*W*ill you look at them now?" said Reuben Waller in a hushed but approving whisper.

"They do make a sight, don't they?" replied Seamus Donegan.

Both men stood at the edge of Fort Sill's parade, witness to the strutting, preening pride of the warriors and chiefs who streamed through the post gates and strode regally past the central flagpole, making the great circuit for the large Sibley tent pitched at the south side of the parade.

Half the strength of H Company, for the moment under the command of Sergeant Waller—the second half under command of Captain Louis H. Carpenter himself—joined the other three companies of the Tenth U.S. Cavalry ringing the fort in readiness. Mounts stood saddled, a shell in the breech of every carbine, and sidearms loosened.

If there was to be fighting this day, as Lieutenant Colonel Davidson had predicted, the Tenth would be ready when trouble raised it hoary head.

The huge, conical Sibley tent had been pitched in front of Davidson's headquarters along the south wall of the stockade. It was here both the Texas and In-

dian Bureau officials would formally meet with the
Kiowa and Comanche leaders who slowly came forward in small groups and seated themselves on the
ground in the order of their importance.

Behind a series of tables, the white officials settled
in ladder-back chairs, watching the unhurried, delib-
erate assembly of the head men from both tribes. Off
to the side, in the middle of a crescent of buffalo
soldiers, sat the stoic Satanta and Big Tree.

It was some time before the chiefs, head men and
the young warriors had all seated themselves and appeared ready for the grand council to begin. Philip
McCusker whispered in Davidson's ear, prompting
the lieutenant colonel to rise and address the colorful, feather-adorned assembly. From his spot at the
end of the tables, where he could position himself
between the two groups, McCusker began to sign for
the Comanche and translate in Kiowa.

"I am Lieutenant Colonel Davidson of the Tenth
U.S. Cavalry," the officer began. "We have called you
here today to listen to the words of some important
officials of our governments regarding the future of
both your tribes: Kiowa and Comanche. Without fur-
ther delay, I introduce to you Mr. E. P. Smith, the
Great Father's commissioner of Indian affairs back
in Washington City."

As Smith rose from his chair, there came a smat-
tering of applause from the other white men, while
none of the buffalo soldiers clapped. The assembled
Indians looked on without emotion as the government official began his proclamation.

"I come this morning with greetings from the
Great White Father for his Kiowa and Comanche
children," Smith said, then halted a few moments to
allow for McCusker's translation. "There are many
important matters for us to discuss today between

your tribes and our government officials. But perhaps the most important of these is the release of your two chiefs."

Smith glanced at Davis, finding the governor watching him intently. The commissioner wiped some sweat from his upper lip and continued self-consciously, clearly ill-at-ease before the painted, feathered assembly of plains raiders. "The man I will now introduce comes from far away in the land of Texas."

As Smith paused, McCusker translated and signed. That singular word was muttered and re-echoed among the proud red crowd.

"Tehas!"

"This one is chief of Tehannas?"

When McCusker nodded at him, the commissioner continued, "He is the leader of the people of that state, and as such comes to discuss the release of Satanta and Big Tree with you. I now have the honor of introducing Governor Edmund J. Davis, the esteemed governor of the sovereign state of Texas."

Davis rose to the applause of his staff and most of the Texas stockmen who had come north in hopes of locating some of their stolen cattle. With a hand held in his vest as if to strike a commanding pose, the governor peered over the crowd for a few moments in a manner of assessing it for political advantage before he began to speak. When he started, it was with a nod given to Philip McCusker, as if he were granting the interpreter permission to begin his part of this highly charged drama.

"Allow me to begin by telling the great leaders of both the Kiowa and Comanche peoples that the white citizens of the state of Texas want only peace with your tribes." As Davis spoke he walked slowly to his right, down behind the line of officials seated at the table, his left arm held out theatrically while he drove home his words.

"It is indeed unfortunate that the history of the state of Texas . . . truly from the time of our independence from Mexican rule and domination, has been a history of bloodshed and hatred and prejudice beyond any man's imagination. But we of today—truly, we of this *very* day, have before us the opportunity to change this bloody trail we both find ourselves upon. We can begin anew, today."

Theatrically, he came to a stop behind the two captive Kiowas, laying a hand on Satanta's shoulder, the other on Big Tree's. "Behold, your chiefs. See how they have fared while they were in our care. They have not missed a meal. They have not suffered from want of sleep. Nor suffered for want of anything at all. We arrested them for their crimes against a private civilian on the soil of Texas. And now, the time has arrived that they can be turned back to their people."

When the last words tumbled from McCusker's lips, there was a rapid stirring among not only the Kiowas, but the Comanches as well. Like the flushing of a large covey of quail from the brush, or the scattering of turkey toms from the mesquite, the air grew charged. This was to be a great moment, Seamus Donegan realized. A chance at last for the white man to live up to his word given to the Indian.

"But first," Davis continued as he stepped away from the chiefs, steepling his fingers together thoughtfully, his countenance much more subdued, "I must present you with the terms of their release."

McCusker's translation brought confusion to the red faces where an instant before there had been a tangible joy. Low, thunderous voices rumbled as the group whispered among themselves, their dark eyes growing murderously dark once more, glowering not only at Davis, but at every one of the other white men at the table.

"I will free the chiefs, releasing them from the custody of the soldiers—allowing them to return to their people on this great reservation—if your tribes will subscribe to the following conditions."

Only stony silence now met the once enthusiastic throng of red men seated upon their blankets before the tables, or standing stock still on the Fort Sill parade, an impressive array of armed, warrior might.

"Where are the Comanche among this gathering?" Davis asked of McCusker.

The interpreter began to translate automatically, then realized his mistake. Self-consciously he pointed out the left side of the great assembly pouring across the grass and gravel parade.

"Good," Davis said, nodding and stepping down the front of the long tables for the first time, placing himself between the other white officials and the Indians. "We are aware that recent war-parties of Comanche warriors have illegally left this reservation and crossed the Red River into Texas—striking our settlements, stealing our stock, murdering innocent citizens of my state. Now, listen to me carefully . . . as I tell you that the Comanche must deliver up to my hands five of their warriors responsible for these recent and bloody raids into Texas."

McCusker anxiously delivered the condition, his own eyes filled with its terrible message. As the ultimatum sank in, the Indians stirred. Shifting uneasily, the buffalo soldiers brought their weapons up in a noisy rattle that prompted Carpenter and Waller to whisper among their men.

"Hold on! Just stand by . . ."

At the same time, the white officials at the table

appeared to be trying to make themselves as small as possible in the event of calamity as a puffed-up Davis plunged ahead.

"In addition," the governor continued, holding an arm up which he waved over the assembly, "both the Kiowa and the Comanche must return all the stock that can be identified as coming from the ranches of Texas citizens."

Ignited up by the white man's incendiary words, the young men near the back of the assembly began exhorting for resistance—shouting, waving lances and bows, unashamedly exhibiting their guns, pointing them at both the white men and black soldiers the warriors clearly outnumbered at this tense moment. Some of the old men, undoubtedly concerned themselves about the harsh condition placed upon them by the white men, nonetheless turned and attempted to regain order and calm over the young hotbloods threatening to turn the assembly into a bloodbath.

"Finally," Governor Davis continued, his loud voice raised over the hubbub, "the tribes must guarantee the U.S. Army and our varied government bodies that they will always camp close to their agencies and will no more ride into the sovereign state of Texas . . . they must agree that they will obediently draw their annuities as distributed by the Indian Bureau . . . and the bands must submit to a roll-call system to determine if any warrior or family has fled the reservation between the occasions of distributions of those government rations."

It was clear to Donegan that McCusker found this translation distasteful, if not downright dangerous. The interpreter glanced at Satanta and Big Tree, who were whispering between themselves.

"The tribes must understand," Davis shouted over the clamor, "that we are requiring them to adhere to

these conditions within thirty days. That is thirty suns
. . . or the two chiefs will not be released."

With the translation, Satanta and Big Tree leaped
to their feet, shackles rattling, both ankle and wrist.

There came an almost immediate surge of the
young men. Their chiefs were shouting as loudly as
the rest—with McCusker attempting to translate a little of the angry rhetoric that blued the air of the Fort
Sill parade that sixth day of October.

Then a new voice arose above the clamor—drown-
ing out most of the others, quieting the rest. Lone
Wolf, the aging war-chief who, along with Satanta,
had been held hostage by Custer and Sheridan five
winters before, hurried to stand at the front of the
assembly, his blanket looped over one shoulder and
under the other arm for gesturing.

"You figure that old sharp-eyed one's got a gun under that robe?" Seamus asked of Sharp Grover and
Jack Stillwell.

"If he don't," Grover replied, "then Lone Wolf
ain't the sort of chief the Kiowa want leading 'em
anyways. From what I know of that devil, he's packing iron, that's for certain."

Stillwell whispered, "I heard how Lone Wolf
stepped up to General Sherman right here on this
ground, pointing his rifle at the general back to 'seventy-one when the army arrested them two chiefs,
Seamus. You best believe that's a bad one with an
oily reputation and he doesn't come out of his lodge
less'n he's swaybacked with weapons."

In the uneasy hush brought about by Lone Wolf's
demand for quiet, the Kiowa chief began to speak.

"Let the white man know we want peace with him.
But we want a strong peace—forged between two old
enemies who respect one another. Not a peace of one

powerful adversary over his weaker neighbor. This cannot be."

He stepped slowly through the front rows of the chiefs and head men who remained seated on the ground, coming to a stop in front of the Texas governor.

"Let the white man know we will adhere to the terms he has laid down for us to live on this reservation and to receive our presents from his government. But let the white man know too that he must release our two chiefs . . . but not in thirty suns. Not in one sun. We must have our chiefs back *now!*"

There arose a sudden whipping of fury from the young warriors who cried out their war songs, yelping and yipping like hungry coyotes for blood. Across the next anxious moments, the older men slowly quieted them, then waited for the haughty Davis to respond to Lone Wolf's angry demand.

When he had crossed his arms over his chest defiantly, the governor said, "I will not be dictated to by you, Lone Wolf—or any other Indian savage. You yourself have been a criminal. A known murderer and a butcher and a thief. You will not tell me what to do. Instead, I have come here today to tell you and your people what I want you to do for the white man!"

Lone Wolf's eyes narrowed on the tall white official, those eyes the only betrayal of his emotions. "We have nothing more to talk about. Perhaps I was an old woman when I told my people to come here and listen to the words of the white man. Perhaps I have told them the wrong thing to pay heed to what you had to say, because there is little sense and reason and courage to your words."

"Courage?" Davis shouted, his own eyes narrowing. "I'll show you courage! Look around you, Lone Wolf!"

"I see your soldiers. But are your eyes crusted shut, white man? Can't you see our warriors ready to turn this ground red with your blood?"

Already on his feet and just then scurrying to Lone Wolf and Davis was Enoch Hoag, central superintendent of the Indian Bureau. He stepped boldly between them, glaring up at the taller Davis, jabbing a finger in the governor's silk vest.

"By damn, Davis," he hissed, face red with anger, a Quaker not easily given to profanity. "Your refusal to release these two prisoners at once blocks the way to achieving peace right at the outset. For, if Satanta and Big Tree are not released here and now, we'll never get agents among these people ever again. The bands will scatter across the prairie, making it a job for the army to gather them once more. And that bloody war will be on your hands, Davis!"

"What the hell do you think we have now, Hoag?" Davis spat. "You figure we've got us a picnic of things down there in Texas? That what you think of things now?"

Hoag shook his head angrily, licking spittle from his lips as Smith and Cheyenne agent John Miles rose from the table, headed for the scene. "You listen to me you pompous prig. If these two chiefs are released, then agents can go among them and begin working on the path to peace: distributing presents, counting families, holding roll-call for them."

Instead of paying heed, Davis grinned mockingly and rocked back on his heels, gesturing over the anxious, muttering crowd of warriors and chiefs. "If they are so warlike as all that, Mr. Hoag," the governor replied, "then we had as well fight them here and now, at once!"

Lone Wolf turned away on his own accord, wagging his head in bitter frustration, and took his seat, not able to understand the white man's words, more so unwilling to talk with someone so dead set on bringing ruin to this council and any last chance of peace.

E. P. Smith hurried up to his superintendent and Davis as the old chief turned away. "Governor, would you consider it a sign of good faith on the part of the Indians—and therefore agree to release the two chiefs—if the tribes bring in five of the warriors guilty for the raids into your state?"

Davis rubbed his chin thoughtfully, glancing over some of his staff and then letting his eyes rest on the stockmen who had come north from their ranches in Texas.

"Yes," he quietly answered in the end. "I suppose I would see it as a sign of good faith from them."

Smith immediately turned back to the haughty, muttering crowd of ignited red men. "Listen to me!" He held both his arms up, demanding quiet of the huge assembly threatening to explode into bloodshed. "You can have your chiefs back if you will listen to me and do as you are told!"

Pointing to Satanta and Big Tree, Smith continued, raising his voice to announce to all, "Bring us five of those guilty of the raids in Texas . . . within twenty-four hours—one more sun from now—and the chiefs will be freed!"

He waited a moment while McCusker translated and some of the words sunk in. More and more of the head men murmured among themselves.

"You must go back to your lodges," Smith added. "Go there now and discuss this among your leaders. You must do nothing else but talk about this matter

. . . and decide what you will do to bring in five of the guilty raiders to us."

Lone Wolf stood, his hair black with no iron belying his sixty-plus winters. Few wrinkles marred his thoughtful face. "We will go talk now. Yes. And we will return with our answer. If we have not decided by tomorrow at this time, we will be here the day after. We go now."

As if on that cue, the rest, both Kiowa and Comanche, arose with a rattle of weapons and a shuffle of blankets and robes, a tinkling of hawks bells, heading off the parade and out of the gates as slowly as they had come earlier that morning.

Seamus watched the bead of sweat slowly fall down the black flesh of the sergeant's immobile, muscular neck minutes later as the last of the warriors strolled beyond the gates. Only then did he realize he himself was sweating, his palm plastered to the wood handles of the army model .44 he carried over his left hip, butt forward.

Waller sighed. "Damn, but I figured we was dog meat, Seamus."

"Me too, Reuben." He looked over the rest of Waller's squad. While the strain of events clearly showed on their faces, there appeared to be no fear. "Your men held up well, Sergeant."

Reuben turned suddenly and saluted. "Thank you, sir—Sergeant Major Donegan."

On instinct, Seamus saluted, a little self-conscious as his fingers snapped against his brow. "As you were, Sergeant Waller."

The black soldier wagged his head slightly as his eyes went back to watching the warriors disappear through the trees. Only then did he reply in a doleful tone. "I don't . . . don't think things is ever again gonna be the same as they is now, Seamus."

Chapter 20

October 7–8, 1873

*I*n the Moon of Falling Leaves. The end of the raiding season and the coming of another winter.

Lone Wolf despaired for his people. Many times he had gone the way of his heart—fighting the white man, leading the war faction of the Kiowa bands along with Big Tree and Satanta. His voice the strongest in calling Kicking Bird an old woman for dealing with the soldiers and cuddling up with the white peace-talkers.

But now something inside the old chief told him the sun was setting on his people.

It was the autumn of the white man's year 1873. Perhaps too this was the season of the yellow leaf for the Kiowa.

This was a betrayal all the more difficult to deal with because even Kicking Bird remained silent, staring at the flames of their council fire in Lone Wolf's lodge. The Wolf sat surrounded by the others who talked and argued and debated for long hours that night. Yes, now even Kicking Bird believed the white man had lied and proven himself faithless.

First they had been guaranteed the two chiefs would be freed more than seven moons ago. Anger set in among the Kiowa, but with Lone Wolf's help, Kicking Bird had quieted the warriors and the noisy women—convincing them to wait out the time specified by the white Tehannas. They never had any other choice: it was always the white man's schedule for their lives.

Gone the time of the short grass of their lives. No longer was it merely the march of the seasons and following the imperatives of the nomadic buffalo from rut to hunt, to calving and to hunt once more. When life was simple not so long ago.

Now even old Kicking Bird hung his head in confusion, if not outright shame, that he had been lied to as well as the war-chiefs.

"We could have told you, Kicking Bird!" cried Eagle Heart, giving voice to much of the denunciation heaped on the old chief's shoulders.

"Yes! The white man talks from one side of his mouth when he is afraid of our strength . . . and he talks from the other side of his mouth when he demands something of our weakness!" added Big Bow, a powerful war-chief among the Kiowa.

Red Otter, Lone Wolf's brother, took the talking stick, impatient to speak his heart. "Why do you spend so much of your strength beating Kicking Bird's shoulders and head? Is he to blame for our troubles?"

"We would not be caught in this now if we had not listened to Kicking Bird in the beginning!" White Horse shouted.

Many others agreed, laughing, jeering, snorting and pounding their flat hands on their thighs in concert.

"It was not Kicking Bird who fooled you," Lone Wolf said, agreeing with his younger brother, Red Otter, and instantly quieting the noisy ones. "The white man is the one to blame. He—not our chief—should be made to pay."

"We are trapped now! What can we do?" asked Tau-ankia, Lone Wolf's eldest son.

"Yes, what can we do, Lone Wolf? You have told the white men we would agree to whatever they demanded of us. What now?" asked Gui-tain, the nephew of Lone Wolf.

His eyes glowered at the young warrior, coming to share a place of power and respect among the Kiowa. "I agreed with what the white man wanted—so that he would free Satanta and Big Tree. While one is young, and has many winters left to him . . . the other is like me: growing old. A man never knows when he will enjoy his last summer. His last autumn. Perhaps never again to see the melting of another winter's snow. Maybe never to feel himself grow strong within the moist pleasure of a woman. This is what guides my thoughts when I attempt to free Satanta."

"There is more than one way to free our chiefs," Eagle Heart said quietly above the hush come over the lodge at the end of Lone Wolf's words. "More than one way."

The old chief gazed across the fire at the warrior. Nodding slightly, Lone Wolf said, "What is it you speak of, Eagle Heart?" He grinned slightly, sensing his heart leap with anticipation.

Eagle Heart grinned back. "The white man does not want to give us back our chiefs. This is plain to see. If he does not—we simply take them."

"How do we do this?" Kicking Bird asked, for the first time raising his eyes to face the rest of the council.

"Yes—I must know how we do this without causing a lot of Kiowa blood to spill."

"Lone Wolf," said Big Bow, seated beside Eagle Heart, "we can do nothing brave if we are not ready to spill Kiowa blood."

His pride was pricked. He, a proven warrior of many battles with not only the Caddo, Tonkawa and Pawnee, but with the white man as well. Lone Wolf's back straightened. "Do not lecture me, Big Bow. There is not a morning that will come as long as I live that I cannot match the bravest of you here. There is not a night fire to come that the stories of my coups will not overshadow the coups of any man in this lodge. Only Satanta's record in war is greater than mine! Not yours—not any man's here. Do you wish to challenge that truth, Big Bow?"

"Big Bow is only zealous, Lone Wolf," explained Eagle Heart, placing a hand on his young friend's shoulder. "He meant no challenge—"

"I must hear it from his lips," Lone Wolf demanded.

Big Bow struggled at first, then finally relented with an apology, "I meant no challenge to my chief."

"We are all as one in this," Lone Wolf told the hushed ring of counselors and head men. "No man must shy from the very good prospect that he will die when next we go into the white man's fort. It will be then that we free our chiefs!"

Most keened their war songs or trilled their tongues with victory shouts or yipped like coyotes.

"We must bring a few women with us!" shouted Gui-tain.

"Why?" asked Lone Wolf.

"The white man will see the women and never be suspicious of our plans to fight."

"This is good," Lone Wolf agreed. "Bring a dozen women to come to the white man's council with our warriors. And give those women guns to carry under their blankets."

"Will the Comanche join us in our plan?" asked Red Otter.

"You must ask them," Kicking Bird replied before anyone else could. His voice had grown hard, for the first time in many winters, like the sharp edges of granite. "Go to them in the morning and tell them of our desire to include them in freeing our chiefs. They will be there when we pull our guns and shoot the white men at the tables—the Comanche deserve to know that we plan to spill our blood rather than bend down to kiss the dirty boots of the lying white men who have betrayed me for the last time!"

"Tell the Comanche we will make war together!" shouted Eagle Heart.

"Just as we have in days gone by," said Big Bow, "Kiowa and Comanche fighting side by side! It is powerful medicine!"

"Then we are all agreed on this plan?" Lone Wolf asked, looking at his old friend.

"Yes," answered Kicking Bird in that lodge heavy with renewed silence. "All we must do is to decide on the details. If the white man will not do as he promised, if he will not give us back our chiefs voluntarily —then we will take Satanta and Big Tree back by force."

While the Kiowa and Comanche were meeting to plan war, the white man met to smooth the way for peace.

As much as Davis had promised his constituents back home and those influential stockmen who had accompanied him north to the reservation that he would hold firm to his demands of the Indians, the governor finally gave in under a relentless crusade led not only by Commissioner Smith and Superintendent Hoag, but with the lobbying of the Kiowa-Comanche agent, James Haworth himself.

"After all, Davis told them," explained Sharp Grover, just back from a late-night meeting in Lieutenant Colonel Davidson's office, "Haworth would be the man on the spot, right here—the one responsible for making the whole bargain work for both the tribes and the government."

"You think he can do it?" Seamus Donegan asked.

"I figure he's got the cut of a man who'll give it a hell of a try, Irishman."

"What's Davis and his crowd think now?" Stillwell asked Grover.

"He's been persuaded."

"Finally, eh?" Jack said.

"What they going to do now?" Seamus asked. "They left the tribes pretty stirred up over that matter of the army keeping the two chiefs if the camps didn't bring in five hostages."

"From the looks of it, Davis realizes now he backed the tribes into a corner—where they had no choice but to cower or fight. Damned politicians anyways," Grover muttered. "They can't get it through their thick heads that a Injun cornered ain't about to turn tail."

"He'll fight if he's cornered, won't he, Sharp?"

Grover nodded at Stillwell. "The army can't catch 'em—but them warriors aren't running just because their bowels turned to water. They're running to stay ahead of the soldiers and to fight another day."

"Looks like Davis and the army got to convince the tribes to sit back down for another peace council now," Seamus said.

Grover nodded. "The lieutenant colonel is sending Phil McCusker to the villages this evening to ask them to come in for another talk tomorrow morning."

"That soon?" Jack asked.

"This thing goes on any longer," Grover replied, "tempers getting hotter and hotter—it's likely to mean some blood spilled on that parade out there."

The eighth of October. An autumn sun shown brightly on the many-hued leaves of the surrounding countryside encompassing Medicine Bluff and Cache creeks. The air itself captured the coming of winter, if not the chance of hope.

This time the chiefs and warriors from the two tribes assembled on the ground near the white man's tables in a much more sullen and hostile mood than they had for the last council. Women were among the crowd, making Seamus feel a bit more at ease, although he did not like the eyes of most of those warriors who milled about between the seated chiefs and the cordon of buffalo soldiers Lieutenant Colonel Davidson had ordered out to ring the parade.

Something did not feel right as the Irishman stepped up beside Jack Stillwell and Sharp Grover, waving them behind the council tent with him.

"What is it?" Grover asked in a whisper.

"I don't know," Donegan admitted. "I just don't like the idea of you two being up there with all them officials if all hell breaks loose."

"You figure there's trouble brewing, don't you?" Stillwell inquired.

"Just humor me, boys. And come with me over to Sergeant Waller's outfit."

The pair followed Donegan as the council got under way.

This time Governor Davis rose and addressed the tribes without any preliminaries or introductions, beginning even before Satanta and Big Tree had reached their chairs near the end of the long tables.

"I wish to announce to the great leaders of your tribes that I have reconsidered my demands delivered two days ago. Instead of waiting for the five raiders to be turned over to us . . . instead of waiting for all your people to come in to the reservation— I will now turn over your chiefs to your care."

At the governor's direction, the guards shuffled their two prisoners forward. With a rustle of chains, Davidson's buffalo soldiers helped the chiefs from their shackles. The pair stood but a moment, rubbing wrists while the soldiers removed the irons from their ankles. That done, they looked with uncertainty at the Texas governor.

"You are free to return to your people," Davis explained magnanimously, then waited for McCusker to translate. "Tell the two they are free men—yet they remain responsible to us for seeing that their men do not raid into Texas any longer."

With a wide grin and undisguised pleasure, McCusker translated the decree into Kiowa. Seamus watched apprehensively as the chiefs made their way to their people. Everyone seemed stunned, except Davis and his staff, all of whom stood smiling at the reunion. It took a moment for the sudden release to sink in before the Kiowa rushed forward, chattering, singing, greeting their chiefs with joy.

"McCusker," called Commissioner E. P. Smith, waving the interpreter over. "I want you to inform the chiefs that I will be holding a meeting with them about three o'clock."

"You want them here?"

"Yes."

"Should I tell them why you're calling them here again?"

Smith appeared agitated at the answer. "All we've done is free the chiefs, McCusker. We haven't begun to make a lasting peace with these people. Tell them the demands still hold—and Lone Wolf's guarantee of those demands will stand as well. We have done what we said we would: releasing their chiefs. Now it is up to the tribes to do what they said they would to satisfy all our demands."

McCusker flicked his knowing eyes at Grover, Stillwell and Donegan as the trio came up.

"I figure there's no better time to give an Injun bad news than when he's celebrating good news—is there, Sharp?" McCusker joked sourly.

"Let's hope the Kiowa and Comanche decide to go along with what Lone Wolf guaranteed these government fellas here," Grover replied.

When the sun had slipped halfway from mid-sky to the western horizon that afternoon, the chiefs and warriors again assembled, but not on the parade by the Sibley tent this time. Instead the Indians were directed by buffalo soldiers to the Fort Sill commissary, where blankets had been spread for the red dignitaries. What was more, this time Satanta and Big Tree sat squarely among their fellow leaders, looking gravely on the long table of white faces above starched collars or blue tunics. So many Indians had come that fully a third had to watch the proceedings from outside the commissary, contenting themselves with standing on the porch, where they crowded at doorways and windows when Commissioner Smith rose to speak.

"We do not need to be here long," began the stern Quaker, glancing at McCusker to begin his translation. "You will remember the demands the government made of your bands two days ago. It is most important that you remember that you guaranteed to turn over to us five of the raiders who stole and killed across the Red River into Texas."

There arose a disquieting murmur and shuffling among those Indians crowded into the tight commissary. Donegan eased his hand beneath the holster flap, finding the pistol butt small comfort at this anxious moment. Blankets were being loosened among those in the room.

"You have been asked to turn five of the guilty over within twenty-four hours," Smith continued. "But you have failed to live up to your end of the bargain. You now have the next twenty-four hours to comply with this demand. Until this time tomorrow and no longer."

"Or what?" demanded Lone Wolf, who stood suddenly from his place beside Satanta. "Or you will try to take back our chiefs?" He laughed loudly. "I think not, white man. We gave you our word that we would bring you five of the guilty Comanche . . . but that was when we were told our chiefs would be freed."

"We freed your chiefs. But you did not bring us the five murderers."

"You freed our chiefs this morning, white man. We are not so foolish as to think your demands began two days ago!"

"Lone Wolf is a fool if he thinks we will not put teeth into this demand," Smith snapped, attempting a show of muscle. "You promised—and you will be a liar if you do not comply!"

McCusker had a hard time spitting out the word for fool, especially the word for *liar*. Those two expressions crashed harshly on the ears of those in the room and on the porch.

Lone Wolf waved down much of the angry, noisy protest as many blankets slid from the shoulders of both Kiowa and Comanche in the crowded room. Seamus glanced at the windows and doorways, realizing this would be a bad fix when it came to shooting in a matter of heartbeats. Not knowing what could save the bloodshed, he listened helplessly to McCusker's translation of Lone Wolf's next words.

"You gave us one day to bring you the five raiders. We will bring you five at this time tomorrow. No sooner. And, as true as I am to my word—no later than that. I will not play foolish with you . . . the way the Tehan chief played liar for us."

"You sound like a crybaby, Lone Wolf!" sneered Smith. "Complaining that you don't have enough time."

McCusker had trouble translating the white official's expression into Kiowa, but when it came out with the interpretation of a squalling, spoiled infant, exactly as Smith had intended it to, Lone Wolf appeared stung for the first time.

At the doorway, many of the young men who had overheard the explanation of the term clamored to get into the tight room. Some shouted to spill white blood in general.

Eagle Heart's voice rose above the others' as he cried out. "Lone Wolf—let me kill the old white fool who wants to kill our young men who go raiding into Tehas!"

"Blood's gonna spill—you don't shut your mouth, Commissioner!" growled Philip McCusker.

"How dare these savages question me!" Smith roared back above the commotion in the room heated with too many bodies and sudden anger. "I'm the one who can save their godless souls!"

"McCusker's right!" said Lieutenant Colonel Davidson. The officer raised one arm, yelling for silence, while with his other he started to nudge Smith to the rear. "Calm them down best you can, McCusker."

"Take your hands off me!" Smith snapped, drawing back from the officer.

"Your kind always does this, don't you, Commissioner?"

"What are you—"

"Goes and gets trouble started because of your pigheaded attitudes . . . then leaves it for the army to come in and clean up your idiotic mistakes."

As McCusker was hollering above the first rows of council delegates, Lone Wolf and Kicking Bird were shouting as well, all three attempting to calm the enraged warriors.

"You will each get a chance to talk when your time comes," McCusker tried to explain to the youthful hotbloods. "When the chiefs have talked, then you will have your say."

"I wish to speak to the white peace-talker with the heavy tongue."

McCusker and the others, both white and Kiowa, turned to find a young Comanche chief getting to his feet amid the rest of his people seated on the plank floor.

"You are Cheevers?" asked the interpreter.

"I am," the young warrior answered.

"Who is this?" inquired Superintendent Hoag.

"He is a powerful chief of one of the Comanche bands," replied agent James Haworth. "I'm praying he can calm things. Phil, tell Cheevers he can talk."

The young chief with expressive eyes and a rigid spine stepped from the crowd with a rustle of his blanket and stopped before the white peace delegates.

"Tell this Washington chief that I am a Comanche and that my people have been doing no wrong. We should not be asked to pay for any wrong done by the young men of other bands. I know there are bad men among all people—among white men as well as among red men. But among my people there are those who persist in doing these bad things contrary to the orders of the chiefs. These warriors are rene-gades whom we have cast out from our villages. They are the raiders who are bringing all this trouble onto our shoulders."

"Do you know where they are, Cheevers?" asked McCusker.

The Comanche chief regarded his own warriors be-fore he answered. "You will find them west of the Antelope Hills. Have your buffalo soldiers round them up soon. Understand that you may keep them as long as you choose, but do not ask these good men of either tribe to sacrifice themselves for the evil done by others."

"No!"

The room reverberated with the shout, every man turning his attention to Black Horse, a war-chief in Cheever's band.

"Yes—this must be, Black Horse!" argued the chief.

"Let the white man come to understand pain, Cheevers!" Black Horse repeatedly beat his chest with a fist, his other hand shaking his repeating rifle provocatively. Many of the other warriors from both tribes were stirred by this demonstration, muttering angrily, readying weapons for the showdown sure to come.

But just when all seemed ready to spill into a bloodbath, a half-dozen old Comanche warriors rose as one and pushed their way through the crowd of youthful belligerents to ring Black Horse. There, without a word, they seized the young provocateur and escorted him roughly from the council room. His angry protests gradually faded from the parade as an uneasy quiet settled over the entire assembly.

Into the unsettling quiet Kicking Bird rose and agreed with what the Comanche chief had declared to the white man. When he sat, a Kiowa sub-chief, Woman's Heart, spoke his mind, in sympathy with Cheevers' words.

Then the Comanche chief stood to speak again, looking this time not at Commissioner Smith, but at Lieutenant Colonel Davidson. "I make this offer to you, soldier chief. I—Cheevers—will lead your buffalo soldiers toward the Antelope Hills in search of the renegades who are responsible for all this trouble between our peoples and the Tehannas."

"You aren't going to get anything better than that, Mr. Smith," Davidson advised. "You'd better take this chief up on his offer, or prepare to have your Quaker peace policy go up in smoke down here on the southern plains."

"I don't think the whole program—"

"I've said my piece, Smith. And, by God, I'm going to let Washington know what I think of your pig-headed priggishness. Now, tell Cheevers you're agreeing."

It was clear to everyone in that room watching the commissioner that Smith had trouble swallowing down his pride. At last he spoke in subdued tones to the assembly.

"Cheevers will lead the colonel's soldiers in search of these raiders causing all the trouble. I will give the Comanche chief thirty days to bring in five of those renegades responsible. If, after the end of thirty days, there are no results—then I will withhold monthly rations and not issue annuities to all bands."

"You would not feed our children?" Kicking Bird asked, staring incredulous at Smith.

The commissioner sneered, finding himself in possession of the upper hand once more. "Bring me the raiders—and your children will not go hungry."

Chapter 21

"*Y*ou seriously think that Comanche chief will find any of the raiders?" Seamus Donegan asked the other two civilians at their smoky breakfast fire.

Jack Stillwell looked up, wagging his head "Cheevers is a Yamparika. They might be looking for warriors from other bands—but I figure he and his bunch will lead Reuben Waller's brunettes on a merry chase, but never find nothing."

"No matter where Cheevers leads Waller," added Sharp Grover, nodding, "they'll never find a sign."

"So he's pulling a fast shuffle on the government officials?"

Grover shook his head. "No. It's just because he's a Yamparika."

"What's that?" Donegan asked.

"One of the Comanche bands," Grover answered.

"And a Yamparika will never be able to track down and find the Antelope Eaters."

"So who are these Antelope Eaters?" Seamus asked, rising, stretching and tossing out the last of his coffee gone cold.

"The worst of the lot," Stillwell answered. "Called Kwahadi. Running under a chief named Quanah.

Word has it his mother was white as you and me. Took from her people when she was a girl. Growed up with the band. But make no mistake, Seamus— from the stories I've heard, this Quanah can't have a single drop of white blood in him, from the way he's sworn to kill white men."

"You figure it's time to go, Jack?" Grover suggested, rising as well. "This is your show, but I consider we should get moving south. You're the one needing to be back at Fort Richardson before the last week of the month."

"That's when the easterners I'm guiding, Pierce and Graves, ordered me to be back," Stillwell explained, kicking dirt over the firepit and smothering the flames. "Besides, that's when the new escort assigned us should be riding in from Fort Griffin to relieve that first bunch."

"You got any better idea who the hell this Pierce and Graves are?" Grover inquired as all three laid saddle blankets atop their mounts and began saddling up.

Stillwell shook his head. "They been real close-mouthed about everything but their names—and that they're the ones giving out the orders."

"Jack loves a secret," Grover said to Donegan with a wag of his head. "Damn, but them two make a man suspicious of what they're up to. Government fellas out here where they don't belong."

"They surveyors you figure?" Seamus asked.

"No," Grover replied. "For sure they got themselves a passel of maps, they do. But—they ain't like any other government fellas I ever knew in many a year of working for the army. Damn well keeping their secret squeezed tight in their grubby little hands, ain't they?"

"That's just what this is, Sharp—a secret," Seamus

replied, drawing up the cinch. "They're government, no doubt of that. And the lieutenant in charge of the last escort let it be known them two work for the bureau."

"Indian Bureau?" Grover asked.

"The only bureau I know of," Stillwell replied. "Those last few days there in Jacksboro before we rode over to Dallas to fetch Satanta and Big Tree—I can't remember them two doing anything else but camping out over at the telegraph office."

Donegan nodded. "Day and night. Sending and receiving. Would make a man wonder, I'll say."

"Who they wiring to?"

"Don't know, Sharp. They're playing everything so close to the vest."

Stillwell nodded as he finished strapping his bedroll behind his saddle. "They don't let them canvas valises of theirs out of their sight at all. Right under their arms or plopped on the table beside them when they eat."

"Bet those pilgrims sleep with the valises too!" Grover hooted.

"And their maps," Donegan added.

"They got maps?" Grover sounded intrigued.

"I suppose that's what it is they keep rolled up in a long, leather tube," Jack said. "Saw one of the maps once—walked in on 'em before they knew I was coming to tell 'em we were pulling out. They both rolled it up quicker'n quail spooks into flight."

"What I can't put straight is what the government's looking for down south toward Mexico anyway?" Donegan inquired.

"That where they're gonna lead you two?" Grover asked.

"They informed me of that back in Kansas—that this trip of ours might take them as far south as the

Rio Grande," Jack answered. "Said that if they had to cross on over into Mexico—they'd see to it we got the required papers for the military escort to cross the river and push on into foreign country."

Grover scratched at his jawbone, taking up the reins to his horse. "Mexico. Well, my friends. Sounds serious—and it looks like it could be a long trip for you both."

"For Jack," Donegan protested as he climbed to the saddle. "I came along to see you, Sharp. Not to go riding off to Mexico."

"Shit, Irishman," Stillwell said, smiling as he nudged his mount away from their camping spot on the south bank of the Red River, once more plodding south, deeper into north Texas. "If I was to tell you about the aquardiente them Mexicans make down there—you'd likely do more'n just lick your lips for a taste."

"What's aquardiente?" Seamus asked. "Some type of Mexican food?"

Grover chuckled. "Hell no, Seamus. That's Mexican whiskey so powerful it comes on like a crack of lightning. Brewed from corn and strong enough to pop the top of your skull."

"Sounds mighty good, fellas. Where's a man gonna find some aquardiente?"

"Plenty of it down south where we'll likely head," Stillwell said. "But since you plan on busting up this partnership—looks like I'll just have to drink your share."

"Bring some back with you, Jack," Donegan suggested with a grin.

Grover chuckled, then said, "How 'bout one of them dark-skinned señoritas too, Seamus?"

"Mexican women any good once you get 'em

skinned and down in the blankets with you, Jack?"
asked Donegan.

Stillwell shrugged. "I wouldn't know, Irishman.
Never had a Mexican gal before."

"And besides, the Irishman won't be dealing with
no Mexican whores," Sharp protested, "Seamus
Donegan is already called for."

The other two looked quizzically at Grover. Jack
was the first to speak. "What you mean—Seamus is
called for?"

"Samantha Pike's got her mind set on making the
Irishman a honest-to-goodness husband, appears to
me."

"Appears to you?" Donegan squeaked.

"She's aiming to make you hers, Seamus. Plain
and simple," Grover declared.

"Samantha tell you this?"

"She didn't have to. Rebecca told me."

Donegan felt his face go flush, becoming hot and
prickly, wondering if Grover knew . . . or Rebecca
knew . . . maybe Samantha actually had told her
sister of the night that began on Sharp Grover's
porch and ended up on a few blankets tossed care-
lessly atop some freshly mown grass stacked in the
corner of Grover's lopsided barn.

For the longest moment Seamus studied the older
man, peering at him for any clue that might betray
Grover's knowledge of that night.

"Reb . . . Rebecca told you about Samantha
wanting to get her hooks in me?"

Grover nodded, grinning as he threw a punch at
the Irishman. "Stupid mick. Where the hell you think
I come up with an idea like that—all on my own?
Samantha told my wife!"

Donegan shrugged. "I suppose I'm just a bit put-off
at the woman talk behind my back, is all."

Then Seamus studied the country ahead as it opened up to them, helplessly thinking on Samantha Pike. Remembering with such vividness the full, vital fleshiness of her body and how she had given herself to him so willingly, with such a fury that it had startled him.

With a hunger that had matched his own. A ravenous, insatiable hunger.

Simon Pierce had gladly escaped a muggy summer in Washington City.

And now that the promise of success loomed that much closer on the horizon, Pierce believed the excruciating discomfort he had suffered traveling through this savage frontier might not all be for naught.

The ancient map might not be a hoax.

At first he and other scholars had truly believed it was some very sophisticated and well-executed ruse. Nothing more than a well-contrived hoax on the world's scientific community, but albeit an elaborate hoax dating back centuries . . . a historical practical joke nonetheless.

Now, it appeared of late that the brittle parchment map and its cryptic promise were not some ancient jokester's plan to laugh at them from beyond the grave.

Simon Pierce had been brought onto the small team at the Smithsonian when the map first made its appearance, and only then because he was the country's foremost scholar on the most ancient of Castilian dialects.

But by the time Pierce had been brought down to Washington City from his native New England, the others had covered a lot of ground. Enough of it by then that Pierce and fellow researcher William

Graves could plan a trip to the Great Plains, far from the security and creature comforts of the East Coast that was all the two men had ever known.

From his study of the ancient dialect used on the map, Pierce grew certain of its richness, either as a joke or as a true linchpin in locating what would prove to be an unbelievable treasure. A mother lode, only hinted at and whispered about in every schoolboy's history of the exploration of the New World. Until now, Simon knew the map could only have been compiled by one who had a command of the old tongue—the language of the most royal of Spanish conquistadors.

But in the last two days conclusions the two had come to here in this hovel called Fort Richardson and highly secret discoveries made back east in the lamplit cellars and dusty archives of the institute itself told Pierce and Graves that the map had to be genuine. The ancients were pointing their fingers to Indian country where untold wealth beckoned from beyond the grave.

The pair would soon be walking on ground where the great explorers once stood . . . looking at the landforms as the conquistadors had. Not for the purposes of discovery in this new and foreign land had the Spaniards come but to look instead for a place to hide their most valuable treasure.

It was enough to raise the hairs on the back of his neck—to one day soon be close enough to feel the presence of those ghosts, countless soldiers left behind on the long marches, their bones left to bleach in the eternal sun.

Pierce pitied those expendable men, the mighty right arm of the ancient Spanish Empire. But now that military might had eroded and Spain was nothing more than a mere shadow of what greatness it had once experienced. Simon understood the need for expendable men—the soldiers and civilians who guided early explorers across the trackless wastes of this godforsaken land. Those guides too were most expendable when the time came.

Yes, with Spain's economy a thin shell of what it once was, it had not been hard to convince the poor and venal Spanish scholars to free the map once enough American money had been coughed up and put on the table.

That's where Graves had come in, and proved his worth.

A member of a wealthy family from which he inherited a sincere interest in ancient Spain and exploration of the New World three centuries before, William Graves had both redeeming and despicable qualities, if Simon Pierce was to admit it. While Graves was indeed born to countless riches accumulated through generations of savvy entrepreneurs who bankrolled America's early decades, Graves had known enough of the ancient archaeology to actually make himself invaluable to the entire research project as well. And, when a great amount of money was needed by the institute to purchase the map—more so to bribe the Spaniard in Barcelona who said he would let it slip through his hands if the price were right—William Graves assured the institute he could put his hands on the required amount.

In a week Graves was back with every last American dollar required by the institute to secretly acquire the ancient map from its Spanish caretaker. The money, and a contract that required signatures of the institute's directors, demanding a four percent per annum charge for the luxury of borrowing against the possibility that the map might actually be the genuine article.

Graves had known all along, Simon Pierce thought now as his fingers once more brushed lightly over its parchment surface. He looked at the bowed head of the other man as Graves studied more of the northwest corner of the map, comparing and recomparing the lines and landforms and watercourses between it and the most recent of surveys performed by government crews sent out to prepare the way for the coming of the railroad to Santa Fe.

The railroad had been laid—from Kansas down to the territory of New Mexico . . . across the corner of a stretch of unforgiving wilderness some called the Staked Plain, what others called the Llano Estacado. And little had those filthy-rich railroad barons known that they had passed through a country rich with possibilities.

Pierce did not like Graves that much, but he would never tell the man. For all his upbringing, all his wealth and position, Graves was a renegade historian —not content to believe and study and reinforce what his betters had proven to be scientific fact. History was, after all, just that—scientific fact. But then, Simon thought, only the wealthy had enough aplomb, or downright nastiness to go against the established grain. And only then if they had the venal side William Graves did.

But that was exactly why Simon Pierce liked Graves at times. Because they had that trait of venality in common. Both had begun this quest fully realizing it as the search of the centuries: a chance to turn the scholars of the civilized world on their ears. And by now, what with the correlations of the Barcelona map to the most recent topographical surveys, along with the continuing efforts to decode the inscriptions at the border of the map by scholars back at the institute in Washington City—it appeared both Pierce and

Graves stood not only to make themselves a reputation that would shine resplendent in the scientific and historical texts for all time, but stood to make themselves some of the richest men in the history of the world.

"Excuse me, Mr. Pierce?"

Graves and Pierce quickly drew the sheet of crimson velvet over the old map as soon as the first syllable had come from the soldier's mouth when he presented himself at their tent flaps. Simon turned, disturbed.

"Yes? What is it?"

"Colonel Mackenzie asked me to come over to see if you'd care to dine with him again this evening."

Pierce looked down at Graves, who was gazing up at him, smiling.

"Yes. I believe we will," William Graves answered. "Don't you think it would be a good idea, Simon? Tonight is, after all, our last night here at dear old Fort Richardson."

"There, you have your answer . . . Lieutenant, isn't it?"

"Yessir. Colonel Mackenzie's adjutant."

"Thank you, Lieutenant," Pierce said. "I never served myself, so I never got the meaning of the different ranks. You were in the war, Lieutenant?"

"No, sir," the young officer answered with resignation. "Wasn't old enough before Appomattox. But I satisfy myself by listening to the colonel's stories. The others regale me with their experiences whipping the Johnnies in fine fashion, from Manassas to the Georgia campaign."

"I bought my way out," Graves said, quite matter-of-factly. "Money can do that, you know. As far as I understand, the taker of my bounty was killed at Gettysburg. A nasty affair I've heard."

The young officer blanched, his mouth moving wordlessly until he said, "I'll see you both for dinner at the colonel's quarters."

"Will Mackenzie have that soldier who plays the mouth harp there, as well as the one who sings so beautifully?" Pierce asked, remembering past dinners at the colonel's.

"Yes," the lieutenant answered. Clearly distressed at Graves's disclosure, the young man fled and the flaps fell behind him in his leave-taking.

"Why did you do that, Graves?"

He looked up at Pierce, his face as innocent as the day he had been born. "Do what, my dear Simon?"

"That young man idolizes those other, proven soldiers. He probably dreams of campaigns filled with gleaming sabers and daring men and mighty, painted red savages screeching past on horseback."

"And what, Simon? Did I puncture his martial fantasies—let the air out of his schoolboy's dream by giving him a dose of cold reality? Yes, and I damned well enjoyed it too. These military types bore me. Were it not for the fact that we need them, and those unseemly civilian guides—"

"What, William? What would you do? Go off on your own into that savage country . . ." and Pierce jabbed a finger down on the map usually protected from view, wrapped in the blood-colored velvet he began to stuff inside the long leather map tube, "go off by yourself into that land teeming with evil, grinning Comanches?"

Graves grinned that charming, handsome smile of his, pushing one of the black curls back out of his eyes. Pierce hated Graves for his good looks. It seemed the wealthy did have it all.

"Simon . . . dear Simon. One of these days, we won't have to worry about needing anyone else to help us. One of these days—and very soon—you and I will be rich enough . . . we'll own our own god-damned army—because you and I will own and run our own goddamned country!''

Chapter 22

Late October 1873

"You . . . you want me to guide you two where?"

Jack Stillwell had trouble with few of his faculties, and hearing simply wasn't one he had ever experienced problems with in his life. In fact, his acute sense of hearing had protected both him and old Pierre Trudeau back to '68 when they walked more than a hundred miles on foot through Cheyenne-infested high plains wilderness to deliver word that the survivors of Major Sandy Forsyth's fifty white scouts were pinned down on a nameless island in the middle of a nameless river.*

So Jack had heard Simon Pierce plain enough the first time.

"I said we have changed our plans, Mr. Stillwell," said the older man. "Or, more to the point—our plans have been changed for us. We need you to take us north by west from here. At each night's camp we'll review with you the march for the following day."

"You'll review for me the march for the following

day?" Jack asked, disbelieving his ears, as good as they were.

"Every stream and creek and river we cross," Pierce went on. "We'll tell you where to go from here."

"I'd like to tell you where you can go, Pierce," Stillwell snapped as Seamus Donegan came up, having finished saddling his horse for departure. "Both of you with your starched collars and nasty tones."

"To Hell, I imagine," William Graves said in that engagingly civil tone of his.

"As a matter of fact—"

"You aren't planning on going down toward the Rio Grande and Mexico now?" Donegan asked the two easterners.

Pierce glanced at him as if the Irishman was an unwanted intruder. "No. We no longer need to explore territory south toward Mexico." He turned on Stillwell. "Are you going to lead us, Mr. Stillwell? Or am I going to have to acquire the services of another guide here at Fort Richardson or in nearby Jacksboro?"

"There's a lot of 'em might think about taking your money and guiding you from here south to the Rio Grande," Jack told them. "But if you're hoping to find a guide to lead you northwest of here—I doubt you'll find any takers."

"The money's very good," Graves added, regarding an old scab on the back of his hand.

Stillwell gazed a long time at the strikingly handsome, black-headed William Graves. "I don't doubt that the money is very good. And I planned on having me some of it. But I plan on living long enough to enjoy that money you two say the government's going to pay me for guiding you. So, thanks . . . but no thanks. You'll have to find yourself another fool."

Stillwell had turned, shoving past a bewildered Donegan, the Irishman's face showing only confusion, when Simon Pierce's voice stopped him in his tracks among the pack animals Jack was breaking out.

"The money aside, Mr. Stillwell . . . you still understand this is government business."

"It might be, Pierce," Jack replied, flinging his voice over his shoulder as he worked to free the knots binding his belongings to the cross-buck pack saddle. "But it's none of my business any longer."

"That means the federal government, Stillwell," Graves spoke this time. "The army. Federal prison. And I have the power to put you there. Do you understand now, Stillwell?"

Jack turned, feeling his neck gone hot with rage. Nothing else could possibly be the cause, as the sun had barely peeked over the horizon this hazy, cloudy morning. "I see your point, Mr. Graves," he replied, striding back up to the civilian with a grin that evidently put both Graves and Pierce at ease. "If I don't guide you—you'll have me arrested and thrown in Mackenzie's guardhouse on some trumped-up charge, because you've got the power to make these soldiers dance."

Pierce wagged his head, rubbing his hands together and clearly enjoying his advantage. "Not some imaginary charge—a very real one. You were hired by the federal government to do a job. You don't walk out in the middle of that job without suffering the consequences."

"C'mon, Jack," Seamus said. "It's nothing to become riled about. In fact, I'm relieved we aren't marching south all the way to Mexico. Never really wanted to see the place anyway, meself."

Jack looked at Donegan. "You don't realize where they want us to head, do you?"

Seamus shrugged. "Northwest of here. That makes it Texas, unless you push all the way to Colorado. And I've been there before."

Stillwell shook his head. "We'll never make it to Colorado Territory, you dumb Irishman."

"Why not?" Donegan's brow knitted up. "What's out there in Texas got you so riled up?"

"The federal government fellas back in Washington City may think of that stretch of country out there as Texas. Everyone might call it Texas. Yeah, and Governor Davis and his Texicans may think of that panhandle as Texas too. But that don't change things a hoot when it comes to who really runs things out there."

"Only buffalo and a few old Indians on their last legs—unable to relinquish their ancient practices," Pierce sneered, then chuckled with Graves.

"There's buffalo there, no doubt about it," Jack said.

"I'm hungry already," Donegan said, apparently not understanding.

"But Seamus—the Indians out there aren't old. And there's more'n just a few of 'em."

"What bands roam and hunt out there, Jack?" Donegan asked, his eyes gone serious.

"Renegade Kiowa—young warriors bolting off the reservation from Satanta's and Lone Wolf's bands." He waited a heartbeat. "And the Kwahadi Comanche. They're led by Quanah Parker—and that's one chief never come in for a white man's present, or eaten a mouth of white man's food yet that I know of —unless he ate it from a settler's wagon or soddy before his warriors burned it to the ground."

"Yes, Quanah Parker is the name," Pierce replied.

"He's the leader of the Antelope Eaters band that roams the Llano Estacado."

"Llano?" Donegan asked.

"Staked Plains," Pierce answered.

"In all likelihood," Graves said, "the landform was named for the tall stakes that Coronado had his soldiers drive into the ground to find their way back out of that trackless, mapless wilderness."

"Hold on a minute," Seamus said, shaking his head dully. "You want Stillwell to lead you someplace where some guy named Coronado put some stakes in the ground to find his own way back out? How can Stillwell guide you if this Coronado needed some bleeming wooden stakes to lead him back out? And why don't you just go find this Coronado fella to guide you in there—so you'll leave me friend Stillwell alone."

Jack watched Pierce and Graves chuckle at that, before Pierce got serious once more.

"We've got work to do, gentlemen," Pierce said. "There is no one else who will do. And, for your information, Mr. Donegan—Coronado is currently unavailable to guide us."

Graves laughed sharp and harsh, as if it were his own private joke shared only with Pierce. "He's dead —some three hundred years, Mr. Donegan."

"Three hundred—"

"Are you going to guide us, Mr. Stillwell?" Pierce asked, cutting off all other conversation. "Or shall I call for Colonel Mackenzie so that I can prefer federal charges against you both?"

"You don't understand, Pierce. What you're asking—"

"I understand you aren't going to guide us." He turned and immediately started toward the post commander's headquarters.

Stillwell snagged the older man's arm in desperation, hoping in some way to convince him of the danger. "You don't have no idea what you're going into, Pierce." The civilian glanced down at Jack's hands on his arm as the scout continued, "That's bad country out there. Never really been to the Llano myself, but I know enough who have, or knowed those who never came back."

"We have an escort, Mr. Stillwell."

"Them soldiers are just more honey for the bees, Pierce. Soldiers attack Injuns. And Comancheros. And the Injuns and Comancheros turn things around a time or two."

"What are Comancheros?"

Graves was there to answer, startling both Pierce and Stillwell with this obscure bit of knowledge for a rich man from the northeast. "Comancheros are Mexican renegades, Simon. Am I right, Mr. Stillwell?" He waited until Jack nodded. "They are the middlemen of the southern plains. Dealing in stolen property of all descriptions: cattle, horses, trade goods. Even human flesh."

"Human flesh?" Pierce asked.

"Slave trade . . . human misery—prostitution, if you will," Graves replied, a twinkle in his eye.

Pierce turned to Stillwell, his eyes boring into the young scout's. "Are these Comancheros any worse than Parker's Comanches or the renegade Kiowa running off the reservation?"

"No, not really. They're no worse. Like the Comanche, the Comancheros love killing just for the sake of killing."

"Then we won't be deterred, Stillwell," Graves said, turning on Pierce. "Simon, let's get this guide placed in the guardhouse so we can acquire the services of another."

"You're asking everyone who rides along with you to take a gamble on getting killed out there," Stillwell pleaded, as afraid of the guardhouse as he was of what was out there on the Staked Plains. "It's suicide you're asking. There's more murderers and butchers out there than there is fat, blood-sucking ticks on an old bull's hide."

"Are you guiding us or not, Mr. Stillwell?" Pierce snapped. "We don't have time to stand here talking about buffalo hides with you."

"That's Injun country out there. Give to the Comanche and Kiowa and Southern Cheyenne fair and square by treaty."

"What's your point, Stillwell?" asked Graves.

His eyes pleaded with the two civilians. "White men aren't allowed out there in Injun country."

Pierce laughed a moment. "White men may not be allowed, Stillwell. But the army is. And where you're going to guide us, that land—that great buffalo range —is still owned by the United States government. Not by some smelly, red savage reeking of urine and tallow. It belongs to us, Stillwell—men like Graves and me. Now, are you two guiding us there or not?"

Jack looked at Donegan a moment before answering, then turned back to the two government men.

"If you're dead set on rooting around until you find something out there in Kwahadi country, I'll guide you where you want to go. But I want you both to know you're probably going to come up with more out there than either of you ever bargained for."

Pierce smiled broadly and clapped his hands together, excited as a child on Christmas morning. "That's exactly what we want to do on this journey, Mr. Stillwell. To come up with more than either of us ever bargained for."

* * *

North to the Red River they followed Jack Stillwell.
After crossing into the southern fringe of the Kiowa-
Comanche reservation, they marched along the north
bank of the Red, an ancient trail that took them west
by northwest, ever toward the northern reaches of
the Staked Plain, the great wilderness haunted by the
Kwahadi Comanche and the Kiowa.

That Indian country had now become the southernmost reaches of the "Great Slaughter Pen," as the
buffalo range was becoming known. With alarming
rapidity the animal was disappearing from its normal
ranges. Two years before that fall, the U.S. Biological
Survey had sent out an expedition staffed with pro-
fessors from Yale University to survey the great Republican herd roaming along the Platte River in
Nebraska. George Bird Grinnell was camped west of
Fort Kearney when he had the chance to count what
remained of the herd—no less than 500,000 head.

Yet at the rate the hide hunters were cutting
through the herds, Grinnell estimated the buffalo
were nonetheless clearly in their final days.

In 1872 a government reconnaissance party had
marched south from Fort Dodge to Camp Supply in
Indian Territory and had never been out of sight of
buffalo. Hide hunters were as thick as ticks along the
Arkansas River itself, their big-bore rifles bringing
down the beasts as they came to water. By the end of
that season, when the buffalo migrated south for the
winter, both banks of the Arkansas reeked with rotting carcasses for more than fifty miles in either direction.

By the next year the hide-men were having to con-
template the wisdom of moving deeper and deeper
into Indian country, south of the dead line.

A minimum of two thousand hunters had spread
across the buffalo range, from the Dakotas to the

Staked Plain when the green grass burst forth from the brown breast of the prairie that spring of 1873. Many of those never did succeed as hunters: either their bones lay bleaching beneath the sun that year—a victim of one war-party or another—or they had simply "seen the elephant" and gave up the notion of making their fortune in hides.

Instead, most men with families to feed turned once more to farming. Anyone with around fourteen dollars, the price of a filing fee, could stake his claim to 160 acres of grassland where he would park his wagon, unhitch the milk cow, set free the chickens to scratching for bugs in the dirt, and begin digging at the tough soil to build a soddy on those immense plains. Better to face the incessant wind and rattle-snakes and grasshopper plagues and the alkali water . . . than face the screaming Comanche and the Kiowa.

Because of the exploding numbers of hunters, more than a few citizens on the western frontier began to express alarm. While Congress debated but never did pass any legislation banning the hunting of buffalo, Kansas, Wyoming, Idaho and Montana each passed laws either restricting or outlawing the killing of buffalo altogether. Lobbying against any attempt at this sort of legislation proved strong: the hide hunters had powerful and well-heeled allies in the railroad barons and their millions. For most months out of the year, at most railroad sidings in Nebraska and Kansas, rows of huge sheds stood filled to their rafters with not only hides but the bones as well—waiting for empty freight cars and a trip east.

If the Great Slaughter Pen was to be closed down, the railroads stood to lose a fortune.

But in the end it was not the railroad barons' money that turned the tide in Texas—it was the unvarnished sentimental appeal of none other than Lieutenant General Philip H. Sheridan himself.

When he learned that the Texas Legislature was preparing to enact a bill to outlaw the buffalo hunter within the state boundaries, Sheridan was carried nonstop, night and day by rail to Austin, there to stand before the assembly of legislators and protest the impending law. Impassioned, Sheridan flung his words at the lawmakers, telling them in no uncertain terms that instead of driving the hide hunters from their state, they should instead issue a bronze medal to each one who had crossed the dead line with his Sharps rifle.

"On one side of that medal you should engrave the image of a dead buffalo," Sheridan roared in their assembly. "On the other, the image of a starving Kiowa or Comanche!"

The bandy-legged Irishman repeatedly pounded his fist on the rostrum for quiet from the assembly he was hoping to sway with his sentiment.

"These hide-men have done more in the last two years, and will do more in the next year, to settle the vexed Indian question than the entire regular army has done in the last thirty years. The buffalo hunters are destroying the Indians' commissary; and it is a well-known fact that an army losing its base of supplies is placed at a great disadvantage. Send them powder and lead, if you will, but for the sake of lasting peace, let them kill, skin and sell until the buffaloes are exterminated! Then your prairies can be covered with speckled cattle and the festive cowboy, who follows the hunter as a second forerunner of an advancing civilization."

There was little debate when Sheridan stepped from the dais. The legislation once thought to be enacted into law failed to pass and the little general passed out cigars to the back-slapping state legislators.

The Secretary of the Interior, Columbus Delano, had also been deluged with complaints against the buffalo men. Yet he too approached the matter with clear-headed logic when he told his critics that the quicker the end to the buffalo, the quicker the Indian would learn to appreciate the merits of hard work and Christian industry.

There were few in that fall of 1873 who would take up the clarion on behalf of the Plains Indian. It was therefore left for the Kiowa and Cheyenne and Comanche to defend for themselves the hunting ground they had been granted by treaty.

The buffalo that roamed that great expanse of the Staked Plain belonged to the Indian who had for generations hunted them. To the nomadic horsemen, any white hunters who came to slaughter the beasts for their hides and occasionally the tongues were nothing more than common thieves. And the Indian had had himself enough experience living near the white man and his settlements to know what the white man did with rustlers and trespassers and thieves.

The Kiowa and Cheyenne and Comanche were learning at least one important lesson from the white man in what should be done to any and all of those trespassers who came to butcher the buffalo.

They would kill them.

Chapter 23

Moon of Deer Rutting, 1873

*T*he skies had turned a cold blue, and that meant the yellowleg soldiers would likely not be stalking the villages.

The Kwahadi had been harried for each of the past three summers, so much so this past summer that the bands had spent little time together after the great sun-gazing dance. Better that the bands disperse across the great vastness of the Staked Plain, to confuse the Tonkawa trackers who scouted for the yellowlegs.

Already the first winter storm had come to blanket the land. The snow had gone nearly as fast as it had come while the weather grew warm enough for the great buffalo hunt to begin.

But it had been many days now since Quanah Parker had sent out the young scouts to search for the herds. While they could ride quickly across the Staked Plain on their ponies, the village traveled much slower, dragging travois and the old ones along. When buffalo were spotted by the scouts, they were to set large signal fires, the smoke of which would serve as beacons for the village to follow.

There had been no signal fire for more than twenty days.

Again Quanah counted the knots he had tied in the long, thin rawhide whang he carried stuffed under his belt. One knot tied each night his people had failed to find signal smoke on the far horizons. Each night he prayed, and morning as well, that the new day would bring discovery of the great herd, for this was most strange—not finding the buffalo moving south toward its winter range.

"Quanah!"

Unmoving as he sat in the cold wind, the chief had been watching the young scout riding up on his winded pony for a long time now, having first found the youngster breaking the northern skyline far, far away.

"You have seen some smoke from the signal fires?" Quanah asked hopefully.

"No," and the youngster shook his head as he came to a halt. "No smoke."

"You have winded your pony for no reason?"

"I have seen something from the hill . . . there," and he pointed to the northeast, toward the land of the river the white man called the Canadian. "You must come see."

"Is this a good thing you want me to see, young one?"

Again the scout shook his head, as if ashamed, even afraid, to answer. He looked away, unable to confront the chief's gray eyes. "Come, Quanah. And behold."

Even before they reached the top of the ridge, Quanah knew.

One gently sloping hill after another they had put behind them, but he knew before they reached the top of the last one what the young scout wanted to show him.

Above, against the clear, winter sky, hung the lazy, big-winged birds. Predators—circling. The blue above was filled with their noisy protests and beating wings.

At the crest of the ridge, he saw. His pony fought the rawhide surcingle, its nostrils flaring at the overpowering stench. Both ponies attempted to back down the slope, but were held in check by their Comanche riders.

Littering the small valley that seemed to stretch endlessly below him, Quanah saw the thousands of carcasses.

So many of them, Grandfather Above! he thought to himself.

Around every one fluttered the busy vultures, while still more hung like black-winged evil against the sky above them, crying out in complaint, as if worried there would be no meat for them. Quanah knew there would be plenty for all the carrion eaters.

"Look at them, young one," Quanah said quietly, covering his mouth and nose with a bandanna and one hand to keep out what he could of the strong stench of this place. "The birds grow so fat on the rotting meat that they can hardly fly."

The young one nodded, his reply written in his moist eyes.

Even upwind as they were, the stench grew overpowering and burned a man's eyes. Never before had Quanah smelled anything so bad. Nor had he ever seen destruction this extensive. Even the time the strange cloud shaped like a tinkling tin cone had tongued its way out of the clouds above and stuck its thorny finger down among a herd of buffalo already on the run, frightened by claps of thunder.

He had been sixteen summers.

The sky had grown black with threat, driving a great wind before it. Quanah and others had been out hunting, practicing with their bows when they heard the thunder of the hooves, recognized the roar of their bellows as the beasts rumbled across the rolling hills of the Staked Plain. They had watched from a bare hilltop much like this one as the storm raced toward them faster than even Peta Nocona's pony could run, without a rider.

The wind grew more and more furious with the land, until the boys could no longer stay atop the hill and turned to find shelter among some trees. But upon mounting, Quanah looked back over his shoulder, being the first to see the swirling black funnel sweep its evil finger down out of the clouds to tear along the ground through the herd. It sucked the huge animals up as if they were no more than the small mud figures he crafted as a boy on the banks of the rivers and creeks where the Kwahadi always camped. Spinning, spinning the huge, bellowing beasts up into the sky like some great magic performed by a tribal shaman.

By the time they reached a dry, eroded washout near the base of the long, gentle slope, the rain had commenced. Not a gentle rain falling from the sky, but a violent, painful slashing coming at them from the four directions, flung against them so hard the six could hardly keep their feet. Time and again the young warriors stumbled and fell to the muddy, slimy earth. Time and again their ponies were nearly thrown over as well with the might of that great windstorm.

In that shallow washout the six huddled like insignificant sowbugs Quanah had found beneath an overturned buffalo chip when he was a curious child.

Above them the trees and the brush grew to a deafening roar with the great wind—reverberating with a thunderous pounding that drew ever closer.

Then the wind had passed, slowly fading in the distance across the great Staked Plain.

Yet the rains fell, driving like a gray wall behind the great funnel cloud. Then came the rumble of thunder he heard in the ear he had pressed against the floor of the washout. He knew the cloud had been a warning. He hollered into the might of the wind, again and again, screaming so the others would hear his warning. They did not. The wind took his words from his lips and stole away with them.

Quanah had to struggle on hands and knees to each one of the other five with him—touching them, pointing, unable to say anything for the deafening noise. It was hard enough keeping their eyes open in the swirl of pelting rain as they clawed up the slippery, slimy side of the washout onto the flat prairie.

The last young warrior to struggle up the side was not so lucky. When the giant wall of churning, foaming, brown water roared down the washout, he clung in desperation to a tree root. His pony was caught in the wall of water, screeching in fright as it tumbled out of sight in a matter of three frantic heartbeats.

The young warrior clung there to his tree root, the brown monster churning and slashing inches away from his heels, as Quanah and the others made a chain of themselves and pulled their friend to the edge of the prairie.

They stayed the afternoon in a stand of trees that had been battered by the storm, constantly watching the sky as the dark clouds rumbled farther to the east. Just as the sun dipped out below the black underbellies of the clouds, the rain suddenly tapered off and stopped. And with it, the wind died as mysteriously as if it had not held such powerful dominion over this land for the past few hours.

"I must see," he remembered telling the others. "See if I can find where the great black cloud took the buffalo to hide for itself. If we know where it took them, we can go there next time we are hungry and want to hunt. The black cloud wants buffalo for itself. We want the buffalo as well."

Back atop that knoll, they scanned the horizons with their farseeing eyes. The herd was gone. Driven off with the wind and lightning and frightening funnel cloud. But directly through the middle of the valley where the herd had been running when Quanah last saw them now lay a wide, deep scar of torn earth. It looked as if some huge creature had raked the ground with a monstrous stick, perhaps its own incredible fingernail.

"We will follow this track of the cloud monster," Quanah had told them. And paid no attention to the fear he saw in their faces.

Miles away, as sunset descended upon the land, they had found the buffalo—those animals that hadn't made it out of the cloud's path. For several hundred yards the carcasses were stacked in crazy fashion along the wide-open plain that had been stripped clean of all plant life. Some of the buffalo had eyes sucked from their sockets, most had their tongues lolling from the sides of their huge jaws. In their midst lay a few antelope and deer and wolves and coyotes. All dead.

"This is a place of great mystery," one of Quanah's young friends had said to him, clearly trembling. "We must go."

"I do not feel good standing here either," spoke another. "Let us ride far from here."

Quanah had laughed at them, acting like such nervous children. "There is nothing to be afraid of here—"

Then he saw the wolves—a pack of them loping off to the side of that huge, brown-black ridge built of thousands upon thousands of carcasses and muddy earth scooped right up out of the prairie. Whereas these wolves should have been in among the dead, eating on the bounty of meat that would last for many weeks, this pack of wolves was instead slinking off, tails tucked and glancing guardedly over their shoulders in great fear of this place.

"Yes," Quanah had replied. "We must go far and fast from this place. There is great evil here."

From that day until this, he had never seen anything like that great destruction. Yet there was no mystery here. No black funnel cloud had dipped out of the lowering heavens to sweep up the thousands of buffalo as if they were children's toys made only of mud.

Quanah knew what had caused this great obscene blight on the prairie.

"White hunters," he told the young scout now as their ponies fought their bits and struggled to be gone from that place.

"The white man would waste so much?"

Quanah nodded. "For only the hides and a few tongues—they do this to our brother, the buffalo."

"They should be made to pay, Quanah," the young one vowed, smashing a fist against his palm.

"One day—the white hide hunters will pay," he vowed. "Pay for taking the food from the mouths of our women and children!"

Quanah led the scout from the hill, his heart as cold and filled with hate as his belly was empty.

By the time another six days of journey had passed, the women and children were growing desperately hungry. Scraps of something to eat were scraped from the bottom of parfleche bags the women used to store their jerked meat and pemmican. There was plenty of sun to warm the ache of the cold from their bones each morning as they slowly plodded around to the south in a wide arc that took them those six days to complete.

Then one morning an outrider spotted a signal fire. Then a second column and a third. Almost due east from the marching village, toward the land where the sun was born every morning. The young camp guards rode out and returned with word that afternoon—the advance scouts had located a small herd. Nothing as big as what they were expecting to find, but enough to provide meat and hides for the coming snows of winter, bone scrapers to flesh those great furry hides, along with sinew to repair old clothing and fat to mix with charcoal to smear beneath the eyes of the hunters, protecting them from sudden blindness when they went out in the coming season of snow. There was enough, so there was much rejoicing among the village when word of the discovery traveled from lips to lips.

Again Quanah reminded ten of his best hunters on the fastest ponies that they had been chosen to kill buffalo for the old ones and those who could not hunt for themselves. His people would always take care of one another, and he would see to their needs before caring for the needs of his own family.

In the fading winter light of that day, Quanah ordered the column to halt and make camp, for in the morning the hunters would mount up and make meat for them all.

Before dawn they were ready. These young horsemen, having tied up the tails of their favored buffalo runner as they did with a war pony before going into battle. Most wore little bundles of personal medicine tied behind an ear or around their necks, perhaps over one shoulder, under one arm or the other. Powerful stuff to make the young warrior shoot straight and keep him from harm among the slashing hooves of the herd they would soon put on the run. Dust or ashes or a sprinkling of puffball spores were scattered over the buffalo ponies—to give them wind and courage among the huge beasts, to give them swift hooves to carry their riders into then out of danger at the slightest tap of the brown knees that climbed atop those ponies now and followed Quanah and his camp police away from the village.

Slowly marching to the east, where the white man had named the river *Canadian*, Quanah followed the buffalo scouts.

Farther still to the east, beyond the horizon, lay the Cheyenne-Arapaho reservation. And only a long day's ride to the north lay the land of the white man and his smoking wagons and the yellowleg soldier camps and the land of the hide hunters.

When the herd was sighted, Quanah halted the great assembly of riders and divided them into two groups under capable leaders. One he sent to the north side of the herd, the other to the south, both coming in from downwind as quietly as their ponies could move, without disturbing the great beasts until the two groups formed a great, sweeping arc behind the feeders.

With a wave of Quanah's white blanket, the four hundred horsemen broke into a furious gallop from the outskirts of the herd.

In surprise, the animals tore their heads from the prairie where they had been grazing while meandering along to the south. The half-blind, poor-sighted beasts sniffed the air, hearing the pounding pony

hooves and the excited yelps of the young hunters
and hammering of the few guns—then lurched into
the rocking-chair gait so typical of the huge animal.

A sudden, frightening, snorting stampede that filled
the valley.

Ponies swept in and out of the fringe of that throbbing herd as one after another of the animals went
down, chins into the ground, tumbling rump over
horns, never to rise while the hunters rode on, firing
one arrow after another, hundreds upon hundreds of
them fired into the thundering herd. Arrows whispered from the horn and Osage orange bows, arrows
driven up to the feather fletching, some fired with
such might they drove right on through the buffalo,
shafts that were trampled under the hooves of those
falling, stumbling, cascading buffalo.

A time or two Quanah watched as a rider spilled,
urging his pony too close to bull or cow—perhaps
getting a dull horn driven up and into the belly of the
pony with a shower of red and a tumbling waterfall
of intestine as the rider picked himself off the cold,
hard prairie and ran for cover, ran to escape the on-
rushing beasts mindlessly lurching ever southward.
One rider did not make it in time, his own belly
opened up by a slashing hoof.

Others, riders too young to hunt, rushed forward
now to drag the wounded, bleeding warrior from the
scene, where he could be tended to by one of the sha-
mans who laid his skeletal, veiny hand over the great,
gaping, crimson flap of skin that had exposed the in-
ternal organs, and began shaking his rattle in time
with his prayer chant.

When the first of the hunters had turned about to
claim their kill, there was a profusion of carcasses
more than a mile long. The young men turned their
ponies over to family members then went about the

business of searching for particular markings on the arrows. When a beast was found to have a warrior's arrow in it, the hunter called out. The women and men too old to hunt came running, their butcher knives glinting in the cold, winter sun of the Staked Plain. Time for work had come.

The children reveled in the glory of it, hungry as they were. Slices of liver sprinkled with gall from the tiny, yellow bladder were passed out to be sucked juicily by the little ones. Long strips of gut were gobbled and gummed by the old, toothless ones. With blood up to their elbows, splashed on their knees, the women dove into the carcasses time and again, pulling meat and organs from the white, fleecy carcasses.

Like a rich offering made to a royal king, one of Quanah's wives brought him a long bone she had skinned out and cracked to expose the rich, yellowish marrow. As he watched the butchering and listened to the happy voices, Quanah scraped the marrow free with a finger and sucked the rich, greasy buffalo butter with delight.

By twilight beneath the cold winter sky, the celebration had rolled into full swing. Over every merry fire roasted hump-ribs or thick roasts speared on a sharpened stick. The men played drums and sang their songs of thanksgiving, the women trilled with happy voices. The children laughed and ran and cried out with the warmth of full bellies. Quanah could ask nothing more for his people than this—that they be allowed to roam the buffalo land, allowed to find enough buffalo to feed themselves for time beyond his grandchildren's grandchildren.

Food, clothing, shelter, weapons . . . what more could his people want? Quanah asked himself.

So it was the following morning before the sun found its way out of the east that the Kwahadi chief had awakened himself and left in the freezing pre-dawn darkness, carrying a selected green hide in his lap as he rode to the crest of the highest hill for miles around, smelling the pungent air of winter's cleansing hand upon the land.

Reverently he laid the green, heavy hide on the browned, autumn-dried grass and unrolled it. Atop he laid a little tobacco stolen in raids among the settlements, a bit of powder and a lead ball from his pistol. In the end he slowly drew the edge of his knife along his left palm, opening up a tiny laceration that beaded with blood then began to ooze more freely. Quanah squeezed and squeezed his wrist, milking the hand until the blood would drop, bit by bit, until he had a crude circle made around the articles of thanksgiving on the green hide.

"These we offer to you, Grandfather Above!" he cried out into the pinking sky far to the east of him where the white man was said to number like the stars.

"May you accept all this, and the blood of a Kwahadi warrior in thanks for your gift of the buffalo to my people. We will always return the blessings you have given us with gifts of our own for your kindness to The People."

The harsh wind came up, tussling his long braids and worrying the fringe of leggings and shirt.

Although the wind was clean, Quanah nonetheless suddenly smelled the killing field they had run across a week ago. It was as if the power of the wind spirits now commanded him to scour the land clean of the white man.

"I will do as I am asked," Quanah Parker vowed. "To drive the white man from our land. And those who will not turn about and flee—we will kill."

Chapter 24

Early November 1873

Seamus couldn't remember ever before seeing that color in the sky. More so, he couldn't remember ever seeing that color before at all.

He figured nowhere else would a man possibly find that radiant lavender hue to the hulking winter clouds as the sun drained out of their gray bellies into the far west. And for a bittersweet moment he thought on Uncle Ian O'Roarke, Dimity and their five children, living beyond the Rockies and Sierras too.*

In a matter of minutes he knew Jack Stillwell would be stopping the group for the coming night.

Already the air was growing cold as the sun lost its short-lived power over this wide land of never-ending horizons. And Seamus figured he knew the spot Stillwell would choose for their camp—down there along that meandering creek, most likely among that stand of stunted trees on the far bank.

Autumn had begun to chant its death song across these southern plains. Winter silence would seal its fate.

The tall, red-gold grass brushed the stirrups as his

---

* The Plainsmen Series, vol. 5, *Devil's Backbone*

horse pushed through it, wading belly-deep mile after mile through this dying, inland sea. Long ago stripped bare of leaves by the incessant wind on these plains, the trees and brush stood skeletal, austere, and ultimately lonely in the cold, fading light. Except for the quiet hoofbeats of the horses, the brushing of the grass beneath the riders' stirrups and the rumble of the iron-tired wagon over the uneven ground, all sound was quickly swallowed by the coming darkness and the immense, aching wilderness. Every bit as quickly, the approaching night worked to draw the last vestige of warmth from the land.

By the time all the riders were across the narrow creek, the commissary sergeant leaned into the brake and halted his wagon. The escort's commander, Lieutenant Harry Stanton of the Fourth Cavalry, ordered two soldiers to help the sergeant unhitch the eight mules. Two black and brown sharp-eared animals were always rotated out of hitch each day, halter-tied to the back of the wagon to enjoy their stint at leisure. The other six mules were used to pull the high-walled freighter which contained the party's rations: beans, salt-pork, hardtack and coffee, along with bedrolls and tents, extra weapons and two thousand rounds of ammunition for each of the twelve soldiers. In addition to having enough cartridges in the event the group was surrounded and put under siege, Lieutenant Stanton had requested that one of the young troopers assigned to come along on the escort would have blacksmithing skills. Crossing the hard, sun-baked prairie like this, there was no telling when one of the army mounts or wagon mules would throw a shoe. Out here, that could mean a slow, lingering death for a man as sure as anything else.

Small fires were the order of the day, started at the bottom of holes they dug out of the hard, unforgiving soil so the flames would not be seen from any distance. Three of such fires was all Stillwell allowed, and those only long enough to boil coffee before dirt was kicked back in to snuff the red embers. Cold, almost tasteless salt-pork and the big, dry squares of hardtack served as supper for the weary men who took their canteens to the narrow, muddy creek and refilled them before settling back against their saddles and bedrolls as the sun disappeared for good and night-black descended upon over the land.

"Look yonder," said one of the troopers, pointing as he strode back from the nearby brush where he had relieved his trail-hammered kidneys.

Most of the rest turned to look, rising from the ground where they had been squatting, filling pipes or rolling smokes. Seamus saw it too, over the tops of the rain-grayed canvas tents, over the backs of the horses they picketed close in to camp, wary of pony-hungry horse thieves.

Across the whole of the western horizon the sky glowed brightly, giving an iridescent orange-pink to the gray underbellies of the winter clouds suspended overhead.

"What you make of that, Jack?" Donegan asked as Stillwell came to a halt beside him.

"Prairie fire."

"Makes a pretty sight, don't it now?"

Stillwell nodded, only slightly. "We'll have to keep an eye on it, Irishman. That sonofabitch stew is coming our way."

"Sonofabitch stew?"

"Fire drives everything in front of it—critters of all kind: four-leggeds, birds, every bug that flies. All them get churned up together hurrying to skeedaddle so's they don't get cooked. That's what they call son-ofabitch stew out here on the prairie."

Donegan stared back at the dimly lit, long red line faintly shimmering on the far horizon. "It's coming our way?"

He smelled the air. "Take a sniff. Smell it? We're sure as hell downwind of it. No chance I'd bet against it—that fire's coming right for us."

"How long do we have?" asked Philip Graves as he strode up to the others.

"I don't rightly know for now."

"Perhaps we should strike camp and move off— away from the flames, Mr. Stillwell," suggested Simon Pierce.

Donegan looked at the pair holding their valises, Pierce clutching that long map tube like it was life itself to the man.

"We've got time. Besides, it could snuff itself out for all we know."

"And if it doesn't?" Graves prodded the young scout.

"Then we'll have to make a run for it. But for now —that stew's still a long way off."

"Will it be here before morning?" Pierce asked.

"No," Stillwell answered. "Too far off. Plenty time for breakfast."

"Come along, Philip," Graves said, turning and pulling his partner by the elbow. "I have something to discuss with you—in private."

Seamus watched the pair go, then found his eyes naturally returning to the fire. "How fast does it travel?"

Jack stooped only slightly and tore off up a handful of the tall, seed-headed buffalo grass. He smelled it, then crumpled it between his gloved hands. Then smelled it again. "Mighty dry."

"That fire will eat right through this grass, won't it, Jack?"

He nodded. "Mighty dry, Seamus. Let's go get Stanton's men to understand they've got to keep an eye on that red horizon off yonder when they stand their turns at watch through the night."

With the soldiers understanding they were not only to watch and listen for possible horse raiders, but to monitor the progress of the prairie fire itself, Stillwell joined Donegan in their small tent. No more than any other night on this journey, the canvas rattled and snapped quietly beneath the hand of the wind as the camp settled down into slumber. Donegan tossed and turned in his blankets, still brooding on what brought Pierce and Graves out here to Comanche country.

From time to time Seamus was aware of the camp guard walking about outside the frost-rimed canvas tent he shared with Stillwell. Sleeping as light as he did, the Irishman awoke with each changing of the guard. Throughout the long night, he dozed and listened to the two troopers stomping about in an attempt to stay warm while standing their watch.

Realizing he had finally fallen asleep, Donegan slowly grew aware that the quality of light had changed in their small tent. But it was deliciously warm inside where he had burrowed his head down in the heavy wool blankets. There came a quiet rustle of voices outside, then one of the soldiers poked his head through the doorway, his announcement shattering Donegan's peaceful reverie.

"Mr. Stillwell? Lieutenant wants to see you."

Both of them sat up. Seamus saw the young trooper's thick breath-smoke fogging up the tiny tent.

"What is it, soldier?" Jack asked.

"Says he wants to show you something."

"The fire?"

The young soldier's head bobbed. "He wants to know if it's time for us to make a run for it."

"I'm coming," Stillwell muttered, throwing off his blankets, pushing back the canvas bedroll.

It was only when the soldier left that Donegan first became aware of the change in the wind—its power now something clearly definable, a presence announced with a sharp tang to the air. This was no longer the clean smell of the prairie. This wind had in it the stinging, acrid smell of blackened death.

His breath-smoke fogged before his face in thick tissue as he jammed his feet and pants down into the tall, stovepipe boots and pulled on the heavy, blanket mackinaw and leather gloves. Seamus followed Jack from the flaps and stood, turning up the tall collar to keep the brutal cold from his ears which instantly began to ache with the bone-numbing temperature.

"I don't need to see more, Lieutenant," Jack called out to the backs of the soldiers on the other side of their camp.

The lieutenant turned. "You see what I see?"

"Yes—let's get this camp struck." Jack turned to Donegan. "Roll Pierce and Graves out, Seamus."

Stuffing the upper part of his body through an opening in the tent flaps lashed together against the wind, the Irishman announced, "Gentlemen, it's time to rise and shine!"

Pierce was the first to poke his head out to greet the predawn cold. "What's the meaning of this intrusion, Donegan?"

"Fire, gentlemen. We have company coming this morning—and it'll be here before breakfast." He watched Graves awaken groggily and pull the blankets back from his face. "If you plan on coming with us, start moving now."

"Fire? Did you say the fire was coming?" Graves asked.

Seamus pulled his head from the tent flaps as the

civilians argued between themselves, snappish. Those
two had secrets enough to eat a man up. He turned,
drawn magnetically to the west where the whole horizon had gone from a faint, thin line of red reflected
off the belly of the clouds overhead to a wild orange
glow painting the whole sky as far as he could see in
three directions. A sliver of moon was preceding the
sun—a bright, crimson ball rising out of the icy cold
sky in the east.

That fire was due to make things warm here
shortly.

At the perimeter of camp the horses and mules had
begun to protest their hobbles and picket pins, growing more wild-eyed with every passing minute, snorting, their nostrils flaring as they filled with the heavy
stench of blackened death carried on the growing
wind. Then everything fell quiet for the space of two,
maybe three heartbeats—only long enough for a man
who paid attention to such things to hear.

Seamus listened to the unmistakable sound rumbling in from the west. Almost like a distant freight
train roaring along its tracks—drawing closer and
closer still.

Then that distant sound of the all-consuming prairie fire was swamped over by the rustle of wings beating thunderously overhead, the whirring of tiny
insects and the pounding hooves of a large herd of
antelope that came racing for their camp, veering at
the last moment. The wings of another flock of jays
reverberated just over the treetops, while wrens and
swallows and magpies swooped across the ground
only long enough to peck at a mouthful of the insects
driven before the fire before they took wing for a few
more yards, then swooped down again on this hearty
feast of retreating creatures. Everything that could
escape was trying to, driven east in a headlong rush

of noise and panic, galloping along the west bank of the stream, most taking the easy route: pointing their noses to the southeast along the bank instead of crossing the stream directly.

As he watched in utter amazement, the whole sky now seemed swallowed by some black monster—smoke clouds boiling overhead, their underbellies growing even brighter crimson as he watched in sheer wonder and fascination.

"Donegan!"

"Here!" Seamus answered Stillwell's sharply edged call.

"Get saddled! I need your help, dammit!"

The Irishman burst into action, tearing his eyes from the huge globe rising off the eastern horizon, first orange, then yellow, and finally becoming a bright red disk as it climbed into the fire's smoky remnants of the canopy overhead.

As he threw the hard, frost-stiffened blanket over the horse's back, more wild animals burst past the campsite. Deer bounded by, tongues lolling in exhaustion. More antelope, their doelike eyes filled with mortal fear, a few clearly scorched, blackened, oozy red wounds scorched on their legs where they had escaped only by bounding through the devastated grass itself. Rabbits hopped around the outskirts of the bustling camp. Skunks and badgers waddled past. Everything that could move was on its way.

"Let's just get this outfit across the stream!" hollered the lieutenant. "We'll be safe there, Mr. Stillwell."

Jack grabbed the young soldier by his wool coat. "That goddamned stream is too narrow to protect us from a fire this size!"

Stanton swallowed, his eyes narrowing first on the

scout, then widening at the oncoming fire. "Then what the hell do you suggest we do?"

Jack wagged his head. "All we can do is get out of here as fast as we can. Cross the stream and keep running till I can find us some place to put in till it passes over us."

"P-Passes over us?" stammered Simon Pierce as he rushed up.

Stillwell whirled on them. "Are you two ready to ride?" he snapped.

"No. I came to—"

"Get your horse saddled or you aren't going to make it out of here!" Stillwell interrupted.

Seamus nearly tripped over the half-dozen cottontails that had sought some haven of safety between his legs as he stood working beside his nervous mount, setting the saddle atop the stiffened blanket. The hares bolted away, ears and noses twitching frantically, eyes roaming at both sides of their heads, sorting out a direction to take to safety.

There seemed to be none as the blackened ash began to sift down from the low-hanging smoke clouds. The air filled with debris and cinders, stinging the lungs, making him hunger for nothing more than a single clean breath.

"Get those canteens filled!" Stillwell shouted at the soldiers who turned from saddling horses. "The rest of you, get those two water barrels topped off. We're going to need all the water we can carry in a bad way —and real soon."

"Lieutenant!" Seamus called. "Help me get the wagon cover tied down."

"The hell with that—let's get out of here!" Stanton growled, clearly filled with panic.

Stillwell snagged the young lieutenant's coat again. "Do as the Irishman says. Tie the goddamned cover down over everything. If we plan on saving the wagon and supplies, we'll need that cover."

"C'mon, Irishman," the lieutenant growled as he bolted toward the wagon. "I don't know why we can't just leave this wagon here and make a run for it with the mules."

"I figure Jack will try to save everything he can save before he gives up."

"So he wants to die becoming a hero?" asked Stanton as he lashed down the last loop on his side of the wagon.

"Jack Stillwell was a honest-to-goodness hero five years ago—when he was a pup of nineteen."

"He kill some Indians?"

"He saved the lives of over forty men, Lieutenant. Walking across a hundred miles of prairie wilderness just like this to take word that Major George A. Forsyth and the rest of us was pinned down by more than five hundred Cheyenne and Sioux on the Arickaree."*

The lieutenant's face blanched. "Sounds like you both were there?"

Donegan nodded. "But it was Stillwell who was the hero at the end of those nine bloody days. He carried word and Forsyth's map that eventually brought in the Tenth Cavalry to raise the siege."

For a moment the lieutenant turned to look at the young scout who was then directing the filling of the two water barrels strapped to the sides of the high-walled wagon. "I suppose he doesn't have to prove a damned thing to any man now," Stanton said, with some genuine approval in his voice. "I see he already was a hero."

"And he will be again," Donegan said as he yanked

* The Plainsmen Series, vol. 3, *The Stalkers*

hard on the half-hitch he tied in the last loop over the
wagon cover.

"Soldier! You there!" Stillwell called out, patting
one of the blanket-wrapped water barrels. "Fill that
coffeepot and bring it over to splash on these kegs."

"Water 'em down?"

"Yeah," answered Stillwell. "Soak the blankets
real good. I'm afeared we're going to need everything
as wet as we can get it pretty soon."

Donegan turned to find the lieutenant staring at the
flames just now breaking over the near horizon to the
west. No longer did the underbellies of the low winter
clouds and blackened, stifling smoke overhead appear painted with a crimson brush. Now the whole
world had gone brighter as more ash and soot fell
from the thickening air. Their whole world had become a bright orange-yellow as the hungry, consuming tongues of flame licked at the sky from horizon to
horizon. Lapping at the dry, brittle grass that until
now had been awaiting only the snows of winter.

Without satiation this monster was greedily consuming the prairie and all the life it had held season
after season. A roaring, snarling freight train of a
sound that assaulted the Irishman's ears.

"Into the creek!" Stillwell shouted, still on foot,
waving his arm.

"You heard him!" Seamus hollered as the commissary sergeant clamored aboard his wagon and
slapped leather down on the rumps of the six mules
lurching into motion. "Cross the bleeming creek!"

Donegan watched the two government men ride
behind the wagon among the extra mules. Those valises and that map tube remained with them as always while they prodded their anxious mounts down
to the bank and into the water.

Now only Jack and Seamus remained on the west

side of the creek. He saw Stillwell vault into the saddle, his young face already smudged with smoke and blackened cinders. More and more sparks drifted past them now, carried before the stiff wind that had grown much, much warmer in the past few moments.

"Into the creek, Irishman!"

Seamus closed his eyes and made the sign of the cross. "Hail Mary, full of grace—"

Chapter 25

Early November 1873

"*I* can't find it!" William Graves shrieked, arousing the attention of every one of the soldiers.

"Find what?" asked Simon Pierce.

Seamus turned in the saddle, finding the two civilians halting their horses, allowing Stanton and his ten horsemen to pass as the wagon rumbled out of the narrow creek and onto the prairie, driven east, away from the prairie fire.

Graves patted his coat pocket, his eyes filled with panic. "I always carry it here."

"What?" Pierce repeated.

"The . . . the—" and Graves skidded to a verbal halt when his eyes caught the Irishman staring at the two of them. "I've got to go back, Simon!"

Pierce glanced at the advancing wall of flame. "You can't. What can be so damned important that you—"

Graves grabbed Pierce's arm, almost pulling the smaller man out of the saddle, whispering huskily. "It's what this whole damned expedition is about, Simon!"

Pierce flung off the arm. "You're insane, William.

Always feared you would be. But be that as it may—you can't go back. See for yourself.''

Graves studied the far side of the creek as the fire roared closer, the air become heavy, stifling with live cinder and ash. He turned back to study the wagons and horsemen continuing away from the creek, onto the open prairie at a rapid clip.

"Go with me, Simon!" he begged. "I'll show you something that will knock you back on your heels. Just go with me to find it.''

"I don't know what *it* is. Forget it—and come on.''

Graves shook his head. "Donegan. Come back with me—I beg you.''

Seamus almost felt sorry for the man. "If you left it —it's gone for now, Graves. We don't have much time—''

Donegan watched Graves hammer his heels into his horse's flanks and saw the reins about, galloping the animal back to the creek.

"Goddamn you," he muttered as he kicked his own horse into motion and plunged past a darkly amused Simon Pierce.

Graves had his mount out of the stream and up the west bank before Seamus got to him. When the Irishman reached out for the civilian's elbow, Graves yanked his arm back, his eyes gone wild.

"Help me!" he screamed, dropping to the ground, his fear-filled eyes scanning the campsite.

"I will help you! Get on your horse and we'll get out of here.''

It was hard to hear much of anything now, even a man's loud voice. The roar of the all-consuming fire bore down on them, blotting out most of the light with clouds of suffocating smoke, the air alive with cinders like fireflies on a summer night.

"Yes! This is where our tent stood!" Graves

shouted, falling to his knees and crawling about through the dusklike darkness, muttering, his hands feeling along the ground as he inched forward, not stopping even as the ground around him began to smoke, the dry grass catching fire from the meteor shower of flaming cinders.

He winced in pain, slapping out the smoldering flames on his wool coat, his wool britches. His bare hands blackened as he groped through the brittle, dry grass, his face a smear of sweat and smoke, wide, fear-tinged eyes white in his darkened face.

"What can be so bloody important to you, Graves?"

The man looked over his shoulder at Donegan for only a moment then said, "It's what I've worked years for—something my family just didn't hand to me. Mine, all mine. But I don't expect you to understand that. Besides . . . it's something that's already cost a lot of people their lives—I must find it!"

"Tell me what it is . . . what I'm looking for, so we can find it and get the hell out of here!" Donegan flung his voice into the roar of the onrushing prairie fire.

"The damned things's wrapped in a bit of corduroy fabric," Graves explained breathlessly, eyes wide in his blackened face.

"What color?"

"Brown . . . no—gray-brown."

"How big?"

"Does it make any—" Graves snarled. "This big," he said, holding out his two palms less than six inches apart. "It's small."

"You'll never find it," Donegan said, beginning to climb down.

"I must find—" he started, then his hands filled with something he held up before his eyes. As if sud-

denly aware of the Irishman's presence, Graves
turned his back on Donegan and unwrapped his
prize only enough to be sure it was actually back in
his possession.

"You found it?"

"Damn right I did!" He rose clumsily, for the moment unaware of the danger.

Donegan saw the danger first, how the fire suddenly leaped from the ground a few yards off, cinders
flying all around Graves, enveloping him in smoke
and ash. And when the civilian emerged coughing,
sputtering from the dense wall of smoke, he was on
fire, the back of his wool coat fully aflame. Shrieking
like a madman—

"Drop it, dammit!" Seamus ordered

But the frightened man refused to drop his prize.
Instead he clutched it to his breast and took off running, screaming, his whole back being whipped into
furious flames.

Seamus hammered his heels into the horse, taking
off after Graves. As they both reached the creek,
Donegan surged past the civilian and kicked the man
in the back of the shoulders with the heel of his boot.
Crying out in panic, in surprise, in pain, Graves went
spilling into the shallow stream. The Irishman was
off the right side of his horse into the cold water,
kicking Graves over, again and again, scooping handful after handful on the back of the man's head,
across his legs, everywhere that still smoldered after
the soaking in the icy water.

Looking up, Donegan found his horse on the far
side of the narrow stream, tossing its head in fury at
the air filled with burning cinders. The government
man's horse was nowhere to be found. Reaching
down, Seamus snagged the back of Graves's collar
and dragged him across the pebbled stream bottom

then up the bank as Stillwell appeared out of the thick smoke.

"He dead?"

"I don't think so," Seamus replied breathlessly. "Just a good soaking."

"Where's his animal?"

Donegan shrugged. "Looks like I'll have to carry him meself till we reach the wagon."

"They're covering ground. I came back when Pierce told me he was turning 'round to find something he'd left—and that you was coming back to help him."

"I came back to save his bleeming hide, Jack."

"Looks like that's what you've done," he said, dropping from the saddle and grabbing hold of the civilian. Unconscious, Graves still growled, an animal-like sound at the back of his throat.

"Is he coming to?"

"Sounds like it," Jack said, hoisting the man up as Donegan pulled on the civilian's arms until they had him slung over the Irishman's legs.

"He ever find what he was willing to die for, Seamus?"

"Figure he did: I saw him pick something off the ground—but I still don't know what it was he tucked under his arms just before the fire got to him."

"He's still holding it," Jack said.

Sure enough, Graves clutched his cloth-wrapped treasure beneath one arm, the other drooping off the far side of the horse.

"Was it worth the trouble, Graves?" Stillwell asked after he came around Donegan's horse to take up his own reins.

Graves growled again, a wordless, predatory sound as the air filled with suffocating heat.

"Let's get, Seamus!" Stillwell hurled himself into

the saddle without using the stirrup. He wrenched his horse around and was off, slapping the rear of the Irishman's mount.

The fire was starting to jump the creek in fits and starts.

Above the dry, leafless brush and trees, the air grew choked with soot and live embers, driven across the stream on the back of the tireless wind. A wind made hotter and stronger by the fire itself. A wind that acted like some monstrous tongue of heat searing everything in its path even before the flames came in to finish the destruction.

Behind Donegan now arose a renewed rumble, the fire regaining strength and speed as it lurched across the stream and grabbed hold on the east bank after faltering for only a moment. Like a phoenix rising from its own ash, the great wall of flame rose once more, yellow-red fingers clawing at the prairie grass, almost laughing as it strained to run down more of the wild, frightened creatures driven before it's death song.

Far ahead of them through the smoky haze, Seamus could make out the wagon and the horsemen, gold dust spun up from the four iron tires as the sky continued to darken. Behind him arose the rumble of what he recognized as thunder. A low, long blat that for but a moment overpowered the roar of the grass fire. Splitting the air with its might, then gone as quickly as it had come.

Stillwell reined around at him, his face taut with strain, waving Donegan on frantically. "I gotta leave you behind!" he spat his voice into the robbing wind. "Don't wanna," and he pointed at the soldiers far ahead, "but that bunch is going off in the wrong direction!"

"Go—I'll come along as fast as I can."

Stillwell glanced down at the semiconscious Graves slung across Donegan's saddle. His eyes found the Irishman's, showing his grave concern and earnest affection. "You have to—just leave the bastard behind. Get yourself out."

"Go on, Jack! Get!" he shouted into the oncoming roar of the fire that already heated the cold winter morning beyond anything the sun itself could do.

"That way!" Stillwell shouted as he leapt away, an arm out. "Point yourself that way!"

Cinders and ash, antelope and deer and cottontails all hurried past his plodding horse, handicapped and sidestepping with the ungainly double weight.

"By the saints," he muttered to himself, feeling the heat growing at his back, afraid to turn around and see for himself, "I've got the notion to leave you behind myself, Graves."

"But you won't, will you?"

Seamus was surprised at the answer to his question. Seamus said, "Coming to, are we?"

"I've never experienced such exquisite pain before!" he growled. "Just hurry this blasted horse up or we'll both have problems."

"No—*we* won't, Graves," he replied, shifting the smaller man's weight across his thighs. "You give me any trouble, I'll leave you off here for the fire, just like Stillwell—"

The words caught in mid-sentence as he felt a twinge of something unexpected and looked down at William Graves, finding a derringer jammed into his rib cage, just below his heart.

"Just a reminder, Donegan—how badly I want to make it out of here alive, you see. Now ride, goddammit!"

The minutes crawled by and still there was no change in his odds. The army escort and wagon and Stillwell all had disappeared beyond, somewhere in the rolling swales of prairie grassland soon to become blackened wilderness. And behind him roared the angry flames. For but a moment he thought back to another moment of helpless fear he had managed to swallow down—another fire he had stared in the face, set that time by Cheyenne Indians near the hayfield corral a few miles from Fort C. F. Smith on the Bighorn River, M. T. Montana Territory.*

Praying now in his own way that the wind would come up as it had then. Just such a wind to slap at this fire, snuffing it before it came any closer.

But this time the wind conspired in deadly partnership with the flames, driving them to a fury, speeding them on their eastward path, swallowing everything in their wake.

The prairie ahead of him was alive with the small creatures, throbbing, falling, running over one another to escape the searing heat. Some had patches of hair burnt off, ugly patches still smoldering as they scurried past, falling then rising to run again blindly. Some with paws reddened, bloody flesh raw from running across blackened, smoking grassland in making their escape from burrows and dens.

"Seamus!"

Through the haze of black smoke and fiery cinders that burnt his eyes to the point of blindness, seared his lungs to the point he hesitated taking his next breath, he thought he heard Jack Stillwell's voice.

"Here! Over here, Irishman!"

There was a second voice yelling to him. Then a

* The Plainsmen Series, vol. 2, *Red Cloud's Revenge*

third and fourth, screaming out—giving directions in the murky light.

A gust of sudden, shifting wind brought another low blat of thunder to his ears, somewhere behind him. Odd that it would rain this time of the year, he thought, his weeping eyes still straining into the darkness ahead for the disembodied voices.

"Goddamn you, Seamus."

Then Stillwell was beside him, yanking on the weary horse's bridle. A pair of soldiers were dragging Graves off the animal and into their arms, half carrying him, half dragging his half-burnt body toward a dark scar on the prairie.

"Where the divil—"

"Just c'mon—it's our only chance!"

Stillwell did not wait for a reply but began to run faster, his boots kicking up the dry dust in shallow puffs as he pulled on the Irishman's bridle. Seamus let the horse have its head, clutching the horn in sudden, overwhelming weariness as they reached the steep edge of a dry washout. For a moment he saw Jack's face swim before him in the black smoke billowing over them like grease smoke off a pork fire. But he could not hear a word the scout was saying—so loud was the hammering freight train of the on-rushing flames now. So close behind them that he felt it on his neck like never before, smelled the acid stench of hair burning and didn't know if it was the horse or if he were on fire.

Really didn't matter when the animal suddenly collapsed on its rear haunches just over the abrupt lip of the washout, catapulting the Irishman against the far side. He shook his head, clearing his eyes to find the horse sliding on its side coming down to the bottom, its legs thrashing, its tail smoldering.

Jack was pulling on his arm, forming wordless,

open-mouthed orders he could not hear. But he understood. Without looking back, they hurried together down the washout toward the others, already clustered in the deepest part.

For the past few minutes the soldiers had been busy at what Stillwell had ordered them to do: some to haul out the thousands of rounds of ammunition and hurriedly bury it a hundred yards down the narrow washout, bury it as deeply as they could in the time they had left them. Others he ordered to pull free the canvas wagon cover; drag out a blanket for every man, including the Irishman and Graves; splinter open the tops of the water barrels and use cups or coffeepots or their kepis, but use something to soak the canvas and especially the blankets. The commissary sergeant and another soldier freed the last of the animals, slapping them into motion, driving them on down the washout.

"We gonna lose the animals, Jack?"

Stillwell nodded. "Likely we will."

Seamus ground his teeth, feeling the surge of fear rise in him like vomit. "It'll be all right, Jack."

A brave grin crossed the scout's face. "Damn right, it will." He whirled on the others. "Everyone got their blanket sopping wet?"

A chorus of frightened men answered. Their eyes smarted, flecks of burning grass and fiery cinder drifting down into the sharp-sided coulee, dancing on the furious wind created by the prairie fire.

"We ain't got no more time to do anything more!" Stillwell shouted. "Get under the wagon! Every one of you." They started moving, slowly. Too slowly. "Hurry up, dammit!"

"Wrap yourself in your blanket when you get under the sowbelly!" Donegan ordered, the skin on his cheeks reddened with the unimaginable heat, stretched taut like rawhide. He could barely hear himself talk, not knowing if anyone else could.

"It's your turn!" Jack hollered.

"You first, son!"

"Don't be no hero again, Irishman!"

"Me?"

Then the roar of those flames jumping the coulee slapped Donegan to the ground, with one blow hammering the air from his lungs. He was stunned, shaking his head, robbed of breath as he realized the others were pulling him under the soaked, dripping canvas wagon sheet.

"Sweet Mother of Jesus," he muttered. "I've fought the best of 'em—but I've never been knocked down like that."

"You've never fought a bitch woman before," the old sergeant's voice growled in the darkness beneath the wagon and canvas.

"You're daft, ol' dodger! I'd never fight a woman."

"Just what the hell you think Mother Nature is, if she ain't a bitch a'times."

Some of them laughed, and the laughter died quickly, swallowed, sucked right out of them all, by a renewed rush of roaring fire passing overhead, consuming everything. Even the air they desperately needed to live.

The fire took his breath away, the super-heated air searing his lungs. Seamus didn't know if he could hold out. He heard some of the others crying in the sudden, frightening darkness, and he knew how they felt. He did not want to die here in the darkness either. Better in the light of day, staring down your enemy.

Instead of crying, Donegan bit down on a bit of the soaked blanket he had wrapped around himself and chewed, sucking air through it. Chewing to loosen some more water, then sucking in another breath of air.

Time passed. How slowly time passed.

Chapter 26

Early November 1873

*H*e was sniffling, his nose weepy, eyes burning with the smoke, knowing this must truly be Hell —at least purgatory itself . . . when he finally realized the deafening roar was fading.

Seamus Donegan swallowed hard, then took another small breath. The air not so hot now.

Slowly he peeled the hot, damp blanket back from his face. Peering up at the bottom of the wagon and the canvas sheeting they had stretched out tent fashion to drape over them all.

"Jack?"

Stillwell poked his head out like a tortoise emerging from his shell. He blinked, cocking his head to listen. "I think it's gone over us, Seamus."

"Praise God and the Virgin Mary."

"You pray while you was under there?"

"By damn, we all did, son!" growled the sergeant who came out of hiding.

"Is it safe now?" asked Lieutenant Stanton.

"Let's go see for ourselves, Irishman," Stillwell suggested. "Rest of you wait here."

Throwing back the edge of the canvas wagon cover, Seamus squinted into the murky light, brighter now than it had been ever since yesterday at sunset. This morning's sunrise never had a chance to light the land.

Donegan felt like a boiled potato wrapped in the steamy, wet blanket—his clothes heavy with dampness, his skin tight and tender, seared by the severe heat. The air was still warm, but every now and then arose a rattle of breeze rushing along the floor of the washout—cool enough to remind them that winter had indeed come to the southern plains. Seamus dropped the blanket and stood, his eyes blinking, looking up the coulee, then down, finding Stillwell doing the same.

"You look a sight, Irishman," said the young scout, grinning.

"Don't look so bad yourself, Jack, me boy." He wrapped Stillwell in his arms fiercely. "Thanks, friend. You saved my arse again, didn't you?"

"Someone's gotta watch out for you, that's for sure."

Donegan sighed, turning back to the wagon and sticking his head beneath the canvas. "C'mon out."

They came out singly and in pairs, most still clutching their soaked blankets, shedding them only when they truly believed they were safe, that the fire had passed over them. The only celebration they allowed themselves at that moment was to mutter relief to one another.

"We'll go up, Lieutenant," Stillwell said. "See what there is to see."

"What about our horses? The mules for the wagons?" asked Stanton.

"Like I told you—the odds are they didn't survive. I told you it might come down to the stock or us."

The lieutenant finally nodded. "Don't know what's worse, Stillwell," he admitted. "Getting burned alive

. . . or being out here in the middle of Comanche and Kiowa country—set afoot like we are."

"Don't rile the rest," Donegan warned in a whisper. "We've got to do the best we can—with what's left us now."

"I suppose we can do that," the lieutenant agreed. "You two made it through that siege at Beecher's Island on the Arickaree—you'll see that we make it through this too."

Stillwell and Donegan turned and walked quickly down the coulee to a gentle slope still scarred by the wagon tires in its wild descent. They struggled up the slope, digging in toes and clawing with their hands until they gazed over the lip of the washout, gazed across a surreal world.

The fire was gone, far to the east now. Greasy smoke filled the air like a murky wall on that distant horizon. All that was left behind was a blackened world. Streamers of bluish smoke steamed up from tufts of buffalo grass and matted buffalo chips, all still smoldering, burning slowly after the intense flames had passed by.

Bursts of translucent, saffron sunlight shot down from the sky overhead, while to the east, darkness greased the horizon. To the far west, the first gray storm clouds threatened, drawing closer as he watched.

But below that great, multicolored canopy there was no living thing to be seen from horizon to horizon to horizon.

"Where you figure the horses went?" Seamus asked, sensing the despair in his own gut.

Jack shrugged. "Run off—if they're still alive."

He sighed. "You think we have a chance of finding them?"

"Don't know." Stillwell seemed as morose as Seamus had ever seen the man.

"I suppose you're right, Jack. We won't know, if we don't give it a try."

Stillwell smiled, cracking his smoke-blackened face. "Let's go tell the rest . . . have the lieutenant form up a few search parties. We might find some of the stock before sundown."

Jack had made sure he told all the soldiers who were going out in groups of three to give themselves enough time to make it back to the washout before slap-dark.

Most of the young soldiers looked worried, a few downright scared when they were hit with the lieutenant's orders to go in search of some of the missing horses and mules. Two dozen animals they needed to account for. And though he never said it to the others, Stillwell knew the chances were damn slim they would find them all together, if at all.

He couldn't blame the soldiers, most of them his age or older. Some of them German, a few Irish. All of them poor, and this frontier army the surest way to assure themselves of two squares a day and a blanket each night. But the thought of going out into this trackless wilderness of rolling tableland now covered by the black scar of the prairie fire's passing was enough to give pause to even a well-seasoned plains scout.

"What you do is pick out something far off in the direction you're going in," he had told them all after they had climbed out of the washout and stood in the middle of that black desert ready to depart the questionable safety of the commissary wagon. There were four groups of them. Seamus and Jack would walk south. Three parties of soldiers would take the other cardinal points of the compass—three troopers in each group.

"That way, you won't get turned around until you need to stop and come back for the night. If you don't find sign by the time the sun is two hands above the horizon—like this," he showed them how to hold two flat hands side by side off the far western edge of the earth, "then get your asses on back here, using another high point on the land to guide you in."

"The sergeant here will have a flag rigged up and flying over the washout for us," the lieutenant explained. Then Stanton assigned two soldiers to the sergeant: to stay with the civilians and protect the supplies.

"Good luck to all of you," Jack told them as he and Seamus Donegan waved good-bye and set off to the south.

What Stillwell did not say aloud was that he was praying for those first few hundred yards of march into the blackened, smoking, smoldering Hell created by the prairie fire. Praying that they would run across some sign—hoofprints . . . anything—something to hold on to with more than mere hope.

So it was they had walked, and walked some more, without much said between them. Each man carried a pistol and a rifle—Jack's a Spencer repeater that gave him seven shots in each Blakeslee reloading tube. Jack was packing ten of those heavy tubes along in the haversack strapped over his shoulder. Donegan cradled the big, heavy, brass-mounted Henry repeater over the crook of his shoulder, extra cartridges gently rattling in the huge, slash pockets of his blanket mackinaw.

Each of them deep in his own thoughts, perhaps his own pain, more so despair for their lot at this moment.

"Jack—it's time we headed back," Seamus said late that afternoon.

Stillwell stopped and sighed, standing inches deep in the blackened ash that had drifted up into his nostrils and eyes and had coated his tongue with its acid all day long. Hot, stinging, rancid.

"All right," he replied, turning around completely on that spot. "See that knob off yonder?"

"Yeah—but it looks to be a little west of north."

"Just keep walking to the right of it some," Jack explained, "we'll get back to the wagon and the others."

"I pray the others get back to the wagon," Seamus said as they set off on the back trail, able to follow their outbound footprints for more than a mile.

It was after that first mile or so that it grew difficult to see the bootprints. The ceaseless wind saw to that —blowing away all traces of their passing from the scorched prairie. Only hours after the fire, herewith beginning the healing of this wilderness.

By now the sun was shining only through a few patches of open, blue sky above. Yellow light streamed down on the cold land like saffron streamers from a forbidding gray canopy. Far off to the left gathered some ominous clouds with black underbellies. The sky thickened, like Cheyenne blood soup, blotting out the setting sun completely.

"We don't have as much time as I figured we would," Jack admitted. "We got to walk faster, Seamus. I was counting on us having some light from the sun even after it went down. But with those storm clouds hanging up there in the western sky—we're going to have to push it to get back to the wagon before dark."

"You set the pace—I'll keep up," Seamus said.

"And keep your eyes moving too. Don't want to be caught out here."

"What the divil a difference it make, Jack? There's no place we can hide that I can see. We'd just have to stand them off."

Stillwell smiled back at the Irishman's blackened face, those gray eyes twinkling as they regarded Jack. "Yes," the young scout sighed. "I suppose we've done a bit of standing off Injuns before, haven't we, Seamus?"

On into the fading light of dusk they pushed at a renewed pace, until at last, more to their right, Jack spotted something in the distance, fluttering, waving on the horizon.

"You make out what that is, Seamus?"

He squinted, blinking his red, swollen eyes some. Rubbed them, then looked again. "It ain't really moving. Don't look like a Injun, though—on foot or sitting top his pony."

"You think it could be the sergeant's flag?"

"Pray it is, Jack. Let's go."

The closer they drew to that high point of land, the clearer it became, until they both could make out the flapping of the old sergeant's handmade flag: a large strip of greasy hand towel from his kitchenware. Jack had to admit that nothing had ever really looked that good to him since the day he spotted the black faces of those buffalo soldiers who rode up to him on the dusty road between Cheyenne Wells and Fort Wallace.*

"Hurry!" A voice was hurled at them from the figure standing beside the flag, waving them on.

They rolled into a clumsy, weary trot, their feet sweating from the heat of the ground, their lungs

---

* The Plainsmen Series, vol. 3, *The Stalkers*

stinging from the acrid smoke and ash still drifting up from the burnt grass like wounded ghosts of the fire's passing.

Jack could make out the words as the soldier turned to the side and hollered down into the wash-out.

"They're coming, Sarge. Two of 'em."

There was a pause, likely while the old sergeant said something, then the soldier yelled back in reply. "It's them two scouts. Just them."

"Anyone else come in yet?" Jack asked when he was close enough to shout.

"Just the bunch from the west. Got in here a short while back."

"The lieutenant still out?" Seamus asked.

The soldier's head bobbed up and down as the two civilians ground to a halt near the wash-towel flag.

"Hurry, fellas—the sarge needs you bad."

"Goddammit!" came the old sergeant's growl from below them. "I don't need 'em—but this pilgrim from the east sure needs help."

Jack and Donegan came to the edge of the coulee and peered down at the men gathered about William Graves.

Simon Pierce turned around to gaze up at Stillwell and Donegan. His eyes pleaded with them. And then it was that Jack realized William Graves was being held down by two soldiers and Pierce himself.

"We're trying to dress this wound he has," Pierce explained as the two civilians skidded down to the bottom of the washout.

"How'd he get hurt?" Donegan asked.

"That's a nasty looking one—he get bit by some critter?" Jack inquired, glancing up then down the coulee.

Pierce nodded. "This morning, not long after all of

you left—I heard William cry out. Sounded like he was in pain. We all looked up, found him standing there holding his arm—like this. When I asked him what was wrong, he said he was bit."

"What bit him?"

Pierce gazed at Stillwell. "The sergeant shot it— soon as Graves could get out of the way."

"It was a mean sonbitch, boy," explained the sergeant. "But I blowed it to kingdom come. Popped it —just like that. Shoulda seen it."

"What was it, dammit!"

"A skunk," the sergeant answered snappishly.

"Where is it?" Jack asked, glancing down at Graves with a bit more concern now, the confusion gone from his eyes.

"I throwed it down there," the sergeant answered, pointing up the washout.

"It smell strange to you?"

The old soldier shook his head. "No worse'n a pole-cat skunk will smell anytime."

"Get me some lye soap."

"I already washed the bite, Stillwell," explained Pierce. "I tried to do everything I could think of."

Stillwell pulled the government man aside by the arm to whisper, "You figure it the same way I do?"

Pierce nodded. "I had no idea—"

"Skunks carry that poison in 'em . . . it makes the critters fearless. I imagine the fire scared hell out of it anyway, and it found a place to hide out somewhere in this washout with us while the fire crossed over. Then Graves likely did something to rile it."

"He said it came running at him, spitting and hiss-ing—snapping its jaws," Pierce said.

"Skunks don't usually come out in broad daylight —do they?" Seamus asked.

Jack pointed to the sky. "It ain't exactly been full daylight since sunup."

"Rabies is a death sentence," Pierce said quietly to the two civilians, wringing his hands together, fear etched on his narrow face.

Stillwell swallowed hard. "If we're to save him, we've got to burn the wound."

"Purge the poison?" asked Simon Pierce.

"The only caustic we got in camp is fire," Donegan replied. He turned to the soldiers. "Sergeant, get one of your cooking irons out after you've started a fire. We need something red hot."

"You gonna cauterize that bite he's got?" the old soldier asked as he pulled a long iron poker from the back of the wagon.

"Tie him up for now," Seamus said to the others, all of whom had returned, then nodded to the sergeant.

"He doesn't have much of a chance, does he?" Pierce inquired weakly, the strain and outright fear evident in his voice.

"I figure we're going to give him the only chance he's got," Jack replied. "It'll either heal him—or we'll find out it's too damn late as it stands."

Chapter 27

Mid-November
1873

*A*nother two days had turned up half of the mules and a handful of the horses. Two of the army mounts Seamus and Jack Stillwell ran across had hooves burned so badly they were limping and had to be put down.

As for concern about the noise of the pistol shots, Jack said a man would be foolish not to worry that a wandering Comanche buck might just hear the solitary shot they made that second day, another lone shot fired their third day of looking.

"But," Jack had told Donegan, "the Injuns usually go where the white settlers are. And if they aren't raiding the white man, they're hunting buffalo."

"It's for damned sure there aren't any white settlers out here," Seamus had replied, gazing over the blackened wilderness. "And I haven't seen buffalo in so long, that army salt-pork is starting to taste like real food!"

While a fourth day of searching the wide prairie of the Staked Plain did not turn up any more of the stock, nonetheless they had enough animals and human muscle to sweat the wagon out of that coulee. Hitching the four mules to the tree took care of all of the sergeant's wagon stock they had managed to find. And after the lieutenant claimed his animal, along with Donegan and Stillwell given mounts for tracking purposes, that left only three soldiers who would not have to ride in the wagon with the two civilians.

That fourth night after the fire, they were back by the stream where they had been camped the morning the flames pushed them east. Water had never been a problem. Finding wood, even unburnt buffalo chips to heat coffee over, was a different matter altogether. As the horses and mules were turned up, the men would take one along each morning they went out in search, using the mount to carry back to camp any and all firewood and chips they could find at the end of the day.

"A man might do without a lot of things out here," the old commissary sergeant announced that fourth night as the sky grew as black as the burnt scar of never-ending wilderness they found themselves surrounded by. "But he won't do without his coffee."

Sure enough, Seamus figured, he could choke down the half-raw salt-pork and hardtack with some water. Time was he had even chewed on some coffee beans for the pure, heady flavor. But nothing in the world could replace the pleasure of a steaming cup of coffee in the morning, and another in the evening when the day was done and he was back among friends and the cold, prairie night closed in about them like a tightening, frosty fist swallowing them up.

They never took the ropes off William Graves. Even though it seemed he had lucid moments, but only in between the increasing fits of laughter and rage, the fits of convulsions. Even in those rational moments when he begged and pleaded and bribed and cried and cursed as sane as the next man, even then no one took the ropes off Graves.

And Jack Stillwell had made sure the lieutenant assigned a man to shoot Simon Pierce first—if Pierce was caught trying to release his companion.

"They have their secrets, Lieutenant," Donegan had agreed with Stillwell. "And there's no telling what Graves, or Pierce for that matter, might offer a man to get himself released. But the man's done for."

"It's for the best that all your men stay away from him now. Let Pierce see to his needs until the poison works its way to his heart," Stillwell suggested, trying his best to explain what he had seen happen to others more than a dozen times since childhood.

"There's no chance he'll heal—no chance that he can fight it off?" Pierce asked, walking up to the group that fourth night after Graves had fallen into a fitful sleep, anchored against a wagon wheel with a short tether.

Stillwell shook his head. "I've seen some of those get bit what don't get hydrophobic until months later. Folks thought they was cured—by some magic potion. But of a sudden one day—they was wild and most of them run off. Never heard tell of 'em again."

"Damn luck of it all," Pierce said.

"This change your plans?" asked the lieutenant.

"No, it doesn't. We'll go south to reoutfit, back at Richardson. Then I'm under orders from my superiors so we'll turn right around and come back out here."

"What about Graves?" Donegan asked.

For a moment Pierce regarded his colleague lashed to the wagon wheel some thirty feet away. "I only hope he'll last until we can get him to a doctor."

"Don't count on that," Jack said. "Not a thing a army surgeon can do for him."

Pierce wagged his head. "At least by getting him

back to Fort Richardson he won't be a danger to me any longer."

"You think he'll do you harm?" asked Lieutenant Stanton.

The civilian's face went grave with concern, his eyes pleading for understanding. "Don't you know how bad it makes me feel to see my friend, compatriot and co-worker in such dire distress? Don't you see how it kills something inside of me to see him tied up like an animal? But what with the way he's been acting—there are times when I wonder if he would not turn on me, turn on any of us. How I pray there was something, even some magic, that could cure William of this curse."

"I've known some who think there is magic to cure hydrophobic," Jack said quietly. "They're real hard to find, but some carry mad stones—shaped like an egg, pale-colored like a egg too. A man finds one in the belly of a white doe or white buffalo cow."

"What good is a stone to a man dying of hydrophobic?" asked Stanton skeptically.

"Word says that a mad stone grabs on to the bite wound if there's hydrophobic poison—and a man can't pull it off while the stone is sucking out all the poison. And when the poison's all sucked out, the stone turns a green color—about like the color of the juice in a gut pile when you get through dressing out a buffalo carcass."

"My lord!" Pierce exclaimed quietly, his hand over his mouth in astonishment. "I rhetorically asked for magic—but what you've told me is nothing more than pure paganism."

"The best part of the whole story is the milk," Jack went on. "I've heard from some of the old buffalo hunters who made their living chopping through the Republican herd that the mad stone had to be cleaned in milk after it had sucked all the poison out of a hydrophobic wound. Some of them hide hunters told me they've killed a wet buffalo cow just to milk her udder dry then drop the green mad stone into that warm milk."

"Did the stone turn back to white?" Donegan asked in the hushed silence.

Jack nodded. "After some time in the milk, a man can take the mad stone out and she's as good as new. Ready to keep a man safe again."

Pierce swallowed. "I'm willing to try anything for William. Where do you think we might find such a stone?"

Stillwell glanced at Donegan a moment, then studied Graves tied at the wagon. "Mr. Pierce, your friend there's too far gone. It's been four days now. The poison's gone to his head now—ain't no doubt. You saw how he acted this evening when we pulled him down from the back of the wagon." He looked into Pierce's eyes. "I'm sorry."

Pierce bit a knuckle. "Dear God in heaven—poor William."

Seamus watched the civilian walk away, going over to sit beside Graves as the man slept against the wagon wheel.

"You believe Pierce really cares about saving his partner, Jack?"

Stillwell considered it. "He does make a fine show of it, don't he? But I figure I know enough about men to know when a man's more interested in himself than he is interested in a friend who's done in every bit as sure as if that friend had been bit by a rattler."

"You ever know anyone bit by a hydrophobic animal before?" asked Seamus.

"Yeah—a fella I hunted with back in 'seventy-one.

Lemoy was his name. We was up west of Fort Dodge. Next year, in 'seventy-two, he worked his own outfit. Two of his skinners was bit, so Lemoy went right off and camped by himself on a little sandbar in the middle of the Arkansas River so he'd be safe from the skunks and badgers that was hydrophobic. But he got bit anyway. For all his trouble, he got bit on the cheek. Come the next morning, he built him a fire of some driftwood and heated his knife blade—cauterized the wound before he rode on in to Fort Dodge to see a surgeon. The doctor told him he couldn't done a better job himself."

"So, Lemoy got healed from cauterizing the wound like we did to Graves that first night?"

Jack's face drained of color. "Lemoy was a good man. Drank a might too much. But a good man all the same. No, Seamus. He died too—even after his face healed up nice where he'd burned out the wound's poison. Always was proud of the fact that he could still grow a beard to hide the scar—but he never had much of a chance to get that beard fully growed. He died less'n three months after he got bit. Tore off his clothes in camp one afternoon and run off onto the prairie. We tried to find him—but never did."

"Maybe that hydrophobic does something to a man's soul, Jack. Drives him right on back to the wild things."

"All I know is that last year up on the Arkansas was a bad year for skunks, Seamus. Some fellas put out bait meat with poison—and ended up getting a lot of wolves and coyotes through the summer and into the fall. Hides wasn't worth a whole lot neither. But after last winter, we started to find a lot of dead skunks around—really nothing more'n some dried-up black and white hides and a few bones. Found the carcasses everywhere: in the forts, out by the hide ricks, right at the edge of our camps. Downright spooky, it was."

"The skunks were all gone? Just up and died?"

"Until now, I thought that was so," Jack replied. "But now I'm worried this is turning out to be the beginning of another season of them hydrophobic skunks."

"I suppose we'll never know about them two," Seamus said, watching Graves whispering in Pierce's ear, and Pierce shaking his head. Graves lunged at Pierce, struggling in vain to get loose from the ropes that tied both wrists to the wagon wheel before he sank in enraged frustration to the ground again.

"I'll be happy when we get back to Richardson with this outfit," Jack said. "I don't figure Camp Supply is any closer than heading southeast would be."

"Pierce will turn you back around when you do start heading this outfit in to the fort," Seamus said. "By the saints, it'll be the dead of winter when he drags you back out here. But you best be prepared for more argument and threats from that one."

"No—I don't figure Pierce will be able to do that," Jack replied. "Not with Colonel Ranald S. Mackenzie having anything to say about what happens to his soldiers and where they go and when they march. No, Mackenzie's the sort will tie that badger-faced Pierce up in knots so tight he and his Washington friends won't be able to get loose until spring anyway. By then—yes, I'll come back out here with Pierce. And so will you . . . just to see what it is we came out here to do in the first place."

"You're so damned sure about me joining you, ain't you, Jack Stillwell?"

"I am at that, you bloody Irishman," he cheered. "Unless you've got marrying on your mind."

"M-Marrying?"

"Samantha Pike? Ain't you gone soft on her now?"

Donegan choked. "She's a pretty thing and a real joy to smell and hold, she is—but . . . marrying is a whole different matter now."

"Best you explain that to Sharp's wife—Samantha's sister. I figure they've all three got you measured for a marrying suit, Seamus Donegan."

"I'll have no more such talk," the Irishman protested, clapping his hands over his ears.

"All right then—it's time for me to find my bedroll anyway," Jack replied, strolling off. "Have yourself some sweet dreams, Seamus—filled with that doe-eyed Samantha Pike."

"Sweet dreams, indeed," he growled, dragging out his own canvas bedroll and pulling back the wool blankets inside the waterproof sacking. Winter was come to the southern plains, and all warmth would again be drawn from the ground with another nightfall. The cozy cocoon felt good to him, despite the unrelenting hardness of the ground where his hip and shoulder lay.

And, try as he might to fight it, Seamus did fall asleep thinking on Samantha Pike—thinking on her ravenous hunger that had surprised him there on the blankets and hay in Sharp Grover's lopsided barn.

At the crack of the pistol Seamus was up and kicking at the blankets, his own pistol drawn and cocked as he came awake.

Overhead the sky still domed as black as the inside of a cast-iron kettle, but along the eastern rim of the world stretched a long, gray line of winter's light.

And standing in the dim glow of last night's coals

was Simon Pierce, his pistol hung at the end of his right arm, smoke curling from its muzzle. At his feet slumped William Graves, blood oozing from both bullet wounds: the one fired at close range between his eyes, blackened with powder burns; and the messy, bigger exit wound that glistened the back of his head as he sagged against the rope tethers binding him to the wagon wheel.

"What the hell you doing, Pierce?" demanded the lieutenant, pulling on his wool coat against the stiff, bone-numbing wind heavy with the smell of snow. He hurried over and yanked the pistol from the civilian.

"I . . . I," he started, then dragged the empty pistol hand beneath his drippy nose. "I had to. He . . . William asked me."

"Asked you to do what?" Donegan demanded.

Pierce glanced up, looking for the moment like a wounded animal. Seamus almost felt sorry for him. Then the eyes went cold again.

"Asked me to kill him." Pierce knelt beside the body, picking up one of Graves's hands in his, stroking it like a sick child's. "He said he couldn't take the pain anymore. He was frightened of the uncertainty. Not knowing when the insanity would come."

"You're the one what's crazy," Seamus growled, suspicion eating a hole in his gut. "I've a mind to turn you over to—"

"This is a government expedition, Donegan," Pierce snapped, glaring up at the tall Irishman. "These soldiers are my personal guard—and you'll do well to act the same."

"Is he right, Lieutenant?" asked Jack Stillwell.

Stanton nodded grudgingly. "Unless someone prefers charges against Mr. Pierce, there won't be an inquiry into the shooting. You, Mr. Donegan?"

Seamus glanced at Jack. Stillwell shook his head slightly, almost imperceptibly.

"I . . . I suppose not, Lieutenant," Donegan found himself saying, as much as the gall rose in his throat to say it.

There was something inside his belly that hammered away at him, something that made Seamus believe Pierce had shot his partner to keep him quiet. Perhaps out of the fear that with Graves slowly growing insane with every passing hour, William Graves would indeed spill his guts about something. To shut the man up . . . and then Seamus looked at Jack Stillwell again.

Maybe there was a good reason Jack did not want him to protest, to ask for an inquiry. Maybe Jack knew something . . .

"Very well," the lieutenant replied, a look of extreme worry crossing his face. He turned and called for two soldiers to abandon their bedrolls, to cut the dead man loose from the wheel and get him wrapped in two blankets.

"Ain't he gonna start to smell if we don't bury him, Lieutenant?" one of them asked.

"Not in this cold, sojur," Seamus answered, shivering.

"Snow's coming—soon," Jack said, smelling the air. "You want the man buried in the morning, Lieutenant?"

In turn the officer looked at Simon Pierce. "Mr. Pierce—are we to bury your companion here before we pull away in the morning?"

He was a few moments in answering, finally dropping the limp hand of William Graves. "By all means, Lieutenant. We'll give him a decent burial here . . . in this wild country where we had both hoped to make the discovery that would rock the civilized world."

"You heard the man," Stanton said to his soldiers. "Wrap the body up and we'll bury it in the morning. And the rest of you, back to sleep. Damn, if it doesn't feel like winter itself is coming down on us at that."

Chapter 28

**Mid-November
1873**

*G*raves was mad . . . raving mad.

Although his face didn't grow distorted there at the last, in the cold, winter darkness beside the glowing coals of the fire—although he did not rant and rave like a lunatic . . . Graves was mad nonetheless.

Simon Pierce was sure of it. As sure of it as he had ever been of anything.

Oh, for sure Graves was an intelligent being—very likely savvy enough to control the creeping, incipient insanity. That's the only reason he hadn't appeared or sounded crazy there at the last.

Perhaps it was only what he had told Pierce that was crazy. Yet what he said with that wild, consumed look in his eye proved that the cartographer was downright insane.

But Simon didn't need the map expert any longer. As much as he had watched Graves brooding over the fragile Castilian parchment, as much as Graves himself had innocently and stupidly shared all the map's secrets with Pierce—Simon no longer needed Graves along. If things had turned out differently, there would have been more than enough to divide between the two of them. But now, with Graves unwittingly providing his own untimely exit, Simon Pierce found himself center stage at this singular moment in history, no longer compelled to share with any man the limelight, the fortune, and the ultimate in raw power that would come from that treasure.

Who knows? Simon Pierce thought to himself as they rolled through the growing darkness of midday, marching northwest on a course away from Fort Richardson and Jacksboro, where Lieutenant Stanton and the others had wanted to go after the prairie fire—marching away from the safety of the settlements . . . north by west because Pierce ordered the party to continue its march across the Llano Estacado.

Yes, he thought. Indeed, there have been rumors of great distress in Mexico. Perhaps they are ready for a benevolent leader—one who can buy his own army and navy, a presidente who will not take any guff from the big bully to the north. Perhaps the time was right, the stars in alignment, the fates smiling on him —everything ready to make a very wealthy American the president of Mexico and, who could say? Perhaps with a well-paid army and navy, El President Pierce could reach out and absorb the riches of Central America as well.

Why stop there? He could easily defeat the ignorant Indians of South America with his unstoppable military. By then there could be no telling how much power one man might hold.

Money was power, he knew. And by controlling the world's greatest wealth, Simon Pierce just might possess the greatest power in the world.

"Are you warm enough, Mr. Pierce?"

"What?" he asked, surprised, of the lieutenant who had ridden back to the rattling wagon crowded with soldiers, their dwindling rations and camp supplies. "Oh, yes. Thank you. Warm enough."

Simon found the eyes of the soldiers in the wagon glaring at him. Indeed, he was the warmest, having selected the softest spot among the bedrolls for himself. The rest squatted precariously atop campaign gear while he was rocked in the lap of luxury. At least enough luxury that the dropping temperature and icy flakes lancing down from the lead-belly sky bothered him very little. He could tell the rest of the soldiers were miserable. Perhaps it was time to spread some cheer.

"Thank you for your words over William's grave this morning, private," he said to the young soldier squatting to his left. "I was most happy you remembered so many kind thoughts and scriptures to repeat over his final resting place."

The soldier sniffled, his nose red in the angry wind. "My mama taught me the bible at her knee. Likely I've heard the burial service said over and over again more times than I have years, Mr. Pierce. But you've no need to thank me—every man deserves to have the proper words said over his mortal remains."

"Yes—dust to dust . . . ashes to ashes," he sighed thoughtfully. "We are all but temporary wayfarers, aren't we?"

The young soldier never did answer his poetic flight, but looked away instead, resuming his watch of the darkening sky churning out of the north with the others.

To hell with you then, soldier, Pierce thought. Let them believe what they will. Any of them—including those two civilians. Especially that big Irishman. There was no way any judge or court of law could convince a jury that Simon Pierce had killed William Graves with anything but the most humane intentions . . . simply to ease a troubled and fellow wayfarer from this earthly veil, at his own request. And besides, who was there who could testify to, much less prove, that William Graves hadn't begged Simon Pierce to shoot him—to put him out of his great and unfortunate misery?

Certainly not that Irishman who Pierce sensed was suspicious, and therefore clearly enough a threat. Perhaps not even that young Stillwell, who, while quiet, showed great distrust in his eyes for how Pierce had explained the killing.

It mattered little now—for after William's burial, Pierce had ordered Lieutenant Stanton to turn about and head northwest once more—against the protests of both Stillwell and Donegan. Simon was not about to be deterred now—and if that meant placing the two guides under military arrest, he would see to that in the days to come.

Low food supply? Nothing more than an inconvenience. Simply have the soldiers find some game in this veritably unpopulated countryside. There were clearly no Indians to be found, Indians scaring off the animals. Stanton's soldiers could surely find game enough to sustain the party.

What of the incoming storm? Listen to the carping! Were they not soldiers? Simon had jeered. Did they not have tents, bedrolls and the wherewithal to survive in all conditions of nature?

No, for all the protests Stillwell and Donegan raised, Pierce had answered them in due course. He was, after all, much smarter than they. Oh, either one of them might have more experiential knowledge of the land and its native inhabitants, and possess more of the requisite survival skills. But nonetheless, Simon Pierce was clear and away much smarter than either of those bumpkins.

The lieutenant and his men were soldiers, trained to take orders from their superiors—and Simon was clearly the superior mind remaining in the party now . . . what with William's unfortunate tangle with that hydrophobic skunk. With the lieutenant and his obedient troopers allied behind him, Pierce had only to concern himself with the two guides. They were the unknowns, the variable factors to this great scientific expedition. They were ultimately the men Pierce had to monitor most closely.

Those two . . . yes, and keeping the discovery of the treasure a secret until he could find its exact location, return to Jacksboro where he would hire on an entire team of laborers who would be protected by a mercenary army Pierce would enlist and bring along to make sure none of the wealth slipped through his fingers.

No, William Graves might have been many things . . . he might even have been raving mad there at the end—but there was surely one small piece of his sanity the man clung to with all his might right down to the bloody end.

Graves realized he was slipping, like a man on a mud-soaked slope, with no place to dig in his toes, nowhere to claw with his hands. Graves realized it—felt compelled to tell Simon about the blood money he had paid to acquire a small piece of the treasure from a Mexican Comanchero, a bandit who had murdered a Tonkawa guide for it, who in turn had killed a Kiowa warrior for the small but heavy treasure that now rested in the dirty scrap of corduroy Graves said it was wrapped in when he had struck his bargain with the Comanchero.

Only moments before Pierce had killed Graves, the cartographer had explained how, in his putting the pieces of the old Spanish puzzle together, he had spent more than two years sniffing around in Mexico, and finally came up with the band of Comancheros who knew something of the ancient legends about El Llano Estacado. With the wealth of the Graves family, William had promised one of the bandits a small fortune for that single piece of treasure two men had already died for.

When Graves finally had the treasure in his hands, and the Mexican bandit had his money, the two marksmen and bodyguards William had hired killed the Comanchero. No mess. And no great expenditure of his family's wealth. And William Graves had one of the last pieces needed in the great Castilian puzzle.

But now Simon had to grin with the thought, four men had paid with blood for this piece of the unimaginable treasure to come this close to returning home. First the aging Kiowa warrior who had originally owned the sacred object, handed down to him through six generations of warriors. Then in turn the Tonkawa and the Comanchero bandit . . . and finally William Graves. Every last one of them had been killed for their silence. More men might need to be murdered perhaps—to assure their tongues would never wag.

The Spanish had come halfway around the world to claim the riches of the New World as their own: Indian gold.

Simon Pierce stuffed a cold hand inside the flaps of his wool coat, feeling beneath his fingers the reassuring firmness of the treasure he had taken from William's effects—still wrapped in that scrap of gray-brown corduroy, and now safely ensconced under Simon's shirt.

A bar of it: not much bigger than the width of his palm. Smooth and hard, and heavy as a brick.

Indian gold—said to be taken right from the tall,

gleaming walls of Coronado's fabled Seven Cities of Cibola.

Winter Man must be very angry with The People.

There was no other explanation that Quanah Parker could think of as he struggled to keep his pony pointed in the right direction. It struggled against the rein, wanting to quarter to the wind, bringing its rump around. But that would mean he and the warriors would not find their village in the fading light here at midday with the dark clouds sodden with ice and snow looming over the nearby hills. Ever closer.

Already it was the beginning of the Moon of Deer Shedding Horns. A season grown old with cold and stiff muscles.

They had been moving in a slow, lazy arc ever since leaving the village more than a moon ago. Quanah led all those young warriors who wanted to make one last ride before winter squeezed down hard on the land. It was even more of a struggle now to control the pony than it had been when they had set the grassfires before the wind many suns ago.

Oh, to have that warmth now as Winter Man's angry breath howled out of the north.

Quanah's scouts had come back to the main party with word they had discovered a small band of soldiers and a handful of other white men riding northwest across the Staked Plain.

"How many is small?" Quanah had asked.

The young scout held up his five fingers, then struck that right hand across his left forearm three times.

The Kwahadi chief had peered over his warriors, almost ten-times-ten of them, all wrapped in blankets or robes, their hair streaming in the wind. Each one of them anxious for coups. Many howled in disappointment when he told them there was no honor in wiping out the small band of yellowlegs.

"But what of the white hide hunters we have killed, whenever we run across them in Kwahadi buffalo country?" asked one of the older warriors.

"They are something different," he had explained. "Something evil. I will always kill the hide hunters who come only to slaughter the buffalo and take food from the mouths of our families."

"How can you be sure these yellowlegs do not mean trouble?" asked one of the others.

"*Aiyeee!* Let us kill them quickly, Quanah!" said a third.

"Yes! We can always use more soldier guns," said another.

"No—whenever we attack the yellowlegs, they always send more," Quanah had explained solidly. "Don't you remember the lessons taught you yet? The soldiers always come, always. It is not they who are the problem now. It is the hide hunter who comes out of the north. Not the yellowlegs who come from the south and east."

"Then let us make sport with them!" a warrior demanded.

Another howled, "Good—we can scare them and turn their pants to water!"

Quanah had waited while they all had their laugh. "Perhaps we can scare them—but not by attacking them. The soldier guns shoot far and they can shoot straight. We might have fun, meaning only to give them a good scare . . . but the yellowlegs will not know that, and one of you might be killed—all for a little fun? No," he told them. "We will only scare them away. Drive them back east, where they belong and are to stay."

"How do we do this?"

Quanah had turned to the young warrior and said, "We will build a fire—between us and the soldiers. The wind at our backs will drive the flames toward them."

"A big fire?" asked another excitedly.

"Yes—it is late in the season and the buffalo have gone south. Make this a big fire and let's see how well the soldiers run from it. Perhaps a wild thing like a prairie fire will turn their bowels to water and make them cry for their mothers!"

"Hi-yi! Hi-yi!" they yipped in excitement, worked into a lather to set the flames that eventually spread across countless miles as the horsemen carried firebrands both north and south, igniting the grassland sucked dry of moisture with autumn's arid winds.

Come spring he would have to return to that country to see what he could find of the blackened remnants of the wagon—or see if the yellowlegs had indeed escaped the rushing flames.

Now their great arching march was reaching its completion, the arc that had swept north toward the Canadian River, turning east and sweeping southward again into the land where they found the yellowlegs and started the fire. And now Winter Man was showing his unhappiness with The People. Why else would he roar down on them so early in the season?

Perhaps Winter Man, like the other spirits, were angry with the Kwahadi because the Comanche had not driven the hide hunters from their country. Perhaps.

Why else this terrible vengeance come on the back of the cruel wind that was the breath of Winter Man?

If that was so, Quanah did not understand the spirits. It was not a warrior's way to slaughter a small, outnumbered band of soldiers. But it was the way of

the Kwahadi warrior to slaughter the small, outnumbered bands of hide hunters wherever his warriors
could find them.

Yes, he told himself now, pushing the long hair
from his face and tugging the furry buffalo robe more
tightly against his cheek where the wind scoured and
bullied his skin, giving it the feel of scraped rawhide
worked with an antler fleshing tool.

Yes.

And the idea began forming itself in his mind as the
brutal cold sought to numb every other part of his
body. He had the beginning of a plan to stop the
white man from crossing the dead line, a plan to
drive the white man from the northern part of the
Staked Plain for all time. Perhaps it would work—
one concerted effort between the Comanche, the Kiowa, and the Cheyenne as well. To attack in force
those camps of buffalo hunters and make it too ex-
pensive in lives lost for any of the white men to again
dare venturing south of the Cimarron River.

To rid the Kwahadi buffalo country of this spreading disease that was turning their land into a slaughter yard—a place of stinking, rotting carcasses,
where only the huge-winged, black birds of prey
would travel. This was becoming a place where the
air was no longer sweet and where the water tasted
foul on the tongue because of the carcasses lying rancid in the creeks and streams where the great buffalo
had come only to drink—but found instead the white
hunters waiting with their big rifles.

No more would Kwahadi land be a place where the
white hunters could roam and slaughter with freedom. When Winter Man was done squeezing this
land between his cold hands, when the short-grass
time had come and their ponies were sleek and fat
once more on the green shoots raising their heads

from the brown breast of the earth all across the prairie—then Quanah would lead the three warrior bands against the hide hunters.

They would find the hide hunters where the hide hunters gathered.

And in one fell swoop, wipe them all off the face of the earth.

Chapter 29

**Mid-November
1873**

*A*utumn was gone in less time than it took a man to eat his breakfast.

Winter had arrived, battering the land with a snarling, wind-driven rage.

Seamus felt Stillwell tugging on his arm.

"Now I know why we didn't see any buffalo for the past two weeks!" Jack shouted into the fury of the wind that whipped icy flakes at them like tiny, painful arrowpoints.

"The buffalo knew this was on its way?" Donegan asked.

Stillwell only nodded.

Once more they both pulled the wool mufflers back over their faces so only their squinted eyes were visible below their hat brims.

A day ago there had been a little warning, Seamus recalled. The wind—quartering around out of the north. It presaged the dark, forbidding presence looming along the northern horizon ahead of them. But mostly it had been the change in the wind. Something to its smell. Not only the sudden cold this time.

More the smell of death carried on the wind's icy wings.

It was during the noon break yesterday, and then again when they had stopped to make camp last evening, that Jack had convinced the lieutenant to have his men scour the prairie in all four directions for buffalo chips. With orders for each man to take along a blanket to carry the chips in, the soldiers dispersed in a wide circle, returning near dark with their prairie firewood.

Seamus thought now how fortunate they had been that Jack had made that suggestion to the lieutenant and his soldiers. No sooner was the last trooper back in camp than the sky turned loose with a torrent of wind-driven rain. And once everything was good and soaked through and through—clothes, tents and bedrolls—the temperature started to drop dramatically, quickly changing what had only been a chilling rain into a freezing, life-robbing, man-killing sleet.

They had huddled together for warmth under the wagon cover stretched to the ground from the wagon's high-wall, and somehow got through that night in their wet clothing. By the next morning not one of them wasn't sniffling, runny-nosed and red-eyed from more than a sleepless night. A smoky fire brought them little cheer, and a cup of hot coffee only made a few complain of their gnawing bellies.

At least at Fort Richardson, the soldiers grumped, they damned well knew what there was to eat. It was hot, and usually there was plenty of it to go the rounds. Here they had nothing.

Shivering in his soaked clothing, Simon Pierce silently glared back at each of the complainers, from all appearances making note of those who proved less than enthusiastic about his unswerving dedication in pushing on to the Canadian River.

"What's up there, Jack?" Seamus had asked Stillwell that very morning while they saddled their two horses in the driving, freezing drizzle. A man crackled as he walked about, bent his elbows, worked his shoulders throwing blanket and saddle atop his uncooperative horse.

"Up where?"

"On the Canadian."

Jack shrugged, pulling his dripping hat down tighter on his curly hair with his gloves, which were soaked through. "Don't know."

"You been there?"

"Couple times. With buffalo outfits—first time was two years back, it was. Then last year."

"That's out and out Injin country, ain't it, Jack?"

Stillwell swung his arms. "All of this is, dammit." He looked up at the Irishman, his face softening. "I'm sorry. You didn't deserve that."

"It's all right—I understand," Seamus replied. "It's that bleeming Pierce got us all in this bind. I've got to figure a way out before we all go the way Graves did—stark-raving mad."

"I'm not so sure you should try anything, Seamus. I don't know what power a government man has on any of us in something like this."

"He don't have the power to make us die for something," Donegan whispered.

Stillwell wagged his head. "What's the difference, Irishman? We rode along with Major Forsyth—and he had the power to ask us to die for something . . . didn't he?"

Drawing a deep breath so cold that it burned its way into the dregs of his lungs, Donegan's thoughts swam with his uncle Liam O'Roarke and Sharp Grover and that hot, sandy, bloody island in the middle of the Arickaree, with Major George A. Forsyth down and suffering three festering bullet wounds while Lieutenant Fred Beecher lay dying in a hollowed-out riflepit surrounded by the bloated, stinking army horses they had shot for breastworks . . . the flies forever buzzing and laying their eggs in the untended wounds of those asked to fight and very likely die in this nameless, unmapped place on the high plains.*

Seamus sighed, his face stinging with the crackling cold of the wind-driven sleet. "I suppose you're right, Jack Stillwell. When it comes to army matters—men like you and me just don't have much say in anything has to do with our living or dying."

Completely saddled, only then had they untied their horses, lashed one to the other since nightfall. All the stock had been paired in that manner before twilight had arrived, bringing with it the driving sleet and the phosphorescent lightning that rendered the whitening, ghostly sky a pale, greenish color. It was an old plainsmen's rule to lash a pair of animals together, in addition to using the individual hobbles before each soldier drove an iron picket pin into the hard, crusty earth—in the hope that all their precautions would slow the horses and mules from wandering far from their miserable camp beneath the wagon shroud that slapped and cracked on the brutal wind.

They hadn't been up and on the march for more than three long and weary hours now, nosing almost straight on into the wind, when Jack grabbed Seamus's arm again, signaling the Irishman to rein up. Stillwell pulled down his faded muffler and hollered into the force of the gale, his eyes blinking with its cruel blast beneath his crusted hat brim. Every shotgun flurry of icy snow made a man's eyes smart with cold pain.

"This is fool's work, Seamus!" he hollered. "It's

---

* The Plainsmen Series, vol. 3, *The Stalkers*

getting too deep . . . and bound to start drifting worse."

"What do you fix on doing? Make camp here?" Donegan asked, his own stinging eyes moving quickly across the diminishing horizons for something that might beckon as a suitable place to hunker down for the brunt of the blizzard.

"Make camp here and hope for the best."

"Here?" Donegan asked, disbelieving.

"You got any better ideas—best spit them out now, Irishman!"

"Here," Seamus repeated. "Here is where we'll make camp and *pray* for the best, Jack."

Stillwell nodded. "C'mon, let's go give Pierce the bad news."

They reined around and backtracked through the eight new inches of snow resting atop at least a half dozen of old crusty snow, all of it becoming wind-scoured in the short time they had been on the march that morning. Fifty yards behind the two horsemen, in the blinding swirl of icy, stinging white buckshot, loomed the dark shapes of the wagon and the four mounted troopers.

"Lieutenant! We best make camp!" Stillwell shouted.

"Where?" asked Stanton.

"Right here!"

The lieutenant glanced at Donegan as if he thought Stillwell might be crazy.

"There's no place any better than this we can find," Seamus said. "And the sooner we get at making ourselves comfortable for what's coming, the better off we're going to be."

Stanton appeared to chew on that a moment. "What makes you an expert on prairie blizzards, Mr. Donegan?"

"I've been through my share, Lieutenant. The first I got through was a killer—and I doubt I'll ever forget what winter can do up on the Bozeman Road."

"Bozeman Road? When were you up in that country?" he demanded in a doubtful tone.

"Fort Phil Kearny," Seamus answered, his voice almost stolen by the howling wind. "December, 1866."*

"You knew Fetterman?"

"A good soldier, so I was told," Seamus replied. "A might lacking in good sense on that bleeming, bloody day."

The lieutenant's face went taut. "Was it . . . was it true what the rumors said ever since?"

"What rumors?"

"That a lot of Fetterman's men killed themselves on Lodge Trail Ridge?"

Seamus shrugged, dragging his wool glove beneath his tearing eyes, both of them stinging with the icy snow. "I imagine they fought as long as it looked like they had a chance. But from what I saw of the place just after, those sojurs didn't have a chance at all. The few of us who saw the bodies scattered up and down that ridge know why the fight was over so bloody quick. But that bit of news isn't something the army wants being spread around among its sojurs, Lieutenant."

"All right, gentlemen," Stanton sighed. "We'll camp and pray we make it through this. Let's go tell the others what you need them to do."

In the swirl of snow some twenty feet behind them waited the rest of the soldiers and Simon Pierce, all huddled in the wagon. Like two dark coals positioned atop his muffler, the civilian's feral eyes glared with

suspicion when Stillwell and Donegan appeared out
of the white swirl on either side of the lieutenant.

"We're stopping here, Pierce," Stanton announced.

The coal eyes flared. "Why?"

"The storm's worsening."

"The horses and mules are getting us through it for
now, Lieutenant."

Jack nudged his horse closer to the wagon so he
could be heard in the howling wind that stole voices
across the endless prairie. "Yes—for now they can
make it—"

"Then we'll keep on until we can't go any longer,"
Pierce snapped matter-of-factly, declaring an end to
the discussion.

"No, Pierce," Donegan said.

Pierce shot the Irishman a look of unconcealed hatred. "Lieutenant, I want this man placed under arrest for insubordination."

Stanton tore his eyes from the government official
and looked first at Stillwell, then at Donegan. Finally
he gazed again at the shivering Simon Pierce.

"No. Like I said, we're stopping here. I have the
lives of my men to consider." He turned to the three
others on horseback, waving his arm to bring them
in.

"Goddamn you, Lieutenant—I'll have your bars!"

"You may have my bars, Mr. Pierce. But, by damn,
I'll save the lives of every one of these men I can . . .
and maybe yours as well."

"You arrogant prig!" Pierce vaulted to his knees
and swung around in the middle of the wagon,
shrieking at the rest of the soldiers to obey his orders.
"Place your commander under arrest! It's treason!
High treason!"

"All of you—get out of the wagons and start mov-

ing—now!" shouted the lieutenant. "Put your backs
into it like you've never done before. Some of you,
pair up the stock. The rest of you, lash up the wagon
cover like we did last night. Erect the tents if you can,
double-staking against the wind."

Stillwell and Donegan were on the ground, tying
their horses off to a wagon wheel as the old commissary sergeant clambered down from his seat stiffly,
banging his arms on his sides and dancing to get
some circulation back in his legs.

"Soldier!" he hollered at the closest trooper hunch-
ing past in the white swirl. "Be sure you drag in that
sowbelly of buffalo chips when the rest of them got
the shroud up!" The sergeant turned to Donegan and
winked, which creased half his frozen, windburned
face. "Boys, looks like I'm going to try to build the
most important damned fire I ever started in my
life."

As quickly as the tents went up, each one filled with
wind-driven snow—billowing, then sucking empty as
a flattened bladder, then puffing full again with fury
—they ripped free of their double stakes one by one,
to go tumbling off to the south, disappearing. No man
went after them. They had their hands full beneath
the wagon and canvas shroud, the wind grown so
strong it threatened to topple it onto them.

For the moment most of the soldiers were gathered
around the old sergeant as he struggled, one match
after another, to light the fire in the lee they formed
with their shivering bodies.

"Goddamn you!" Pierce wailed suddenly, lunging
forward and with his gloved hands flinging the char
and buffalo chips one way then another.

"Get that sonofabitch and tie him up!" snarled
Donegan.

"Put him over there!" Stanton ordered, yelling

from behind a shoulder he raised to protect his face from the stinging snow.

"Let's pull the wagon over," Jack Stillwell suggested. "It'll make a windbreak for us where we can get under the shroud as the snow builds up."

For a moment the lieutenant thought, then agreed. "Throw everything out of the wagon, here! Then put your backs behind it."

"Leave my belongings—" Pierce shrieked, tearing away from the two soldiers restraining him, darting to the open gate at the rear of the wagon and vaulting himself up.

"Get him now!" the lieutenant shouted.

"These are mine!"

Donegan watched as Pierce scrambled over bedrolls and extra tack, snatching up the long leather map tube and his canvas valise with one arm. Without fail the other arm never moved from Pierce's midsection, as if he were clutching something to him, hidden there beneath his coat.

Roughly the soldiers dragged the man out of the wagon by his ankles. He rolled onto his back clumsily, the map case and valise tumbling from his hold on them. Pierce lashed out with his boots, connecting with a soldier's jaw, and sent the trooper sprawling. The other soldier, bigger and stronger, began to twist the civilian's ankle to control Pierce.

Pierce cried out, gritting his teeth in pain, and pulled his right hand from his coat pocket. The pistol roared, muzzle-flash bright in the murky gloom of the descending blizzard.

With only a look of shock, the soldier took a stumbling step backward, his mouth moving wordlessly as he slowly turned to the others as if asking for help, a neat, blue-black hole in his forehead that began to

ooze sluggish blood. He collapsed into the small
snowdrift forming behind the wagon.

Scooping up the valise and map case, Pierce held
the pistol on the others as he clambered down from
the wagonbed.

"I don't need you now, Lieutenant," he said, wagging the pistol to herd the soldiers into a tighter
bunch. "The Canadian isn't far."

Seamus had seen that same light in the eyes of a
few others in his time. A crazed, empowered light
that would suffer not other men, nor suffer something so insignificant as a winter blizzard attempting
to darken the glow of its madness.

Stanton took a step toward the fallen soldier.

Pierce brought up the pistol, his hand trembling
terribly. "Stay where you are. He's dead."

The officer halted as suddenly. "You . . . you're
going to the Canadian now? In the middle of all
this?"

Pierce nodded. "All of you can stay here. With your
precious wagon and animals. I'm going on. And
when I've made my report to Washington City—
there's not a man of you won't be rotting in jail for
the rest of your miserable lives."

"You'll die out there," Stanton said.

His eyes widened as he laughed. "Die? I think
you're mad, Lieutenant. As mad as William Graves
was. And you've become a man I see I cannot trust
now. So, you'll be the first to suffer disgrace when I
return in triumph to Washington City . . . New York
and the world!"

Pierce turned halfway to the beckoning, white prairie, clutching his few precious belongings beneath his
arm, waving the pistol at Donegan, who inched toward the dead soldier.

"Stay away! Or you'll get the same, Irishman!"

Seamus wagged his head. "A shame the blizzard is going to claim you, Pierce. I'd love to watch you die myself."

He laughed, a crazed cackle that he had to swallow down with a breath-robbing, howling gust of wind. "You'd love to kill me yourself—admit it, you insolent, brainless mick!"

"You're right about something for once, Pierce. Yes —I'd like to kill you myself."

"C'mon then. Show these soldiers how brave you are. Take me."

Donegan stared at the muzzle of that pistol, flexing his fists, anxious to try it, assessing the odds of crossing the drifts of icy snow, perhaps dodging one shot . . . but by putting the bullet between the soldier's eyes, Pierce had proved himself too good a marksman. Tonguing down the gall of his disappointment, Seamus resigned himself to allowing the land and the storm to take Simon Pierce.

"Afraid, aren't you?" the civilian shrieked. He began backing away, the thin veil of swirling white between him and the rest growing thicker with each step into the storm.

Pierce laughed. "The ancient conquistadors had far more courage than any of you . . . more than all of you put together! They braved this wilderness without a whimper—as I am now to do. So don't you see? The untold wealth that awaits me can't belong to anyone else—I alone am brave enough to walk in their footsteps. I alone can possess the wealth I will find in the walls carved with gold—where the ancient peoples will anoint me their new king! Hail to the mighty monarch!"

The hair raised on the back of Donegan's neck as he listened to the civilian's fading, maniacal voice. It had a ghostly quality as it was bullied by the growing howls of the storm.

"I alone will rule the fabled Seven Cities of Cibola!"

"You're insane, Simon Pierce!" Seamus flung his voice back at the gauzy apparition as Pierce disappeared into the blizzard.

"You'll wish you would have gone with me, Irishman! One of these days you'll pray you hadn't crossed me! I'll have power . . . such great power!"

Chapter 30

Late November
1873

*N*ever had he seen a blizzard like that in his young life.

Jack Stillwell had been through his share of northers on the prairie, but nothing had prepared him for the vicious rage of that capricious winter storm that roared down on the southern plains in the early winter of 1873.

By sawing a spare double-tree in half, the soldiers had formed two poles they used to prop up one side of the wagon they had tipped over for shelter. There beneath the wagon shroud, with the wagon itself keeling on its side to cut most of the life-robbing wind, they huddled through the next two nights while the world shrank around them, becoming more white and silent as the endless hours passed.

From time to time one of them would complain of the cold, or grumble about his gnawing belly, but there wasn't a one of them who complained for very long at a stretch. Someone else would remind them of the specter of Simon Pierce out there, somewhere in the storm—likely dead already.

Or someone might remind the grumbler about Malley—the soldier Pierce had killed before the civilian took off into the teeth of the blizzard.

Beneath the flapping shroud and their wool blankets and the deepening cavern of snow swallowing them, the men stayed warm enough. While they could still see their breath suspended in gauzy sheets before their faces, they realized at least the skin on those faces hadn't frozen to the stiffness of buffalo rawhide.

Throughout those two days of waiting for the raging howl of the storm to pass, the old sergeant or Donegan or Jack or the lieutenant keep feeding small chunks of the dried buffalo chips to the smoky coals that gave off enough heat to cut most of the chill sneaking through the exposed wagon planks or seeping behind the edges of the wagon shroud, showering them at times with a dusting of icy, white silt.

But through the hours that stretched into more than two days, the soldiers told jokes, regaled one another with memories of the war, told favorite stories, sang a few songs and learned some others, besides making use of a greasy, well-wrinkled pack of cards the old sergeant always carried. With nothing for chips, they played for all the wealth in Washington City, for all the gold near Sutter's Mill or in Cripple Creek or up north along Alder Gulch in Montana Territory.

And they would sleep a lot. It did not matter when, what with the little light coming through the canvas like watered-down milk to let a man know if it was day or night. All they had was the lieutenant's pocket watch to know that time really was passing. Too slowly, but passing all the same.

"You hear that, Seamus?" Jack asked, nudging the big man huddled beside him, snoring quietly with most of the others. Stillwell had kept himself awake, feeding the little fire that had likely saved the lives of thirteen lucky men.

Donegan stirred, cocking an ear for a moment before he turned to the young scout. "No—don't hear a thing."

Stillwell rose to his knees, joints stiff with cold and lack of movement. "That's just what I mean, Irishman!"

"By the saints and the Virgin Mary!" Seamus cried, lunging at Stillwell. They embraced fiercely as the others began to stir.

"What's going—" Stanton started to ask. Then his eyes grew wide. "Is the . . . is it over?"

Jack's head bobbed. He sensed the sting of salty moisture at his eyes. "I think so, Lieutenant."

Most of the others were howling now, happily. Now that the noisy, wind-driven blizzard had passed, their voices and laughter and the hearty slaps they delivered to one another echoed within the tiny shelter that had kept them cramped, but alive, for more than two days on the Staked Plain.

"Suppose I go see how the world looks outside, fellas," Jack told them, then turned to the Irishman. "You wanna come have a look for yourself, Seamus?"

"Anything to stretch my legs."

As Donegan turned and started to pull aside the canvas wagon shroud, a shower of snow tumbled into their shelter.

"Watch it, you dumb mick!" howled the old sergeant. "Move aside and let a old file show you how to dig hisself out."

"That's right, Donegan," said one of the troopers. "Sarge there is about small enough, and he knows how to tunnel real proper—just like a barracks rat burrowing down in my tick."

"You got rats in your beds, have you?" Seamus asked as the sergeant squeezed past him.

"If'n we wanted anything else as warm and squirmy as them rats in a bed," declared the sergeant, "a soldier's gotta go visit one of them whores over to Jacksboro!"

In a few minutes all they could see of the sergeant was his boots. Then a moment later he let out a muffled whoop and began scooting back down into the canvas and wagon shelter. He turned around, his eyelashes and the five-day growth on his cheeks frosted.

"There's sunshine out there, boys!"

"Thank you kindly, sergeant," said Stillwell, slapping the old soldier on the shoulder as he eased by in the cramped space and began clawing his way up the tunnel dug by the sergeant.

Even before he had made it to the top of the drift, Jack could see blue sky, and the light grew so bright it hurt his eyes for a moment. He blinked them clear, then started back down the tunnel, where he bumped into Donegan.

"Aren't you going out to greet this glorious day, Jack?" Seamus asked, allowing Stillwell back into the shelter.

He grinned. "Damn if I ain't. We been like rats here in this dark hole for more'n two days. That sun's too damned bright—my eyes can't take it all at once."

Dragging off one of his wool gloves, Jack dipped a couple of fingers in the black soot at the center of the shelter where the buffalo chip fire had kept them warm. He smeared the soot beneath one eye, then dipped so he could smear a fat gash of black beneath the other eye.

"You fellas best do the same—you fix on coming out to see the world with me," Jack said.

"Can we, Lieutenant?" one asked.

"That's right—we gotta go up some time, sir."

"Let's all go," Stanton sighed, then grinned. "We might as well take a look at the work that awaits us."

"Damn," growled the sergeant as he smeared black soot at the tops of his cheeks, "ain't that just like a officer now? Reminding a soldier of a work detail—and taking all the fun out of our little celebration!"

Jack clawed his way back up the gentle slope of the shaft cleared by the sergeant, slowly widening it for his shoulders as he went, packing the snow beneath him for the men coming behind. He heard their muffled clamor and friendly joking.

And he felt like he was being reborn.

It had to be like this, he figured, not knowing any different. Coming headfirst through the passage, so the old sawbones surgeons said. Headfirst into the world between your mama's legs. Squinting and blinking and everything so damned bright. The air so cold it took his breath away as his head broke the surface. Its shock burned his chest until he pulled up the wool muffler and started breathing beneath it.

For a long moment he just hung there, his shoulders out in the morning merely looking around the bright, sunlit new world. White in every direction. The horizons stretched endlessly now, a deep, cornflower blue beginning there and stretching overhead with such a reflected brightness that for a moment Stillwell felt as if he had resurfaced here the first day after God had created the world, and he the first one allowed to look at what the Lord had created just for him.

He felt an insistent nudge on the bottom of his boot.

"You going up today?" Seamus asked right behind

him. "Or you fixing on staying right there—plugging the hole for the rest of us?"

Pulling himself on out through the hole, Jack brought his legs up and twisted his body around, loosing his grip and sliding down the six feet of icy, wind-sculpted drift that had been formed of driven snow alongside the freight wagon. He landed in a spray of loose snow piled at the bottom. Laughter greeted him as he picked his face out of the cold.

"It safe to come out, Jack?"

He gazed up the slope to find the Irishman half out, staring down at him.

"Just a little clumsy, I guess."

"Is that it now? I was thinking you was just having yourself a little fun!"

By the time Donegan slid down the icy slope, Jack had found his legs and was rolling them around, kneading the kinks out of them so that he felt more confident in walking. The Irishman stood beside him, then gasped quietly as his eyes grew accustomed to the light, and his heart took in the pristine sight of a world made clean and new.

"It makes a man want to pray, don't it, Seamus?"

Donegan clamped an arm around Stillwell's shoulder, drawing the younger scout close. "It does at that, Jack. Makes a man want to get down on his knees and thank God he's alive. Almost like the bible story me mother told me back home when I was a wee one."

"Which story was that?" asked the old sergeant as he poked his head out of the hole.

"The story of Lazarus, of course," Seamus replied. "Returning from the dead." He sighed. "Ain't this just like being a Lazarus?"

"I've never been one to mind getting down on my own prayer bones and taffying up to the Lord with you," growled the sergeant as he heaved himself free of the hole and slid down the slope.

As he stood, the lieutenant, then the rest came out to greet the brightness of this new, white, brutally cold world.

"Any chance we have some of the stock left?" Stanton asked, pointing at five partially covered brown carcasses, stiffened in death and cold where the wind had kept much of the snow leed off the collapsed animals.

"The rest might be buried under the bigger drifts," Donegan said.

"And then again—they might not," Jack said. "If your men are up to it—we need to find out. They might have drifted on south, driven by the storm."

"If they were—how far could they be by now?" asked the lieutenant.

Stillwell shook his head. "No telling. Might be no more than a mile . . . or maybe even on their way to Mexico by now."

The lieutenant sighed and shrugged. "We've got to try, I suppose." He turned back to the wagon. "We have a chance of pulling this free, if we get enough muscle behind it, then we can right it."

"But we need stock to pull it," one of the soldiers said.

The lieutenant nodded.

"We don't find any still alive," Jack told them, "we'll be walking south out of here on our shanks."

"Maybe we ought to try pulling the wagon south ourselves," the lieutenant considered.

Donegan shook his head. "These men—wore down the way they are—they're in no shape to drag that bleeming wagon through these drifts. Better you have them carry what they can each one. That wagon shroud. What's left in the way of vittles. Assign a couple of them to drag that sowbelly with buffalo chips in it."

Jack agreed. "We've got a lot of walking to do, Lieutenant. And there's many a fire we'll still be needing to make with those chips."

"All right," the officer sighed. "Sergeant, you stay here with another, and keep the fire tended inside. The rest of us, we'll try to run across some tracks . . . find some of the stock."

Stillwell went with Donegan, the both of them choosing to strike out to the north, more so to see if they could find sign of what had become of Simon Pierce. The lieutenant divided the rest into three squads to work the other points of the compass. He himself would lead the detail going to the south, where the faintest of crusty, snow-filled hoofprints indicated the stock had indeed wandered before the wind, driven east by the storm.

As cold as it was, the sun felt good on Jack's cheeks as they plodded north, slowly picking their path between drifts of snow, trying their best to stay on ground blown clear by the blizzard's passing fury.

"You figure that's him?" Donegan asked hours later when Jack stopped, pointing at something he had spotted many yards ahead of them—something dark, contrasting with the snow.

Stillwell only nodded, then set out again, his feet growing colder with every yard they had tromped across the unforgiving winter plain.

A man's leg protruded from the edge of a snow-bank. His stocking had been worked through, the flesh of the exposed foot blackened with frostbite.

Jack tapped it with his gloved fingers. "Solid as ice, Seamus."

Donegan said, "Let's see who it is."

"We know already," he replied as he knelt and be-

gan scooping snow from the upper body. "Poor bastard lost one of his shoes and his foot was so froze he
didn't even know it. Kept right on going, instead of
turning around and coming back to where he could
have stayed warm till the weather blew on over."

They had a struggle pulling the stiffened body over,
frozen as it was to the ground at the edge of the snowdrift that had formed against it during the height of
the storm.

"Simon Pierce."

They could tell it was the government man, even as
blackened as was the flesh on his face. The wool muffler Pierce had tied over his head, knotted beneath his
whiskered chin, was so stiff there was no removing it.
The frozen lips were drawn back in what looked like
a grotesque smile. But it was more the freezing re-
traction of the skin than it was anything Simon
Pierce wished to communicate from beyond the pale
of death to the two scouts.

"He kept everything to the last, didn't he?" Donegan asked, pulling the long map tube from beneath
the dead man's arm. Next came the valise.

"Pierce acted like he had something else with him,
inside his coat," Jack said.

Together they pulled apart the frozen, stiffened
wool coat.

"Gives me the willies," Seamus said quietly, "going through a dead man's clothes."

"I heard a lot of the soldiers in the war did that
with the enemy dead."

Donegan nodded. "Not just the enemy dead, Jack
—but their own too. An extra shirt or jacket. Maybe a
new pair of shoes or boots. A dead man didn't need
'em no more." He shrugged. "There's nothing here."

Jack rocked back on his heels. "I was sure there

was something . . . check that valise. Maybe he put it in—"

"What the divil is this? Weighs like a rock, it does," Seamus declared as he pulled forth a heavy, brick-sized object wrapped crudely in a tattered, greasy piece of gray-brown corduroy.

"I didn't know better," Jack said, sniffing at the smoke-scented cloth before he helped pull the frozen shards of cloth from the object, "I'd say this was in a Injun camp at one time."

"Lord!"

They both just stared at it for the longest time, sitting there as it was across Donegan's palms, brilliant in the new sunlight of this midday in winter on the Staked Plain.

"It's got to be real," Jack said finally.

"No doubt of it, Jack. Pierce was protecting it from the rest of us. Likely he killed Graves for it—or because of it. Here." Donegan gave the crudely-cast gold bar to Stillwell and began digging around in the valise.

"You understand any of this writing?" Donegan asked, shoving some papers to the young scout.

He didn't. "Looks like it might be Spanish, Seamus. I don't know that tongue."

"Who would—anyone you know?"

"Only one Mex I know. He's got a place up at Dodge City now. Runs him a whorehouse. Keeps Mexican girls, nigger girls too, for the buffalo hunters come in. They pay good to dip their stingers in a moist honey pot."

"Shutup, Jack," he said with a grin. "That's just what a man like me has to keep his mind off of way out here in the middle of nowhere."

Jack chuckled. "I s'pose you're right. But he's the only one."

Seamus went through the papers, page by page, until he came to a stack of telegram flimsies. "While I read these, why don't you see what's in that tube. Might explain what Pierce and Graves come looking for."

"I don't know if we ever will know, Seamus. All Pierce told us was he had to get up to the Canadian."

Donegan looked at him a moment before saying, "And up there is where you said the Comanche and Kiowa are thick as ticks on a bull's hide."

"I suppose so—'cause that's where the warrior bands figure they'll have to stop the hide hunters from coming any farther south."

With the two buckles freed, Jack pulled aside the top of the leather tube and shook out the stiffened map printed on a large sheet of ivory-colored stock. As he unrolled a map of the central and southern plains, an old parchment map, somewhat smaller, slid into his lap.

After a moment of studying the newer map, Jack said, "Looks to be government work, Seamus. Here's the surveyor's seal. And they have the railroads marked in, some of the reservation boundaries. A few of the forts. But look here—seems Graves or Pierce marked something of their own on the map."

"Right on the Canadian," Seamus replied. He looked down at the old drawings. "What's that?"

Setting the new map aside, Jack picked up the old parchment. "By Jesus, this is old, Seamus! And writ in Spanish too. You think this has something to do with the gold bar?"

Donegan wagged his head. "Pierce was crazy. I know that. But maybe not all he said was crazy."

Jack remembered the mad talk, those final, almost unheard ramblings, that crazed babbling carried to them on the ghostly wind about gold walls and the seven cities and the Spanish conquistadors.

"And you remember Pierce saying he was going north to find the entrance to the road that would take him to the Seven Cities?" Seamus asked.

"Cibola?"

"Yeah, that's it."

"Shit—now that's just some old talk, what some call a legend, Seamus."

Donegan shook his head, pulling free one of the telegrams. "Maybe . . . maybe not, Jack." He looked into Stillwell's eyes. "You ever hear of an old trading post on the Canadian River?"

Jack nodded. "I heard tell of it. Goes back a long ways. Bents had a operation there. Kit Carson fought a battle with Injuns there back to 'sixty-four."

Seamus studied the telegram a moment more, then looked at Stillwell. "Is the place called . . . Adobe Walls?"

"Damn, if it ain't."

Chapter 31

**Early December
1873**

"*T*hen it's decided. That's where we're going—up to the Canadian," Seamus declared, stuffing the official documents, correspondence and telegrams back in the ice-stiffened canvas valise.

Jack Stillwell shook his head. "Whoa—hold on now. Not till we get some answers from the Mexican fella in Dodge City."

"One runs the whorehouse?"

"Louie Abragon." Jack rolled the small parchment map inside the larger U.S. survey map, both against his coat. He slid them into the leather map tube as he said, "Abragon will translate this map for me."

"You don't plan on telling him about the gold, do you?"

Stillwell replied, "I wasn't planning on it."

Seamus looked down at the frozen corpse. "What you figure we should do with Pierce?"

"Nothing. If we can get the wagon righted, and round up some stock—I suppose Stanton will want us to fetch Pierce's body."

"Good—because I'm not dragging this frozen bastard back across those drifts for no one, Jack."

"And if they haven't found any horses, we'll just have to leave him here."

Donegan nodded. "That means the lieutenant will have to report him dead when we get back to Fort Richardson. And he'll have to explain why he didn't bring in the body."

"You were in the army too damned long," Stillwell said. "All that fuss, all that paperwork. The lieutenant damned well has a good reason for leaving that bastard out here. Pierce killed two men: one of his own, and one of Colonel Mackenzie's soldiers too."

The sun was in the last quadrant of the sky by the time the two came within sight of the wagon camp, following their deep bootprints hammered into the wind-scoured snow. The closer they got, the more it appeared there were too many men moving around the wagon. Seamus's eyes swam with the bright light. He blinked, trying harder to focus—concerned that the Comanche, who were not known to move about in the deep snow and bad weather, much less a blizzard, had raided the camp in their absence.

But as they drew closer, inching from snowdrift to snowdrift, both Seamus and Jack discovered why there were too many men in that camp. And animals to boot.

The old sergeant was regaling with a squad of buffalo soldiers laughing and joking around a smoky fire. The crusty soldier was the first to notice the two civilians coming back across the snowy plain.

"Donegan!" he called out. "Stillwell—both you come on in. We got us company!"

"Seamus Donegan, you say. As I live and breathe!"

That call brought the Irishman up short. "Reuben? That really you, Sergeant?"

"In the flesh. You half froze for a hug?"

He watched the tall brunette soldier hurrying toward him. "From you, anytime!"

They back-slapped and pounded heartily between the three of them until each was breathless.

"By the saints, is it really you? What you doing out here in the middle of the blizzard?"

"Mama Waller's boy knows better than to get hisself caught in a blizzard, Seamus," Waller explained with a smile. "We stayed behind it, moseying slow out of eastern New Mexico as it pushed on ahead of us."

"Why were you out there in New Mexico?" Jack asked.

"Following horse thieves."

"You catch any?" Jack asked.

Waller wagged a finger for the two scouts to follow him. He stopped by the canvas wagon shroud and pulled it back to expose two white men, lashed back to back in the dark, out of the cold.

"Shut that flap, nigger!" one of them snapped.

"Damn you, Sergeant Coon—that wind's cold!" the other growled. "You give me a knife, I'll show you whose balls I can cut off, boy!"

Waller dropped the canvas and turned to his friends, smiling.

"What's this all about?" Stillwell asked.

"Horse thieves—like he told you, Jack," replied Donegan, turning to the sergeant. "You went all the way to New Mexico after them?"

"Had a good trail to follow—so we followed," Waller answered. "Tracks led right off the reservation."

"Those white fellas steal Injin horses?" Seamus asked.

Waller nodded. "We're taking 'em back to the Kiowa."

"Whose bunch they belong to?"

"Lone Wolf's band. These two and a half-dozen others rode in a while back and stole about fifty head of Kiowa stock."

"What happened to the rest of the horse thieves?" Jack inquired.

"We shot three when we caught up to 'em in New Mexico. Couldn't stop to give 'em decent burying 'cause the other three took off with a high tail behind —like they wasn't ever going to stop."

Donegan glanced over the group of some twenty brunettes. "You lose any of your men?"

Waller appeared to swallow down the pain of owning up to that. "Two of my own—H Company." He nodded to the west while he dug his heel in the snow. "We buried 'em out there. Someplace no one will ever know—out there."

"That's only fitting," Donegan replied quietly. "Those men fought out there on the Staked Plain. They died where they fought—like soldiers. It's right what you done, to bury 'em there, Reuben—with the sky to look down on 'em for all of eternity."

"One of the men said some words over the graves," Waller said quietly. "And them words made me think, Seamus—think on when you and me carried the body of your uncle up to that high place looking down on the island where you and the rest waited for nine days."*

"A man like me uncle Liam chooses to live his time in this open country, Reuben—it's right he should be allowed to rest out here for the rest of all of God's time."

"So what you do with them two now?" Stillwell asked, throwing a thumb back at the canvas shelter where the prisoners waited out of the cold.

* The Plainsmen Series, vol. 3, *The Stalkers*

"We'll take those two on back to stand trial before Colonel Grierson at Fort Sill," Waller told them, "after a side trip to Fort Richardson."

That surprised Donegan. "Why so far south?"

Waller grinned, his teeth bright beneath the fading light in his dark face. "Here, and I took you for being a smart man, Seamus. We got us a heap of horseflesh here to tend to, and your lieutenant ain't got a single animal. How can I live with myself, I don't ride on in to Richardson with you, then turn my bunch north back to Sill from there?"

Seamus looked at Stillwell. "Reuben makes a lot of sense to me, Jack. Don't he?"

They laughed and pounded shoulders once more as the old commissary sergeant strode up, his pipe smoking in a thick wreath about his head.

"We'll get this wagon over before the rest of the lieutenant's men come on back—I'll have us some warm vittles to greet their bellies with," the old soldier told them.

Waller put his men to work with their mounts and several ropes and in short order had the wagon righted and what camp goods the commissary sergeant had left squared away. The brunettes then devoted their efforts to enlarging the buffalo chip fire as the sun eased toward the far west and the last of the search parties straggled in to celebrate new faces and horses and a warm meal among friends with all the rest.

Twilight deepened into a shocking purple as the cold stars came out one by one by one overhead, like a saloon keeper in Dodge City would turn on his oil lamps come sundown. The smell of hot food and fresh coffee made the Irishman's belly gnaw all the more.

"We ain't et proper in more'n two days, Seamus,"

Jack said as he squatted beside Donegan with a couple cups of coffee.

Seamus took his. "Whatever Sarge is cooking going to be fine with me. Smells good, don't it?" He sipped at the scalding coffee, then asked, "When you figure we can head north to Dodge City to get some answers from that Spanish map, Jack?"

"We could fight our way north anytime," Stillwell said. "But I been figuring it might be a better idea to wait until late winter. Weather might be more predictable. And . . ."

Donegan looked over at Jack, waiting for the rest. "And what?"

"And," he got a sheepish look on his face, "with us spending the winter down near Jacksboro with Sharp Grover like he asked you to, well . . ."

"Spit it out, Stillwell," he growled, blowing steam off his coffee.

"All the better for you to burrow in for the winter with that pretty Samantha Pike."

Seamus sputtered on the hot coffee. "Jack—not you too! First Sharp's trying to marry me off to the woman. And now you! Saints preserve mother Donegan's boy if I stand a whore's chance in Sunday mass with you two matchmakers around!"

Prologue

Moon of Deer Shedding Horns
1873

"*T*here are only six of them, Quanah."

Quanah Parker nodded, still staring into the distance at the austere ocher and white snow-covered ridges. The winter wind nuzzled his long, braided hair this way and that, gently clinking the silver conchos he had woven into that single, glossy queue almost long enough to brush to the back of his war pony.

"You waited long enough to be sure there were no more inside?" Quanah asked the scout who had ridden back across the snow from the valley southeast of where the Kwahadi warriors waited anxiously this bright, cold winter mid-morning.

"Six."

"How many of the white man's log lodges?"

"Two. One in front. The other in back, with the wood pen for his horses and two of the spotted buffalo."

Quanah turned his nose up at that. Spotted buffalo. The white man's cattle. Docile and spineless. With less courage than even a buffalo cow. Good only for milking. And he wondered what the white man saw in milk anyway. If the Grandfather Above gave the milk to the cow, why then did the white man drink it?

If he was so fond of milk, why didn't the white man suckle at the breasts of his wives?

It was not as if Quanah had never tasted human milk. He had. Many times. For a moment now, here in the cold of this open land, with the brutal wind moaning out of the west like a death song upon the Llano Estacado, it was good to remember. At times he had thought about taking a second wife, but his first filled his life with all that he needed.

She satisfied him even more now than ever before. Mother to their three children, he recalled how her belly had grown swollen with that first child. Thought about how he still made love to her when she grew as big as a antelope doe. How she had never been shy about expressing her hunger for him . . . the warm softness of her fingers as they encircled his excited flesh, kneading him into readiness. How he would roll her over, bringing her up on her hands and knees, that ripe belly of hers and those swollen breasts suspended beneath her as he drove his hard flesh into the moistness of her own warm readiness.

Quanah always answered her rising whimpers with his own growl of enthusiasm in the coupling, for none had ever satisfied him like she.

And after he had exploded inside her, Quanah would suckle at first one, then the other of her warm breasts. It seemed she was never without milk from the birth of their first child. And it had always been a warm, sweet treat for Quanah—after making warm, sweet love to his wife. This drinking of her milk from her small, swollen breasts—something that often made him ready to mount her again.

He had never understood that . . . yet had neve
questioned it either.

Quanah shook his head, feeling the cold blast o
winter air once more. Something that reminded hin
he was not in his warm lodge, wrapped in the furr
robes with her.

Perhaps he needed her badly.

He acknowledged that he had been away from the
winter village for too long perhaps. He was thinking
on his wife and that sweet, warm and moist rutting
he shared with her, when he should be thinkin
about those six white men down there in that valle
less than two miles off.

Many suns ago he had led a large hunting part
away from their village to hunt buffalo. The Coman
che were running low on dried meat. With a disap
pointing fall hunt, Quanah's Kwahadi band wer
forced to hunt much earlier this winter than they nor
mally would have to hunt. More than a moon before
he and the warriors had killed a few white hide hunt
ers they found south of the dead line, that plac
where the white treaty-talkers said the white buffal
hunters were not to cross.

But more and more the Comanche, Kiowa an
Cheyenne were discovering the white man south o
the Arkansas River, on the hunting ground guaran
teed to the Indian as his own. A worthless, heartles
act, this talking treaty with the white man, Quanah
thought.

Ever since the time the old chiefs had signed that
talking paper up on Medicine Lodge Creek six winters before, it seemed the white hunters were crossing south of the Arkansas in greater numbers,
crossing south too of the Cimarron. And Quanah
feared they would one day soon come to the Canadian River—what he rightly believed was the last

stand for his people: that northern boundary of the great Staked Plain, the Llano Estacado of the ancient ones with metal heads who first brought the horses to The People of the plains.

Besides those hide hunters they found and killed more than a moon gone now, his scouts had also returned with news of a small group of soldiers marching northwest onto the Staked Plain. Quanah knew that killing the soldiers boded no good for his people. The army would only send more next time. And the yellowlegs never found the roaming warriors—instead the army's Tonkawa guides sought out the Kwahadi villages filled with women and children and the old ones.

Rarely were the young warriors punished by the white soldiers. It was their families who were made to suffer—losing lodges and blankets and robes, clothing and meat and weapons, when they ran quickly to flee the white man and his Tonkawa trackers, who led the soldiers to the valleys and canyons where the Kwahadi always camped to escape the cold winter winds or to find shade come the first days of the short-grass time.

No, he had told his warriors. We are not going to kill these soldiers. Which had made them howl in angry disappointment.

"But we will drive them out of Kwahadi land," he had instructed them, "by burning the prairie!"

For miles in either direction along a north-south line, the horsemen set their firebrands to the tall prairie grass dried by the arid autumn winds. The winter wind did the rest: whipping the sparks into a fury that forced the yellowlegs to turn about and flee to the east for their lives.*

* The Plainsmen Series, vol. 6, *Shadow Riders*

However, in the days that followed, his scouts reported finding no sign of the soldier party. No charred wagon or burnt carcasses.

From time to time the mystery had made Quanah shudder: to think that those white men had merely vanished into the cold air of the Staked Plain. But if they had, he argued with himself, where would they find food for their animals?

And besides, that great storm that thundered down upon the plains, riding in on the bone-numbing breath of Winter Man, leaving behind tall snowdrifts and many hungry bellies, would surely have killed the white men so unprepared for such a blizzard.

While he was certain that storm had killed the retreating soldiers, it had also driven the buffalo farther and farther south. The little ones in Quanah's village cried with empty bellies. The women and old ones wailed as well. It was only the warriors who could not cry out in the pain of their gnawing hunger—for it remained up to them alone to go in search of meat to lift the specter of starvation from the Kwahadi.

After many days of endless riding to the south, Quanah and his hunters found themselves near the southernmost reaches of the Staked Plain, without having seen any buffalo or antelope. It was as if Winter Man had wiped all before him with his great, cold breath.

As the days of searching grew into many, they had come across a few old bulls partially buried in a coulee here, frozen in a snowdrift against a ridge there— no longer strong enough to go on with the rest. A few had been left to rot by the passing of winter storm . . . like the white hide hunters left the thousands upon thousands to rot in the sun.

Where had the rest of the herds gone? Farther and farther south still—to the land of the summer winds?

If they had, they would likely not return until the short-grass time on the prairies, when the winds blew soft and the Grandfather Above once more told the great buffalo herds to nose around to the north in their great seasonal migrations.

"You wish to attack these white men?" asked the young warrior sitting beside the Kwahadi chief.

He blinked, his reverie broken and brought back to the now. "Yes." Quanah turned to his scouts. "You tell me there is a hill looking down on the place where the white man built his log lodges?"

The scout dropped quickly to the ground, his buffalo-hide winter moccasins scraping snow aside from a small circle. In the middle he formed up two frozen snowballs. Circling the snowballs on three sides he mounded up some of the snow he had scraped aside.

"Yes, Quanah," he said, gazing up into the bright winter sun behind his chief. "These are the white man's two lodges. And these are the hills."

"Where are we?"

The scout pointed with the butt of his rifle.

"It is good," Quanah declared. "We will have the wind in our faces and the sun at our backs as we ride to the top of the hills."

After dividing his force of more than ten-times-ten warriors into four groups and instructing each in its role, Quanah led them away in silence, moving swiftly across the hard, frozen ground.

Behind the low hills he halted them, ordering off three of the groups, then sending off the fourth to guard the all-important opening in the small valley. If the white man was to flee, he told his warriors, it would be through that saddle. They were not to attack. Instead, they were to wait for any of the white men to come their way once the settlers were flushed like a covey of quail.

When all was in readiness, Quanah took the small quarter of a red trade blanket that he sat upon and nudged his pony to the top of the hill. There he waved it against the pale, winter blue of the sky, watching the two white men turn from their work on something in front of the first log lodge.

Immediately the three groups burst into motion, yelling, screeching, riding at a gallop for the two wood buildings.

The two men outside in the open, grassy yard threw down the tack they had been soaping and repairing, sprinting for the cabin.

Puffs of smoke began to rise above the warrior groups.

One of the white men skidded to a stop, reaching behind him to claw at his back before he fell face first into the dry grass dotted with wind-drifted snow. Some of the first warriors leaped their ponies over him, attempting to get to the second man before he reached the cabin. He grabbed his arm, crying out as he stumbled—yet he disappeared through the doorway and slammed it shut as the red horsemen galloped by, their bullets thudding dully into the heavy planks.

As that first wave passed the cabin, puffs of smoke appeared from the windows. From where Quanah sat, there were three windows used by the white riflemen. With one of the settlers already killed—his warriors had only to flush the other five.

Quickly Quanah brought the red blanket over his head and held it there in the steady breeze. Two warriors obediently broke off their attack and sent their horsemen to a safe distance from the cabin while they rode to talk things over with the war-chief atop the hill.

"Burn them out," Quanah told them. "If we attempt to ride past their windows and kill them—the chances are very small we will kill them. This would be a bad thing, for the chances are very good the five who are left will kill many, many more of us with their big buffalo-killing guns. Burn them out!"

The two returned to their bands, calling forth the Fire Carrier—the one who kept his hot coals smoldering in a protective gourd when they marched from camp to camp, fire to fire. A dozen of the warriors quickly made firebrands using the dried, belly-high prairie grass.

The torches glowed and smoked smudgy trails against the blue sky as the warriors raced in. This was the most dangerous work of all, Quanah admitted. His men were riding in defenseless, not shooting arrow or bullet while their hands carried the firebrand. And the horsemen had to ride close—very close—to drop the torches through the windows—right where the white man squatted like a badger in his hole . . . with those big-barreled buffalo guns of his.

Rider after rider rode by the windows. Some of the torches fell short. One horseman was knocked off his animal and dragged across the ground to safety by the rawhide rope lashing him with his pony. Most of the firebrands fell against the sides of the log lodges. Only two of the torches made it into the cabin.

They were enough.

It did not take long for the smoke to begin wafting from the chimney, pouring thick and greasy from the three windows Quanah could watch. Then as the smoke darkened and grew thicker, he instructed his warriors with his blanket to await the bolting of their prey from its den.

A few minutes more and two of the white men

burst out of the cabin, coughing, their rifles still held
up at the ready.

Warriors hammered their ponies into action, in-
tending on running the white men over. But first one,
then a second horseman fell to rifle fire. And from the
looks of it, those guns were being fired from the second of the white man's log lodges.

A pair of white men had been in the second log
lodge all the time, and his scouts had missed them.
Quanah grew furious inside, his hatred seething for
these settlers come to Kwahadi ground.

The two who had fled from the cabin sprinted
across the wide, grassy yard and found safety in the
barn. Three more white men appeared at the door of
the cabin, driven out by the thick columns of dark
smoke issuing from every window.

As the Kwahadis galloped in to make the kill—the
three white men bolted headlong for the barn, while
the four already there laid down a covering fire.

His anger grown to a rage, the war-chief became a
warrior once more. Without waiting for any of the
rest to take the initiative, Quanah put heels to his
pony and raced off the hillside for the cabin. At a full
gallop he reined his pony toward the front window,
leaning off the side of the animal to sweep up one of
the burning firebrands that had not made it inside the
first log lodge. Bringing his pony around in a broad
circle, Quanah rode for the barn with the torch smoking and hissing, sputtering sparks on the cold winter
breeze.

Bullets whined angrily overhead like noisy black
wasps on a spring day. He felt the sting of one of
those bullets at the moment he pitched the firebrand
through the narrow opening at the back of the barn
where the white man had pitched his tall pile of
grass.

Sawing the rawhide reins hard to the left, Quanah urged his pony away from the white man's guns—but not quickly enough.

He sensed the flutter in the pony's heart . . . a misstep, then the animal pitched forward suddenly, throwing its rider clear.

Quanah rolled and rolled across the dry, smothering grass and frozen, crusty patches of snow, coming to a stop at last far from the white men who had killed his favorite war pony.

On all four sides of the small valley, his warriors set up a great cry of rejoicing, for the firebrand had gone in and quickly ignited some of that dried grass the white man foolishly stored for his stock.

With smoke billowing from doors on both sides of the barn, the seven white men darted into the open in a tight group, hurrying for the skimpy timber along the little nearby creek.

With their quarry flushed into the tall grass, the young warriors had great sport with the settlers who no longer had any place to hide.

It was over quickly.

Quanah watched as the noisy young men laughed and joked over the eight bodies, counting coup and scalping, stripping them of their clothing to try it on, then cutting off hands and feet, and finally the manhood parts. Each of the eight were left facing the sky —for they had fought hard to the end and were worthy enemies.

"Do you claim any of the white man's horses, Quanah?" asked one of the older warriors.

"I should look over the animals in the log corral. If I don't find one that will let me ride it on this hunt—I will have a long walk home!"

"That gray one looks strong," suggested the warrior.

"Quanah!" yelled a young scout riding in off the nearby hill. "Soldiers—they come!"

"Where?" he asked. "How many!"

The scout pointed to the east, his face grave. "Ten times ten. More," he replied, striking his left forearm twice.

"Tonkawa trackers lead them?"

The scout nodded, his eyes filling with great concern.

Sweeping his red blanket from the ground, Quanah turned to some of the others. "Open that horse pen and bring the big gray horse. Drive the others away when you leave." He brought the blanket over his head, waving it swiftly from side to side. "Ride, my brothers—soldiers come! Ride now!"

Two mounted warriors brought the prancing gray horse up, its eyes wide with fear at the smell of the Kwahadis, its nostrils flaring as it tested the cold wind.

"You do not like the smell of Comanche, do you, my new friend?"

Quanah tore the concho slide from the bandanna at his neck and looped the bright yellow cloth over the horse's eyes, tying a knot securely behind the animal's jaws. As the two warriors held the big stallion, the Comanche war-chief leaped on its bare back.

When it attempted to rear, Quanah instead drove his heels into its rear flanks. The horse bolted off, followed by the last of the raiding party to leave the scene of the attack.

"You will do, my new friend," Quanah whispered into the horse's ear as they raced up the snowy slope. "We will learn much from one another."

"Between now and the short-grass time when the Kwahadi will join the Cheyenne and Kiowa in one great fight against the buffalo hunters . . . you and I will hunt many buffalo together and learn much about each other."

The cold breath of Winter Man whipped tears from his eyes as the great gray horse surged ahead of the other ponies, its hooves tearing up clods of frozen ground and crusted snow.

"Then, I will proudly ride you when I lead a thousand warriors down to drive the white hide hunters from the Staked Plain—for all time!"